RANDOM HOUSE

LARGE PRINT

THE
FARM

THE
FARM

A NOVEL

JOANNE RAMOS

RANDOM HOUSE
LARGE PRINT

All rights reserved.
Published in the United States of America
by Random House Large Print in association
with Random House, an imprint and division
of Penguin Random House LLC, New York.

Cover design: Lynn Buckley

The Library of Congress has established a
Cataloging-in-Publication record for this title.

ISBN: 978-1-9848-8694-1

www.penguinrandomhouse.com/large-print-format-books

FIRST LARGE PRINT EDITION

Printed in the United States of America

10   9   8   7   6   5   4   3   2   1

This Large Print edition published in accord
with the standards of the N.A.V.H.

FOR MY MOTHER, ELVIRA ABAD RAMOS

THE
FARM

JANE

THE EMERGENCY ROOM IS AN ASSAULT. THERE ARE TOO MANY people, and the din of their voices is too loud. Jane is sweating—it is hot outside, and the walk from the subway was long. She stands at the entrance, immobilized by the noise and the lights and the multitude. Her hand instinctively moves to cover Amalia, who still sleeps on her chest.

Ate is here somewhere. Jane ventures into the waiting area. She sees a figure that resembles her cousin. She is dressed in white—Ate will be wearing her nursing uniform—but the woman is **Americana,** and too young. Jane scans the seated crowd and begins to search for Ate row by row, feeling a growing apprehension, though she tries to stifle it. Ate always says Jane worries too much and too soon, before she knows anything is even wrong. And her cousin is hardy. She did not even get sick from the stomach virus that swept through the entire dormitory over the summer. It was Ate who took the lead in nursing her dorm-mates back to health—bringing ginger tea to their bunks, washing their soiled clothes—even though many of them were half her age and most much younger.

Jane sees the back of another woman's head: dark hair threaded with silver. Jane makes her way toward her, hopeful but not entirely convinced, because the head is angled in the way of someone sleeping, and Ate would never sleep here, under these bright lights and around all these strangers.

Jane is right. It is not Ate but a woman who looks Mexican. She is short like Jane's cousin, sleeping with her legs splayed and mouth open. **As if she is in the privacy of her own home,** Jane can imagine Ate saying with distaste.

"I am looking for Evelyn Arroyo," Jane says to the harried-looking woman behind the registration desk. "I am her cousin."

The woman glances up from her computer with an impatient expression that softens into a smile when she sees Amalia in the baby carrier on Jane's chest. "How old?"

"She is four weeks," Jane answers, pride blooming in her heart.

"She's a cutie," the woman says just before a man with a shiny, bald head cuts in front of Jane and begins to yell that his wife has been waiting for hours and what the hell is going on?

The woman behind the desk tells Jane to go to Triage. Jane does not know where this is but does not ask, because the woman is busy with the angry man. Jane walks down a hallway lined with cots. She checks each bed for Ate, embarrassed when the man or woman lying there is not asleep but looks her directly in the eyes. One old man begins to speak to her in Spanish as if beseeching her for help, and Jane apologizes that she is not a nurse before hurrying away.

She finds her cousin farther down the hall. Ate is covered in a sheet, and her face against the softness of the pillow is pinched and hard. Jane realizes she has never seen her cousin asleep before, even though Jane rents the bunk right above her—Ate is always on the move or away on a job. Her stillness makes Jane fearful.

Ate collapsed on a baby-nurse assignment, in the Fifth Avenue apartment of a family called the Carters. This is what Dina, the Carters' housekeeper, told Jane when they finally spoke. Jane was not entirely surprised by this. Her cousin had been suffering from dizzy spells for several months. Ate blamed them on her blood-pressure pills but did not make time to see a doctor, because she was booked in back-to-back jobs.

Ate was trying to burp Henry Carter, Dina said with a hint of accusation in her voice, as if the fault lay with the baby. This did not entirely surprise Jane, either. Ate had described to Jane how Henry would not burp in the usual positions: sitting on Ate's lap, his floppy neck snug between her fingers and his body stretched over his sticklike legs; or slung over her shoulder like a sack of rice. He only burped when Ate was walking and jiggling him and patting his back with the flat of her palm. Even this way, it could take ten or twenty minutes before Ate succeeded.

"You should put him down, so you can rest," Jane had urged Ate when they spoke only two nights ago, while Ate was having a hurried dinner in her room.

"Ay. But then the gas wakes him, and his nap is too short, and I am trying to get him on the sleep routine."

Dina told Jane that before Ate collapsed, she managed to place Henry safely on the sofa. The mother was out exercising even though she was still bleeding and Henry was barely three weeks old. So it was Dina who called 911 and held the baby while the men wheeled Ate into the service elevator. Dina was the one who scrolled through Ate's phone looking for someone to call and found Jane. In her voicemail, she said only that Ate was in the hospital and that she was alone.

"You are not alone now," Jane tells her cousin,

feeling guilty that it was hours before she checked her messages and returned Dina's call. But Amalia was awake much of the previous night, and when she fell asleep this morning after her feeding, Jane allowed herself to rest, also. The others were already at work, so they had the room to themselves. Jane slept with Amalia on her chest, the sun streaming through the dirty windows, undisturbed.

Jane smooths Ate's hair, gazing at the deep lines around her mouth and her small, sunken eyes. She looks so old. Jane wonders if a doctor has already come but does not know whom to ask. She watches the men and women in colored scrubs stride past, waiting for someone she can approach, someone with a kind face, but they all rush by, preoccupied.

Amalia begins to stir in the sling. Jane fed her before they left the dorm, but that was over two hours ago now. She has seen the American women breast-feeding their babies openly on benches in the park, but she could never do this. She kisses Ate quickly on her forehead—Jane would be too shy to kiss Ate like this if she was awake, and the gesture feels strange—and goes in search of a bathroom. In a clean-looking stall, she covers the toilet bowl with tissue paper before sitting and takes Amalia out of the baby carrier. Her daughter is ready to latch, her wet mouth open. Jane looks at her, the eyes black as night that take up half her face, and is overcome with a tenderness so vast it is almost suffocating. She guides Amalia to her nipple and her baby latches on with ease. It was hard in the beginning, but they know how to do this now, the two of them.

"THE EKG DETECTED AN ABNORMALITY, SO WE'RE GOING TO order an echocardiogram," the doctor tells Jane. It is at least an hour later, maybe more. They stand in front of Ate's cot in a makeshift room created by green curtains hung from the ceiling. Behind the curtains Jane can hear Spanish being spoken and the bleep of machines.

"Yes," Jane says.

Moments earlier, Ate stared around the room with glazed eyes, but now she is alert.

"I do not need another test," Ate says. Her voice is weaker than usual, but sharp.

The doctor adopts a gentle tone. "You are almost seventy, Ms. Arroyo, and your blood pressure is high. Your dizzy spells could mean—"

"I am fine."

Because the doctor does not know Ate, he continues to try to reason with her. But Jane knows he is wasting his breath.

When she is released, after hours of "observation," it is the middle of the night. The nurses tried to convince Ate to stay longer, but she snapped that if they had not observed anything problematic after the day she had already wasted, then she was well enough to go home and rest there. Jane averted her gaze when Ate spoke this way, but Ate assured her afterward: I am doing them a favor; I cannot pay, and now they have a free bed.

One of the nurses insists on wheeling Ate down to the street in a wheelchair. Jane, ashamed of Ate's earlier rudeness, tells the nurse she can push her cousin herself. Ate explains loudly that it is not the nurse's kindness that prompts her to help with the wheelchair but a hospital rule.

"This is the **protocol**," Ate utters, pronouncing the last word carefully. "If you push me, Jane, I might fall, and then I could sue the hospital for millions of dollars."

But Ate smiles at the nurse when she says this, and Jane is surprised that the nurse smiles warmly back.

At the curb Jane hails a taxi, ignoring Ate's grumbling that it is a waste of money and they should take the subway. The nurse helps Ate into the car and has barely begun clattering away with the empty wheelchair when Ate begins pestering Jane, as Jane knew she would. "Mrs. Carter will need help with the baby. You must replace me. Only temporarily. Will you do this?"

Of course Jane cannot leave Amalia, who is barely one month old. But she is too tired to quarrel with her cousin. It is the middle of the night, and Jane only wants to go home. She makes a show of searching for the seatbelt clasp, and by the time she is strapped in, Ate has dozed off.

The road, rutted, is under construction. The taxi

hits a bump, and Ate's head is jolted, landing in an angle so acute it looks as if her neck has snapped. Jane rights her cousin's head, taking care not to wake her. She holds it gently against her shoulder as the car continues to lurch its way to the highway. In the sling Amalia squirms but does not fuss. She has been so good today, even after all the hours in the hospital, crying only when she was hungry.

It is late, the sky outside black beyond the reach of the city lights, the sidewalks empty of pedestrians. Jane would like to sleep. She tries, willing her eyes closed. But they only keep fluttering open.

JANE CALLED ANGEL, WHO IS IN BETWEEN JOBS, FROM THE taxi. She is one of Ate's closest friends. She sits waiting on the front steps of the squat brown dormitory where they live. The street is dark except for the twenty-four-hour bodega where Ate sometimes buys her Lotto tickets. As the taxi nears, Jane sees Angel jump up and hurry to the curb.

"Ay, Ate, Evelyn," Angel exclaims upon opening the taxi door. Her voice, normally loud, is muted. Her face folds into a tentative smile before she bursts into tears.

"**Nakapo,** Angel! Too old to be crying!" Ate shoos Angel's outstretched hand. "I am **fine.**" But Ate cannot get out of the taxi on her own.

Jane waits until her cousin is out of the car to pay the driver. Ate was right; the ride to Elmhurst is expensive. Jane watches Angel lead Ate into the dormitory—recalling suddenly that back in the Philippines, Angel worked as a nurse's aide. Jane is struck with the disorienting sense that she is seeing her—silly Angel, with her dating schemes and ever-changing hair color—for the first time.

They cut through the kitchen, where a new renter is playing a videogame on his phone at the table, past a bedroom in which three bunk beds are squeezed side by side so tightly that to get to the middle bunks you have to crawl over the outer ones, and into the living room. It is dark, filled with the soft rumbling of many people sleeping. The bunks Ate and Jane rent are on the third floor, but Ate is too weak now to climb so many stairs. Angel has ar-ranged for Ate to borrow the first-floor sofa rented by a friend who is on a 24/7 baby-nursing job and will not return to the dorm until the weekend.

"By then you will be strong," Angel whispers to Ate, who grimaces and looks away.

"I am thirsty," Ate says, and Angel scurries to the kitchen to fetch a glass while Jane unties Ate's shoelaces.

"Jane. You did not answer me. Will you go to the Carters'?"

Jane looks up at her cousin. It is difficult to dis-agree with someone so old without being disrespect-ful. "The problem is Mali. I do not trust Billy to care for her." Only saying the name of her husband leaves Jane with a sour taste in her mouth.

"I will take care of her. I will like that. I have

not gotten enough time with Mali since the Carter job." In the dimness, Ate smiles.

"It is not easy to have a baby in the dorm."

Two bunk beds away someone coughs, a phlegmy cough that sends billions of germs rushing through the air. Jane glances down at Amalia, still sleeping in the baby carrier, and turns her back to the cougher even as she knows the germs will find her daughter anyway.

Only three weeks ago Jane was still living with Billy and his parents in a basement apartment on the border of Woodside and Elmhurst. When she discovered that he had a girlfriend, that his brothers and mother knew and had known for many months, she moved into the dorm. Amalia, only one week old, came with her. The bunk above Ate's was available. Ate prepaid Jane's first three months' rent.

Leaving Billy was not easy. He was all she had known since coming to America. But Jane is glad to be free of him, as Ate said she would be. She does not miss his pinching hands and cloying breath or the way he turned off his phone when he was out at night so she could never reach him.

It has not been easy here, either. In the dorm, there always seems to be a line for the bathroom whenever Amalia soils herself; Jane is constantly afraid her baby will roll off the narrow bunk they share, even though Amalia is still too young to roll. In the night, when Amalia cries, Jane is forced to seek refuge in the stairwell or the kitchen so as not to wake the others. And Jane has no plan for what comes next.

"Everyone will help me," Ate remarks. This is true. There is always someone in the dorm—resting before the night shift, off work for the weekend, biding time before a new job. Almost all of them are Filipinos and a good portion of them are mothers who have left their own children back home. They dote on Amalia, the only baby in their midst. The only baby with a mother desperate enough to bring her child to live among them.

"And, I can see if Cherry will let me share."

Each of the dorm's three floors holds two shared bedrooms and a living room, each room housing a half-dozen renters and often many more. But at the back of the upper two floors there is a single private room. On the third floor, this room is rented by Cherry, the longtime nanny of a family in Tribeca who hails from Cebu. Her room fits only a bunk bed and a set of drawers, but there is a door that can be locked. There is a window, next to which Cherry keeps a clay bowl of violets and several potted herbs that she shares with the others for cooking. There are framed pictures on her walls: of the Pope's visit to the Philippines, three of her children grinning in front of a sea of the pious; of her youngest grandchild with a dimpled chin like a movie star; of the two American boys she has raised since they were babies, grown now. They stand against a wall of bamboo on their expansive terrace, the Freedom Tower behind them, the older boy in a graduation robe with one freckled arm looped around Cherry. He holds in his free hand a scarlet banner reading STANFORD.

Ate shivers and her eyes drift closed. Jane pulls a sheet over her, surprised at how tiny she seems. In motion she looms large, much larger than her five-foot frame. "Ate" means **big sister** in Tagalog, and that is her role at the dorm: the mediator of fights, the provider of loans when someone is in a lurch, the only one who dares approach their landlord when there are complaints—mice in the pantry, another leak. At work, Ate speaks with authority to million-aires who in the presence of their babies turn into children themselves, reduced to clumsy beings who seek Ate's help to get their newborns to eat, or sleep, or burp, or stop crying.

But lying on the sofa with a sheet stretched over her like a tarp, Ate looks as if she could fit on Jane's lap.

WHEN ATE ACCEPTED HER FIRST BABY-NURSE JOB MORE than twenty years ago, she had never worked with babies—at least, not the babies of other people. She showed up on the doorstep of the Prestons' vine-covered brownstone in the rain. She held an umbrella in one hand, a bag in the other, and she wore a white nurse's uniform. "Like a brown Mary Poppins," Ate liked to joke, though Jane always thought it must have been intimidating, even for Ate—to be in a new country, her family so far away, starting a new life when she was already in her forties.

Ate had found the job through her friend Lita, who long ago returned home to the Philippines. Lita was then the Prestons' housekeeper. After work, when she and Ate and whoever was around the dorm were making dinner, she liked to tell stories about her bosses. The husband was okay, always working, but Mrs. Preston was strange. She liked her money, but she also despised it. She spoke witheringly about the "ladies-who-lunch" at her social club as if she was not one of them. She hosted black-tie parties in her bare feet. She took the subway to visit artist friends in Brooklyn and Queens but in the city she always used her driver, and before her baby was born, Lita heard her announce to her girlfriends that it was unnatural to outsource motherhood.

It took only two weeks for the baby, a boy, to convince her otherwise. He suffered from colic and cried night and day, inconsolable unless you held him in your arms and walked with him, up and down the townhouse stairs. When you stopped, even for a short while, he would begin to cry again. Finally, in desperation, Mrs. Preston begged Lita: "Find someone to help us."

Lita immediately thought of Ate, who she knew needed the money. She told Mrs. Preston that her friend was a nurse and an expert with babies. This was truer than not. In Bulacan, Ate had worked in the church's free clinic in the summers, and she had raised four children almost entirely on her own.

Because Ate had no expectations, she could be patient. She did not mind walking the baby up and down the stairs, sometimes for hours, kissing his mottled face as he raged and whispering ocean sounds to remind him of the comforts of the womb. She took him on long walks in Central Park even when it was drizzling and cold. In the stroller, with the earth bouncing beneath him, the baby grew calm. He sucked on his fingers and stared up at the moving sky. Back in the townhouse, when the afternoons wore thin, the baby would arch his back and begin wailing anew, and Mrs. Preston would become agitated. Then, Ate would send her upstairs to rest and begin the walking—up and down, up and down, the baby pressed to her chest.

Ate was hired to stay with the Prestons for three months, but Mrs. Preston extended Ate's term once, then again, and still again until the baby was almost a year old. Mrs. Preston told everyone Ate was a savior and that she would never let her go. But when her friend Sarah bore a baby girl and also developed postnatal depression, Mrs. Preston asked Ate to help her. Ate worked with Sarah until her baby was ten weeks old. After that she moved into the penthouse of Sarah's sister Caroline, who kept Ate for twelve weeks. Caroline passed Ate on to

Caroline's husband's friend from college, Jonathan. This family recommended Ate to Jonathan's colleague at the bank, the one whose wife was carrying twins, and so on. In this way, Ate became a baby nurse.

Because Ate had the Prestons' baby sleeping through the night at eleven weeks, despite his colic and fussiness, and Sarah's baby at ten, and then Caroline's at nine, she became known for her sleep routine. This was the reason families fought each other to hire her, she told Jane. There were couples who called as soon as they found out they were expecting or even earlier, when they were still hoping to conceive. Ate would tell these parents that she did not book jobs until the fetus was twelve weeks along. "This is the only way to be fair to all the others," she explained, although she admitted to Jane that this was not the real reason. The risk of miscarriage in the first trimester was too high; how could she schedule her work around wishful thinking with rents to pay and mouths to feed?

Ate also understood that for parents such as these, who had everything and more, being unavailable made her more desirable.

Ate began enforcing her sleep regimen when the baby was very small, just two or three weeks old. Without training, a baby of this age feeds often, every hour or so, and it constantly seeks comfort on the mother's breast. If you hired Ate, though, she would stretch out the feedings right away, so that your baby fed every two, then three, then every four hours. By eight weeks or ten she would have your baby sleeping through the night, depending on the baby's sex and weight and whether it was born prematurely or on time. For this the mothers with the arms like ropes and whipped-cream skin called Ate "the Baby Whisperer." They did not know that Ate stood all night over the crib in the darkened nursery holding a pacifier to the baby's lips. When the baby fussed, Ate lifted him to her drooping chest and rocked him until he was drowsy but not yet asleep. Then she would put him down again. Night after night, this way, until the baby was accustomed to eating only during the day and falling asleep by itself at night. After this, sleep training was easy.

Over the years Ate developed a sterling reputation. "My jobs are the best jobs with the best people," she liked to say. This was not a boast, at least not an empty one. Ate's clients were not just rich—anybody who could afford a baby nurse was rich—but very, very rich. While the other Filipinas took jobs where they slept on a futon in the corner of the nursery or on a pullout sofa in the client's den, Ate almost always got her own room, often with its own bathroom. There might be a terrace or a yard where she could sun the jaundiced babies to rid them of bilirubin. There were five or six toilets and sometimes more, and so many rooms that several of them had only one use—a library for books, a gym for exercise, an alcove just for wine! Ate had been on private planes where she and the sleeping baby had the whole back section to themselves, where she was served meals at a table with cloth napkins and heavy silverware as if she were at a restaurant. "No commercial for me," Ate joked, and it was true. Without papers she could only fly private. In her white nurse's uniform, she accompanied families to Nantucket and Aspen and Palo Alto and Maine in airplanes as big as a house.

Ate attracted the best clients because, somehow, she understood them. Jane believes it is this understanding that allowed the mothers to trust Ate and leave their rings and bracelets scattered carelessly across the countertops and urge their friends to hire her.

"I have **relationships,** not only clients," Ate often said. To prove her point, she would pull from under the bed she rented in the dorm for three hundred and fifty dollars a month a see-through plastic bin full of holiday cards, some over two decades old. Each card featured the smiling children of a former client posed at the beach or balanced on skis in front of a snow-covered mountain or perched in a jeep with the African savanna stretched behind them.

Chase—ah, he was an easy baby, and his parents, so kind! They gave Ate a big bonus and, even years afterward, sent Ate money on her birthday. And now, look how big he is! And how smart, studying to be a doctor!

The Levy twins—they were born small like mice,

each fit in one palm. And crying, crying all the time from gas. But by the time Ate left they were fat, with double chins! See how pretty now? They have grown into their noses!

With trusted friends, Ate liked to take out the "parting gifts" she stored in a separate bin that she sealed and resealed with duct tape for safety—a silver picture frame engraved with both Ate's initials and those of the baby she cared for, a leather purse she used only for Christmas Mass. She enjoyed describing how the mothers often cried when they bid her goodbye after a job, as if Ate were a lover going off to war. "And then, always the gift! From Tiffany or Saks or Barneys. Always too expensive." Ate would shake her head, smiling.

Ate did not often mention the slights or indignities she suffered in certain homes, nor the illimitable tiredness that worked itself deep into her bones when she was on a job. She once told Jane about Mrs. Ames, who did not speak to Ate for the entire twelve weeks Ate lived with the family except when she was annoyed (about Ate's choice of outfit for the baby, about the cashmere sweater that shrunk in the dryer), who stared through Ate like she was made of glass. There was also Mr. and Mrs. Li, who did not allow Ate to eat their food, even just a little milk with her morning coffee, and did not repay Ate for the formula she purchased—so many cans, and so expensive—with her own pocket money because the housekeeper never bought enough.

What is the point of remembering these things? she would ask Jane, although she was the one telling the stories.

"EAT NOW!"

Angel is standing in front of the sofa holding a tray. Someone has opened the blinds, and in the newly brightened room Jane sees that the two bunks nearest to her are now empty, the beds hastily made. She must have dozed off herself.

Angel helps Ate sit up and places a plate on her lap. It contains the leftovers from last night's dinner—shredded carrot, peas, a little ground beef—held together by egg. Angel is famous for making omelets out of anything in the fridge. She hates waste of any kind. From her employers, she collects take-out food containers from the recycling bins and brings them back to the dorm. Every few months, the large shipping container that several of the women share to send things home to the Philippines is filled with stacks of these emptied plastic bowls and platters and trays that at one time held the dinners of Angel's clients—poached salmon, egg-drop soup, spaghetti all'amatriciana—and that soon, across the world, will be piled high with **pancit** at church gatherings and school picnics.

Ate thanks Angel for the omelet, though she does not eat it. She turns to Jane, who has begun to feed Amalia under cover of the bedsheet. "The

Carters are VIPs! It is good for you, too. To make relationships."

Ate was first hired by the Carters two years earlier. Mrs. Carter miscarried when she was only four months along, still slender like a sapling's branch. She never even felt the baby move. The second time the Carters hired Ate, Mrs. Carter carried a baby boy, and the Carters decided to call him Charles, after the father's father. When Charles was thirty-seven weeks in utero, with lungs that could breathe and fingernails that could scratch, he stopped moving. Mrs. Carter became worried when a full morning passed without feeling him kick. In the hospital she was rushed to an operating room, Mr. Carter running alongside her. But the cord had already twisted itself around the baby's neck, denying oxygen to its heart, its brain.

When Mr. Carter called from the hospital to cancel on Ate this second time, Jane was visiting the dorm because it was Angel's birthday. "Long life to me!" Angel sang as she ladled **pancit** noodles into bowls. She was in a good mood. Her eyes were still rimmed in black from the previous night, when she had gone dancing with yet another man she had met online. She was trying to find an American to marry her. She wanted citizenship so she could return to Palawan to meet her newest grandchild; she could tell from the pictures the baby was the whitest of them all, with the best chance of becoming Miss Philippines. Maybe even Miss Universe.

"You will get caught. Immigration knows these tricks," Cherry scolded Angel. Cherry was almost as old as Ate, and old-fashioned. She did not approve of Angel and her many dates with old American men. She also did not approve of how Angel, who was celebrating her fifty-first birthday, dressed for these encounters, in short skirts and leather boots to the knees.

"It is not a trick. I will only marry a man who loves me," Angel answered, then added, slyly, "It's only **I** may not love **him** back!" She tossed her head and laughed, exposing the many gold fillings at the back of her mouth. Cherry pressed her lips into a straight line and said nothing, and Jane fought the urge to smile.

"Dios ko," murmured Ate, sliding her cellphone into her pocket. "The Carters."

"Let me guess," said Angel, always with an opinion. "They canceled again."

Ate sighed, nodding.

"I knew it! These people!" Angel made a noise like she had eaten bad fish. "They do not think how they affect others."

"No." Ate shook her head. "No, the Carters, it is not their fault." And she told them about the baby and the hospital and the umbilical cord like a noose. She told them how Mr. Carter insisted on giving her one month's pay to tide her over until she found another job. How he offered to introduce her to his wife's friends who might need her services.

How he asked her to come to the apartment for a few days to help Mrs. Carter with the adjustment.

"A few days? Ha! You will be there all month," predicted Angel. "These people do not give money for nothing. That is why they are rich!"

Jane cleared the plates while Ate began to iron her uniforms. She packed them in her overnight bag, along with her blood-pressure pills, pens, and notebooks. She was on the F train within an hour of Mr. Carter's phone call and at the Carters' doorway before two hours had passed.

Dina was clutching a tissue and sobbing when Ate first met her. The Carters were still in the hospital. Dina told Jane later that Ate's response was characteristic: "Enough crying! There is work to do!" And she pushed past Dina into the apartment.

Ate started with the nursery. She put the monogrammed pillows and blankets and towels in the closet, along with the size N diapers and onesies stacked on the changing table. She flitted to the mother's room, emptying the drawers of nursing bras and clearing the baby books and ultrasound pictures off the nightstand. She moved the bassinet and the plush, stuffed bears out of the library, removed the lactation tea and pregnancy vitamins from the kitchen shelves, piled the breast-feeding pillow and glass bottles and baby monitor into grocery bags and stored everything in the utility room.

When Mrs. Carter arrived home from the hospital, she was hard with milk. Ate helped attach the rubber plates to her heavy breasts and showed her how to use the pump. She did not allow her gaze to linger on Mrs. Carter's patchy face, her puffy eyes. When the milk slowed, Ate detached the tubing and bottles and round breast plates and told her to rest.

"Someone on the street congratulated me," Mrs. Carter said, her arm shielding her still-large belly.

Ate bowed her head and left the room to pour the still-warm milk down the stainless-steel drain.

"YOU ARE WASTING YOUR MONEY ON ME," ATE ANNOUNCED TO the mother on her fourth day. She disliked being idle, and there was little for her to do. She had spent the morning watching the gardener trim the trees on the terrace so that they did not block the views of the park below.

But Mrs. Carter insisted she needed Ate's help to work the breast pump. She pumped her breasts every four hours, six times a day. She pumped even in the middle of the night, doing so in Ate's small room with Ate by her side because she said she did not want to disturb her husband.

"But there are many other rooms in this apartment," Ate confided to Jane on the telephone, whispering.

Several days passed before Ate attempted to quit again. Angel was ill and had asked Ate to replace her in a baby-nurse job. The family was nice and paid well.

Mrs. Carter had just finished pumping in the study.

She held up the bottle of milk for Ate to admire. "Eight ounces. Not bad, don't you think, Evelyn?"

"I believe, ma'am, that we should slow down," Ate ventured, taking the bottle from Mrs. Carter and capping it. "We should allow your milk to begin to . . . dry up."

The mother's blouse hung open. Ate noticed she wore a nursing bra.

"It just seems a waste not to save the milk." Mrs. Carter flushed. "In case we have a baby."

"You will have a baby, ma'am. And you will make milk then. You produce well."

"I read somewhere that breast milk is good for up to a year if it's stored in a deep freezer," Mrs. Carter continued almost dreamily.

Ate began to put away the pieces of the pump as she waited for Mrs. Carter to finish.

"I hope you will help us, Evelyn. I hope . . . if we have a baby . . . that you can help us."

Ate told Jane later that Mrs. Carter's voice crumbled as she spoke, so that Ate had to strain to hear her.

"You will have a baby, ma'am. I believe this."

Mrs. Carter turned her face toward the window. She stayed that way for a long time, so long that Ate lost the courage to mention the other baby-nurse job, and quitting. As she left the room to store the milk, Ate looked out the window to see what it was that had transfixed her client. But there was nothing there. Only treetops and the empty sky.

———

WHEN JANE WAS NEWLY PREGNANT, SHE VISITED ATE TO help her pack boxes for the Philippines. Ate's bunk was piled high with clothes—outgrown or out of fashion—donated by the clients of the women in the dorm. The phone rang, and Jane heard Ate exclaim, "Congratulations, ma'am."

It was Mrs. Carter. Only months after losing her baby, she was pregnant again.

"You will help us, Evelyn, yes?" Mrs. Carter asked. "For six months! Please?" She was on speakerphone so that Ate could continue sorting the clothes by size.

When Ate asked Mrs. Carter how far along she was, Mrs. Carter giggled and confessed she was barely pregnant.

"Call me in three months' time," Ate said kindly.

Not even ten minutes later, Mr. Carter rang from a business trip in London. He, like his wife, asked Ate to promise to work with them when the baby came, offering to double her daily rate "as an inducement."

"What is paramount is that Cate feels safe," he said. "And you, Evelyn, make her feel safe."

Ate told Jane afterward it was this comment that made her break the twelve-week rule. The trust, insisted Ate, not the money.

But it is the money Jane considers almost a year later, with Ate resting on the sofa and Amalia, sated, dozing in Jane's arms. At the double-rate, even if she replaced Ate for only one week, she would make thousands of dollars. Two weeks or three, and she would have more than enough for a deposit on a studio. Something near Rego Park, perhaps.

Jane can already envision the apartment. It would be at least three floors up, not underground like Billy's parents'. There would be no mice, no mold, no moths chewing holes in her sweaters. In her own home Jane would not have to fish the hair of twenty people out of the drain every time she bathed with Amalia. She would not lie awake late in the night while Angel coughed and coughed in the bunk beside because of her acid reflux.

"Will you be my substitute? Until I am stronger?" Ate is awake again, her voice insistent.

In Jane's arms, Amalia shifts. Jane draws her closer, pressing her face to her baby's soft cheek. Her daughter is sturdy. At her last checkup, the doctor said she was gaining weight well.

Jane feels the heaviness of Ate's gaze, but she is not ready to meet it yet. She looks only at Amalia.

ATE

ATE TURNS ONTO HER SIDE ON THE SOFA, WATCHING JANE, and sighs.

The problem is that Jane does not yet understand. She is a mother, yes, but so new. Still nervous, still scared. She holds Amalia like she is made of glass. Every time Amalia cries, even little cries that mean nothing—Jane runs and picks her up. But babies are stronger than people think, and smarter. This is important to know to be the best baby nurse, with the best clients.

Angel has more experience than Jane, and she is loyal. But Angel talks too much. She talks to her clients as if they are friends, gossiping with them about her other clients! When Ate warns Angel that the clients will not trust someone with a flapping, too-big mouth, Angel grows defensive: this mother likes to **chismis** with me! She likes my stories!

Ay, Angel. Of course the mother will gossip with you to learn the secrets of her friends: which ones leave the baby to shop all day; which give the baby formula instead of the breast; which ones fight with their husbands about money. But such a mother will not truly trust Angel. Never, never. She will not ask Angel to stay in her home for very long or recommend her very much to her friends. Because this mother—even as she laughs at Angel's jokes and listens to her secrets—she knows that Angel's eyes are too big, her mouth too loose.

Marta, Mirna, Vera, Bunny—Ate considered them all. They are more serious than Angel. But Ate has not known them as long or as deeply. Will they give up a job as good as the Carter job—and all the money the Carters pay—when Ate is ready to return?

Because she does plan to return. The doctor told her to "take it easy" for at least a month. He said this smiling, as if he were giving her good news. But Ate has never taken it easy in her life! Even when she fell sick over the years—this was rare; she is strong—Ate did not lie in bed all day doing nothing. Because the children still needed to eat, the clothes still needed to be washed.

After sixty-seven years like this, Ate is supposed to rest? And with what money?

No. Ate will return as soon as it is possible to Mrs. Carter, who is paying her the double-rate for six months. Only thinking of it makes Ate feel stronger.

Until then it is Jane who will replace her. She is green, but she is the best choice: she is respectful, and she works hard. She will not fill the head of Mrs. Carter with ideas—that Ate is too old or too weak or too sick—as the others might. And she will leave the job when it is time.

"I only need to train you," Ate says to Jane, who is not listening.

To catch her attention, Ate reminds Jane that with the double-rate, she will make more money in several weeks with Mrs. Carter than in many months working in the retirement home for her minimum wage. She reminds her that Billy is no one to depend on, and she must now think about what is best for Amalia.

"Big money cannot be ignored. Life holds surprises," Ate says, thinking of Roy, her youngest.

Jane is quiet. Ate can tell from her expression that she is thinking. Her mother also had this look, like she was somewhere far away, when she was deep in thought.

Ate waits. She can hear her own heart beating.

When Jane says, "Ate?" Ate's eyes fly open. And when Jane says yes, as Ate knew she would—she is a good girl; she tries to do the right thing—Ate smiles.

THIS IS WHAT ATE TELLS JANE, IN A VOICE THAT IS URGENT, BE-cause they do not have much time:

You must wear a uniform. If mine do not fit you—most likely they will not, you are still chubby from the baby—then you must go to the uniform store, the one on Queens Boulevard. I will pay. Buy two or three, the kind with matching pants. Only pants with big pockets for the pacifier and the milk, the aspirator. Things like that.

The baby is not yet sleep trained, so expect to work all day and also night. When do you sleep? When the baby sleeps of course! But only in the evenings. During the day, if the mother or father is around, you must stay busy—even if the baby is napping. Otherwise, you will look lazy.

Sundays are the day off, but for the first week you should not take it. Mrs. Carter will insist, but you must refuse. Tell her you prefer to stay and "get to know Henry." She will always remember this. She will tell Mr. Carter, and they will be pleased you are my replacement.

You will miss Mali, I understand this. I will send you pictures, many videos. But you must only check them in your room. You see the babysitters from the islands on their phones at the playground, not watching the children? Do not be like that. You do not get double-rate for being like that.

I will tell Dina you are coming. She will help you find what you need. Cabbage—the leaves are good for when the mother's milk duct gets plugged. Lactation tea—the mother should drink it several times a day. Multivitamins, also every day. A beer called Guinness—this is good for milk production.

But, Jane, speak to Dina only in English. No Tagalog, even if the parents are in a different room. Otherwise, they are uneasy; they feel like strangers in their home.

I do not mean to scare you, Jane! Mrs. Carter and Mr. Carter are very nice! It is only that you need to show respect. They will tell you to call them "Cate and Ted," very American, very equal—but it is always "sir" and "ma'am." They will tell you to "make yourself at home"—but they do not want you to make yourself at home! Because it is their home, not yours, and they are not your friends. They are your clients. Only that.

Mrs. Carter, she is the type of mother who feels guilty. She likes to be with her baby; but she thinks she likes to be with her baby more than she likes to be with him. Do you understand? And this makes her guilty, because she believes love and time are the same. But that is not true! I have not seen Roy, or Romuelo, or Isabel, or Ellen in many years, but my love for my children is the same. Mrs.

Carter does not understand this. So she is guilty. Guilty if she leaves the baby for half the day to do her haircut; guilty when she learns her friend did breast-feeding longer.

Be careful of the guilt, Jane. Do not allow it. At times, Mrs. Carter will tell you: **I will take Henry, go nap, you were up all night.** But most likely she is only feeling guilty about you! You must give her an excuse to leave the baby. For example, you can say: it is time for the baby's bath; or, it is tummy time.

Or in a joking voice you can say: can I please have a turn with Mr. Handsome now?

If she insists she wants him, okay. But then the baby must be full of milk and already burped and happy. Not hungry, or tired, in a crying mood. If he fusses with her, she might get jealous. This can happen—if the baby smiles at you more, if he is comforted by you faster.

And you must stay nearby, one ear listening— but not just standing. Always busy: washing bottles, folding clothes. Otherwise the mother begins to resent you. For only taking up space while she is the one with the baby.

The father? He is working at a bank. He works very hard, very long hours. Keep your distance, Jane. Be polite, but do not look him in the eyes. And do not smile at him. No, he is nothing like Billy! But Mrs. Carter, she is still fat from the baby. And you are young, and pretty.

The book! This is important! These are records, you see? This is where you record—in a chart, the clients like charts—what the baby drank, how much, breast milk or formula or mixed, and when. It is also where you record the bowel movements. Pee-pee or poo-poo. If the poo-poo is runny or hard.

This information will help you with the sleep routine. I will explain. When I left the Carters, the baby was drinking every 120 minutes. See? In this column? But we are trying to make him eat every four hours, little by little. When he is drinking enough in the daytime—26 or 28 ounces—then he does not need to eat at night. Then it is time for the sleep training.

Another example. What if the baby is crying all day? Mrs. Carter wants to know why. Look at my book! Did Henry pee-pee enough? No? Then maybe he is thirsty. Did he poo-poo today? Yesterday? No? Maybe he is constipated!

These types of parents, Jane, you must try to understand: they are used to controlling things. This is what their money gives them. But with a new baby, what happens? The parents pick the day to induce. The father takes the day off work. There is the new car seat, the baby's clothes folded so nice. And then the labor comes, and then the baby comes and: **Pah!** No control! The baby cries, and they do not know why. The baby will not latch. Why? How to force it? But you cannot force it! The baby spits up, poo-poos, will not poo-poo, has a rash, gets a fever, will not sleep—no reason, no control!

Jane, please listen; this is important, maybe the most important. To be the best baby nurse, you must show the parents you are in control. When the baby cries or vomits, when the mother shouts because her breast is hard like stone and so painful— you cannot be surprised. Only in control, with all the answers.

This book—it is not only a book. You understand? It means for the parents that there is an order. That the world is not random.

This, Jane, will make the parents trust you.

And touch the leather. See how soft the cover is? They are not cheap, these books. But they are a nice keepsake. I have found that the mothers love them.

JANE

THE FIRST TIME JANE MET MRS. CARTER, HER HEART POUNDING
in her chest, her heart aching for Amalia, Mrs.
Carter hugged her. Jane was not expecting this. At
the retirement home the residents sometimes em-
braced Jane, but their children, when they visited,
kept a distance.

When Mrs. Carter hugged Jane, they were standing in the foyer, on a marble floor in the pattern
of a checkerboard. Jane still held her bags in her
hands. Mrs. Carter smelled of perspiration—she
had just returned from an exercise class—and perfume. She murmured in Jane's ear, "I'm sorry about

Evelyn," and then she asked Dina to take her to the maid's room.

The maid's room was in the back of the apartment. It was small, but it was more than Jane had ever had to herself. When she lived with Nanay, her grandmother, they'd slept in the same bed. Years later, when Jane joined her mother in California, she slept on the pullout sofa in the family room near the television. In the maid's room Jane found Ate's spare uniforms folded neatly in the dresser. Sticking out of the gilt-edge pages of her Bible was a snapshot of Amalia from the day she was born.

Jane first understood what money could buy at the Carters'. She had been with the family for a week when Henry developed a fever and a strange, barking cough. While Mrs. Carter called the doctor in the library, Jane prepared Henry for the trip. She slipped him into his Patagonia jumpsuit, packed extra diapers, and warmed his milk.

"Ma'am, we are ready whenever you are," announced Jane when Mrs. Carter was off the phone.

"Ready for what?" asked Mrs. Carter blankly. She was still in her yoga pants, cross-legged on the couch.

"To go to the doctor?"

"It's a petri dish over there," Mrs. Carter explained, wrinkling her nose. "Henry's too young."

Half an hour later, the doctor arrived carrying a satchel filled with her instruments. She left her shoes in the foyer and examined Henry in the nursery in slippers, using a skinny flashlight to peer into his ears and throat. She wore thin gold bracelets with blue stones in them that jangled while she worked. When she was finished with the exam she called the pharmacy on Third Avenue with the prescription, then chatted with Mrs. Carter as she packed up her things. They were old friends from Vail, where they had spent Christmases for decades. The doctor said she and her husband were thinking of joining the Game Creek Club but balked at the fees. Mrs. Carter assured her that the upfront cost was worth it; the food was so much better than in the lodges, and you never had to wait in line. And the slippers! Divine.

After the doctor left, and once Henry was sleeping, Jane put on her coat and asked Mrs. Carter if she would like anything at the pharmacy besides Henry's medicine. Mrs. Carter explained that they paid a concierge service to run their errands, and the medicines would be dropped off with the doorman.

"Rest; you were up with Henry all night," she said kindly.

Over the weeks Jane watched as the world, like the doctor, came to the Carters' home. Dry pasta and raw almonds, unscented body cream and baby wipes, wicker baskets full of fresh vegetables and meat from local farms, cases of wine, fresh flowers every Monday and Thursday, Mr. Carter's work shirts boxed like gifts, and new dresses for Mrs. Carter draped on padded hangers and sealed in long zippered bags from the stores on Madison Avenue—all delivered to the apartment's back door and put in their proper places by Dina without the Carters ever noticing. There was little reason to leave the apartment, and Jane barely did, except for the twice-a-day walks around the park with the baby.

The first time Jane and Mrs. Carter and Henry ventured into the world outside together was for a weekend trip to Long Island, where the Carters owned a house. The mother of Mr. Carter was hosting a party for Henry at their country club in East Hampton. The morning of the trip, Mrs. Carter and Jane and Henry descended the building's main elevator and slipped into the waiting Mercedes, in which Henry's car seat was already strapped and their bags already stowed. The driver brought them to the heliport on the East River, and they were transported to East Hampton in half an hour. There, another car swept them to the Carters' sprawling, shingled house, which was invisible from the road because of the high hedges that surrounded it. Jane remained on the property the entire weekend except for the three hours she spent at Mrs. Carter's country club for the party.

It was a self-contained world, one built to withstand the shocks and storms of life, Jane realized over the weeks. A world all but divorced from the one she and Amalia and anyone Jane really knew inhabited. And until she was paid by the Carters—

six weeks at the double-rate, just as they had promised—Jane had thought it was wholly unattainable for someone like her.

But when Jane went to the bank to deposit her money, she learned that she qualified for a new kind of account. A Savings-Plus one, with a minimum balance of fifteen thousand dollars and an interest rate of 1.01%. Jane confessed to the bank teller that she did not understand what an "interest rate" was. He took out a calculator and explained that it was the rate at which her money would grow for leaving it in the bank.

"For doing nothing?" Jane asked, just to make sure.

"It is called 'compounding.' You understand how it works now?"

For Jane, the fact that her money would grow by itself was a revelation. It was as if a door previously closed to her had been opened—just a crack—and for the first time she could imagine a way inside. If her money could grow just by sitting still, then she needed more of it. Not the dollars and dimes that she made at the retirement home, but big money, like she made at the Carters'. If she was careful, this big money would grow, little by little, all by itself. Into a fortress.

MRS. CARTER USED TO DRINK GREEN SHAKES FOR BREAKFAST every morning. She had Dina make them out of frozen blueberries and leafy greens and various seeds and spices—cinnamon, turmeric, chia. One day, Jane's second or third on the job, Mrs. Carter offered Jane a sip. Jane was surprised, but Dina said later that Mrs. Carter was like that. Nice, and not snobby like her friends. The next night Mrs. Carter invited Jane to watch a movie in the screening room because her husband was working late. They sat side by side on deep leather chairs, hands dipping in the same bowl of popcorn while Henry slept.

Maybe this was why Jane felt it was okay to borrow the breast pump. Because Mrs. Carter and she were becoming friends. But no; this was not true. Jane never even told Mrs. Carter about Amalia, because Ate said it would make her feel guilty. And Jane always knew, inside, that borrowing the pump was a violation.

The first time she used it, she had worked for Mrs. Carter for only six days. Henry had been fussy all afternoon, and Jane had not found time to empty the milk from her breasts since the early morning. As soon as Henry was down for his nap, Jane rushed to her room. She stripped off her shirt, stuck a bowl in the sink of the adjoining bathroom and leaned over it, ready to milk herself like a cow. _he was by then already saving her milk in plastic bags borrowed from Mrs. Carter and storing them in the second freezer in the pantry, the one the Carters only used for big parties. Already then, Jane planned on bringing the frozen milk to Amalia on her first day off.

Mrs. Carter was out exercising. Jane believed she was exercising too much and eating too little, because her milk production was weak. Jane's eyes fell on the breast pump on the desk in her room. It was hospital-grade, stronger than the kind in the stores. It pulled the milk from Mrs. Carter with such force that her nipples behind the breast plates were stretched long, like pinky fingers. Mrs. Carter worried constantly that the "contraption" would leave her chest ruined, but she still preferred it to feeding Henry on the breast because he was so slow, sometimes taking an hour to get his fill.

Jane made a decision without consciously making a decision. She locked her door. She turned on the radio. She moved the baby monitor to the desk and attached herself to the pump. In moments her breasts were being pulled like taffy beneath the pump's plastic plates. Jane did not mind the ruination. She did not expect anyone to touch her. Even Billy had not touched her often, complaining her breasts were too small to be fun.

Jane closed her eyes and pictured Amalia—Mrs. Carter said thinking about Henry while she pumped made her produce more milk—and she was right. It took only fifteen minutes for Jane to empty herself, and she made many more ounces than when she used her hands. Through the baby monitor, Henry never stirred.

After that, Jane used Mrs. Carter's pump several times a day. Over the weeks the feeling that what she was doing was wrong faded, like a bright T-shirt washed too many times, but it never entirely disappeared. Jane began to put some of her own milk into Henry's bottles, because Mrs. Carter's supply was low, because Jane overflowed with milk, because doing so helped Jane believe that, maybe, the borrowing was good for everyone.

"I CAN'T IMAGINE HOW TINA AND ESTER MUST FEEL, WITH THEIR children so far away in the Philippines, living with a family like ours," says Margaret Richards.

She is the pretty college friend of Mrs. Carter, with big blue eyes and hair so light it is almost white. She holds Henry over her shoulder, and he is drooling on her shirt. Jane wipes Henry's face with a spare burp cloth without Mrs. Richards noticing.

Mrs. Richards is describing the documentary she is making about the Filipina nannies of her two young daughters. She has never made a documentary before, but she met a struggling filmmaker at a benefit for MoMA PS1, and he is "thrilled" to help her.

"What we're trying to sort out is how big a role the kids and I should have," Mrs. Richards says, seeming not to notice that Henry is beginning to fuss. Jane checks her watch and notices worriedly that it has been four hours since he last had a bottle.

Mrs. Richards continues, "I think it would add

relatability to show us with them, how they're a part of our family. It might be easier to hold the audience's interest with us in it. Not just nannies."

"It's brilliant to see you back to work with the girls so small! Clay keeps me so busy I couldn't **imagine** going back to work anytime soon," exclaims Emily van Wyck, the college friend who left her child at home with her nanny. Jane overheard Mrs. Van Wyck warning Mrs. Carter that she was crazy to let someone as young and attractive as Jane into her house. **Why tempt Ted?** Mrs. Van Wyck asked, not knowing Jane was around the corner in the library picking up the Cheerios that Mrs. Richards's girls had spilled on the carpet.

Jane offers to take Henry, who is whimpering and gnawing on his fists, but Mrs. Richards acts like she does not hear her. "Of course, Xander's getting cold feet. He says it looks bad. You know, a privileged Upper East Sider married to a successful businessman making a film about her help—"

"But it's **how** you do it," interrupts Mrs. Carter. "Harriet Beecher Stowe wasn't black. Art is a leap of empathy!"

"**Exactly** my point," agrees Mrs. Richards.

Henry begins to cry. Jane retrieves him, berating herself for not feeding him right before Mrs. Carter's friends arrived, even if it was a little earlier than the feeding schedule. Ate has told Jane that mothers like their babies to be "easy" in front of their friends, not fussing and crying.

Before Jane can slip away, Mrs. Richards asks, "Are you Filipino?"

"Yes, ma'am," Jane answers reluctantly. She needs to feed Henry before he becomes overhungry, and he will not drink here. There are too many people.

"You don't look like it."

"Well your dad's American, right?" Mrs. Carter smiles at Jane.

"Were you born there?" asks Mrs. Richards at the same time.

Jane takes the bottle of breast milk she warmed earlier from her pocket and brings it to Henry's mouth, praying that he drinks, but he shoves it away with frantic hands. "Yes, ma'am. My father is American. And, yes, ma'am. I was born in the Philippines."

Mrs. Carter interjects, "But not in Manila. That other island . . . Ted used to scuba dive there when he was with Morgan Stanley. Where was that again, Jane?"

"I am from Bulacan," Jane answers, nervous, because Henry now grabs his ears, as he does when he is overstimulated.

"Oh no, I was thinking of the island with the Aman resort . . ." Mrs. Carter shakes her head. "In any case, Jane's dad was stationed at an American military base—"

"Probably Subic Bay," Mrs. Richards interrupts with breezy confidence. "We've already done a great deal of research. There are a lot of mixed marriages like this, an American soldier becoming attached to a local. Is that how your parents met, Jane? Through the base?"

Jane's face prickles. Her mother was sixteen when she became pregnant with Jane, a scandal that Nanay wielded throughout Jane's youth to explain her strictness. Jane's father left the Philippines soon after Jane was born, but this did not sour Jane's mother on Americans or their military. The last Jane heard, her mother was living in the California desert with her newest husband, a former Army pilot who worked construction.

"I am not sure."

"Why is that?" asks Mrs. Van Wyck.

Jane looks to Mrs. Carter for rescue, but she is discussing what to make for lunch with Dina.

"My mother left to America when I was small . . . My grandparents—they raised me."

"Did she come here to rejoin your father?" asks Mrs. Richards.

Jane lies again. "No, to find work."

"As a nanny?"

"First cleaning. Then later she was a nanny."

"So . . ." Mrs. Richards says thoughtfully. "So your mother came to America and found work as a nanny. And now here you are working as a nanny. You followed her path. Imagine if **you** had a daughter and she—"

"Like recidivism," says Mrs. Van Wyck. "Generations of black men going to prison because their dads did."

Henry bursts into a prolonged wail.

"Margaret, you can interview Jane later for your movie. Henry needs to eat. Jane, do you mind?" Mrs. Carter asks.

Jane bolts out of the room. She does not stop walking until she is safe in the nursery, planted at her favorite spot in front of the window. She jiggles Henry until his cries subside, then slips the bottle into his mouth. In the nursery's quiet, he drinks. She listens to the sound of his slurping, her heartbeat slowing. Soon these trees will change colors, she tells him. She thinks of Amalia and wonders what she is doing at this exact moment.

The door bursts open and the two Richards girls, Lila and Lulu, careen into the room.

"Shhhh! Girls! Henry is sleepy!"

The girls are hyper. Dina should not have given them the sugared Cheerios. They press against Jane's legs, begging to touch the baby, too noisy. Henry stops drinking.

Where are Tina and Ester? Do they expect Jane to take care of the girls while they **chismis** with Dina in the kitchen?

"Go play! See?" Jane points to a shelf filled with Henry's toys, which to Jane seem more like decorations: carved, wooden, expensive-looking things in the shape of toys.

Lila, barely three years old, runs across the room screeching about a ball. She grabs a carved globe from the shelf and, without warning, flings it at her younger sister, smacking her in the face. For several seconds, Lulu stares at her sibling without speaking. Then her face crumples, and she begins to scream.

"Why is she crying?" asks Ester, Lulu's nanny, who stands in the nursery doorway holding a cup of blueberries.

Jane tries to soothe Henry, who has begun to cry also, and tells Ester about the globe. Ester examines Lulu's face, announces everything is okay, and begins to feed Lulu her fruit, even though she is still wailing.

"Lila! Mommy says to eat your blueberries!" Tina calls as she enters the room.

"Mommy does say that!" sings Mrs. Richards in the lilting voice she uses with her girls. She trails behind Tina holding an upturned iPhone in her hand. "Blueberries are a superfood!"

There are too many distractions. Jane is about to leave the nursery when Mrs. Richards stops her.

"Give Henry his bottle here, Jane. Don't mind me. I'm just making a movie!"

Using her phone, Mrs. Richards films Tina as she hand-feeds blueberries to Lila, shifts to Ester, who is still trying to comfort Lulu, and pans slowly across the nursery until she comes to Henry and Jane.

"Jane, can you move away from the window? The

backlighting makes you look too dark," directs Mrs. Richards, before intoning, "Three Filipinas. Three babies. Three stories."

There is a whimper followed by a hacking sound.

"Lulu's choking!" Mrs. Richards cries.

Ester begins pounding on the little girl's back. Lila, frightened, begins to cry. Henry's wails grow shriller. Suddenly, a stream of half-chewed blueberries explodes from Lulu's mouth.

"TINA! ESTER!" Mrs. Richards yells, the iPhone limp in her hand. "Those. Blueberries. Will. STAIN."

Jane rushes out the door before Mrs. Richards can stop her again. In her room she holds Henry close until his sobbing quiets. He snuffles against her shoulder as she checks her phone messages. There is one from Ate about Amalia's doctor's appointment. Amalia barely cried when she had her shots, and she is tall for her age. Jane swipes through the pictures Ate sent—of Amalia in a new hat, of Amalia on the examination table. By the time Jane puts down her phone, Henry is asleep.

Jane sighs, annoyed with herself. She should not have checked her phone for so long. Henry did not come close to finishing his bottle, and now Jane will have to throw the milk away. Ate says that it is only good for up to two hours at room temperature; after that bacteria starts to form. Jane considers defrosting more milk and waking Henry to keep him on schedule. But he is sleeping so peacefully, and her breasts are already tingling, which means it is time to pump. And what if she runs into Mrs. Richards on the way to the kitchen?

Jane places Henry on her bed against the wall. As she goes to lock the door, he begins to squirm. She runs back to the bed, piling pillows on his exposed side to buffer him. She turns on the white-noise machine, peels off her shirt, and attaches herself to Mrs. Carter's pump. Within minutes, her milk begins to flow. Jane listens to the rhythmic suction and thinks of Amalia and relaxes.

Suddenly, Henry shrieks. He shrieks so violently it is as if the air in the room is being ripped in two. He burps—Jane forgot to burp him before laying him down!—and shrieks again, then again, dissolving into a ferocious wailing. Jane, heart battering her chest, quickly unlatches herself from the machine and sweeps Henry off the bed. His hands claw at her skin.

"Sh . . . sh," she whispers urgently. Pressing Henry against her chest, Jane uses her free hand to detach the tubes from the bottles. Henry's mouth closes on her nipple, which oozes milk.

"No, Henry." Jane tries to pull him off, but he only clamps down harder, gulping milk the way a drowning man, once saved, gulps the air.

Stubborn boy! Jane slides her pinky into the side of Henry's mouth and pries open his jaws. Henry, bereft, tips back his head and bellows so fiercely his splotchy face goes white.

"Henry!" Jane's insides thunder. She pushes him against herself to muffle him, and when he begins to suck on her again she lets him. Just until she can clear away the pump, which she should not be using. Just until she can dump the old milk from his bottle into the sink and rinse it and fill it with her fresh milk. Just until she can screw on the rubber nipple. She works as quickly as she can. Her breast, the one free of Henry's hungry mouth, drips onto the floor.

Jane is walking to the bed, a bottle finally in hand, when her door flies open. The doorknob bangs against the wall.

"Jane, I just wanted to—oh my God!"

Mrs. Richards stands in the doorway, filming phone in her hand.

Jane stares, words jumbled in her mind out of order. Only Henry makes a sound, sucking hard on her breast with greedy snorts, like a pig.

MAE

THE CAR IS LATE, WHICH MEANS MAE WILL PROBABLY BE late. And if there is traffic—and there often is, the Taconic being a crappy road, too narrow, too curvy, too fast, site of countless car-crash-inducing crossings by deer and other woodland creatures— then she will definitely be late. And Mae **loathes** being late.

"Eve!" Mae calls to her assistant through the open door of her office. "Have you found the car yet?" Mae takes care to hide her annoyance, to keep her voice serene but commanding. During the corporate retreat in Mexico last month, the new girl in

Investor Relations had exclaimed that Mae "never looked ruffled." Mae likes this image of herself and seeks now to cultivate it: calmness in a maelstrom, sangfroid in a crisis.

The retreat was a first for Holloway. Leon, Mae's boss and the company's founder and chief executive, felt it was critical to convene the heads of Holloway's various businesses to share learnings on how best to satisfy their customers—the ultra-rich. "Only the paranoid survive," Leon declared at the opening meeting, a PowerPoint slide illuminated on the screen behind him showing the impressive upward slant of Holloway's annual profit figures.

General Managers of the Holloway Clubs in New York, San Francisco, Dubai, London, Hong Kong, Miami, and Rio were flown into Cancun for the gathering. They were joined by the Managing Directors of Holloway's art consultancy, the yacht and private-jet management company, the real-estate management outfit, the family-office advisory— and Mae, the only female business head of the bunch, representing Golden Oaks. The "gestational retreat" is Holloway's newest venture and, in Mae's mind, its future.

Mae grabs a tissue box off her desk—it is half-empty, she has suffered from a torturous head cold ever since the ski holiday she and Ethan took over New Year's—and stashes it in the hidden cabinets behind her chair. She straightens the orchid that sits askew on her desk, a gift from Ethan, and stands back to admire her workspace.

"Any word, Eve?" Mae asks again, shrugging on her cashmere coat—twenty percent off at Bergdorf and it **still** cost a fortune—and grabbing her bag. She's supposed to meet Reagan McCarthy in the Village at six, and at this rate she'll be lucky if she gets there by six-thirty. She tries never to be late for a Host—doing so implies that irresponsibility is condoned, and if there is one thing the gestational carrier of a billionaire **cannot** be it is irresponsible—but it's especially bad form when meeting a Host she is still actively courting.

Eve is still on the phone with the driver. Mae, stifling a frown, tells her to text when he arrives and strides toward the front of the Main House. Dammit. Mae messages Reagan that she needs to push back the meeting as she walks, the hallways of Golden Oaks so familiar Mae doesn't need to look up from her phone. Out of habit, her steps slow in front of the painting she has come to consider hers. It's a small landscape, one of six hanging in the main hallway. Years ago, Mae found an image of the painting in one of her art books at home. She immediately called her friend at Sotheby's to guesstimate its value and was told it could go for mid–six figures at auction, possibly more. The story goes that Leon bought the hallways' half-dozen paintings on a whim, years ago. He was driving along a dusty back road, lost somewhere in rural Massachusetts on his way to Newport, when he stumbled on an estate sale. Leon convinced the doddering old widower affixed to a wingback chair in the sitting room to sell him all six paintings for a bulk discount, and although as a group they are similar—dark, earthy colors, paint layered in thick slabs, depictions of rustic scenes—**Mae's** painting is worth multiples of the other five put together. "I guess I've got a nose for value!" is Leon's punchline when he recounts the story to Clients, pointing self-deprecatingly to his prominent, slightly crooked, and strangely attractive nose.

Every few weeks Mae devises a different theory as to why her painting is a standout. This week she noticed a smudge beyond the clouds, green-black, like a new bruise. She also observed that the trees in her painting are thicker than in the others, the density of them almost palpable. Do these things matter? Is value correlated to smudges and density? The truth is, she doesn't know, and months ago she added **Enroll in Art Appreciation Class** to her Long-Term, Nonurgent-but-Important To-Do List. Now, though, she thinks she placed it too far down, sandwiched as it is between **Organize B-School Golf Weekend** and **Digitize Tax Returns.** The renovations to Ethan and Mae's apartment will be finished sooner than expected, and they aim to host their engagement party in their south-facing, natural-light flooded, six-hundred-square-foot living room. Before then they'll need new art for sure.

Mae's cellphone bleeps. It is Eve texting that the driver is pulling up. Mae breezes through the waiting room, making sure to wave to the receptionist, and pushes through the heavy front doors. She darts to the car, where the driver apologizes for his tardiness repeatedly, like an incantation: "I'm so sorry I'm late, so sorry, so sorry."

"I'm fine. Let's just get going." Mae's tone is more severe than she means, so she shoots a half smile at the driver's rearview mirror.

Even in the dead of winter, the countryside around Golden Oaks is beautiful. A checkerboard of pastures that in warmer months yields alfalfa and corn and grass for haying rolls past Mae's window, fringed by snow-dusted sycamore and oak trees, some hundreds of years old. A small brook, frozen now, cuts through the side fields, accompanied by a rambling stone wall. The sky above is a hard, dusty blue, like an inverted Wedgwood bowl. Mae knew from the second she saw Golden Oaks Farm, when she and Leon were scouting upstate New York and nearby Connecticut for potential sites, that it was perfect: a place unspoiled in its natural beauty, lush and wholesome—and yet a mere two hours' drive from the best hospitals in the world in Manhattan.

Mae allows herself to enjoy the scenery until they hit the highway. Then she gets down to work. She brings up her To-Do List on her phone.

#1: Finalize Madame Deng Pitch

Mae feels good about this one. She is already about ninety-five percent ready for the meeting tomorrow, having spent the past several weeks devouring every article she could find on Madame Deng, even plodding through a handful in Chinese—no small feat given that Mae's father, although born outside of Beijing, refused to speak anything but English to her at home. Mae's near-flawless Mandarin is the result of years of dedicated toil starting her freshman year in college, when she made the bet that mastering the mother tongue of the world's fastest-growing economy would someday pay dividends. Years later she was proved right when millionaires and then billionaires began sprouting up across China like weeds, craving the Western-made luxury goods and services that Mae's staked her career on.

The salient facts, wrung from Mae's painstaking research: Madame Deng is the world's reigning Queen of Paper and Pulp. She was born in a tin-roofed hut in a squalid village in Hebei Province to uneducated farmers. Through smarts, sweat, and a helpful marriage to a well-connected lieutenant in the Red Army, Madame Deng created a globe-straddling, paper-recycling behemoth in little more than a decade. Her company, Eight Heavens, owns a string of factories in coastal China that buys scrap paper by the ton from facilities in the West, treats it, cleans it, smashes it into sludge, and turns it into the containerboard and other materials used to wrap/box/package the torrents of cheap, mass-produced Chinese products that are exported daily to the West. There, acquisitive but increasingly eco-conscious consumers pop their used containerboard/cardboard/paper into bright-blue recycling bins to be sold back to Eight Heavens. Through this cycle of use and reuse Madame Deng has accumulated a fortune that the **Journal** estimates at well over eighteen billion American dollars. She is the richest woman in China and the richest self-made woman in the world. And she is considering an investment in Holloway Holdings.

Normally, Leon and the newish Head of Investor Relations, Gabby, would host Madame Deng in New York, at the Holloway Club on Fifth Avenue. But this pitch is different. Madame Deng is not only considering investing in Holloway, she may choose to have a baby—it would be her first, she is pushing fifty—at Golden Oaks, using a Host handpicked by Mae to carry one of the dozen frozen embryos Madame Deng has stored at the eponymous Deng Center for Reproductive Health Studies at MIT.

Leon, in a masterstroke, asked Mae to host the pitch at Golden Oaks, a first. He reckoned its pastoral prettiness and clean, limpid air would stand in sharp contrast to the pollution-clogged skies and tainted groundwater that Madame Deng is accustomed to in Beijing.

"And **you,** Mae. You always make a great impression," Leon had said warmly.

Mae is almost faint with excitement at the opportunity. **This** could be her chance. Since the hard launch of Golden Oaks three years ago, Leon and the Holloway Board have insisted on keeping the surrogacy operations subscale—arbitrarily limiting Mae to only thirty Hosts, give or take, at any time even though the beta phase succeeded beyond expectations.

But there are eight bedrooms gathering dust in the east wing and crying out for occupants. If Golden Oaks simply did away with private rooms—a policy Mae has recommended time and again; she firmly believes Hosts should be paired up so that they can keep tabs on each other, and of course more Hosts per bedroom means fatter profit margins—the site could accommodate at least another two dozen Hosts.

But first, Mae needs to land Madame Deng. She would be by far Mae's biggest get from the Mainland, and she would prove to Leon the enormity of Golden Oaks' potential.

Mae fishes earphones out of her bag and plugs them into her phone. "**Huanying dajia!** Welcome, everyone. **Xiexie deguanglin!** Thank you for coming," chimes her recorded voice. Mae plans to begin tomorrow's presentation for Madame Deng in Chinese, then segue into English for the benefit of Leon and the others. She has been practicing her intro with her Beijing-based online tutor for days, and the hard work has paid off—the voice blaring Chinese into her ears has the accent of a native.

Mae lip-synchs along with her recorded presentation while flipping through the slim stack of Host applications Eve printed out earlier in the day. She glances through the photos on page one of each stapled packet and frowns. Most of the applicants are from the Caribbean, but she has enough of those. What she is low on are non-black Hosts. Really, Mae muses, what she could use are a few more Filipinas—they are popular with Clients, because their English is good and their personalities are mild and service-oriented. Mae herself is partial to them because her housekeeper growing up, Divina, hailed from a village in the mountains somewhere in the southern Philippines. Divina was a kind, homely woman with a flat nose punctured by bug-sized nostrils and dark skin left cratered by a terrible case of childhood chicken pox. Mae's fair, comely mother tried to use Divina's appearance to scare Mae into wearing sunscreen when she was a child ("You have your father's skin, Mae, do you want to end up looking like Divina?"), but her fear-mongering was ineffectual, at least in those early years, because young Mae didn't find Divina ugly.

She was, though, and one thing Mae has come to learn from her job is that even if Divina were still alive, and even if she were young enough to be a Host, and even though she was trustworthy to the extreme, tidy, and obedient, with a womb as hale as any other at Golden Oaks—no Client would ever pick her. Because of her ugliness. The Clients would never **say** this, of course, at least not the American ones. But when paging through the dozens of online Host profiles in Mae's sleek office, Clients would almost invariably skip past someone who looked like Divina and settle on a prettier Filipina with paler skin, or a Polish girl with a fresh-scrubbed face and freckles across her nose, or a slender Trinidadian with glossy eyes and dimples.

Certainly this does not hold for **all** Clients, Mae concedes to herself. Some really are focused only on choosing a Host with a healthy womb. But not many. Most Clients cannot help but feel that the Host they choose is not only a repository for their soon-to-be-baby but an emblem of the lofty expectations they have for the being to be implanted inside. So they gravitate toward, and are willing to pay a premium for, Hosts whom they find pretty, or "well-spoken," or "kind," or "wise," or even: educated.

This last one initially surprised Mae—that some Clients are willing to pay a gigantic premium for wombs that have graduated from Princeton or Stanford or UVA, as if their fetuses will absorb, along with glucose and proteins and oxygen and vitamins, the acquired knowledge and sky-scraping SAT scores of an expensively educated Host. But it's true: Mae services a handful of Clients a year who will settle for nothing less than a Host with a degree from a top-tier college. Hence Mae's anxiety over Reagan McCarthy, who represents the holy trifecta of Premium Hosts: she is Caucasian (a winsome mix of Irish and German, Mae discovered during their interview), she is pretty (but not—and Mae knows from experience this is critical—sexy), and she is educated (cum laude from Duke University—smart, but not intimidatingly so).

If Mae can convince Reagan to take the job at Golden Oaks and match her with Madame Deng—for whom any price Mae quoted would be a rounding error, an infinitesimally minute drop in the vast ocean of her wealth—Mae would be on track, only weeks into the new year, for a record-breaking year-end bonus. She would use the windfall to redo their bathrooms, which Ethan insisted they leave for "phase 2" of renovations. And she would get her mother a gift so outrageous (a Hermès bag? A Cartier watch? A Cartier watch tucked **inside** a Hermès bag?) it would elicit—**something.** A trace smile of pleasure. An involuntary gasp of surprise.

Although, realistically, her mother would do no such thing. Most likely, she would toss Mae's gift aside with a blithe flick of her wrist, as if she handled fifteen-thousand-dollar bags stuffed with twenty-thousand-dollar watches all day long, rather than hankering for them her whole adult life. How many times had Mae returned home from school to find her mother in the den watching yet another biopic about Jackie O or Babe Paley or some other gilded swan? How often did Mae's mother lament the uncouth flashiness of their nouveau riche neighbor's newest Louis Vuitton clutch only to find her, later, lustily poring over the handbag section of a Saks Fifth Avenue catalog in the bathroom like it was porn?

But this is no good! Mae shakes her head with almost violent snaps of her neck. This is not the time for idle daydreaming and speculation. Mae has work to do. The next twenty-four hours are critical.

Mae finishes rehearsing her presentation once more, this time aloud, speaking crisply into her phone. She emails the recording to her tutor for review during their video session later that evening. She then returns her attention to the Host applications. By the time the car reaches the FDR, Mae has singled out the one or two applicants from the stack who merit further consideration and emailed their names to her team for background checks. With a decisive swipe of her pointer finger Mae deletes both items #1 and #2 from the To-Do List on her phone. Done and done.

Mae is starting on item #3 when her phone buzzes. **Exceed Academy** blinks on its screen underneath a picture of Katie, Mae's college roommate. Mae can envision Katie hunched over a borrowed desk in one of the four charter schools she and her husband established in graffiti-strafed, bullet-punctured, drug-infested neighborhoods across Los Angeles. She'll be calling because of the plane tickets, but Mae doesn't have time to chat and absolutely abhors being thanked, at least by

Katie. When Mae sent her goddaughter a good organic crib mattress as a Christmas gift, Katie and her husband were embarrassingly profuse in their gratitude. Katie, who had minored in visual arts in college, hand-painted Mae an exquisite card, and Ric orchestrated a comedic video featuring himself squashed in the crib in a bonnet and gold chains reciting a thank-you rap.

Mae shudders to think how they'll respond to the round-trip, business-class ticket from L.A. to Miami, where Mae's erstwhile sorority sisters insist on hosting an "epic" bachelorette party for her in several months' time. In fact, it is Katie bestowing the favor. Mae wouldn't last half a day with the Kappa Kappa Gammas without Katie's grounding presence. And Mae likes doing things for Katie, whose life seems drab and hardscrabble compared to her own.

"The traffic is so bad," the driver apologizes. The car has exited the highway and is nosing into the city, slowed by a crush of bikers and taxis, buses, trucks, and pedestrians.

"It's not your fault, don't worry," Mae answers. She does not check Katie's voicemail, not yet. While the car waits for the traffic to untangle, Mae slips in her ear buds again. The sound of her recorded voice rings in her ears, clear and true, blocking out the angry honking that has erupted on the street.

——

THE WILLOWY HOSTESS AT THE RESTAURANT INFORMS MAE she is the first one in her party to arrive. Mae checks her coat and ducks into the bathroom to freshen up after the long drive. Her reflection, she notices with distaste, is ruffled to the extreme—matted hair, smudged eyeliner, her nose bright pink from the car service's abrasive tissues. She sets about pulling herself together. She reknots her hair, dabs stray eye makeup with one of the Q-tips she keeps in a pouch in her purse. She finds the lip pencil she wants in her makeup bag and outlines her mouth in quick pink strokes. Next, she snaps open a jar of whitening powder and dusts a light strip down her nose, making sure to blend in the sides. It is a trick her mother taught her—insisted on, really, particularly on school-picture day—to make her nose, which is her father's nose, look narrower. "More aquiline" is how her mother put it, hovering over Mae with a fox-hair makeup brush, flecks of whitening powder flying into Mae's eyes.

Mae reenters the restaurant and is led to a table near the window. She is reviewing a deck of PowerPoint slides for tomorrow's meeting when the hostess reappears, this time with Reagan. In her peacoat and flat, mud-encrusted boots, Reagan looks uncannily like the photos of Mae's mother when she was a thin, reedy, horseback-riding teenager, although Reagan's clothes are much nicer. Even their hair—dirty blond, careless braid—is the same. "Do you ride, Reagan?" Mae asks without thinking, standing to shake Reagan's cold hand.

"I do. I rode here," Reagan responds. She swipes a strand of hair off her forehead with her fist. She wears no makeup.

"You ride in the city?" asks Mae, confused.

"I just lock my bike outside," Reagan says, adding reassuringly, "It's okay if you wear a face mask and gloves. You barely feel the cold once you get going."

"Oh right," Mae murmurs. "I'm impressed."

Reagan orders a glass of iced tea. A camera hangs from her neck. Mae remembers that when Reagan came to Golden Oaks for her site visit before Christmas, she had peered out of the windows at the pristine snowscape and wished, aloud, that she'd brought her camera. Mae thanked her lucky stars the interview wasn't scheduled for early spring— all slush and mud and a deep, almost fetid moistness, the woods alive with newly awakened insects and scores of ticks freshly hatched and carrying any number of diseases. Reagan might not have found Golden Oaks so picturesque then.

"I busted my camera when I was in Chicago last week," Reagan explained, placing it on the table. "I just picked it up from the shop."

Mae had learned from Reagan that her parents still live outside Chicago and that her mother began to develop early-onset dementia when Reagan was in her teens, so she must have been visiting them. Mae makes a point of understanding the family background of all prospective Hosts before they're hired. It inevitably shapes their worldview and motivations, both critical factors in determining whether a young woman is suited to carry a Client's child.

She simply can't imagine Reagan's formative years, witnessing a parent's unraveling like that. Her own mother wasn't exactly nurturing, but she was there, in mind if not in spirit. Mae and her team agree Reagan's mother's dementia is a prime motivator. Reagan desires to mother, because she grew up essentially motherless. It's tragic, but it bodes well for her capacities as a Host.

"We had an ice storm last week, and I took some pictures for you," Mae says. She leans over the table to show Reagan her snapshots of entire trees iced over, as if encased in silver. Reagan oohs and ahhs.

"Don't you ever just want to move out there for good—to wake up every day to . . . pure beauty? Rather than to **this**?" Reagan gestures outside the window to a pile of yellowed snow next to a wall of garbage bags.

"Oh sure," says Mae, not quite lying; she and Ethan do sometimes speak of getting a weekend house upstate, especially if things continue to go well with Golden Oaks. "But my fiancé's job is downtown, our life is here in Manhattan . . ."

"I guess it might get boring," Reagan concedes.

"Actually," interrupts Mae, "it's very cultural.

Golden Oaks is not far from the Berkshires, where there's Tanglewood, Pilobolus, galleries galore. There are so many working artists living in the area . . ."

"Not that I'd go gallery-hopping a lot if I were a Host."

Mae, noting the "if," soldiers on. "No, probably not toward the end of the incubation period . . . But in the first and early second trimester we do sponsor trips to the Berkshires for Hosts who are interested." Mae is making this up as she goes along. Really, it has never come up—most of her Hosts would have zero interest in avant-garde dance performances and photography exhibits— but why not? Why not hire a car to take the Premium Hosts to nearby towns for a bit of cultural stimulation now and then? Would that breach something contractually?

"Anyway, even if it gets a little boring, it'd be worth it," Reagan says. She mentions that she is trying to get serious about her photography, but her father isn't supportive. "He'll only help with my rent if I'm being **practical** and working a **real job.**" Reagan makes a face.

Her words are music to Mae's ears. Incentivized Hosts are the best Hosts. "Assuming you deliver a healthy baby, which I'm certain you would, your rent worries will be a thing of the past. Along with any other monetary worries you have . . ."

"I'd also love to know that I'm helping someone," Reagan adds quickly, as if concerned that she's come across as overly money-driven. "I mean, that's what's most important."

Reagan was referred to Golden Oaks by the clinic that harvested her eggs in college. She had probably convinced herself then, too, that she was acting out of altruism, that the money was secondary in her decision to donate her eggs. Mae's never understood why people—privileged people especially, like Reagan and Katie—insist that there's something shameful in desiring money. No immigrant ever apologized for wanting a nicer life.

She reassures Reagan that **both** of her motivations are important. "Being a Host will allow you to fulfill your artistic dreams, while also fulfilling the dreams of a woman desperate for a child. It's the best kind of win-win."

Reagan frowns. "You mentioned before, though, that some people use surrogates for aesthetic reasons. I—I'd want to carry a baby for someone who otherwise couldn't have one. I'm not so interested in a Client who's using a surrogate out of vanity . . ."

If Reagan had been a run-of-the-mill applicant Mae would have sent her packing then and there. As if Hosts get to choose their Clients! But Premium Hosts are hard to come by, and so Mae reassures rather than reprimands Reagan. "Should we be lucky enough to have you join us at Golden Oaks, I have a Client in mind for you. She's an older woman, born in abject poverty. She's done phenomenal things in her career but at the cost of her fertility. She's too old to carry her own child."

Reagan's eyes light up. "Yes. Exactly."

Mae's phone buzzes. It's probably Eve. Madame Deng's assistant had warned Mae that she might need to move tomorrow's lunch meeting to breakfast, which would mean Mae needs the car to pick her up at her apartment well before five a.m. This in turn will determine whether Mae attends the gala at the Whitney this evening. She already bought a dress for it, a gorgeous, size-10 Yves Saint Laurent found on a sale rack at Barneys and tailored down to Mae's size. "I'm sorry, Reagan. I've been waiting on a call from Eve."

Mae picks up her phone. Eve informs her that the Deng meeting has been moved to seven thirty the next morning. Dammit.

"How's Eve?" asks Reagan.

When Reagan visited Golden Oaks, Mae asked Eve to have a chat with her. Mae had a hunch that pretty Eve, with her troubled backstory—her mother raised three little girls single-handedly in the projects—would appeal to Reagan, who is a lost soul seeking meaning. Understandably so, given her childhood.

"She's well. Still working toward her degree in the evenings."

Reagan fingers the sugar packets she has scattered across her placemat. "You know, when I went to

Golden Oaks, I wasn't sure fully how I felt about it. I noticed I'm not the typical Host."

Mae meets Reagan's gaze with steadiness. She decides that Reagan is the type that respects forthrightness; bluntness to blunt bluntness. "You worry that the other Hosts at Golden Oaks are mostly women of color. Am I right? You worry that there's something potentially . . . exploitative afoot." She speaks mildly, as if reading aloud from the menu.

Reagan laughs, a nervous laugh. Mae's directness has put her off-balance. Good.

"Well, I wouldn't have used the term 'exploitative' . . . Although my roommate—if she knew about Golden Oaks—she'd agree with that." Reagan pauses, then adds, as if it were an explanation in itself: "She's African American."

"Did you ever study economics in college?"

"I minored in it, but I hated it. My dad made me. Because it's **practical.**"

"It's not particularly practical if it's taught badly. Which, unfortunately, it often is." Mae smiles. "It's actually quite fascinating. At the macro level, economics is less science than philosophy. One of its core ideas is that free trade—voluntary trade—is mutually beneficial. The exchange has to be a good deal for both sides, or one party would walk."

"Yes, but it could be that **one party** has no other options. I mean, the 'exchange' for that **one party** might not be a 'good deal,' but only the best choice among a bunch of choices that are all total . . . well, crap." Reagan forms quotation marks in the air with her fingers; her voice has sharpened.

Mae remembers having similar arguments with her father when she was young. Dinner-table debates about Ayn Rand and Wall Street and unions and communism. Her father inevitably played his trump card: the hopelessness he had felt living in communist China; his salvation and rebirth in capitalist America. Even after things soured for him—after his import-export business foundered, after he went to work as a pencil pusher at a no-name company an hour's drive from home to pay the mortgage on the McMansion her mother insisted on keeping—he extolled America's virtues. He never blamed his adopted country for his failures, only himself.

"Agreed," Mae responds calmly. "But the trade, as you just admitted, is still the best option available. And without the trade, without this relatively better option, the **one party** would be worse off, don't you think? It isn't like we force our Hosts to be Hosts. They choose to work for us freely—I'd argue: happily. They're treated extremely well, and they're compensated **more** than adequately for their efforts. We certainly didn't force Eve to stay on with us after delivering the Client's baby."

"That's exactly what I found so interesting," Reagan says, shifting tone. She leans forward, speaking quickly. "When Eve told me she'd been a Host, I was shocked. She's so . . . professional. She told me working for you is like winning the lottery."

"Eve's really special. I'm glad you got a chance to chat with her. But she isn't an isolated case. A significant number of Hosts decide to carry second and even third babies with us. A few have gone on to work for their Clients after delivery. For someone with drive, Golden Oaks really can be a gateway to a better life."

Mae omits the fact that, except for Eve, no other Host has transitioned to a white-collar job. They tend to be hired for childcare or household services.

Reagan is nodding. "Just the money has to be life-changing."

Of course, Reagan's earning potential is many multiples that of a typical Host, but that's simply because she brings very special attributes to the table. It's basic supply and demand. The regular Hosts are more or less interchangeable. Not that Reagan needs to know this.

"It certainly is a lot of money to them," Mae agrees.

"It's a lot of money to **me**. And I don't need it nearly as much," answers Reagan.

Mae makes a mental note to talk to Research. She knows they track Hosts postdelivery to ensure they are abiding by the non-disclosure agreements; it can't be that hard to figure out which ones have visibly improved their lives post–Golden Oaks. A list like that would be useful beyond Reagan.

"How can I be of help as you make your decision?" asks Mae.

Reagan bites her lip, staring out the window. An old man buttressed by a stout African American woman, probably his caretaker, hobbles past. "I think I already have . . ."

"Yes?" Mae asks calmly, although inside she is cartwheeling.

"Yes."

JANE

WHEN ATE FIRST TOLD JANE ABOUT GOLDEN OAKS, JANE HAD been without steady work for almost three months. Her position at the retirement home had been filled while she was at the Carters', and her old supervisor could only get her sporadic shifts. Jane was getting desperate.

"Mrs. Rubio is using Golden Oaks for her fourth baby. She had too many troubles with the other pregnancies. Preeclampsia and hemorrhoids and bed rest!" Ate explained.

Golden Oaks hired women to be surrogates. If you were chosen to be a Host you lived in a luxury house in the middle of the countryside where your only job was to rest and keep the baby inside you healthy. According to Mrs. Rubio, Golden Oaks' clients were the richest, most important people from all over the world, and for carrying their babies Hosts were paid a great deal of money.

"I would take this job if I could. The work is easy and the money is big! But I am too old." Ate sighed.

"How much money do you mean?" Jane asked, resting one hand on Amalia's belly so she would not roll off Ate's bed.

"More money than you made with Mrs. Carter," Ate answered, without judgment. "And Mrs. Rubio says if the Client likes you, you can make much more."

Ate pressed a pale-gray business card into Jane's hand. On it, there was a name, MAE YU, and a phone number. "Maybe, Jane, it is a new beginning."

APPLYING TO GOLDEN OAKS WAS TIME-CONSUMING BUT NOT complicated. There were forms to sign. Jane had to agree to a background and credit check and send copies of her citizenship papers. There were rounds of medical examinations at a doctor's office near the East River and a battery of other tests, odd ones, at a smaller office on York.

Jane surprised herself by enjoying the latter tests, in part because the silver-haired woman who conducted them assured her there were no wrong answers. Jane was first shown a series of splotchy shapes and asked to describe them. The silver-haired woman then asked her questions—about what it was like being raised by Nanay, and what made her angry. Afterward, Jane took a computer test where she only needed to mark whether she agreed or disagreed with a list of statements.

Any trouble you have is your own fault.

Jane thought of Billy, of Mrs. Carter, and clicked: **Strongly Agree.**

I do many things better than almost everyone I know.

At this, Jane laughed aloud. She did not even finish high school!

Strongly Disagree.

I don't mind being told what to do.

Agree.

Several weeks later, Jane received an email from Mae Yu, Managing Director, Golden Oaks Farm, informing her that she had passed the first two stages of the "highly competitive" Host Selection Process. She was invited to Golden Oaks for a final interview in early January.

Jane was overwhelmed. She was busy looking for apartments so that she and Amalia and Ate could move out of the dorm if she got the job—how would she have time to study? Ate, as always, took charge. She bought a stack of pregnancy books and showed Jane how to make study cards. She searched the newspaper classifieds for no-fee apartments and brought Amalia with her when she visited them, so that Jane could prepare for the interview undisturbed. Every night, she quizzed Jane.

"What are the correct foods to eat when pregnant? What is the best music for the fetus to be smart? What exercises make labor easier?" Ate asked, sitting at the dorm's kitchen table, a candy cane sticking out of her mouth.

"Food high in omega-3; complex classical music like Mozart and . . ." Jane faltered, feeling not only stupid—she was never good at tests, even the easy spelling tests in school—but guilty, because she did not know these things when she was carrying Amalia.

"Kegels," Ate said. She peered at Jane over her reading glasses. "Relax, Jane."

"I am not good at remembering things," Jane said, near tears.

"You will be fine, Jane. They will be lucky to have you."

ON THE METRO-NORTH TRAIN THE MORNING OF THE INTERVIEW, Jane finds a coil of rosary beads in her pocket. Ate probably slipped them into her coat at the subway stop when Jane was distracted by Amalia. After Nanay died—and before Jane knew her mother would send for her—Jane must have said a thousand rosaries straight using the beads she had taken from her grandmother's nightstand. They were smooth from use, like Ate's.

Jane is so nervous she feels ill.

The train does not seem to be moving fast, but it is. Outside, tall buildings turn into shorter ones, blur into houses with small yards, then houses with bigger yards, then fields, wider fields, forests. Jane fingers Ate's beads and tries to pray, but the familiar words only make her sleepy. She forces herself up and sways toward the café car, thinking of the priest in Bulacan, the one with the hunched back who taught catechism to the village children. The priest used to describe how Jesus was so anguished by the sins he shouldered for mankind that, one time standing in a green garden, he sweated blood. Jesus with blood oozing from his pores! Because of our sins!

The priest's normally timorous voice thundered as he described Jesus's agony. For a long time afterward, whenever Jane was naughty—when she broke a plate and hid the pieces in the trash bin, when she lied to Nanay about whether she came straight home after school—Jane was sure her badness would turn her sweat red, too. On those days, she took care not to exert herself and to play in the shade. When she finally confessed her fears to Nanay, she was spanked for blaspheming.

In the café car, Jane orders an extra-large coffee and drinks it quickly. Outside the window farms flash past and, in the pastures, cows, horses, sheep.

The animals of baby books. Would Amalia recognize them? Jane reads to Amalia every day now, as Mrs. Carter instructed her to do with Henry. Their brains, asserted Mrs. Carter, are like sponges.

Jane's stop comes while she is in the bathroom. She almost twists her ankle rushing off the train. In the parking lot, a line of cars idles at the curb. Jane does not know how she will find which one is waiting for her. She walks the length of the line, trying to ignore how her shoes pinch—she has not worn them since her wedding—peering into each window with a mixture of shyness and apology.

At the end of the line someone honks. Jane notices a black Mercedes with a sign in the passenger window spelling REYES. It is the same car that the Carters owned, down to the slightly tinted windows. Jane pulls her coat tighter around herself and hurries toward it. The front door swings open, and a driver hops out and greets her. She means to smile at him but cannot. She slips inside, not knowing exactly where she is going, and tries to pray.

"ALMOST THERE!" ANNOUNCES THE DRIVER SOME TIME LATER. Jane wakes, dazed. She meant to study her cards during the ride.

"Nice, eh?" asks the driver. He meets Jane's eyes in the rearview mirror. They are driving up a hill lined with trees that Jane will later recognize as oaks. Behind them she glimpses a big, white mansion capped by a roof of dark green shingles, thick white columns holding up a wide porch, and windows, so many, all lit. A wooden sign with swirling, green letters reads: GOLDEN OAKS FARM.

Jane thanks the driver, her heart flapping in her chest. She stands for a moment at the mansion's front door, on which a Christmas wreath still hangs, gathering her courage. Before Jane can knock, the door swings open.

"You must be Jane." A pretty lady with blond hair pulled back in a braid smiles at her. She takes Jane's coat, asks her if she would like a drink, and leads her to a large room with butter-colored walls covered in paintings. Jane sits near the fireplace. She stares above her at the wood beams stretching across the ceiling like ribs and thinks of Jonah, the man in the Bible who was swallowed by a whale. But this whale is a five-star one, filled with five-star furniture.

Jane recognizes the actress on the cover of a magazine on the table in front of her. **How to Spend It,** the magazine is called. She pretends to read as she surreptitiously observes everything around her—the chandelier dripping crystal at the far end of the room; the pretty lady behind the shiny desk murmuring into a phone that **Jane Reyes has arrived.**

"Your tea." A different woman appears out of nowhere. Jane springs to her feet, the magazine in her lap sliding to the floor. The woman places a cup and matching saucer on the table and retreats with a smile. "Ms. Yu will be with you soon."

The magazine has splayed open to the centerfold—three panels long, picturing a watch like none Jane has ever seen. In the middle of the watch's face is the earth, the continents deep green and gold against a circle of blue water. Gold clock hands at ten-ten stretch across North America and what Jane thinks is the beginning of Asia. Ringing the earth in tiny, perfect increments are numbers 1 to 24 and, circling these, at the edge of the watch face, are the names of twenty-four cities: New York, London, Hong Kong, Paris, yes, but also cities Jane has never heard of: Dhaka, Midway, Azores, Karachi.

Jane picks up the magazine from the floor. The watch, she reads, costs over three million dollars! It is one of a kind, antique, handmade—and, still, Jane does not comprehend how something so small can be worth so much money, nor how anyone would ever feel comfortable wearing it.

Jane used to have a watch, too—not a three-million-dollar watch, but so beautiful. It had a heart-shaped face and a wristband made of woven silver strands. Ate received it as a parting gift from one of her former clients, and she gave it to Jane when Jane agreed to be her substitute at the Carters'.

"This is to thank you," said Ate, helping Jane with the clasp. "Also, so you will know when the baby must eat."

Jane returned the watch to Ate when she was fired, her head hanging low so Ate would not see her tears. Ate did not berate her, only said in a quiet voice that was worse than shouting, "I will keep it for Mali. Perhaps for her Confirmation."

"HI, JANE. THANKS FOR COMING UP. I'M MAE YU." MS. YU STANDS behind Jane's chair with her hand already extended.

Jane jumps to her feet. "I am Jane. Jane Reyes."

Ms. Yu stares at Jane with friendly interest but does not speak. Jane blurts, "My grandmother's name is also Yu."

"My father's Chinese, and my mother's American." Ms. Yu motions for Jane to follow her. "So I'm a halvsie. Like you."

Jane watches Ms. Yu—tall and slim in her navy dress, the thin pleats in the skirt swishing as she lopes across the room. Her hair, the color of burnt honey, is pulled back in a loose bun, and when she turns to smile at Jane, Jane notices she is as fair as a white person and wears no makeup.

She is nothing like Jane.

Jane is suddenly conscious of her skirt—too tight and too short. Why did she not listen to Ate, who counseled her to wear slacks? Why did she allow Angel to apply her makeup?

She stops in front of a mirror hanging on a nearby wall and starts to rub at the rouge on her cheeks with her fingers.

"Jane?" Ms. Yu calls from the doorway. "Are you coming?"

Jane drops her arm, blushing, and takes mincing steps toward Ms. Yu on her too-high shoes in her too-short skirt.

They walk down a hallway lined, on one side, with ceiling-high windows and on the other with framed paintings of birds. "The floors here are original to the house, from 1857. And those are original Audubons," says Ms. Yu. She points out the window. "We have over 260 acres of land. Our property line extends to that grove of beech trees back there. And those hills beyond, those are the Catskills."

They enter Ms. Yu's office, which is like Ms. Yu herself—simple and expensive looking. Jane takes a seat, feeling her skirt inch higher up her thighs. She tugs the hem lower.

"Tea?" Ms. Yu asks, reaching for a pot that sits on the low table in front of them.

Jane shakes her head. She is so nervous she fears she will spill on the white carpet.

"Just for me then." Ms. Yu pours with her left hand. A huge diamond, her only adornment, flares on her ring finger. She smiles at Jane. "How were your holidays? Did you do anything exciting?"

"I was home," Jane flounders. She and Amalia and Ate attended Christmas Mass; Angel cooked **pancit** and **bistek** and **leche flan,** and Amalia received gifts from almost everyone in the dorm. Not very exciting for someone like Ms. Yu.

"Home is where the heart is," Ms. Yu remarks.

"So, Jane. Your physical and psychiatric exam results were terrific. Passing Phases One and Two isn't easy. Congratulations."

"Thank you, ma'am."

"This interview is meant to let us get to know you a bit. And to show off our facilities here at Golden Oaks!"

"Yes, ma'am."

Ms. Yu studies Jane's face. "Why do you want to be a Host?"

Jane thinks of Amalia and mumbles to her folded hands. "I—I want to help people."

"I'm sorry, can you speak a little louder?"

Jane looks up. "I want to help people. People who cannot have babies."

Ms. Yu scribbles something on the tablet in her lap with a stylus.

"And—I need a job," Jane blurts. Ate warned her not to say this. It sounds like desperation.

"Well, there's no shame in that. We all need to work to support those we love, right?"

Jane stares again at the diamond on Ms. Yu's finger, bright against her dark dress. Billy did not buy Jane a ring. She was pregnant, and they married quickly, and he said there was no point.

"Your references were also outstanding. Latoya Washington . . ."

"She was my supervisor at my old work."

"Ms. Washington was very complimentary. She said you are a hard worker and honest. She wrote that you were wonderful with the residents. She was sorry to see you go."

"Miss Latoya was very good to me," says Jane in a rush. "When I first came to New York, it was my first job. She was understanding, even when I got pregnant—ah!" Jane claps her hand over her mouth.

"That was my next question, actually. About your child."

Ate told Jane not to bring up Amalia, because why would they want to hire someone who is always worrying about her own baby?

"We have no rule barring Hosts from having children of their own. As long as you wait the medically appropriate amount of time before implantation, there's no issue. And it's good to know you've carried successfully to term before." Ms. Yu smiles. "How old is your child?"

"Six months," Jane whispers.

"What a lovely age! I have a goddaughter who's just a few months older than that," Ms. Yu says brightly. The goddaughter lives in Manhattan. She takes a music class where the songs are in Chinese. The father is French, and he and Ms. Yu's girlfriend plan on raising their daughter to be trilingual. "What's your baby's name?"

"Amalia."

"That's beautiful. Is that the Philippine version of Amelia?"

"It is the name of my grandmother."

Ms. Yu writes on her tablet. "Jane, there is

one thing we **do** worry about with Hosts who have their own children: stress. Countless studies show that babies in utero who are exposed to excessive cortisol—which is a chemical released by the body when stressed—end up more prone to anxiety later in life."

"I am not stressed, ma'am," Jane says quickly.

"We'd need to be sure Amalia is well cared for, that you wouldn't need to worry about her while with us at Golden Oaks. Should we select you as a Host, what are your plans for her?"

Jane tells Ms. Yu about the one-bedroom she located in Rego Park in a no-fee apartment building. She will share it with Ate, who she will pay to take care of Amalia.

"Excellent. Another thing we ask is that you prepay your rent for the time you're with us. Again, this is to reduce stress during the pregnancy. If selected, you'd come to Golden Oaks at three weeks' gestation, which means prepayment of around ten months of rent," states Ms. Yu. "Many of our Hosts take an advance out of their paychecks to cover rent and child- or elder-care in their absence . . ."

"I have savings," Jane announces, trying not to sound boastful.

"And your husband, how does he feel about all this?"

Jane feels Ms. Yu's gaze on her, and her cheeks grow hot. "Billy? He is . . . we are no longer together . . ."

"I apologize for how personal these questions are.

I'm simply trying to pinpoint any sources of stress with which we can help you."

"He is not a source of stress. He is not a source of anything."

"Boyfriend?"

"No!" Jane blurts, flustered. "I have no time for . . . I have Amalia . . ."

"And how do you feel about leaving Amalia during your stay here?" Ms. Yu's eyes bore into Jane's. "You wouldn't see her for a long time unless the Client allowed it, which I can't guarantee."

There is a pain in Jane's chest, so sharp it is as if she is being cut, but she forces herself to meet Ms. Yu's gaze. She is doing this for Amalia, Ate has reminded her time and again, and this is what Jane tells herself now.

She answers: "My cousin is a baby nurse."

Ms. Yu jots something on her device. "She's in good hands, then. You're lucky. Some of our Hosts have left children in their home countries and never get to see them."

Ms. Yu stands and holds open her office door. "Now for the fun part. The tour!"

"Tour," Jane repeats, thinking worriedly about her shoes.

"Yes! This will be your home for almost a year. You should know what you're getting in to. As wesay: the best Host is a happy Host," says Ms. Yu. "Shall we?"

They turn down a different hallway which

connects the old building to a new one, half-hidden by tall shrubs, Ms. Yu moving soundlessly on flat shoes, Jane's heels clattering on the tiles. "We call this the Dorm. It's where you'll spend most of your time," explains Ms. Yu. She holds a badge up to a square card reader to get through another set of doors. They pass through an airy room with skylights cut into high, blond-wood ceilings where a receptionist greets Ms. Yu and turn on to a carpeted hallway lined with doors. On each door hangs a wooden sign. They pass Beech, Maple, and enter Pines.

It is a large bedroom with two sleek four-post beds covered in thick white comforters, a big square window with views of the hills, framed pictures of pine trees dusted with snow arranged on the walls and a large attached bathroom. "I hope you don't mind sharing a room," says Ms. Yu.

"It's beautiful," Jane breathes. In the dorm in Queens, a dozen people would sleep in a room this big.

Ms. Yu shows Jane the lab, where blood is taken and tested, examination rooms, for the weekly ultrasounds and checkups, the classroom where Hosts learn about best-practices in pregnancy, and the library, where one very pregnant Host reclines on a leather chair, her swollen feet resting on top of an ottoman. Jane stares at her, knowing she is being rude but unable to avert her eyes. The Host glances up at Jane, and Jane, heart banging, turns away.

"The exercise room," says Ms. Yu once they

have reached the bottom of a shallow set of stairs. She holds open the door for Jane. "Daily exercise is mandatory for the health of our Hosts and the babies they carry. You'll be extraordinarily fit when you return to Amalia!"

The room is mirrored on three sides, with exercise machines angled toward a fourth wall of windows. Rainbow-colored yoga mats are bunched in a large basket next to a shelf of free weights. A long glass table near the door holds stacks of folded towels, a porcelain bowl piled high with fruit and a pitcher of water filled with slivers of lemon and cucumber. Two Hosts walk briskly on treadmills and curl small red weights.

"Maria, Tanika, this is Jane."

The Hosts greet her and resume watching the flat-screen televisions mounted on the wall. Jane peeks at them as Ms. Yu describes the daily exercise regime. Ms. Yu then leads Jane to the dining hall, a cheerful room filled with white tables of varying shapes and matching chairs piled with woven pillows in bright colors. In the center of the room, a gigantic chandelier of curving, rainbow-colored glass hangs from the ceiling. Through a wall of windows at the back of the room, Jane notices a group of furry creatures grazing on the grass.

"What are they?" Jane asks, rummaging through her backpack for her phone. "Amalia will like them."

"Alpaca," answers Ms. Yu cheerily, placing her hand on Jane's arm. "Sorry, no pictures. In fact, we disable cellphone signals and Wi-Fi, so you couldn't send the photo anyway."

Jane watches the animals for a moment, feeling inexplicably hopeful.

"Do you know anyone with cancer?" asks Mae abruptly, leading Jane back toward the entrance of the room.

"I do," says Jane, thinking of Vera. She rents a bed on the second floor of the dorm in Queens. Her daughter Princesa, only thirty-two, discovered a lump the size of a grape in her left breast that within four months had ballooned to the size of a child's fist. Vera secured Princesa a tourist visa through a brother in the American consulate in Manila, and now Princesa sleeps in the bunk below her mother's. She Skypes nightly to her boyfriend back home, complaining about the long waits at Elmhurst Hospital, where she is treated for free, her Tagalog riddled with the American names of cancer medicines and television shows.

Ms. Yu gestures toward a Host with glossy black skin who is sitting alone at a table and drinking a green shake through a straw. "That Host there. She's carrying the baby of the CEO of a biotech company that discovered a way to detect cancer cells using nanoparticles." Ms. Yu looks at Jane. "These are the types of people you will be helping at Golden Oaks. People who are changing the world."

Jane is awed but does not know exactly what nanoparticles are and worries Ms. Yu will ask her.

She imagines an injection of glowing specks piercing Princesa's arm, the radiance rushing through her arteries like cars on a dark highway, her veins luminescent against her skin.

"And the Host you'll meet at lunch is carrying the baby of one of the biggest philanthropists in Texas." Ms. Yu leads Jane up a short flight of stairs to a private dining room.

"A Host?" asks Jane, suddenly nervous. Is this another test? To see if she can get along with the other women?

"Yes! As I said earlier—we want you to understand fully what you're committing to. Because once you're impregnated—once there's another **human** living inside you—it's no longer just about **you.** There's no going back." Ms. Yu signals for Jane to sit.

Three green salads sprinkled with pomegranate seeds and toasted walnuts are laid out on the table. Ms. Yu spreads a napkin over her lap. "We have our own chef and dietician—so the food's not only delicious, but really healthy. It's one of the perks of working here."

The door swings open. "I am late. I am sorry," a young woman apologizes. She is short and brown. Her dark hair is tied back in a ponytail, and she wears a T-shirt that hugs her stomach so tightly the wormlike outline of her protruding belly button is visible.

"Jane, this is Alma. Alma, Jane. Alma is twenty-four weeks pregnant . . ."

"Twenty-five, Ms. Yu," says Alma, grinning at Jane and taking the seat next to her.

"Twenty-five weeks pregnant for one of our best clients. They signed up for a three-and-three—three children in three years. Alma carried the first and is now carrying the third."

Jane does not like spinach but forces herself to eat it, chewing the gritty leaves for what seems like forever. No one speaks. The silence is a rebuke, a sign that Jane is failing. She blurts: "The alpaca are nice—"

"How are you feeling these days, Alma?" asks Ms. Yu at the same time. "Sorry to interrupt, Jane. You were saying something?"

Jane shakes her head, reddening.

"Good, Ms. Yu. I feel good. The baby, he is kicking," Alma answers.

"We're really proud that we not only have repeat Clients but repeat Hosts. It says something about the quality of this job that Alma chose to carry another child with us," Ms. Yu says. "Alma, do you want to tell Jane about a typical day at Golden Oaks?"

Jane relaxes as Alma describes her routine—meals, meditation, exercise, doctor visits, pregnancy classes, concluding, "It is good here. It is beautiful. The doctors is good. The people is nice."

"And tell Jane, Alma, what you do with the money you make here."

"With the money, I send it to my father in Mexico. He is a little sick. His heart is no good.

And some I keep here with my husband and my son. Carlos."

"Can you tell Jane about Carlos?" Ms. Yu prods gently.

"Carlos, he is eight and he has . . . **cómo se dice . . . dislexia?**"

"It's the same. Dyslexia."

"**Dislexia, sí.** Now, with the money, we have a teacher especially to help Carlos," concludes Alma. She takes a forkful of salad. "Carlos, he is doing good!"

Ms. Yu addresses Jane. "Of course we make the salary more attractive than the alternatives— nannying, eldercare, even baby-nursing jobs. Our Clients **want** their Hosts to be treated well. But I don't know that money alone is sufficient motivation for this job. You need to have the temperament. And the calling."

"I do," says Jane, thinking of Amalia and all the things she would be able to do for her and protect her from, if only she could get this job. "I do have the calling."

"RIGHT WRIST, PLEASE. SLEEVES UP," SAYS THE COORDINATOR. It is Jane's first day. Her interview at Golden Oaks was only six weeks ago, but in that time everything has changed. An unknown baby lies in her stomach, and she is a hundred miles away from Amalia, surrounded by strangers. The smiling woman who greeted her in the Dorm's lobby this morning took not only her suitcase and wallet but her cellphone, so Jane has no sense of the time, whether she has been at Golden Oaks one hour or seven.

Jane rolls up her sleeve and extends her arm, wondering if she is getting another shot, and why, since she is already pregnant.

The Coordinator straps a bracelet onto Jane's wrist, rubber or rubbery looking, and pushes a button that makes its thin, rectangular screen light up. "This is a WellBand. Custom-made for us. I gave you red 'cause it was just Valentine's Day!"

Jane stares at it. Mrs. Carter used to wear something similar, a circle of blue plastic like a child's toy that looked strange next to her diamond tennis bracelet, the gleaming ovals of her nails.

"It tracks your activity levels. Try jumping."

Jane begins to jump.

"See?" The Coordinator angles the bracelet face toward Jane. The green zeroes that had once filled the screen have been replaced by orange numbers that climb steadily as Jane hops, growing short of breath.

"You can stop," says the Coordinator, but in a friendly way. She holds Jane's wrist and guides the bracelet over a reader attached to a laptop until the reader bleeps. "There. Now you're synched up with our Data Management Team. Let's say your heart rate spikes—this happens, it's usually no biggie, but it can also signal some underlying irregularity in your heart, pregnancy being a strain on your tick-tocker." The Coordinator—Carla?—pauses, waiting for the severity of this possibility to set in. "We'll know immediately, can whisk you in to see a nurse. Or if you're not getting enough exercise, we'll have Hanna all over it." Carla grins. "All over **you.**" Her freckled cheeks fold into dimples. Jane has never seen so many freckles in her life—freckles on top of freckles receding into freckles.

"Hanna . . . ?"

"She's our Wellness Coordinator. You'll get to know her **real well.**" Carla winks at Jane. She runs through a tutorial of the WellBand—its various monitors, timers, the alarm and snooze and panic buttons, the GPS locator, calendar, alerts, how to receive announcements.

"How do you like the clothes?" Carla's eyes rake over Jane, head to toe and back up again. Jane feels her face grow hot. In truth, she has never worn clothes so thin and so soft. Just this morning in her winter coat, she was freezing. Ate and Amalia waited with her on the street outside their apartment building for the car to arrive, Amalia buried under so many layers of wool and fleece that Jane could barely see her face. But here, in clothes light as air, Jane is warm. Jane says so to Carla.

"Cashmere," Carla answers matter-of-factly. "Golden Oaks doesn't skimp, that's for sure."

There is a knock on the open door. "Hi, Jane," sings Ms. Yu, giving Jane a stiff hug.

"Hello, Ms. Yu." Jane jumps to her feet.

"Please. Sit. I just wanted to make sure you're settling in." Ms. Yu takes a seat on the bench next to Jane. "How's the morning sickness? Is your room okay? Did you meet Reagan?"

"I feel okay, only a little tired," Jane answers. "The room is beautiful. So are the clothes." Jane rubs the cashmere on her thigh with her palm. "I have not yet met my roommate."

Ms. Yu frowns slightly.

"But," Jane says quickly, not meaning to get her roommate into trouble, "I had the check-in with the nurse and the orientation. I have been busy."

Ms. Yu's face relaxes. She places a hand on Jane's hand. "I'm guessing Reagan was tied up with an appointment. She'll be around soon, I'd think. This is your new home; we want to help you **feel** at home."

At the word "home," Jane's throat tightens. She wonders what Amalia is doing, whether she notices her mother is gone.

As if sensing Jane's thoughts, Ms. Yu asks, "How's Amalia? Was the goodbye hard?"

Jane is pierced by gratitude that Ms. Yu, who is so busy, remembers Amalia's name. She shifts her gaze to the wall so that Ms. Yu cannot see her eyes, which are teary. "It was fine. Amalia is almost seven months now; she is a big girl. And she has my cousin."

"She's in good hands, then." Ms. Yu's voice is kind.

Jane still does not trust herself to face Ms. Yu. She can hear Carla's fingers tapping on a keyboard.

"I know you know our policy, Jane, which is that we don't allow visitors, and we don't allow Hosts off-site unless at the request of a Client." Ms. Yu leans closer to whisper, "But I think we can convince your Client to let Amalia come see you."

"Really?" Jane blurts.

Ms. Yu puts a finger to her lips and smiles. She asks Jane if she is ready for lunch and, when Jane confesses she was too nervous this morning to eat, leads her to the dining hall. Jane trails several steps behind, wiggling her toes in her new fur-lined moccasins, a tentative sense of well-being creeping over her. Ms. Yu keeps up a constant stream of chatter, pointing out her favorite views of the mountains, giving Jane bits of trivia about the surrounding towns. As they walk, Jane imagines Amalia here—hiding beneath the soft blankets draped on the sofas, mesmerized by the fires crackling in the stone fireplaces.

"Do you think you'll feel at home here?" Ms. Yu asks. She pushes the dining room door open with her shoulder.

"Oh yes," says Jane, and she means it.

There is a short line of Hosts next to the serving table. Ms. Yu introduces Jane to two white women—Tasia, tall and skinny with bad posture, and a shorter, full-figured one named Anya— before dashing away to prepare for a meeting. In her absence, Jane feels nervous all over again. The line moves quickly, but when it is Jane's turn to choose her lunch she cannot decide between the sirloin and the salmon, nor between water and a pomegranate drink, and she has to wait several minutes for the multivitamins to be refilled from the dispenser. By the time she is ready, Tasia is already eating with Anya at a table across the room. Jane grips her tray and walks toward them, the rubber soles of her moccasins seeming to stick to the floor. The room is packed. There is a table of black Hosts to her left and a table of four brown-skinned women on her right. Near the fire exit she notices a group of women who look Filipina.

"Jane. Come eat," Tasia calls, motioning.

"Do you know which baby you carry?" Anya asks even before Jane is seated. Her words are accented. She has the same deep-set blue eyes as Tasia, but her face is leaner, perhaps because she is not as pregnant.

Anya stuffs a large forkful of salmon into her mouth, and the sight of the fish, pink and wet, nauseates Jane.

"You feeling sick?" Tasia asks.

"I'm fine. Just—" Jane tastes bile in her mouth and grips her stomach, praying she does not get sick in front of all these people.

"Ah, I have it bad, too," Anya complains, her mouth still full of fish. "Every day, throwing up, and never in the morning. But all the rest of the day!"

Tasia whips a paper bag out of a polished-steel dispenser at the end of the table and hands it to Jane. "Throw-up bag." She adds reassuringly, "Do not worry, Jane. The first trimester is the hard one."

Jane pushes her tray away and presses her head to the table's cool surface. She had morning sickness with Amalia, too, but it was different then, less frightening. Maybe because the baby she is now carrying is a stranger's, the child of someone who invents cures for cancer, or someone who gives more money away than Jane will ever see in her lifetime.

Anya and Tasia are silent except for the sound of their knives scraping against plates. The surrounding conversations mingle into a wordless buzz.

"Lisa, she is getting fat." Anya's voice cuts through the room's chatter. She and Tasia are staring several tables away at two American girls. One of them, the more pregnant one, is arrestingly pretty, like the actresses on magazine covers.

"It is because she skips the exercise class," says Tasia in a cold voice. "She has not come in two weeks. Ms. Hanna does not report her because Lisa is her favorite."

"You should inform Ms. Yu, I tell you," insists Anya, shaking her head. She turns to Jane. "So then, you have not met your Clients?"

"No," Jane answers, still hunched over the table. She sees Tasia shoot Anya a look. "Is that bad?"

"No, no. Sometimes the Client is busy, that is all.

Or sometimes they wish to wait until second trimester, when there is little danger of miscarriage."

At the mention of miscarriage, Jane's stomach drops. She tries to stay positive, because the Golden Oaks materials she studied say it is better for the baby. But she cannot help worrying. The prepayment for Amalia's daycare is nonrefundable. She is not sure about the rent on her apartment.

"What happens if you have a miscarriage?" she asks. "I know you leave Golden Oaks . . . But what exactly happens with the money?"

"You did not read the papers? Only sign?" Anya scoffs.

In the month and a half since Jane was hired by Golden Oaks, she has been busy moving into a new apartment, and finding the right daycare for Amalia, and getting pregnant. Ate offered to read the documents Golden Oaks sent in a big FedEx box marked CONFIDENTIAL, and Jane gratefully agreed. She simply signed where Ate told her to sign.

"You get paid a little every month," Tasia explains. "But the bonus, the big money Ms. Yu promised you? That is only at the end. You understand?"

Jane remembers that Ate mentioned this. They were seated at the counter in Jane's new kitchen. The room smelled like fresh paint, and they had the windows cracked open even though it was cold outside. Ate told Jane about Golden Oaks' rules on cellphones and email, the privacy agreements, the payment schedules, and direct deposits to her bank.

Jane was so overwhelmed by the flood of information that she did not even begin to consider the questions now jostling for space in her head:

What if a miscarriage is not her fault?

Does she get another chance with another baby?

What if the baby is born but dies soon after? Does she keep her money?

Jane opens her mouth, but the words lodge in her throat.

"Here is Reagan coming," Anya mutters.

One of the American girls, the thinner one, is walking toward them. She has large eyes, gray like a rainy day, and long hair pulled in a loose braid.

"Hi, Jane, I'm Reagan. Your roommate. I completely forgot you were coming today. Pregnancy brain!"

Tasia stands abruptly. "You take my chair. I am finished. And I must see Ms. Yu." Anya also excuses herself. The two wish Jane luck and carry away their empty trays, Tasia towering over her friend by half a foot. Several yards away they burst into shrill laughter.

"How're you holding up?" Reagan asks, settling into Tasia's chair and tucking up her legs.

Jane is overcome. She has been imagining her roommate since receiving the roommate-introduction note in the mail three days ago. She has read it so many times she knows it by heart:

Your roommate, Reagan, graduated cum laude from Duke University, double-majoring in Comparative Literature and Art History. She

grew up in Highland Park, Illinois, and lives in New York City. She is a first-time Host.

Even before Jane searched **Highland Park** and **Duke University** and **Comparative Literature** on the Internet, she knew she and her roommate had nothing in common. Looking at her now, Jane is certain she was right.

"I am fine," Jane mumbles after an awkward pause, wondering for the hundredth time what her-own three-sentence description said, what thoughts ran through her roommate's mind when she read it.

She picks at a glob of hardened mustard on the table's surface with her fingernail. Ate counseled Jane to be polite with the other Hosts but to keep a distance, because no one at Golden Oaks is her friend. They are her colleagues, and carrying the baby is a job. Jane is trying to think of a question to ask her new roommate when she notices, out of the corner of her eye, the slender gold chain encircling Reagan's wrist.

Jane is stricken. What does she have to say that would interest Reagan, who has gone to college and did a double-major and can wear a bracelet like this with such ease?

"It can be weird at first," Reagan says, seemingly unperturbed that Jane is mute. She begins to give Jane tips about Golden Oaks "from my whopping two weeks of experience!" How it is best to visit the media room during dinnertime, when it is not so crowded; how she should take the long way to the fitness rooms to avoid Ms. Hanna's office, otherwise she might waylay you and grill you about your diet; how there is a snack table set out in between meals and in the evenings—fruit and energy bars, vegetable slices with healthy dips, herbal teas and nuts and smoothies—and as long as Jane stays within her weight range, she is allowed to snack to her heart's delight, so it's no problem if Jane does not have an appetite at mealtimes.

Jane listens wordlessly, panicking because she still cannot think of anything to say.

"Lisa! Over here!" Reagan beckons to the pretty American with dark hair and green eyes. Her friend is speaking heatedly to one of the cooks, then grabs something from a platter near the serving window and stalks toward them, muttering angrily.

"Despite what Betsy claims, a bran muffin is **not** banana bread." She glares at Jane as if waiting for a response.

"No?" Jane agrees uncertainly.

Reagan laughs. "Jane, meet Lisa. Feel free to ignore her."

"And the thing that's bullshit is," Lisa continues, still addressing Jane, "we're all **pregnant** and we get **cravings** and it seems that they should get snacks that satisfy our **cravings** which are really the **baby's** cravings. And isn't everything about kowtowing to these babies?"

Jane glances around the room nervously. The

nearest Coordinator stands by the fire exit, typing on her device.

"Mind over matter," Reagan intercedes. "Your cravings are just your hormones, not you."

"I **am** my hormones," Lisa snipes, sitting heavily on a chair and taking a reluctant bite of the bran muffin. She complains under her breath that she detests raisins.

"Jane's my new roommate. And today's her first day."

"Welcome to the Farm," Lisa says dully.

The smile Jane is trying to muster dies before reaching her lips.

"Dammit, every cell in my body **needs** banana bread!" Lisa slams the bran muffin onto the table.

"I . . . I can make banana bread?" Jane offers timidly, looking at Lisa's scowling face with a mixture of nervousness and fascination.

Lisa bursts into laughter. "God, they would never let you near a **stove.** You might . . . singe the fetus!" But her voice has softened. "So. Do you know which baby you're carrying?"

Jane shakes her head, no, and Lisa declares, in a loud whisper directed at Reagan, "Neither. Does. Reagan."

Reagan sighs. "It doesn't matter!"

"Of course it matters!" snaps Lisa.

"Why does everybody ask this?" ventures Jane. "Anya, the one who is Russian?"

"Polish," interjects Lisa. "Don't call her Russian. She'll knife you."

Jane is not sure whether to smile. "Anya asked me this, also. Several times."

"She did, did she?" Lisa perks up. "So Anya is fishing for info. **In-ter-est-ing . . .**"

"Lisa's been carrying babies for Golden Oaks since the very beginning," Reagan interrupts, clearly wanting to change the subject. "She's on her third."

"And that's only because of the money." A grin flashes across Lisa's face. "I'm over the romance of being pregnant, unlike my friend Reagan here—"

Reagan rolls her eyes.

"—who still thinks there's something profoundly **meaningful** about it."

Jane is not used to people speaking like this— the words they use, how fast they fly, like Jane is being bombarded.

"It **is** an incredible thing to give someone life," Reagan says.

"Yeah, but that's not what all of us are doing here," Lisa retorts. "It turns out **my** Client could've carried her babies herself if she wanted to."

"But a lot of Clients can't," Reagan says to Jane. "A lot of them are barren because they're old. Or incapable somehow of—"

"What they **all** want is an edge for their babies." Lisa is looking at Jane, though Jane senses she is talking to Reagan. "I wouldn't be surprised if the

Farm's started shooting up our fetuses with brain boosters. Or immunity enhancers or—"

"Those don't even exist!" Reagan snaps.

"But when they do, are you telling me they wouldn't—"

"Stop it."

"You don't think our Clients would pay anything to make sure their **uber**-babies are—"

Jane's stomach is roiling. She folds over herself again in hopes of quelling the nausea.

"Jane, sit up."

Bewildered, Jane obeys.

"First," Lisa says, "don't lie on the table unless you want a Coordinator up your ass. Second, and more important, you've got to understand what this place is. Okay? It's a factory, and **you're** the commodity. You've got to get the **Clients** on your side—not the Coordinators, and not Ms. Mae. I'm talking the parents and, especially, the mother."

"Lisa . . ." Reagan says in a warning tone.

"I . . ." Jane swallows. What if her Clients do not like her? What if they compare her to a Host like Reagan?

"I have not met—" Jane's eyes fill with tears.

"Well, not everyone does," Lisa says briskly. "Some Clients don't give a shit about their Host. But most do, because they're obsessed with everything related to their babies. It's the new narcissism. That's the Farm's gig: feeding it; **fanning** it."

Jane remains silent, her heart banging, wondering if she has made a mistake. If the job is more complicated than Ate said it would be.

"Whenever you **do** meet your Clients, your goal—your only goal—is to get them to **love you.** You want the mother to feel **good** and, even, **virtuous** about having you carry her baby. You want her to want to have another baby with you and **only** you. And when the parents decide to have Baby Two, and they insist that **you** carry it—well, then. You'll have **leverage.**" Lisa pauses. "Do you know what 'leverage' means?"

Jane, embarrassed, shakes her head.

"It means Ms. Mae has to bend. Bend to your will, if you will. Because the Farm's got revenue targets, and the customer's always right—and if your Client only wants you? Well, that's leverage." Lisa's eyes sparkle. "**My** Clients adore me. And that means I can demand things with this third bambino—like, more money. And my own room. And visits from my man. And, even"—and now Lisa unleashes her voice—"BA-NA-NA BREAD!"

Jane ducks. A Coordinator yells at Lisa to pipe down.

"For fuck's sake!" Reagan hisses, shooting Lisa a dirty look. She turns to Jane, a tight smile on her face. "Don't listen to her. She's not usually this nuts. She's just hormonal."

"I **am** my hormones, I told you," Lisa grumbles.

"Take it one day at a time. Just focus on keeping yourself well for the baby. That's what's most important: your baby."

Jane is engulfed by the desire, so sharp it cuts, to be home. Away from these strangers and their too-fast, too-smart talking. She longs to be in bed with Amalia watching television. She wants to palm her baby's fat belly until Amalia falls asleep, her arms flung up over her head as is her habit, so open and trusting, like the world could never do her harm. The nausea that had receded returns, more forcefully.

"Are you okay?" Reagan's face looms over her, her eyes full of concern.

Jane is reaching across the table for the vomit-bag dispenser when she throws up.

REAGAN

A RIPPING SOUND, METAL RINGS SCRAPING METAL, AND THEN light. Light scything through the darkness. An infestation, Reagan thinks. Behind her closed eyelids, scattered pinpricks balloon into a pinkness so bright it makes her head pound. Fucking Macy. Miss Early Fucking Bird. Even hungover, her roommate wakes with a smile and ties her sneaker laces in perky double knots, ready to pound the concrete along the East River. Reagan braces herself for the inevitable "Rise and shi-ine!"

Instead, footsteps slap past. Someone humming. But not Macy, because Reagan's not in Manhattan.

She cracks open one eye and is engulfed by late morning light. The pounding in her head intensifies, tendrils curling from her ears sprouting vines, sprouting leaves big as palm-tree fronds, wrapping around her head and tightening, her head being shrunk to pellet-size. It's the light, she is sure of it, the light triggering this ravaging pressure.

"Another migraine?"

Reagan stares at the figure in front of her for one blinding moment before remembering who she is. "I think so."

"Sorry," says the Coordinator, sliding the curtains closed again. "I thought maybe you forgot about your ultrasound."

The ultrasound? But she set an alarm yesterday— Reagan glances at her wrist.

"You left it in the basement, by the pool." The Coordinator hands Reagan her WellBand. "It's waterproof, you know. If you keep taking it off they're gonna fuse it on you."

Reagan fastens her WellBand, smiling at the joke.

"I'm serious. Keep it on," says the Coordinator. "You should get moving. I think your Client'll be there."

Despite the hammering in her head, Reagan sits up, a flurry of excitement in her chest. "My Client?"

"Think so. Get going, you!" says the Coordinator as she closes the door.

Reagan checks her WellBand. She's got time. She sets an alarm for herself and drops back onto her pillow, gazing across the room at Jane's bed, already made. Her roommate here's an early riser, too. And extremely tidy. These are the only things Reagan really knows about Jane, even after living with her for two and a half months.

The pressure in Reagan's head suddenly sharpens. She shuts her eyes and attempts the breathing exercises Ms. Hanna taught her the last time this happened, when she asked for an Advil. (We do not medicate the baby; we teach you how to tame your mind, Ms. Hanna had said, wagging her finger.) There's no way Reagan will allow herself to miss this ultrasound. It's her first one in 3-D. Even Lisa admits the images are incredible.

You can see its face, she said. **Every peak and groove.**

And now Reagan's going to meet her Client, too.

She's wondered about her, obviously. Or him— the parents could be a couple of gay guys. She doesn't have a clue, because since arriving at Golden Oaks Reagan's been unable to glean even the tiniest crumb of information about her Client's identity. "Fetal security" is Ms. Yu's excuse, although Lisa insists it's a ruse, a way to keep the Hosts ignorant, because then they're easier to control.

Reagan swings her feet off the bed, head throbbing. A hot bath might help. She wobbles toward the bathroom, catching sight of herself in the full-length mirror that hangs near the door: wheat-colored hair in a limp tangle on her back, her build slim under the Golden Oaks–issued nightgown. She lifts the hem, exposing the length of her legs and the flatness of her stomach. She imagines herself inflating, the hiss of helium and her feet lifting off the floor.

She perches on the edge of the tub and turns on the tap.

When Reagan first heard the baby's heartbeat at the ultrasound appointment earlier in the month, she was overcome by wonder. This flickering inside her; the enormity of her undertaking. A life! She carried a life! She lay on the cot and let the heartbeat wash over her, tears spilling down her cheeks. Afterward, she was a little embarrassed, but Dr. Wilde assured her that "heightened emotionality" during pregnancy was normal. It was the hormones.

But Reagan knows the contentedness, even elation, she's felt since arriving at Golden Oaks is much more than that. It is something entirely new: a clarity. A rootedness after what seems like a lifetime of drifting.

How far along are you? is the first question anyone new to Golden Oaks asks her, and she answers confidently: "ten weeks" or "fourteen." Knowing that in seven days she will be a week further along. Knowing where she is, and what she is doing, and why.

It just shows that even Macy, Reagan's roommate and her closest friend since college, isn't always right. At Duke they agreed on almost everything:

their interests (museum-hopping and books and boys) and hobbies (partying and music and boys) and political views (pro-choice, pro-environment). Now, at twenty-five, Macy is the youngest-ever-black-female associate at Goldman, co-head of the bank's Duke recruiting team, a member of the young patrons committee of a downtown museum, board member of an after-school program for at-risk youth in Queens, and runner of sub-three-hour marathons.

When Reagan confided in Macy about Golden Oaks—a breach of the NDAs, but Reagan swore her to secrecy—Macy had been harsh. They were pregaming before a friend's party, half-empty wineglasses on the nicked coffee table in their living room. An ambulance on Second Avenue drowned out Macy's voice, but only for a moment: "Surrogacy—this kind of surrogacy!—is a commodification, a cheapening! Everything sacred—outsourced, packaged, sold to the highest bidder!"

"Easy for you to say," Reagan had snapped. "You work at a bank! I'm sick of depending on my dad, and I'd be helping someone have a child who—"

"You're letting a rich stranger **use** you. You're putting a price tag on something **integral**—"

"Live-in nannies, baby nurses, wet nurses," Reagan recited, saying whatever popped into her head. "Blood donors, kidney donors, bone-marrow donors, sperm donors. Surrogates. Egg donors . . . Remember those ads for egg donors in **The Chronicle?**"

The Chronicle was their college newspaper, its classified section crammed with job listings for dog walkers, test-prep tutors, after-school babysitters; ads for transcendental-meditation classes, self-storage units; listings for study-abroad programs, student-loan companies, used cars for sale. And, here and there, pleas for egg donors. One of these had caught Reagan's eye her freshman year after yet another snippy phone call with Dad:

> Stable, college-educated Buddhist couple (both Duke graduates. GO BLUE DEVILS!) seeking egg donor. Donor should be 18–24. Preferably student and/or graduate of Duke or equivalent top-tier college. Caucasian. Blond or light-brown hair. Light-colored eyes preferable. Between 5'6" and 5'9". Athletic. Healthy. Spiritually open. Minimum GPA 3.6. $14,000.

She was intrigued. That the couple was Buddhist. That they were so clearly type A but cared about her spirituality. What did that even mean? Would a spiritual donor produce more enlightened eggs? Did lapsed Catholics count?

And of course: Reagan needed money. To escape Dad and his attempts to forge her in his image. Without asking her first, he'd gotten her an internship back home in Chicago. One phone call to his fraternity brother from Notre Dame, a managing director at a big investment fund, and whammo presto! No need for interviews, resumes, none of those pesky hoops to jump through. A favor returned for a favor bestowed. That's why you keep up with your networks, Reagan. It's **who** you know as much as **what** you know.

Dad's presumptuousness was the clincher for Reagan. She went through the whole procedure solo. At night she hid in the dormitory bathroom and injected herself full of Lupron, Follistim, HCG. Her ovaries sprouted more follicles, her follicles sprouted more sacs, each sac teeming with eggs. The day she was harvested she lay on her back and the doctor sucked her dry with a needle. It took half an hour. Because there was no one to drive Reagan home, the nurses kept her in recovery for hours, until she woke clearheaded. Then she took a taxi back to campus and slept straight through until the next day.

"And that's why I could afford to intern in D.C. Remember that summer?" Reagan concluded, downing the remaining wine in her glass.

Macy was quiet long after Reagan stopped talking. She was never quiet for more than a few minutes. Softly, Macy asked, "Did they . . . test them?"

Of course she was thinking about Reagan's genes. It was one of the jokes (that wasn't a joke) that drew them together—that both of them were genetically fucked: Macy, because she could count a half-dozen family members, easily, who were alcoholics, including her mom, who had died in a drunk-driving accident when Macy was young. And Reagan, because of the dementia. They even had a jokey pact that they would both forgo marriage and procreation to spare the next generation from their screwed-up genes, which would leave them time to do huge things in the world, and then they'd grow old together.

"I never heard from them." Reagan shrugged, unwilling to admit how relieved she was when she received the check for the eggs in the mail. Because type A parents like that **would** have checked for every genetic mutation, wouldn't they?

"It just seems . . . hollow. Like selling your eggs was just any old transaction—but they were **your eggs**," said Macy, who spent her days at the bank making trades, one hollow transaction after another.

"They didn't mean anything," Reagan explained, bristling. They grew inside only to be discarded each month, like toenail clippings or hair snippets on a salon floor. Why let them go to waste, when someone else could use them?

"It's not the same thing," Macy answered soberly. "Your hair and your toenails aren't even remotely in the same category."

Reagan sheds her clothes and slips into the water. She sinks to the bottom and resurfaces, her upper body floating. What is it about water that amplifies sound? Reagan can hear the echoey drip drip drip from the faucet. The sound of her breathing fills her ears and reminds her of when she learned to scuba dive. It was in high school, after a volunteer trip to rebuild houses in Asia in a village decimated by a hurricane. She remembers the feeling of weightlessness, sunlight wavering through the water. The only sound, anywhere, was her breathing. Her inhalations and exhalations, and the dark waters below. It was the loneliest sound in the world.

Does the baby feel lonely, submerged in her waters?

Reagan cradles her stomach as she steps out of the tub.

Mom, Reagan believes, would get it in a way that Macy can't: The attraction of the elemental. The peacefulness of life postponed. Mom mentioned once that she'd gone to an ashram in India when she was in her twenties, a silent retreat where she didn't speak for weeks.

In her own way, that's what Reagan's found at Golden Oaks. A capsule of quiet she hadn't anticipated, away from the scrambling of the outside world. She brought her camera, but it was confiscated on her first day. A disappointment, but she's found it's freed her up for other things. She just started **Infinite Jest,** because Macy said she'd love it. And she's been paying attention, as Mom always exhorted her and Gus to do. Reagan keeps a notebook here—not diary entries; words don't often behave for her—but lists of images, ideas for photographs she means to take once she leaves Golden Oaks. Macy would laugh at the lists, because they can read like poetry, and Reagan isn't a fan of most poetry. She never even cracked the binding of the book of Dickinson poems Macy gave her for her twenty-fourth birthday last fall, though she brought it with her.

There is a bleeping from the bedroom, where Reagan left her WellBand. It's the alarm she set. Butterflies in her stomach as she begins to get dressed, because she's about to meet her Client.

THIRTY MINUTES LATER, REAGAN IS ON HER BACK. EVERYTHING throbs. The Calder mobile overhead seems to shudder. The white walls warp and roll. Reagan's head pulsates in time with the baby's heartbeat, dictated by it.

"Headache?" Dr. Wilde's voice.

Reagan nods, keeping her eyes shut.

"Can you lower the volume a little?" Dr. Wilde asks. A command wrapped in a question.

The room quiets but not enough, the underlying beat of the baby's heart still pushing against Reagan's skull, the pressure so intense she is pinioned to the table.

Ba-**BOOM**, ba-**BOOM**, ba—

"Agnes, more, please." The slightest edge to Dr. Wilde's voice, and a welcome quieting.

Ba-boom, ba-boom, ba-boom . . .

The Client isn't coming. The Coordinator who returned Reagan's WellBand got it wrong. Reagan heard Dr. Wilde berate her for getting Reagan's hopes up and for discussing the Client "when Client matters are none of your business."

It's okay, Reagan had laughed it off, feeling sorry for the Coordinator. I'm used to having my hopes crushed.

But Dr. Wilde ignored her. She's different today. There is an aloofness to her, when usually she goes out of her way to be nice. Something almost clinical in how she is scrutinizing Reagan.

Dr. Wilde squeezes gel onto Reagan's bare stomach and begins to move the ultrasound wand across it. Out of speakers that Reagan cannot see, the baby's heartbeat seems to accelerate.

Baboombaboombaboombaboom . . .

Is it a recording?

The thought strikes out of nowhere: that the heartbeat filling the room is canned, a soundtrack played for Clients to reassure them that their babies are vigorous and they're getting their money's worth. One heartbeat sounds like another, after all. It would probably save the Farm money.

The Farm. A Lisa word for a Lisa thought. Lisa's always making snide jokes about Golden Oaks, the monumental efforts taken to make Clients feel good about outsourcing their pregnancies. "Our aim is to **delight** you!" Lisa mocks, simpering smile, hands clasped and head bowed like a novitiate. **Deeee-light.** She makes the word sound like ice cream. "Because having a baby should be **deeee-lightful!**"

Reagan imagines her Client—who is linking in by video from somewhere, maybe a mansion, maybe a private jet. There would be a laptop cracked open before her. Dad at her side, his tie loosened and a full head of hair. Onscreen Dr. Wilde's face bobbing, the baby's heartbeat (the recording of a baby's heartbeat?) blasting from the laptop speakers. Mom and Dad tilting forward, eyes moist, eager to glimpse their **deeee-lightful** future—

No.

She isn't Lisa. It was **her** choice to be here. To carry this baby and care for it.

She refuses to taint her time at Golden Oaks, or the tiny, unformed being inside her, with this kind of cynicism. She worries sometimes for the baby Lisa carries. Forty weeks stewing in her sour broth. How can the child not be affected? Reagan imagines it emerging stunted somehow. Shrunken, like a tree never exposed to light.

"So, Mom, the baby's fourteen weeks today and looks fantastic!" says Dr. Wilde, addressing the camera. She wears a headpiece with the black bud of a microphone positioned directly in front of her mouth. "Are you at your laptop, Mom? Get ready to see Baby in 3-D!"

Reagan cranes her neck but cannot see the ultrasound screen. She is about to ask the nurse to tilt it toward her when Dr. Wilde speaks: "Agreed, Mom. It's a whole different ball game."

She pauses, head cocked and listening, then continues. "Yes, Mom. About Baby. It's a bit over two inches in length as of today, the size of a small lemon. And this here, this is the amniotic sac." Dr. Wilde traces something on the ultrasound screen with her fingertip. Reagan tries to push up on her elbows to get a view, but the nurse frowns at her, and Reagan grudgingly reclines. She can see nothing—not the baby nor the sac, nor can she hear the Client's questions. Only Dr. Wilde's sunny responses, her agreeable laughter.

Reagan stares up at the skylight, feeling strangely unnerved. The ultrasound wand slides back across her belly.

"Let me try to get Baby to move so you can see its face better."

Reagan jumps as a finger prods her belly. Dr. Wilde smiles down at her, cool and reassuring. Another poke, a many-fingered nudge. "There! See Baby squirming?"

Dr. Wilde describes the baby's developmental milestones, her enunciation crisp. "Have you thought more about whether you want to pursue genetic testing?" Dr. Wilde reviews the pros and cons of an amnio. She reassures the Client that the chances of miscarriage are slim—the needle is so very fine, they use an ultrasound to guide them— but the odds of an issue, given the age of the egg, the sperm, the family history, well . . . Statistics follow. On the one hand, on the other. **Mom, have you considered a CVS?** The words, directed elsewhere, run together. Reagan dozes.

"And here she is." Dr. Wilde's jolting voice, and Reagan is yanked upward. Her eyes fly open.

Dr. Wilde and the nurse and the camera face her.

"Mom wants to know how you're feeling," coos Dr. Wilde, an unusual lilt in her voice.

"Great," answers Reagan. She has never spoken directly to the Client before, and she is nervous. The camera eyes her. Reagan smooths her hair and forces herself to speak. "I was really tired and nauseous the first few weeks, but it's been a lot better lately."

Dr. Wilde says encouragingly, "You'll feel more energy now that you're in the second trimester."

Reagan mentions the migraines.

A slight furrow appears across Dr. Wilde's forehead. "But they're less frequent now. It's not unusual. It's nothing to worry about."

Reagan cannot tell if Dr. Wilde is addressing her or the Client.

"When was the last migraine headache?"

Reagan's head still pounds, but the look on Dr. Wilde's face makes her hesitate to say so. "Um . . . Not for a while . . ."

"Do they occur often?"

"Not really."

"Is the baby kicking?" It is obvious that Dr. Wilde is merely parroting the Client's questions. The way she pauses before she speaks, then pauses again for the Client's next prompt. As if Dr. Wilde has no mind of her own but is simply a conduit, a puppet propped on a stool.

Reagan forces herself to look at the camera. "Not yet."

"That's normal, Mom," says Dr. Wilde to no one in the room. "It's the Host's first time carrying, so it will take longer for her to feel the baby move." A pause, head tilted, then to Reagan: "Is your stomach bigger?"

"About the same."

Dr. Wilde instructs Reagan to sit up, to turn. The nurse pulls open her robe before Reagan can stop her, exposing her stomach, her chest. The camera and Dr. Wilde and the nurse study Reagan, unmoved by her nervous fidgeting, the heat in her face.

Dr. Wilde pauses, then laughs. "Yes, flat as a mattress . . . but we'll fatten her up! Yes, I will do that. Thank you, Mom. Until next week."

She hands her headset to the nurse. The nurse instructs Reagan to get changed and places a towel in her lap. They chatter about the morning's appointments and drift away. At the doorway, Dr. Wilde calls, "Keep up the good work." She shoots Reagan an uncharacteristic thumbs-up. Reagan knows the Client asked her to do this.

"And, of course, making it to the second tri means you get your first performance bonus," remarks Dr. Wilde.

"Thank you." Reagan clutches the top of her gown closed and wipes her stomach with the towel.

She waits until the doctor and nurse have disappeared down the hallway before changing into her sweatpants and T-shirt. The headset lies on a tray on the counter. Reagan picks it up, gingerly, and puts it to her ear. Silence. The kind of silence that buzzes.

"I HAVE NEWS."

Reagan is bent over, drying her hair. Between her legs she sees Lisa's bare feet padding across the carpet, toenails painted a bright green.

"**Big** news," Lisa repeats, heaving herself across Jane's bed with a grunt. She begins picking at her toenail polish and scattering green flakes across Jane's bedspread.

"You have to clean that up." Reagan knows she is being bossy, but it irks her that Lisa is always leaving a mess on Jane's bed. Not that Jane ever complains. That irks her, too. How Jane just takes it.

She drops her towel on the floor and pulls a clean robe from the closet. It is newly pressed and smells like mint.

"I need to get it off. The new Coordinator bitched me out for it. Because of the toxins—"

"It is no problem. I can clean it later," Jane offers, out of nowhere. She has the disconcerting habit of appearing and disappearing without a sound, like a cat. She hovers near the doorway now, ready to dart back into the hall at any moment. A thin film of sweat shines on her forehead, and she wears exercise shorts.

"Thanks, Jane. You rock."

"Clean it yourself, Lisa!"

Reagan regrets telling her about Jane's habit of cleaning their room whenever the housekeeping staff is scheduled to come in. Lisa theorized that Jane's behavior is ingrained: the Philippines was colonized for so long that Filipinos got used to serving; generations later, their genes are wired for it; it's why the best hotels in Asia are swarming with Filipino staff.

Lisa swipes the flakes off Jane's bed with her hand. "Happy now? What's with you lately?"

Reagan shrugs. In truth, she isn't sure. Maybe hormones; maybe the headaches. Plus, she's still annoyed that Lisa—queen of conspiracy theories— was so dismissive about Reagan's ultrasound earlier in the week: Dr. Wilde's cocked head as she listened to the voice in the wire; her cold appraisal, as if Reagan were a specimen in a lab. If it had happened to Lisa, she would have ranted about it for days and expected Reagan to listen. But her latest obsession is all-consuming: the "billion-dollar baby," and who carries it.

Reagan rummages in her drawer for underwear, feeling Lisa's eyes boring into her back. She knows Lisa is dying to be asked about her

Big News, but the sheer intensity of her zeal feeds Reagan's indifference.

"Jane." Lisa switches tactics. "I'm going to let you in on a secret. You have to swear you won't tell **anyone.**"

Reagan rolls her eyes. Jane, who is drying the bathroom floor with Reagan's discarded towel, nods.

Lisa begins to tell Jane about the rumor she heard several weeks ago from Julio, the Buildings and Grounds Manager: the richest couple in China is using the Farm to have their first baby. Because their sperm and eggs are old, they will pay their Host an enormous sum of money—multiples of the regular bonus—if she manages to deliver a healthy baby, full-term. And if she delivers it vaginally, the Host will receive an astronomical bonus.

"We're talking serious dough," Lisa says, slowing her words for effect. "Change-your-life money. Fuck. You. Money."

"What's with the vag fetish?" Reagan asks, to needle Lisa.

"It is better for the baby," Jane pipes up unexpectedly. "For the immune system of the baby, vaginal delivery is better than a cesarean. This is because of the good bacteria. The baby gets good bacteria from the mother's . . . ah . . . canal."

Reagan looks up, startled. It's the longest sentence Jane has ever spoken in front of her. And it sounds as if she swallowed a pregnancy book.

"If the baby's going to live in Beijing, it needs all

the immunity it can get," Lisa agrees. "And get this: I've narrowed down the possible Hosts to **three** people." She gazes gravely from Reagan to Jane then back again.

Christ. Lisa's too much.

"Who are they?" asks Jane in a low voice.

"Anya. Reagan. And you."

"And how can you possibly know this?" It slips out before Reagan can stop herself.

Puffed with importance, Lisa explains that according to her latest intel, the billionaire fetus is currently between twelve and sixteen weeks old. "You three are the only ones in that range who haven't met your Clients yet," Lisa says, adding, "You lucky bitches."

Jane perches on the edge of her bed. She is clearly nervous to be so close to Lisa. Then again, she hasn't really warmed to Reagan, either.

It isn't for lack of trying. Reagan has made countless efforts with Jane over the months, all of them rebuffed. She even went as far as swiping a bag of candy for her—peanut M&Ms, her favorite, Reagan overheard her tell another Host. This was earlier in the month, when Ms. Yu took Reagan to see **Hamlet** at a small theater nearby. Reagan stole the candy while the server at the refreshment stand was getting her a glass of water. But when Reagan later handed Jane the M&Ms, Jane only pressed her lips together and shook her head, horrified.

Lisa says Reagan should stop trying so hard, and

she's probably right. But it still bothers Reagan, why she can't break through. She has the sense that Jane judges her. That—based on nothing—Jane has typecast her as just another clueless, rich white girl.

The unfairness of the caricature upsets her. She gets this from her father, too. Every time he mocks "limousine liberals," Reagan senses it is code for her and her friends. Even Macy has teased her about her "white guilt" and her **heteronormative, upper-middle-class white privilege.**

Reagan remembers, though, the expression on Jane's face when she found a necklace of Reagan's—white gold with a single imperfect pearl dangling from it—kicked under the dresser. Reagan hadn't realized it was missing. "I'm actually **trying** to lose it; it's from my loser ex," Reagan had joked—too flippantly, she recognized later.

"You must put it away for safekeeping. Because the cleaners come tomorrow," Jane insisted. "You cannot leave out precious things when they are here."

Reagan was too shocked to reply.

"So, she's racist," Lisa concluded a day later. They were at the snack table before lights out. The pickings were unusually slim.

"Racist?" Reagan echoed.

Lisa picked up a bag of kale chips and shrugged. "Maybe that's why she doesn't like you. Or the cleaning ladies."

"She's not **racist.**"

"She only hangs out with other Filipinas," Lisa responded. "What, do you think only white people can be racists?"

Ayesha, a Host from Guyana with an impossibly high-pitched voice, sidled up to the snack table. "I am too hungry to sleep." She picked up a health bar and began slathering almond butter on it, angling her head in Lisa's direction. "She is right. My mother does not like blacks. Or Chinese people, because they own all the businesses in my country. Everybody is a little racist."

Before Lisa or Reagan could answer, a Coordinator burst into the room and began scolding Ayesha for snacking when she was twelve pounds over her target weight. Ayesha apologized without seeming sorry, tossed her snack into the garbage, and squeaked goodbye to Lisa and Reagan before being escorted back to her room.

"You want me to help break the ice with Jane?" Lisa asked, her mouth full of kale.

"If she's racist like you say, she won't like you, either."

"But I'm better with people than you are!" Lisa asked Reagan if she knew which room Ayesha was in, stuffed several health bars into her pocket, and sauntered out the door.

"I STILL DO NOT UNDERSTAND. WHY WILL A CLIENT NOT WANT to meet the Host? If I was a Client that is the first thing I will do," Jane is speaking to Lisa. Reagan blinks, looking about her with bewilderment. Did she fall asleep? How did Lisa get Jane talking like this?

Reagan finishes dressing, listening to Lisa but pretending not to. She moves to the rocking chair at the edge of the room and idly picks up her notebook from the windowsill. Lisa is boasting about her savviness: how she duped the Coordinators into giving up critical information; how her friends in the kitchen know more than people think because they serve the lunches that Ms. Yu hosts for important Clients. Jane is absorbed. Outside the window, a bird with bright red wings wheels in the sky. Reagan scrawls into her notebook **Black bird/ red wing/bleached sky** even though the image isn't particularly arresting. She notices as she writes that Jane and Lisa are now sitting side by side, and Jane no longer seems so ill at ease.

Reagan feels a twinge in her chest. Lisa's right: she **is** better with people than Reagan is. Reagan's never found it easy to connect with strangers, unless she's drinking. She misses Macy. They haven't spoken in weeks because Macy's been traveling for work.

"What will you do if it's you?" Lisa asks Reagan. Allowing her in, or maybe just expanding her audience.

Reagan looks at her blankly. What would she do? If she carried a billionaire in her belly?

"I . . . I don't know exactly," she answers, stumbling over her words. She chose to be a Host because it was an escape—from her menial job in the art gallery, from her dad. But it's become more than this. At Golden Oaks she's gotten a hint of what it might mean to do what she wants, how she wants, without worrying about **practicality** or whether this month's rent check from Dad is in the mail—a foretaste of freedom that's gotten her excited about photography in a way she hasn't been since college. It's not about the money but the freedom, that's the thing. The freedom to do something real and worthwhile.

"But freedom **requires** money," Reagan says, almost pleadingly. "And the weird part is **too much** money is the exact opposite. It's a cage in and of itself, you know? Because you end up just wanting more and more, like my dad, and then you lose sight of the whole point . . ."

It was Mom who encouraged her to notice. She was always pointing things out to Reagan and her brother Gus—the old woman so bent with age she could only stare at her feet as she shuffled across the street; the poster for a lost cat taped to a lamppost, the letters stenciled, the PLEASE CALL IF FOUND underlined six times.

Mom was artistic, or had been before Dad came along. Dad said it was why he fell in love with her: her way of seeing the world and making it her own. Your mom's no cookie-cutter corporate wife, he boasted back then, and she wasn't. She was funnier than the other wives in their circle, more alive.

She gave Reagan her first camera in first grade, when Reagan was having trouble learning to read. It was a Polaroid that spit out pictures instantly from a slot in the front. Words are only one way to express things, Sweetie, Mom said. She told Reagan about photographers who helped people see the world anew: Ansel Adams with his landscapes, Walker Evans and his photos of the rural poor.

If you don't notice, you can't care, and you won't do anything that matters, Mom used to say. Reagan now thinks maybe it was a jab at Dad.

The first picture Reagan took with the camera was of Mom. Reagan didn't know how to aim, and she accidentally lopped off the lower half of Mom's face. When the blank white square began to take shape, it was Mom's eyes that emerged. Out of nothing, her eyes.

"I messed up," Reagan remembers saying, disappointed.

"But that's me," Mom said, looking at the photo with delight. "You captured me exactly."

"TROY'S VISITING SOON. YOU'RE GOING TO **LOVE** HIM, JANE . . ."

Lisa's acting as if Reagan hadn't just spoken. Reagan tries not to feel slighted. She's seen Lisa do this before, choose someone to subject to her charms, win them over, and add them to her collection. Usually she doesn't do it at Reagan's expense.

Lisa begins bragging about her boyfriend—an artist, a **revolutionary**—she believes in his work so much she pays for his studio space. The problem is, he's so busy preparing for a show at a gallery in Atlanta that he isn't returning her emails. She's feeling horny—that's what happens in the second trimester, just wait for it, Jane, it's incessant, like an itch—and the least Troy can do is reply to her emails with something naughty. To tide her over.

"I've got to come up with a plan," Lisa continues. "Because we're gonna need our privacy so we can **reconnect.**" She waggles her eyebrows suggestively at Jane, who looks paralyzed.

Reagan laughs, surprising herself. It isn't funny, but it **is.** It's all completely ridiculous: three pregnant women carrying other people's babies talking about second-trimester sex pangs and trying to guess which one of them harbors a billionaire's fetus.

"There are cameras all over the hallways. Maybe Troy can get in through the window?" Reagan suggests, trying to catch Lisa's eye.

"I do not think we should be talking like this." Jane looks nervously around the room.

"The bedrooms aren't wired," Reagan reassures her.

"Janie Jane, let's go for a walk!" Lisa says suddenly. "The trails are finally open. Spring's sprung!"

"Me?" Jane looks at Reagan as if seeking confirmation.

"Yes, you. Reagan's happiest with her Infinite Slog." Lisa shoots a withering glance at the thick book at Reagan's side. "And we haven't gotten to hang out yet!"

Reagan's face burns. Lisa doesn't even look at her as she stands and stretches and checks the weather on her WellBand. Jane, clearly flattered by Lisa's invitation, hums as she digs in the closet for a pair of boots that fit.

"I'm ready," Jane says. "Reagan, are you sure you do not want to come along?"

It's the first effort she's ever made, and she's making it out of pity.

"No thanks." Reagan picks up **Infinite Jest** and pretends to read.

Lisa scrutinizes the sky. "Let's get going, Jane. It's sunny now, but it's supposed to storm."

JANE

REAGAN'S NIGHTGOWN LIES ON THE FLOOR NEXT TO A PILE OF clothes. Jane picks it up and places it in the laundry bin. She presses a pair of discarded pajamas to her nose. They are clean. She flaps them several times to air them out, folds them into squares, and places them on top of Reagan's bureau next to a pink bra.

The bed is a tangle of sheets. Reagan was late this morning. She forgot about an appointment with Ms. Hanna, who is strict about time, and did not wash her face or even brush her teeth—only changed clothes and stumbled out the door.

Not that Reagan ever makes her own bed. She

teases Jane that if all the Hosts were like her, the housekeeping staff would lose their jobs. But Jane hates to see a mess. And also: what would the cleaning people think if the room she shared was a disaster? That she is lazy or unclean. That she believes she is better than they are—to kick her socks under the bed for them to retrieve, to leave toothpaste stuck to the sink for them to wipe away.

Jane begins to straighten the sheets, tucking them under the mattress with quick jabs of her hand, working fast. She finds a bracelet under Reagan's pillow and shakes her head, putting it in her roommate's nightstand drawer underneath a pad of paper. Reagan never remembers to put her things away. Jane has warned her that carelessness can cause problems. At the retirement home, Jane was blamed several times when a resident could not find a ring or watch, the accusations stinging like thorns even when Jane knew them to be untrue. Thank God she always found the missing objects— forgotten in the shower, mistakenly thrown in the trash—but until she did, her stomach roiled with fear and shame.

Outside the open window, a bird sings. Jane looks up and smiles. How can she be anything but happy!

Yesterday, when Jane's WellBand beeped with a message from Ms. Yu, Jane was instantly afraid. Was the baby sick? Deformed? Dying? Jane was into her second trimester, but terrible things could still happen. Over the years she had heard so many stories from Ate—about babies stillborn, or born without arms or chins, with weak lungs, shrunken heads, perforated hearts, stunted brains.

But she was wrong—happily, joyously wrong. Ms. Yu welcomed Jane to her office, closed the door, and announced: Amalia will be allowed to visit! Jane burst into tears and could not stop crying, even as she sputtered her thanks.

The plan is this: Ate will take the Metro-North train with Amalia to Golden Oaks next Friday, only eight days away. A car will bring Jane to meet them at the train station and the driver will stay with them all day, taking them wherever they want to go nearby—the freshwater lake past the dairy farm, any of the small towns surrounding them which, says Ms. Yu, are so charming. Only not to Golden Oaks, because the others might get jealous that Jane, a first-time Host, has been allowed visitors.

Several times Ms. Yu made this clear: **This is an exception I am making for you.**

Ms. Yu also told Jane that her Client insisted on paying for the car and the driver and even for lunch ("within reason"). If all goes smoothly and there is a second visit, the Clients would consider paying for a hotel room so that Amalia and Ate could stay the night. Sitting in Ms. Yu's office and learning of the generosity of her Clients—complete strangers, Jane has still never met them—she was overcome with something like love and found herself promising them silently: **I will take care of this baby with my whole heart.**

Of course, the plan was a secret. But Jane was bursting, bursting yesterday after leaving Ms. Yu's office, so full of hope she felt she was floating. Reagan was in their room, sitting on the rocker and writing in the small notebook she kept in her nightstand. And without thinking, Jane confessed everything. As she spoke, Reagan shut the bedroom door and sat close, listening. She promised to keep the secret, and Jane trusted her.

I trust her! Jane marvels at this strange, surprising fact as she plucks a long blond hair from her roommate's pillow and drops it over the trash bin. The hair drifts slowly down, catching the light one moment, the next invisible. Her own nightstand is a little messy, with stray bobby pins and a tube of lotion and several books Reagan gave her when she'd finished with them. Jane sweeps the clutter into a drawer and transfers the books to the shelf beside her bed. She does not even like to read, but she loves these books; she loves that Reagan believes she will read them.

It was not always like this. For many weeks, Reagan made Jane jumpy. She had so many questions: about Jane's childhood, her family, her job. But, mostly, questions about the Philippines, because Reagan had spent a summer there when she was a teenager. She helped build a house and a school; she tried **bagoong** and even **balot,** the fermented duck eggs that Billy loved and that made Jane gag.

They were too different, that was all. Differences only cause problems, and Jane did not need any problems.

Everything between them changed one afternoon several weeks ago. Jane was unwell. Her stomach was unsettled, and she was so sapped of energy she had napped most of the afternoon. She almost never did this. She did not like the thought of anyone—her roommate, a Client taking a tour—seeing her asleep.

When the WellBand began ringing, Jane did not at first recognize the sound. It was a whining, like that of an insect or a faraway jet, filtered by many miles. Even when she realized that it was the alarm, that she herself had set it, it took Jane some time to make her way to the surface. When she did it was almost four o'clock, the time when she told Ate she would video-call. Jane snatched a bottle of water from the small refrigerator in the room and ran, half-asleep and stupefied, to the media center.

The media center was the only place at Golden Oaks where Hosts could receive and send emails and make video-calls and check the Internet. The room—big, well-lit, filled with sleek computers in open-air cubicles or private ones enclosed by glass— was empty except for Reagan, who waved when Jane entered. Jane tensed, anticipating the usual well-meaning assault. But this time, thankfully, Reagan remained in her chair, engrossed in whatever was on her computer screen. Jane hurried into a cubicle and called Ate.

"Hello? Hello?" Ate's creased forehead filled the screen. "Hello, Jane?"

"I am here, Ate. Do you see me? I can only see your forehead."

There was a sharp movement onscreen as Ate re-aimed the camera. The lower half of Amalia's body appeared, as well as a fragment of Ate's lap. "Smile, Mali. Smile at Mama," Ate's disembodied voice urged. Ate lifted one of Amalia's arms and waggled it so that Amalia's hand waved.

"Ate, I cannot really see her. Tilt the camera up a little . . ."

There was a fumbling sound, the image onscreen jiggling, and then Amalia's face appeared. She was smiling and reaching for the phone. "No, Mali. No touch," admonished Ate, her hand pushing Amalia's away. Amalia's dark eyes shone. The tender skin around her right eye was stained a pale blue-violet.

"What happened to her eye, Ate?" Jane leaned forward, now completely awake.

Amalia lunged for the phone, her outstretched hand ballooning on Jane's computer screen. Ate's hand swatted her away. "I took her to the doctor for the ear infection. They gave me the drops. They said it was not a problem."

"But why does she have a black eye?" Jane

persisted. Amalia was now sitting obediently on Ate's lap and sucking her fingers.

"Her eye? It was an accident. She rolled off the table at the doctor's and—"

"Off the table?!" Jane did not mean to raise her voice. Through the cubicle's glass wall she noticed Reagan looking at her. "Amalia fell off a table?"

Amalia began laughing, because Ate was jiggling her. Usually this made Jane smile. Ate answered, her voice soothing, "It is okay, Jane. Mali is okay. She cried for only a short time."

Jane knew this voice of Ate's. It was the one she used for the mothers who wept when they had to supplement their breast milk with formula, the ones who worried when their babies did not sit up according to the development schedule in the books.

"Weren't you watching her?" Jane's voice in her own ears sounded off, razor-thin and too high. But it was Ate who taught Jane the importance of always watching the baby. Because babies roll, and they could fall. Always take the baby with you, Ate instructed Jane before she left for Mrs. Carter's.

"It was an accident," repeated Ate calmly. "Just a small accident. Babies are strong. You are worrying too much, because you are pregnant. I remember one time when I was pregnant with Roy—"

A strange sensation stirred within Jane. Something hot and vaporous rising in her body, spilling into her ears so that she could not hear the rattle of Ate's words. She had never raised her voice at Ate before, but suddenly she was shouting. "I am overreacting? Because you are more careful with the Clients' babies than with your own family?"

Jane, shaking, forced herself to stop. To close her mouth and give Ate space to respond. But no sound issued from the computer's speakers. "Answer me, Ate!" Jane demanded, but her fury was already receding, a wave of shame already rushing in to take its place. The image on her computer screen was frozen: Amalia with one hand tugging a tuft of her hair. Jane jiggled the mouse over the desk and banged on the keyboard, trying to jar the computer back to life. But the connection was broken. Jane shoved the keyboard away, a last burst of anger, and folded herself over the desk, tears wetting her sleeves.

What kind of person yells at someone so old? Someone who is only helping?

"Jane?" It was Reagan.

She placed a box of tissues on the table and stood behind Jane, wordless and solid, like a sentry. Jane lay there, her body shuddering, not even knowing anymore why she cried. After a time, she noticed that Reagan's hand was on her back; not rubbing, but not merely resting, either. It generated warmth.

Reagan handed her a tissue. Jane accepted it and blew her nose.

"She's beautiful," Reagan said, gazing at the computer screen. "She looks just like you."

———

JANE IS FINISHED TIDYING THE ROOM. HER FITNESS CLASS DOES not begin for almost an hour, which gives her time to video-call Ate to tell her about the visit. Since their fight, Ate has emailed Jane dozens of pictures and videos of Amalia—mostly close-ups of her face. Jane thinks Ate wants to prove that Amalia's bruised eye healed quickly, and Jane overreacted. Jane has avoided actual video-calls, knowing her lingering anger with her cousin would show. But today she will look Ate in the eye and say she is sorry. She should not have been so disrespectful.

In the media center, Jane sees Reagan in one of the private cubicles staring at her video screen. Jane waves, and Reagan waves, too, but does not smile. Maybe she is video-calling with her mother. Reagan is often out-of-sorts after their weekly call.

Jane slides into a workstation and picks up the phone. An automated voice says the conversation will be recorded. Jane presses 9 to signal agreement and enters Ate's number, but she does not answer. Jane leaves a voicemail about Amalia's visit, unable to keep herself from smiling.

"I hate my father," Reagan announces. She leans against the cubicle wall and crosses her arms tightly across her chest.

"What is wrong?"

"He's mad that I haven't visited Mom in so long. He pulled this whole guilt trip . . ." Reagan, agitated, begins pacing the short length of the cubicle, like an animal too big for its cage.

Reagan has told Jane about her mother, who was only in her forties when she began to forget things—where she left the keys, the dog, the car. How she no longer remembers her own name or those of her children.

"Maybe Ms. Yu will allow you to visit," Jane suggests.

"My dad doesn't know I'm here. Or that I'm pregnant," Reagan says, her voice thick. "He'd never understand."

Ayesha is passing by. "I am looking for Lisa. I am still not allowed to go to the snack bar, and maybe she can find something for me again?"

Reagan remains silent. Her eyes are red, as if she is about to cry. Jane has never seen her cry before. She tells Ayesha to check the library, and then she leads Reagan back to their room.

The door is barely closed when Reagan starts telling Jane how much she hates visiting her parents. Her father refuses to put her mother in a home, but he barely spends time with her unless he is dragging her to an opera or a vacation abroad, always trailed by one of the nurses he hires to do all the "real work." Sometimes he even hosts dinners for his colleagues with the mother sitting at the head of the table, beautiful as ever, her food untouched.

Jane is astounded. What kind of man can feel a love this big?

"She's just a prop to him," Reagan contradicts her.

"But he stays. Most men would leave." Jane thinks of Billy, then her mother. "Some women, too."

Reagan begins telling Jane about her mother before the sickness. She was the "cool" mom. All of Reagan's girlfriends had a crush on her—admiring how she styled her hair, the "funky" clothes she wore. Reagan's mother let them watch R-rated movies before they were teenagers. She asked their opinions on politics and art, because she believed they had something to say. Once, she let them spray-paint the room above the garage because she no longer used it as her studio. When the father came home from work he was furious, but the mother only laughed.

"She told us street art was real art. Because it's **gritty not pretty.** Like life," Reagan says in an expressionless voice.

By the time Reagan was in high school, she saw her mother differently. Her "quirkiness" was shtick; her father's pride in the mother, proprietary. He liked that she was original, and funny, and smart—but only within boundaries, never too much. Reagan began to disdain it, her mother's constant performance. She was the most brightly plumed bird amid a flock of dull-colored ones. But who gave a shit when she was still trapped in a cage that she herself had chosen?

"Maybe they loved each other in a way you do not understand. Maybe they did not understand their own love, either," Jane says, thinking of Nanay, who was stern and frightening and who rarely showed affection, but whom Jane loved fiercely.

She adds, a little timidly, "And your father is sacrificing everything for her now."

"He hasn't sacrificed anything! It's ego, not love."

Jane listens silently as Reagan tells her about the father's girlfriends—one here, one there, never for too long. She and Gus heard rumors throughout childhood, so how could their mother not have known? And if she did, what did that make her?

Jane finds herself telling Reagan about Billy. When they moved to New York, Jane found a job at the retirement home, and Billy re-enrolled in community college—a precondition set by his parents for letting Jane and him live with them for free. Billy went out with his friends almost every night after class but never invited Jane, and she was embarrassed to ask him to include her. He already thought she was too needy.

One night, Billy forgot his phone in the apartment, and someone kept texting. Jane watched the messages blink on its screen, one after the other:

I'm at the bar. I'm tired of waiting for your ass. I'm not wearing panties. You stuck with your dumb-ass wife?

Jane knew Billy's security code because he never changed it, and when she looked in his phone she found hundreds of texts from her. His girlfriend. She was in school with him, and he had been seeing her for months. In one exchange they plotted how they could take a vacation together in Puerto Rico, where she was from. Billy texted that Jane wouldn't even know where P.R. was.

She's a hi-school dropout. Dumb as fuck.

"You're **smart,** Jane. You just didn't finish school!" Reagan says.

Jane shakes her head, because Billy's words still make her feel ashamed.

"Listen to me." Reagan's eyes are blazing. "Everyone in my family and all of my friends went to college. And what **you** know, the kind of smarts **you** have, they will **never** learn."

Jane is stirred. Her friend seems so certain.

"And you're brave," Reagan continues. "My mom had way more advantages than you, but she stayed with my dad. You had the guts to leave."

Jane shakes her head. "I only left Billy because Ate pushed me."

"I don't believe that."

"I think maybe . . . it is not only one way. Maybe you can love someone even if you do not love everything about them," Jane says slowly, because these are new thoughts, and she has never said them before, even to herself.

"My dad loved my mom as long as she played by his rules. It's the only way he knows how to love," Reagan answers, and there is such harshness in her voice that it hurts Jane's heart.

"I do not think that is love. I do not think your father—"

"**Everything's** conditional. Everything's got strings attached."

"That is not true!" Jane says with a fierceness she did not intend. She averts her eyes, embarrassed, and says more quietly, "I do not love Amalia like that. Family has no strings."

Reagan is quiet. When Jane looks up, she sees that her friend is crying.

"I believe, from your stories, I believe your mother loved you like this, too."

JANE IS ABOUT TO SHOWER AFTER HER EXERCISE CLASS LATER in the afternoon when Lisa barrels into the room.

"Troy just left. We had **no** privacy. The Coordinator—what's her name, the redhead—made us keep the door to my room **open,** like we're fourteen or something." Lisa snorts, flopping onto Jane's bed. "You up for a walk?"

Jane grimaces. On their last walk several weeks earlier, the trails were newly opened after a period of rain, and the ground was wet. At one point, the mud was so thick and deep that Lisa got stuck. Jane had to practically lift her out of her boot, which Lisa left sunken in the trail.

The Coordinator on duty, Mia with the red hair, berated Lisa, who was shivering with cold by the time they arrived back at the Dorm. Her bootless foot was caked in mud, blades of grass clumped between her toes. Mia scolded Jane, too, "It's a buddy

system for a reason. You're supposed to take **care** of each other."

Lisa was whisked away down the hall, and Jane was directed to one of the bathrooms attached to a medical suite and told to take a warm shower. Afterward, she was given hot tea while Mia and another Coordinator dried her hair and examined every inch of her scalp with a magnifying glass. As Mia studied Jane's neck and chest and stomach, she lectured her about the different diseases harbored by ticks, and the other Coordinator scrutinized Jane's backside. She was asked to lie down underneath the lights and spread her legs.

"You'd be surprised where those ticks can get to," Mia joked.

Jane says to Lisa, "I am sorry, but I am meeting Delia soon." It is not a total lie. Jane has not spent time with her Filipina friend in days, and she should visit her.

"But I want to go walking with you!" Lisa exclaims. She clasps her hands. "Please, Janie Jane? Pretty please?"

Jane reddens, flattered despite herself. She knows it is childish, but she likes the nicknames Lisa gives her. She likes that Lisa, who first was Reagan's friend, now considers Jane a friend, too. Two times in front of the others, Lisa flung her arms around Jane and Reagan and called them her **besties.** Jane's Filipina friends say she is becoming a banana ("Yellow on the outside, white on the inside") and tease her that she is getting a big head. But it is not true. Jane knows she is nothing like her new friends. It is only that she likes to be around them. She likes how Lisa and Reagan talk, as if anything were possible.

Jane glances out the window at the sun, still high in the sky. It has been warm for several days. The trails must be dry by now.

"Okay," Jane concedes, and she smiles when Lisa lets out a whoop.

"You're the **best,** Janie Jane. Get dressed and bring a towel so we can picnic. I'll meet you in my room, okay?"

Jane takes care to dress according to the rules this time. She stuffs light-colored pants into tall boots, chooses a long-sleeved shirt and sticks a baseball cap on her head. In a backpack she stuffs a bottle of water and a large pool towel and walks to Lisa's room, which is on a separate hallway. Lisa is already waiting in the doorway. Behind her, Jane notices tall orange flowers with beak-like blooms in a vase on the desk. They look tropical, like something that might grow wild in the Philippines.

"They're called birds-of-paradise," Lisa explains. " 'Cause Troy says I'm his exotic bird. Which I guess makes the Farm paradise." She makes a face.

At the Coordinator Desk a middle-aged woman with singed-looking brown hair scans their WellBands into a reader and reminds them to stick together. "Have fun, ladies."

Lisa and Jane exit through the back door onto a bluestone patio. Large plastic tarps still cover the furniture. They walk toward the trees, their boots crunching on gravel.

"Wassup, David!" Lisa gives a high five to a workman fiddling with a camera affixed to a large map of Golden Oaks' trail system. They talk, Lisa laughing. Jane closes her eyes as she waits, enjoying the sun on her face.

"New plan. Let's take the blue trail to get to the green one instead," Lisa says to Jane, who shrugs, not minding either way.

They walk in comfortable silence as the trail widens, gravel giving way to hard-packed dirt, taller trees casting longer shadows. Birds warble, and there is a gentle wind through the leaves. Jane makes a mental note to remind Ate to bring the baby carrier; it would be nice to take Amalia to a park somewhere and walk through the woods.

Ahead of them, the trail forks around a copse of trees. As they near it Jane notices with a start a man, tall and lean, peeping out from behind an enormous oak. Jane gasps and grabs Lisa's arm. Before she can press the panic button on her WellBand, Lisa is hurrying toward him, her arms flung wide.

"Baby!" Lisa shouts. The man steps toward her. She reaches up for his face with both hands and kisses him hard. Jane remains on the trail, too shocked to move.

"Come over here!" Lisa hisses to Jane, gesticulating wildly. "Don't worry, there aren't cameras on this stretch. David told me!"

Jane hesitates. The man flashes her a lazy, sensuous smile. With one tattooed hand he pushes the hood off his head and runs long fingers through tangled hair. "You must be Jane. I've heard a lot about you. **Magandang hapon.**" **Good afternoon** in Tagalog. He winks at her.

Lisa giggles. Jane has never heard her giggle in this way, like a young girl. "Jane, this is Troy. Who I guess is learning to speak Filipino!"

Despite Jane's anxiety, she feels a flicker of happiness that Lisa has told her boyfriend about her. Jane wipes her sweaty palms on her pants and returns Troy's greeting, **"Magandang hapon."**

Lisa unhooks the WellBand from her wrist. "Janie, can you go for a walk and take this with you? Just for, like, thirty minutes. So Troy and I can have some privacy?" She shoots Jane a radiant smile, dangling the WellBand by her fingertips, and continues, "Stick to the medium loop 'til you get to the creek—there's only one camera on that part of the trail, attached to the trail map. Pass close and walk slowly so you block the camera with your body. Then you're home clear. You can rest by the bank for a bit. It's flat."

Jane stares at Lisa's WellBand. She is already shaking her head. No, no.

"Please, Janie Jane? This is Troy's first visit in

months, and we got **no** time alone together earlier," Lisa wheedles, snaking her arm around Jane's shoulders.

Jane remains silent, her chest tightening.

"I wouldn't trust anyone else. It's only for half an hour. We'll be back at the Dorm before you know it. Okay?" Lisa's large green eyes hold Jane's as she slips the WellBand into Jane's palm.

"You're the **best,** Janie!" Lisa calls, already running back to the trees. "I owe you! Meet you here in thirty!" Troy smacks her rear when she nears him, and Lisa giggles. He mouths **thank you** to Jane, and the two disappear down a slight decline into the density of the trees, leaving Jane alone on the trail.

Wait! Jane wants to shout but doesn't. Should she go after them? Jane takes a step toward the trees and stops, paralyzed. But what if she cannot find them and gets lost in the woods? She looks at Lisa's WellBand in her hand. Should she throw it into the forest and return to the Dorm and confess? But she does not want to get Lisa in trouble. And they are supposed to be buddies—what if the Coordinators blame **her**?

Jane's eyes sting with tears. She peers into the forest and calls to Lisa in a low voice. How did they disappear so fast? And what can she do, now that they're gone? She tries to think of a plan, but her mind is numb. She walks toward the creek, feeling as if the earth might crack beneath her, like too-thin ice. She stands on its bank, feeling exposed. How stupid she is for going on this walk! She should have shouted. She should have pressed the panic button.

Jane squats on her haunches, hugging her knees and staring at the brown creek in front of her. She needs to think, but her mind will not stay still. There is a splash in the water. Are there fish in this small, nothing creek? Two butterflies, white as clouds, dance by her head. Then she hears voices. Far down the trail Jane sees two Hosts, still hard to make out, dark skin peeking out from long-sleeve tunics, both wearing baseball caps. She jumps up, panicked, and retraces her steps, moving like someone hunted.

"Lisa?" she calls at the fork in the path, but she cannot yell, because the other Hosts might hear her. She toes the forest floor and calls Lisa's name again. Almost thirty minutes have passed; why is Lisa not back? What if the other Hosts arrive as Lisa and Troy emerge from the woods? What will Jane say if they find her alone? Without thinking she plunges into the trees, where it is immediately cooler, a dark tangle of low branches and fallen leaves. She stumbles down a steep hill, half-tripping, breathing hard. Just as the ground flattens, she catches herself on a mossy rock. Christmas trees—they look like Christmas trees—stand in a thick bunch in front of her. She pushes through a net of branches.

Lisa does not even see her. She is on her hands and knees, her hair loose around her face, her shirt bunched around her neck so that her breasts swing loose. Her pants are off, the immensity of her stomach exposed. Her hands, planted like hooves in the dirt, paw at the ground. Troy is hunched behind her, shirtless, an enormous bird—a falcon? a phoenix?— blue and green and violet feathers spread across his chest. He thrusts, eyes shut, mouth twisted in what could be pain. His hands anchor her hips, bring her roughly to him, again and again. He grabs her breast, gripping so hard Lisa yelps, then whimpers, writhing, pushing back against him so that he is farther, farther inside. He lets out a moan that is like a growl, more animal than human.

Jane backs away in a panic, twigs snapping, behind the pines, behind the Christmas trees, back to the mossy rock. Even yards away she can hear their breath, sharp and wet, in her head. She can see the grime under his fingernails, the pink scratch marks on her flesh. She begins to climb up to the trail, her thoughts flying so fast they become a blur. She sits on the ground in the clearing where the path forks, not caring anymore if the other Hosts see her. They do not arrive; they must have hiked past while she was in the woods.

Lisa emerges more than twenty minutes later. She is full of energy, almost manic, first proclaiming her love for Janie Jane, then explaining to Troy in great detail where he should meet Julio, who will sneak him out of Golden Oaks. When she and Troy move closer to say goodbye, Jane averts her eyes, and by the time she looks up he is gone.

Lisa chatters incessantly to Jane as she cleans herself—rubbing her hands with baby wipes she has removed from her backpack, scrubbing her face and between her legs. She rebraids her hair, changes her shirt. They walk back to the Farm using a shorter route, Lisa talking the entire time—about sex with Troy, about Tasia, about how Jane needs to stand her ground and assert herself more.

Jane hears but does not listen.

Mia the Coordinator is on duty again. Jane takes a hot shower without being asked. She barely feels the Coordinators' fingers on her. From behind, she feels the slightest scrape on her upper back. The Coordinators speak in hushed voices, a drawer opens and closes. Mia shows Jane the tick, sealed in a plastic bag, ready to be sent to the lab. It is the size of a poppy seed. It looks completely harmless.

MAE

THE PILE OF MAIL EVE DROPS INTO MAE'S INBOX LANDS WITH a thump. Mae switches the screen on her laptop with a flick of her fingers. She didn't hear the knock; she hopes Eve hasn't been standing there long.

"Thanks." Mae pretends to study the spreadsheet now up on her computer as Eve places a steaming cup of tea next to Mae's new mother-of-pearl tissue dispenser. When Eve leaves her office, Mae glances at her inbox. Eve has already sorted the mail into rubber-banded sections, as Mae trained her: invitations, solicitations, bills, catalogs, and magazines. Mae turns her attention first to the invitations, placing the worthwhile ones on her desk (a Central Park Conservancy benefit; a high-profile party sponsored by the St. Regis in the penthouse of their newest luxury condo—a good way to meet potential Clients). She dumps the second-tier ones in the trash, along with a sheaf of solicitations from various nonprofits. She keeps only the donation plea from Trinity, her alma mater; Ethan and she aim to send any future offspring to an Ivy League school, but it's always good to have a backup. Bills, most of them from the interior decorator and the wedding planner, go into their own distressingly hefty pile. She dumps the catalogs into the recycling bin under her desk, skims the bridal-bouquet pictures her mother culled from the wedding magazines she's been stockpiling since Mae graduated from college, and notices with a frown the cover of the latest **BusinessWorld** magazine: **30** TOP LEADERS UNDER **30.**

Ugh.

When Mae, just shy of thirty, was promoted to run the New York Holloway Club—an invitation-only club for the uber-rich and uber-connected and the original business line of Holloway Holdings—she had angled to be included in **BusinessWorld**'s list. Holloway didn't yet have a PR department, so she prodded several billionaire Clients at the Club with whom she had become friendly to push her name with the magazine editor. Leon caught wind of the plan and quashed it, explaining to Mae in the light-filled aerie that is the Holloway dining room that Holloway Clients—and the rich, generally— valued discreetness above all.

Now, with Mae more than half a decade into her thirties, Leon has changed his tune: America celebrates its winners and its winners don't mind the limelight. Today's wealthy are photographed at the best galas, host lavish parties on yachts the size of apartment blocks, unabashedly bankroll their favorite politicians, donate mountains of money to beautify public parks . . . and name the parks after their school-aged kids! All of it documented ad nauseam on the Internet, in countless magazines and TV shows.

Discreetness is out, Leon now declares (as if it had ever been "in").

He still refuses to publicize Golden Oaks, which flies far beneath the radar for a number of reasons, fetal security not least, but Leon is newly happy to promote Holloway's other business holdings. This past autumn he deemed it good business to try and get Gabby—Holloway's new, just-shy-of-thirty Head of Investor Relations—onto the 30 Under 30 list. If she is featured in this issue, Mae is going to vomit.

Mae shoves the mail on her desk into her open briefcase. It is only a stupid magazine. She closes her eyes and breathes deeply, reminding herself that **she** controls her day, **she** can choose which parts to emphasize and which to ignore. She splashes a smile on her face—**act enthusiastic and you'll be enthusiastic!** her mantra since her dad paid her ten bucks to read Dale Carnegie when she was eleven—and reopens the PowerPoint presentation she was working on when Eve arrived with the mail.

Project MacDonald.

Just seeing the presentation's title page makes Mae's pulse quicken. She's been working on this business plan in secret for half a year. She aims to present it to Leon next month—she already booked a meeting with him, ostensibly to go over Golden Oaks' earnings projections—giving him ample time to factor in all her extra work before he decides on her end-of-year bonus.

Project MacDonald, Mae knows, is a risk. Leon and the Board worry that Golden Oaks may be ahead of its time—a cash cow, yes, but too big a leap for the world to embrace, particularly given all the hullabaloo over wealth inequality and the animosity toward the "one percent." Leon and the Board are so wary of a tar-and-feathering in the press, of being misconstrued and then regulated, that they keep Mae's operations sub-scale and straitjacketed.

But they have it wrong! People resent the one percent when there is no story to grasp on to, when the rich are caricatured as faceless fat cats swimming in bathtubs of champagne. But give a zillionaire the right spin—and Americans swoon. Think Oprah, with her childhood traumas and yo-yo dieting, or the Kennedys with their bad luck and tragic beauty, or Warren Buffett, with his aw-shucks charm. Think movie stars and socialites and professional athletes and tech titans. Americans **love** success when they can relate to it.

And they love family.

And that is why Project MacDonald is a slam dunk.

Under Mae's plan, Golden Oaks would embrace—proudly and unabashedly—its essence: a high-end, one-stop shop for the procreation of the men and women—the movers, the shakers, the leaders, the iconoclasts—who are changing the world!

Why shouldn't Golden Oaks, for instance, start an egg and sperm bank for those Clients who have trouble creating life on their own? Why shouldn't it provide embryo storage so that women can pursue their dreams without worrying about their biological clocks? What about postdelivery services, like on-demand antibiotic and allergen-free breast milk or, even, wet-nursing? Why leave baby nursing to freelancers?

And, clearly, Golden Oaks should expand. A West Coast outpost is a no-brainer . . . maybe another one in South America; the aesthetic-surrogacy market there would be huge . . .

Mae swells with pride as she pages through her presentation, each sentence backed by hours of research, reams of data. It is so compelling that Mae has begun thinking that she and Ethan themselves should utilize Golden Oaks whenever it is they're ready for children. She's no spring chicken anymore, and if Project MacDonald takes off, Mae won't have the luxury of slowing down for pregnancy. Why not give their firstborn a jumpstart in life in an environment calibrated **explicitly** to maximize his fetal potential?

Reinvigorated, Mae plucks the magazine out of her briefcase. Project MacDonald could land her on its **cover** someday soon, not just on some stupid list.

She flips to the 30 Under 30 article. Number One on the list is a college-dropout tech whiz, founder of a social-media-virtual-reality dating app now valued at billions of dollars. Mae approves. She gives the thumbs-up to numbers Two to Seven, lingers on the shirtless picture of Number Eight (a former Navy SEAL who started a successful chain of boot-camp-based fitness boutiques), grudgingly approves of Numbers Nine to Twelve, and stops short at Number Thirteen.

Is this a joke?

Mae reads Thirteen's profile: a run-of-the-mill trader at a run-of-the-mill investment bank, just like hundreds, maybe thousands, of other finance types toiling away unheralded on trading desks across the country. Sure, her backstory is terrific: she's a black woman in a white man's game, raised by her grandmother in a rough suburb of Baltimore. But does her trajectory, however uplifting, make her a better "business leader" than, say, Ethan—who does the same job but grew up white in Westchester?

Mae snorts derisively. She's never had patience

for identity politics, for playing up **otherness**—the word du jour—to get ahead. In college, when various Asian American groups tried to include her in their mixers/meetings/protests, she liked to announce that she had more in common with her non-Asian, randomly assigned roommate Katie—shared interests, shared dress size—than she did with a motley crew of people who shared her eye shape.

When Mae finishes reading the list without seeing any mention of Holloway, or Gabby, she clasps her hands and raises them in mock victory.

There is a knock on her door, and Eve pokes her head into the office. "Reagan McCarthy's here to see you?"

Mae asks for five minutes and opens the Host Log on her computer. According to the latest update by Geri, Director of Coordinators, Reagan has been, until recently, a model citizen. But in the past few weeks the Coordinators have reported slight changes in behavior—several instances of tardiness, invasive questions (about the identity of her Clients, about the reasons behind various Golden Oaks policies). Geri wonders if Reagan is being contaminated by her association with Lisa Raines. The two are, according to one entry, "thick as thieves."

Mae feels a headache coming on. Thinking about Lisa is apt to have this effect on her. Lisa—stirrer of pots, maker of mountains from molehills—is the source of almost all of Mae's Host troubles and, by a factor of five, the most profitable Host she's ever hired. Even so, Mae would have cut the cord after Lisa delivered Baby One during Golden Oaks' beta-test phase if it had been in her power. But Lisa's Clients are the type—they almost always live in Manhattan, usually downtown, rich but trying to "keep it real" by occasionally taking the subway and wearing ripped jeans—that feel the need to compensate for their good fortune by propping up the unfortunates around them. They've swallowed Lisa's white-trash-gone-gold routine hook, line, and sinker—going so far as to set up a scholarship fund in her honor (though named after their own boys) at UVA, Lisa's alma mater, where she'd gotten a free ride and which, with characteristic ingratitude, she vocally detests.

Mae messages Geri and asks if she feels a psychiatric check-in might be appropriate for Reagan. She then messages Eve that she's ready.

The door swings open within seconds. "How could you cancel Jane's visit?"

Reagan is clearly itching for a fight. She has also put on a few pounds and looks better for them, but Mae figures it's not the right time to give her this compliment. "Take a seat, Reagan."

Reagan remains standing, her accusing eyes fixed on Mae.

"Please. So we can really talk. I'm flummoxed myself and would love your thoughts."

Reagan seems taken aback. She glances about the office as if getting her bearings and slowly lowers herself onto one of the two curved, midcentury chairs that face Mae's desk. "Jane hasn't seen her baby in months. She doesn't deserve this."

Mae considers going on the offensive and pointing out that Jane was supposed to keep the visit a secret but decides this will only inflame matters. Better to kill Reagan with kindness and understanding.

Mae answers simply, "No, she doesn't."

"So why'd you do it? She's shattered." Reagan's voice is stony.

Mae proceeds cautiously. "All of this is confidential. I hope I can trust you, Reagan."

Reagan uncrosses her arms and leans ever-so-slightly forward in her chair.

"As you can imagine, given the very real risks of Lyme disease for both the Host and the baby, we have protocols we have to follow." Mae looks at Reagan, who gives her a curt nod. "Your WellBands are configured with GPS trackers, which are helpful when Hosts find themselves outside. Jane and Lisa both mentioned they used the WellBand's location function to choose their trail route."

Reagan's face remains impassive.

"Jane's tick turned out to have Lyme disease; it's our first-ever case of it, and we take that seriously. We went back and analyzed the GPS data to understand where Lisa and Jane walked and where we may need to do some selective spraying. They did **not** stay on the trails. For reasons neither of them will adequately explain, they ignored the rules and walked quite deep into the forest, where ticks are prevalent."

Reagan looks as if she is about to say something, then changes her mind. Mae resumes, "Jane will need to be on an IV to receive antibiotics. There is some evidence Lyme can be transferred to the baby in utero. I know that this is completely out of character for Jane. But because she won't explain what happened, I had to proceed with disciplinary action. I went as easy on her as I could. I refused to dock her pay, as protocol demands. Canceling the visit . . ." Mae holds up her hands in a gesture of helplessness. "I thought it was the lesser punishment."

Mae takes a sip of tea, watching Reagan fidget in her chair. The Coordinators found scratch marks on Lisa's breasts and back and slight bruising on her knees but no sperm in her vagina. They failed to test Lisa's anal cavity until a day later. Lisa's boyfriend had visited her the morning in question, but camera footage shows that the two were not left alone for any significant period and that the boyfriend left the premises immediately after lunch. One Coordinator postulated that the boyfriend might have snuck back onto the grounds—but how could he have done so without being caught on camera or tripping the electric fence that rings the property?

"I'm sure there **must** be an explanation, some mitigating factor . . . But Jane won't cooperate."

In a voice so low Mae strains to hear her, Reagan asks, "Did you talk with Lisa?"

"Lisa?" Mae asks, as if Lisa wasn't her prime suspect. "Yes, we did. And she corroborates Jane's story: Jane needed to defecate and was too shy to do so on the trail. They weren't all that far from the Dorm, though. The bathrooms here are surely nicer than going alfresco. In any case, the Clients aren't satisfied with this explanation, and so for now they aren't comfortable letting Jane off-site. It really is a shame."

Mae turns to her computer to tap some made-up numbers into a spreadsheet. Outside a bird screeches. Mae bides her time.

"Was Lisa punished, too?" Reagan finally asks.

"You know I can't divulge that, Reagan."

"She says she wasn't, but she must have been. Because she's . . . because she went into the woods, too."

"We have protocols . . . but we have to balance these against the demands of the Clients. And Lisa's Clients are very . . . liberal with her. The rules simply don't apply to Lisa in the same way."

"So she didn't get in trouble?" Reagan is incredulous.

"I really can't speak to you about Lisa. It wouldn't be fair to her."

"Oh, and this is fair to Jane?"

"There is only so much I can do," Mae answers softly. "It's really up to Jane or Lisa to explain what happened in the woods."

Reagan is on her feet. "This is bullshit."

Mae waits until she is sure Reagan is gone before ringing the Coordinator on duty at the Panopticon and requesting the dedicated feed for Host 82. Mae logs in to the remote application on her computer and watches a real-time image of Reagan walking briskly down the hall. The image cuts out for a second as the footage switches to another camera. Reagan now stands at Lisa's doorway. It is obvious from her gesticulations that she is speaking animatedly. Lisa wears only a T-shirt and brushes her teeth, her face inscrutable.

Mae finds herself wishing, for the hundredth time, that Leon had allowed her to configure the WellBands with microphones, but he refused. His constant concern about the "optics" of the mikes (**how would it look on the cover of** The New York Times **if it came out we eavesdropped on all the Hosts?**) seems to Mae to be pure paranoia. She texts one of the Coordinators and instructs her to do a surreptitious walk-by, in hopes that she overhears something of interest.

There is another knock, and Eve cracks open the door. "Dr. Wilde for you?"

This is shaping up to be a day of stamping out fires. Mae won't make any progress on Project MacDonald, especially as she and Ethan are meeting at the Racquet and Tennis Club at six to try out various entrée options for their wedding-reception dinner.

"Nice flowers," Dr. Wilde says as she strides into the room. She wears an unbuttoned white lab coat over what looks like a Chanel tweed shift dress from last season. She scrutinizes the arrangement on

Mae's desk more closely. "I'm not loving the baby's breath, though."

"My mother sent them. She's angling to be put in charge of the wedding flowers, but her taste is a little . . . countrified."

Dr. Wilde turns grave. "The tests for Host 80 are back."

"And?"

"The fetus has trisomy 21."

Mae takes a breath to clear her head. "Go on." Her voice, thankfully, exhibits none of the disappointment that is currently pooling in her chest.

"The fetus has what's called mosaic Down syndrome. Not all its cells carry the extra chromosome. The good news is that the fetus has a lower percentage of aberrant cells. The bad news is that the prenatal screen can't pick up mosaic Down's with any accuracy."

"What does this mean for the baby?"

"Since a portion of the baby's cells will be normal, the baby may present with less severe or fewer characteristics of Down syndrome . . ."

"So the baby could be mostly normal?" Mae interrupts, already constructing in her mind how she will frame the news to the Clients. They have mountains of money; they can easily afford the caretakers needed to take watch over a slightly disabled child.

"It could . . . or not. Some children with mosaic Down's have very mild features; but others have almost all the features of full trisomy."

Mae manages to maintain a placid expression. "Thanks, Meredith. Give me some time to think about how best to inform the Clients. It may help to have you on the call, in case they have questions."

"Of course." Dr. Wilde stands, smooths her skirt, and excuses herself.

Fuck, fuck, fuck! In Mae's three years at Golden Oaks—five if you count the beta phase—Mae has never had such a series of bad luck. Host 80 is already sixteen weeks along. The Clients will be devastated.

Mae forces herself to focus on the task at hand: information. A decision is only as good as the information it's based on. She texts Dr. Wilde requesting a detailed report of the range of possible outcomes of mosaic Down's as soon as possible. She asks Fiona, her contact in Legal, to check whether the contract associated with 80 contains a fee clawback in the case of a defective child, and how exactly "defective" is defined.

She then skims her available Host pipeline. If the Clients choose to terminate, they may want to implant another fetus straightaway. The problem is that Mae's Host options at the moment are limited. The Clients refuse to consider a black or Hispanic Host, and most of Mae's white and Asian ones are either already pregnant or in the mandatory post-delivery rest period, during which implantation isn't permitted for recuperative purposes. Finding new Hosts is time-consuming—entailing numerous background checks and the hiring of private investigators to ensure candidates are discreet or could be compelled to be discreet if they ignored the nondisclosure agreements.

Thankfully, Mae has cultivated a handful of Scouts who are extremely trustworthy. She texts several of them and asks them to propose at least one viable white or Asian Host candidate within forty-eight hours for a nice bonus over the usual fee. After a moment of consideration, she texts Dr. Wilde and Fiona again, this time to see if it's possible to accelerate the rest period of any of the white Hosts, as they did twice before for Lisa. As long as the Host signs a health waiver, Golden Oaks is legally covered; and acceleration comes with enormous fees . . . though in this case, perhaps Mae should waive them. Because of the trisomy.

Mae turns to the numbers, knowing they are what Leon will be focused on. She puts together a quick spreadsheet with the two most likely outcomes and their permutations in one column and the projected revenue streams for each in successive columns.

Termination, Scenario One (Reimplantation at cost/No Markup)

Termination, Scenario Two (No Reimplantation/ Loss of Client)

Retention of Fetus, Scenario Three (Minimal Trisomy/No Clawback)

Retention of Fetus, Scenario Four (Minimal Trisomy/Clawback)

From a profit-loss perspective, Mae notes in a memo to Leon, Scenario Three is by far the best option, followed by Scenarios One, Four, and Two. Of course, she taps into her computer, the highest priority is to help the Clients make a decision that is right for **them.** In the ideal world, this would dovetail with what is right for Golden Oaks. Mae saves her work and decides to see if Reagan has calmed down from her earlier tantrum.

The Panopticon feed shows Reagan in the fitness room. She holds hand weights and walks on an inclined treadmill. Three other Hosts are exercising next to her, but Lisa isn't one of them. Did they fight? Mae attempts to view the earlier footage, but for some reason the rewind function isn't working. She messages the Panopticon Help Desk to fix the glitch. As she waits, Mae returns a half-dozen phone calls, including one from her father, who is balking at the dance lessons Mae's mother insists he take to prepare for the father-of-the-bride dance at the wedding. Mae reviews a batch of resumes for the new Coordinator position and orders a book for Eve, who is finishing up her second year of night school at a community college in the

Bronx. She is struggling with her accounting class, as Mae did in business school, and this textbook is good. Mae types in the gift-message box: **Because with enough sweat, you can do anything. Aim high and don't ever give up.**

And don't get pregnant, Mae thinks.

What was the statistic that Mae read just this morning in **The Times**? She wanted to share it with Eve. Something about how urban teenagers are much more likely—twice, was it?—than white ones to get pregnant. That's what derails them: having babies when they're barely adults. Eve is attractive— she reminds Mae of a shorter version of the black supermodel who was famous in the '90s—and she has a new boyfriend. The last thing she needs is to get knocked up before she finishes her schooling.

There is another knock. Eve walks into the room and places a package in Mae's inbox. "And Client 33 is on the line."

"No rest for the weary," Mae says brightly. "Put her through."

ATE

ATE SMELLS THE POO-POO AS SOON AS SHE REACHES THE bottom of the stairs.

"Ay, Mali! A poo-poo now?"

Amalia gnaws on her fist. She is teething. The other day she tried to chew the television remote when Ate was making lunch. The back flap of the device was broken, and the battery Ate yanked out of the baby's mouth was slick with drool.

With her sleeve Ate dabs at a patch of dried milk on Amalia's chin and leans the folded stroller against the foyer's scuffed, plaster wall. She frees Amalia from the baby carrier and lifts her in the air to smell her diaper. Ate makes a face. "**Nakapo**, Mali! A big one!"

Amalia smiles, as if in on a joke.

Ate does not want to walk back up the three flights of stairs to the apartment. She is tired today, and they are already late. She told Angel she would be at the dorm before lunch, and it is well past twelve, and the walk takes almost half an hour. Unlike her Filipino friends, Ate prides herself on her timeliness.

Ate squats on her heels, props Amalia on her lap, and shrugs off her backpack. She spreads out the changing pad, takes out wipes and the extra diaper, and lays Amalia on her back. Amalia kicks her legs, smiling a wet smile. She is a happy baby, like Roy was.

"Mali, Mali, Mali. We are already late, late, late," Ate sings. She holds Amalia's legs up in one hand and with the other, folds the soiled diaper closed, wipes Amalia clean, smothers her bum with cream and encloses it in a fresh diaper. Ate hands Amalia a plastic rattle for distraction while she cleans her own chapped hands with Purell, repacks everything into the backpack and slides Amalia back in the baby carrier on her chest, for safety. She carries the folded stroller outside and down the front steps, holding the railing with her free hand and counting each step as she goes. One-two-three-four-five. She does not want to trip again. There is too much to do.

As soon as she slides Amalia into the stroller, the baby begins to wail.

"Mali, Mali, why do you cry?" Ate blows up her cheeks to make Amalia laugh. She tries to buckle the stroller's straps around the baby's flailing legs, but Amalia arches her back and slides down the seat.

"No, Mali. Ate is tired. Ate cannot carry you." The phone in Ate's pocket dings. It is Mrs. Herrera, the bride's mother, texting that there will be twenty more people than expected at the wedding brunch tomorrow. Ate smiles to herself. Good, good.

Until now, the Herreras have only hired Ate to cook for smaller parties, where Ate's food was just one of the many dishes served—the exotic **lumpia** or **adobo** among a table of American meats and salads. But the Herreras' beloved only daughter is getting married to an American this weekend. Ate was hired to make the Filipino desserts at the wedding brunch, which will be held at the Herreras' tennis club in Queens. Hundreds of guests—many of them Filipino doctors and lawyers and each of them potential customers for Ate's fledgling catering business—will attend. It is her big chance!

Ate passes the store where Angel buys and sells her gold—gold chains, mostly, but also gold rings, bracelets. She shakes her head. Angel is not reasonable; that is the problem. She has lived in America for many years, working hard the entire time. With her earnings she paid for the house in Batangas, for her children's computers and Nike sneakers.

And for what? The daughters got married too young, to lazy husbands with nothing jobs. All of them—the three daughters and their husbands and their children—crammed into Angel's house back home living for free. Not even helping with the utilities. Her only hope now is that the grandchildren—nice-looking, light-skinned, with narrow noses—become fashion models! **That** is Angel's backup plan.

Angel's daughters are spoiled; this is the issue. They beg her for money, and she sends it, even though her daughters are grown women! Because when Angel does not send it, they do not call. They let her phone calls ring and ring. When they finally do speak, the daughters cry their crocodile tears and accuse Angel of not being with them when they were young.

As if Angel had a choice? As if any mother **wants** to leave her children?

Ate knows Angel fears that if she does not keep her daughters dependent on her, they will not take care of her when she is old. She is afraid her grandchildren—she knows them only through pictures and video-chat—will not love her without the money she sends for their straight teeth, their iPhones. Imagine: Children not caring for their parents? After all the sacrifice? As if they are Americans?

And also, Angel is afraid of banks. She fears they will steal her money if they discover she has no papers. Ate has told her: they cannot do this. But

Angel does not listen. With any extra money in her pocket Angel buys jewelry. She stores it in a safe that she bought at the P.C. Richard electronics store on sale for $109.99, the kind you open with your fingerprint, like in the spy movies. When Angel needs money, she sells a necklace or a bracelet.

"I get a good price, because Tony knows me," she boasts.

But what kind of savings is that? Because they buy from you at a lower price than they sell to you. Of course they do. That is called business!

Ate advises her—do not waste money on your daughters, on these golden bangles. Buy land, another house! Make good investments so you can take care of yourself when you are old!

But Angel is stubborn. And she likes pretty things too much. Ate has seen her earlobes shining when she leaves for dates with her old Americans. She still dreams of getting her green card in this way, through a foolish husband in a false marriage. So she can visit her spoiled daughters and make everything right.

Ate is different. She owns three properties in the Philippines. The first one is where Roy lives with his **yaya,** who Ate pays good money to take care of him; the second one is a small house Ate rents for income; and the last is the house she is building, also in Bulacan, on a plot of land big enough for another two or three small houses later. She dreams of having a family compound there, with Roy and

Ate in the main house and smaller ones for Isabel
and Ellen and maybe even Romuelo, all of them
together behind a tall fence with an automatic gate.

Before Ate's heart problems, when she was still
working with Mrs. Carter, she made the final payment on the Bulacan land. She was showing Dina
a picture of it on her phone one morning when
Mrs. Carter entered the kitchen, leaning close to
see what was so exciting. The picture was not so
much, just a stretch of ground surrounded by a
metal fence, but Mrs. Carter understood: **Three
properties! Evelyn, you are a real-estate mogul!**

And then, frowning: **But wouldn't you and Roy
be better off in America?**

Of course this is how she thought. Mrs. Carter
only knew the Philippines through her newspapers
and Internet—the tsunamis that washed away vil-
lages; the government full of old movie actors and
boxing champions and greed, so much greed; the
hungry children with big eyes and bloated stomachs
and the crazy Muslims sawing off people's heads in
Mindanao. To Mrs. Carter, the Philippines was a
place of rot and menace, where everything could
fall apart and often did.

But America is not solid for everyone, either. Mrs.
Carter did not see this. How could she? She did not
understand that in America, you must be strong or
young if you are not rich. The old, the feeble—they
are hidden away in homes like the one where Jane
used to work. At Edgehill Gardens there were no

gardens. Only plastic plants that did not need to be watered and old people sitting all day in front of the television, no one visiting or changing the channel. The squat women with thick arms who lifted the old people for a bath—one holding the legs, one grabbing under the armpits—talked in loud voices, but only to each other. And these old people are the lucky ones. At least there is someone looking after them.

In the Philippines, the old people smell good, like talcum powder and soap. Your family takes care of you, and if they do not, your **yaya** will. This is why, when it is Ate's time, she will return home to her big house on her new land and live with Roy, and maybe Romuelo. And, of course, her daughters. Her good girls.

Ate is proud of her girls, though she would never say so. You should not spoil your children, even with words. You should not raise them to be too tender, like little lambs. Small lambs, soft lambs—they make the best meat; they are always devoured. This is where Ate believes she went wrong with Romuelo.

She shakes her head.

Only yesterday a package arrived from Isabel, her oldest. In the small box were several bottles of blood-pressure pills—Isabel is a nurse—and a photograph of Isabel's children, Ate's only grandchildren, at her birthday party. The grandson is tall and handsome, like the weatherman Ate likes on the nightly news. He is an assistant manager at the call center of an American credit-card company, a good job. The granddaughter is Ate's namesake and, **pobre,** she is dark. Like Ate! But she is pretty enough. And she has a good brain; she is studying to be a doctor.

Isabel could have been a doctor, too. She was studying medicine when she fell in love with the first boy who ever looked at her. She wanted to get married right away. What could Ate do from halfway across the world? But at least Isabel became a nurse later on. She is a good one. Very diligent.

Ellen is different. Ate worries about her. She works as a hostess in the rooftop restaurant of a five-star hotel in Manila. (The "head hostess," she always corrects Ate. But a head hostess is still a hostess!) It is there that Ellen meets her admirers, because she is still pretty, even though she is no longer so young. When she was only two years old her picture was chosen from hundreds of submissions to be in an advertisement for Johnson's baby powder. Ate still has a copy in her keepsakes box. The advertisement was in all the magazines at the time.

It was not easy for Isabel, who looks like Ate, to grow up in the shadow of her little sister's beauty. Isabel used to sit at home and study while Ellen went out with suitors. She stood ignored every Sunday after Mass while others crowded around Ellen and complimented her on her hairstyle, the fit of her dress.

But look now. Who is the one with the husband, the children, the good job? Better to be plain and hardworking than beautiful and full of too many ideas. Ellen is still not married, and she is almost forty. She calls Ate every few weeks and tells her about her beaux: the restaurants they take her to, the big jobs they have. Ate ends up shouting into the phone: **Naman,** Ellen! Enough! Just choose one, already!

Ellen did not finish college, and Ate worries these fancy VIPs do not take her seriously. She worries they will throw Ellen away like used Kleenex when they are finished with their fun, and Ellen will end up alone.

Angel acknowledged this possibility only the other day. They were in Jane's kitchen eating empanadas, and Ate was complaining about Ellen again, and Angel said: "But for you it is better if she ends up an old maid."

Ate was shocked into silence, and Angel continued. "Because if Ellen does not find a husband, she will take care of Roy. Even you will not be around forever, Ate."

ANGEL WAITS FOR THEM OUTSIDE OF THE DORM. SHE WEARS red sandals with thick transparent heels, and she has changed her hair since last week. It is now a rusty orange and too curly, like a poodle. Angel laughs at Ate's expression. "Ate, do not look at me like that!

Blondes have more fun! Hahahahaha!" She picks up the entire stroller, with Amalia in it, and carries it up the several steps to the dorm's front door.

After tucking the stroller in a bedroom and making sure that Amalia still sleeps, Ate goes to the kitchen to check on Angel's preparations. On the stove, two huge pots are simmering. Ate takes a wooden spoon from a drawer and tastes, then adds a handful of shredded coconut and a long pour of condensed milk to the filling for the **buko** pie. Angel has set up a workspace on the rectangular table in the middle of the room. On one end are stacks of pie tins lined with fresh-made crusts. On the other are the ingredients for the **bibingka** cake the bride requested. Angel opines that they should make the cake now, because the next morning will be hectic. But the Herreras are VIPs—they live in Forest Hills in a huge Tudor house, and Dr. Herrera is a surgeon. Ate instructs Angel to make the filling today and bake it early the next morning, so that it will be fresh.

Ate turns to the **polvoron,** the crumbly shortbread cookies that Isabel and Ellen and Roy and Romuelo used to eat until they were sick in the stomach, their small faces powdered white. On a folding table, Angel has set three enormous bowls piled high with the **polvoron** mixture— toasted flour and sugar and butter and powdered milk and ground cashews. Mrs. Herrera wants each cookie pressed into the shape of a heart and wrapped in colored paper—take-home gifts for the wedding guests.

"Who is helping with the **polvoron**?" Ate asks.

Angel hurries to the doorway and shouts up the stairs.

Two women, one in her early twenties and one closer to thirty, shuffle to the kitchen, eyes cast downward. The younger one remains near the doorway. The older one greets Ate in Tagalog and, bending slightly, presses her forehead to Ate's hand in the traditional sign of respect.

"Nag mano!" Ate is startled. Is she old enough now to be greeted in this way? It is how she greeted her grandparents every time she saw them, and she raised her children to do the same with their elders. But in America, the gesture feels strange.

Ate makes the sign of the cross and blesses the girl. The girl introduces herself as Didi, short for Diana, and her friend as Segundina.

"You are sisters?" Ate asks, eyeing the younger one.

"No, **po.** We share a bunk upstairs."

They need money then, Ate thinks. She tells them they will receive thirty dollars each for help with the **polvoron.** Angel hands each girl a heart-shaped cookie mold and begins cutting the large sheets of pale-blue paper into squares. After checking on Amalia, who still sleeps, Ate takes a pair of shears from a shelf cluttered with cooking utensils and sits down next to Angel to help.

"How is Jane? Is she still in California?" asks Angel, snipping away.

"She is fine. The baby is easy," Ate lies. She and Jane had agreed that this is the story they would tell the others to explain Jane's absence—that she got a baby-nurse job in Palo Alto, California, and it is so far away she cannot visit. "She will make good money."

"It is good she does baby nursing now. The retirement home does not pay enough." Angel is home from a night-nursing assignment, a job Ate found for her, but she is always eager to make extra money. For her help with the food preparations, Ate is paying her twenty percent of the profits.

"These two," says Angel, "they need jobs also."

The young women do not look up. They continue pressing the **polvoron** into hearts.

"What experience do you have? Do you have papers? How is your English?" Ate asks Didi.

In a quavering voice that grows steadier as she speaks, Didi tells Ate how she came to America—two years ago, through a rich friend of a second cousin, on a tourist visa. The Filipino couple that sponsored her were both doctors. They lived in New Jersey in a big house with a bean-shaped pool in the backyard. Didi cleaned, cooked, and took care of the couple's six-month-old twins. She worked every day except Sunday, when the parents took the babies to church and to visit relatives.

"But they did not pay me, **po.** They gave me pocket change only. I did not have a phone. I did not drive. I could not leave," Didi says. "When I complained, after many months, they said they will call the police. Because my visa is only a tourist visa, and it is expired."

This is not the first such story Ate has heard. A woman who used to rent a bed in the second floor of the dorm escaped from the same situation in Toronto, but at least that time the employers— if you can call people like this "employers"— were Indonesian, not Filipinos. "How did you leave them?"

"I watched the father, **po.** When I cleaned his office, I watched him put the password in the computer. Later I used the computer to contact my sister in Palawan. She sent someone to pick me up at the house one morning, so early everyone was still sleeping. It was more than a month ago, but my sister tells me the police are likely still looking for me."

Ate makes a dismissive gesture with the hand holding the shears. "They did not call the police! Because they would be in trouble also, for bringing you here. Like a slave."

Didi says nothing. Ate studies her for a moment and speaks again, more kindly. "What job do you like?"

"Anything, **po,**" Didi answers quickly.

"I will help you. Cleaning, first. You work hard,

do a good job, learn good English. Then I can find you a better job."

"Thank you, **po.**"

They work in silence, only the crinkle of the papers, the bang of the cookie molds against the wooden table. Segundina has not uttered a word. Ate stares out the grimy window—does no one clean now that she does not live here?—and announces, "I will only place you with Americans. They have softer hearts."

AMALIA IS IN BED. SHE SLEPT EASILY TONIGHT, BECAUSE all day she played in the hot kitchen with anyone who passed through. At bath time Ate noticed a prong of white in the gummy pinkness of Amalia's mouth. Ate took a picture of the tooth, Amalia's first, and emailed it to Jane, so she would not miss the milestone.

Ate is worried about Jane. She is a good girl, but she feels too much. Even before the visit was canceled, she was too full of feelings, screaming at Ate during one video-call only because Amalia had fallen at the doctor's. But babies fall! They will fall their whole lives, again and again, and you cannot always be there to catch them. Ate thinks of Romuelo, wonders where he is, how he earns money now that she does not send it. She pushes the thought away.

Ate was disappointed that the visit was canceled.

She was looking forward to it, a little holiday. She cannot remember the last time she left the city. It must have been four years ago, the baby-nurse job she took in Greenwich, Connecticut. The house was as big as a castle.

The visit would have been good for Jane, too. She needs to see Amalia and hold her in her arms, feel how solid she has grown. Maybe then she could trust that Amalia is okay. The way Thomas in the Bible had to touch to believe.

Ate puts the sponge she uses to wash dishes in the microwave to kill the germs. She watches the blue rectangle turn inside the machine, the soap foaming.

Ate still does not understand what happened. She tries again to remember exactly what Jane told her as she wipes the stovetop with the hot sponge. When Jane video-called Ate to tell her of the cancellation—Ate was already packed, she had set her alarm for six a.m. to meet the car—Jane only cried. The crying made it difficult to understand her explanation—something about the woods, breaking the rules with an American girl. It did not make sense. Why would Jane do such a thing? And what good was crying now?

Ate tried to get Jane to be clearer. But every time Ate asked a question—Why did you leave the trail? Who is this Lisa?—Jane's eyes skittered sideways like beetles. Ate knew these eyes. They were the eyes of someone hiding something. Romuelo's used to move in this way when he would video-call Ate pleading for money—for school fees and books, he said, his insect-eyes shifting. He withdrew from the university without her knowing, taking the money anyway, each year.

Lies on top of lies, and so many thousands of dollars wasted.

Not that Ate thinks Jane is lying about anything as serious as drugs! No, Jane is not like Romuelo. But she suffers from bad judgment. Out of nowhere—**pah!** She will make a bad choice. A stupid choice that you did not expect, did not prepare for or warn her against:

Jane is in school in America, she gets decent marks—and then: **Pah!** She runs away, she is pregnant, she is married! To a nothing like Billy!

Jane works hard for Mrs. Carter, she is making the double-rate, Mrs. Carter likes her and—**Pah!** Jane is back in the dorm. Fired!

On the video-call Ate tried to counsel Jane, because who else will counsel her? **You must be careful. You cannot make more mistakes.**

But Jane would not answer. So stubborn! Like a baby sulking. Like her mother!

Ate should not have grown angry. She should not have shouted. But Jane does not think! She does not see that life is hard and this job is easy. That the big money she will make will change Amalia's life.

"Do you know what I would do for this chance? For Roy? Why do you want to throw it away?" Ate demanded, her voice too loud.

Jane stared straight into Ate's face. Her eyes were sad and, also, afraid. And then she slumped in her chair like she was being drained.

Ate sighs, wondering again if she should have told Jane about Golden Oaks. Jane needs the money. But perhaps it is too much for her to be apart from Amalia.

Ate rinses the sponge under the faucet and begins to wipe the countertop, fighting the desire to cast judgment on her cousin. Cherry, Angel, Mirna, Vera—most of the women Ate knows have left their children behind to provide for them. And she has had clients—American women with important jobs, bankers and lawyers and professors in university—who returned to work when their babies were only ten weeks old, staying so late in the office that they did not see their own children until the following morning.

Does Jane think she is the only one to sacrifice? That only she is needed by her baby? Ate herself has been away from home for twenty years. Does Roy not need Ate, too?

She scrubs furiously at a sticky patch on the countertop. She forces herself to stop; to try to be fair. Jane was young when her mother left her; perhaps that is part of the problem. And Amalia is little. Ate's children were much older when she left: Isabel, her firstborn, was already starting medical school, and her baby, Roy, was already eighteen. It was only after the boat accident, when it became clear that he would not get better, that Roy would always need someone to cut his food, button his shirt—that Ate would have to take care of him until she died and even afterward—that she made plans to go to America.

Ate washes her hands in the sink, dries them, and retrieves a backpack from a hook on the entryway wall. Her friend Mirna is in between jobs and agreed to watch Amalia while Ate is at the Herreras' party. She packs everything Amalia will need the next day and then prepares a separate bag of her own with her blood-pressure pills, her best apron, and the long rectangular box that holds her new business cards.

Ate has great hopes for Evelyn's Catering. She always enjoyed cooking, but she chose baby nursing because there was more money in it. Now of course she needs to help Jane with Amalia. And in truth, and although she would never admit it, Ate is not certain when—if ever—she will be able to return to it. She gets tired so suddenly, sometimes fighting for breath in a way that frightens her. But she cannot stop working yet—the house in Bulacan is not finished, and of course there is Roy. Thank God, she has her backup plans.

First, there are the referrals. Ate is almost like an agency now. She knows many VIPs from her years working uptown, downtown, midtown—and they trust her. When she finds her former clients a cleaner or housekeeper, nanny or baby nurse, she receives a fee—not too big, but fair.

But this is small money, and sporadic, so most of Ate's hopes fall on cooking until Jane delivers the baby. The cooking is not completely new. For many years, Ate ran a stand at the annual Asian fair in Flushing. She sold Filipino dishes—savory ones like **lumpia** and sweets like **halo-halo.** It was through this stand that Ate met the Herreras' housekeeper, who one year bought a small cup of Ate's **pancit lug-lug.** She liked it so much she brought a big foam container of it back to Forest Hills and Mrs. Herrera, upon taking a bite, agreed it was the best she had ever tasted. Ate began to occasionally cook for them, delivering dishes of food for their parties, sometimes staying to help clean up.

But now, Ate aims to make the business big-time. Angel can do most of the day-to-day, and the dormitory is filled with Filipinas who know their way around a kitchen and are looking to make extra money. What Ate brings are the clients and the strategy.

Ay, if only Ate had been born in America! She thinks about this sometimes. She has a head for business, people have always told her so. And she is not afraid of hard work. By now she would be rich—maybe not Fifth Avenue rich, but close. Third Avenue or York or even Forest Hills. Romuelo would be sober. Isabel could finally rest. Ellen would be married. And Roy would have the best doctors—specialists that do not even take insurance. A whole team of them.

Because in America you only have to know how to make money. Money buys everything else.

REAGAN

"IT IS NOT TRUE ANYA HAD A MISCARRIAGE. THEY MADE HER kill the baby," Tasia says.

"Is Anya okay?" Lisa keeps her voice unnaturally low.

They instinctively glance around the room. The nearest Coordinator is twenty feet away. She speaks to one of the new Hosts, who clutches a vomit bag to her chest, swiveling her head back and forth like a latch in her neck has come loose.

"She is Catholic," Tasia answers without emotion. "They made her sleep. With gas. Maybe they worry she might get hysterical."

Lisa drops into the chair closest to Tasia. Reagan remains standing, though the tray she holds is growing heavy, and the seat next to Lisa is empty. Reagan is worried. The results for the last ultrasound were fine, but what if there is something wrong with the baby inside, where no one can see?

Tasia suddenly smiles, a flamboyant smile that consumes half her face. "The Coordinator is watching. I think she is maybe suspicious of me."

"Where's Anya now?" Lisa asks, grinning also. It is jarring, the apprehensiveness in Lisa's voice against the extravagance of her smile.

Reagan rests her tray on the table, feeling queasy. Lisa scooches back to make room for her. The rubber attachments on the bottom of her chair's legs have come undone, and her chair leaves two thin gashes on the hardwood floor.

"I do not ask. I cannot risk trouble." Tasia crumples her napkin in one hand and stands. "We have talked enough. Keep with the smiles, so they will not suspect me, please."

Reagan watches Tasia stop at a nearby table to speak to the new Host, who is also from Poland, her face lit bright as a lamp, contorted by sham laughter. She could be speaking about the Holocaust or a fifty-car pileup and you would never know. Or maybe this time it's real. Maybe mirth truly does well up within Tasia, despite all that happened to Anya, her friend.

Tasia starts toward the trash bins, waddling like

there is a basketball stuffed between her thighs. Someone at the Filipina table calls to her, and she makes another stop. The wattage of her smile, her unrestrained cackling. It's overkill. Jane seems to be thinking the same thing, her expression quizzical as she watches Tasia's performance.

Not that Reagan has a clue what Jane thinks anymore. She's been shunning Reagan ever since the tick fiasco. Almost as if she blames Reagan for her troubles, too.

"Just **sit,** Reag. Aren't you tired of giving me the cold shoulder?" Lisa's mouth is full of avocado.

"I'm not giving you the cold shoulder. I just don't like you as much as I used to," Reagan answers, knowing she sounds childish. But she sits. Her back aches from holding the tray for so long, and where else does she have to go?

"Poor Anya," Lisa says after a time.

Reagan glances at her, wary. But Lisa is being sincere.

"Poor Anya," Reagan agrees, imagining a metal table, the rustle of paper. Anya's stocky legs pried open, mask affixed, dread silence and seeping gas. Waking up sometime later, somewhere else entirely, scooped out like a melon.

"She had crazy morning sickness, do you remember? She was nauseous 24/7. And now—to not even get her bonus." Lisa shakes her head. "Especially if she was carrying the billion-dollar baby."

"Enough!" Reagan explodes, though she meant to keep her distance. "Who cares about that goddamned baby! Do you understand: they **forced** Anya to abort. Like we're in China or something. It's a complete violation—"

"Not of the contract," Lisa answers without missing a beat. "I hear you, Reagan, but all of us signed it. Willingly. It just sucks they didn't catch the defect earlier and spare Anya the heartache."

Reagan swallows hard. She will not be drawn down Lisa's rabbit hole.

"I wonder if she'll reimplant," Lisa muses. "She needs the money badly."

Reagan is silent, unwilling to admit she knows nothing about Anya needing money. Refusing to ask. She knows only that she does not want to be here, breaking bread with Lisa as if she weren't the reason Amalia's visit was canceled.

Reagan shoves fish into her mouth in big forkfuls, only to nourish the baby. She isn't hungry. The roasted squash sticks to her throat, and she washes it down with green juice that is more bitter than usual.

Lisa, oblivious, is prattling on about her Clients. They're total fakes. They act like they're so low-key—making fun of their friends who summer in the Hamptons, driving a beat-up station wagon that is ten years old. But they're just like every other rich person sticking their fetuses at the Farm. They just bought an enormous country estate in the area—did Reagan notice Lisa wasn't at breakfast? Her Clients summoned her to their farm to hang with the Boys, the ones Lisa carried. She had to help the older one milk a cow. The cows are new, along with some chickens, several goats, and a full-time caretaker. The Clients thought living on a working farm, even just on weekends, would be good for the Boys—teach them responsibility, build up their immune systems. Plus, there's a tax break.

"But the kid was too scared to milk the cow. So he sat on **my** lap while **I** did," smirked Lisa. "And he complained afterward that the milk was too warm. Like the cow should have been refrigerated!"

Reagan knows she is supposed to laugh. Only weeks ago, she would have.

"I can't believe I used to think they were different," Lisa says, a twinge of wistfulness before the sarcasm. "Did I tell you they asked if I'd consider **wet nursing** Baby Three?"

Across the dining room, Jane is clearing her tray. Reagan gets up from the table to follow her.

"Don't stay mad. I just missed Troy," Lisa pleads. "I really **like** Jane."

"Then why'd you use her like that? Don't tell me your charm offensive wasn't calculated. You used her because you needed someone to cover for you while you were off fucking Troy. Someone who'd be too scared to say no."

"I tried to help her! All that stuff about taking a shit in the woods was her idea. I went along with **her** because I didn't want to get her in more trouble!"

"You used her."

"You just weren't around. I would've used you, too!"

"You wouldn't have dared. That's what's so awful." Reagan doesn't bother to look back as she leaves. In the hallway, she runs up to Jane and touches her sleeve.

"Yes?" Jane is already drawing away.

Reagan scrambles for an opening. "Did you hear? About Anya?"

Jane's eyes widen and flit to the camera mounted above them on the wall. An almost imperceptible shake of her head, a murmured excuse, and she is hurrying away down the hall.

Reagan blinks, a flurry. She does not want to cry here around all these people. She walks quickly to her room, holding herself together until she is safe in her bed. Only then does she let go. She misses, for the first time in a long time, Gus. When he was little he'd hand her a stuffed animal whenever she cried. Even when he was older, eleven or twelve, he'd sit by her side when she was upset after a fight with Dad. He wouldn't budge until she'd stopped crying.

That was all before her senior year in high school, the thing with Gus's best friend. She shouldn't have done it; she can see that now. But it was flattering, how the boy followed her with his eyes. Sweet, how he blushed every time she came near. He didn't seem like the kind of kid who would talk, and to his credit, he kept it to himself for months.

"She's just looking for something to hold her," Dad explained to Gus one night over dinner. By then Gus knew about his sister boning his best friend, and he hated her.

Reagan was sprawled on the sofa just beyond the kitchen table, headphones on but volume off, the better to hear them. She tried not to look at them, or the carcasses on the table. Veal is baby cows, did you know that? she'd demanded earlier.

Gus brought up the photograph Reagan had submitted to a contest at school, a self-portrait that their know-nothing principal had deemed "pornographic" and rejected outright, even though there's nothing pornographic about mere nakedness. Even though it was good. Pissed, she'd posted it online—it was her senior year, what did she care?—and it went viral.

Gus chewed with his mouth open. Next to him Mom's chair sat empty. She was resting in her room. She'd lost the car at Walmart again, waited hours in the sun until the parking lot emptied.

"No, Dad," Gus concluded, and Reagan could feel him staring at her. "It's that she's a slut."

He reached past Dad for the veal without saying "excuse me" and took a second helping.

———

A FLY BANGS AGAINST THE SCREEN. THERE'S A BLEEP AND THEN another. Reagan sits up, eyes puffy, and checks her WellBand. It's a reminder that her weekly ultrasound is in two hours and another that she is past due for her morning UteroSoundz session.

The UteroSoundz is, at least, something to do. Reagan forces herself to the Coordinator Desk down the hall. She musters a smile for the perky woman dispensing the devices and wanders into the library, which, thankfully, is empty. She scans the hardcovers on a shelf near the library's entrance, looking for something to help kill the time. It used to be that she and Jane and Lisa would hang out while they clocked their UteroSoundz hours, gossiping or watching a movie, not even noticing the devices strapped to their stomachs.

A familiar blue spine, silver lettering, jumps out at her. **Songs of Innocence and of Experience** by William Blake. Mom used to read the poems to her from this exact edition when Reagan was small. Dad forced her to memorize "The Little Girl Lost" and would trot her out in her pajamas at dinner parties to recite it to his friends. She hated the limelight, performing like a circus dog. Afterward, she'd duck from the rain of compliments into Dad's arms, face burning, a dollar slipped into her pocket.

Reagan flops onto an overstuffed chair near the back of the room. She attaches the UteroSoundz speakers to her stomach and enters her code. The week's playlist appears onscreen. It is, as usual, vanilla. Vanilla with white bread and unflavored iced tea. Mozart, of course; Winston Churchill's speeches and the famous commencement address by Steve Jobs; and a compilation of poems read by famous actors in the original language, probably to give the fetus a jumpstart on multilinguality— Shakespeare, Rilke, Baudelaire, and Frost. And then: Li Bai.

Li Bai?

What is he doing here, consorting with the Dead White Men of the Western canon?

Are Reagan's Clients Chinese? Is it possible that **she's** the one carrying the—

She punches Play, disgusted with herself. That she's behaving like Lisa.

She tilts her head and stares at the ceiling, trying to remember what it felt like, not so long ago, when she was happy here. Content in the Farm's quiet erasure; its hermetic calm. But something has changed since the 3-D ultrasound, since Jane's tick and her mean-spirited punishment, and Anya's forced abortion. An unsettling sense that the Farm is a set piece created for the Client on the other end of Dr. Wilde's wire, and behind its pretty façade lies the truth. She's just not yet sure what that is.

It's linked, somehow, to that time at the Tate Modern. Mom and Dad had given her a backpacking trip through Europe for graduation. Macy met her in London for a long weekend of carousing before Reagan set off by bullet train to Paris and Macy returned to New York to start the training program at the bank. They visited the Tate after a night dancing on tables at a posh members-only club in Mayfair. Mascara clotting their eyelashes, bottles of Evian sloshing in their bags. They stumbled onto a side gallery, where the canvases hung: plain, devoid of paint, perfectly framed. And slashed down the center. Only that one swipe. Reagan's eyes were drawn to the fissure. Fontana must have used the sharpest blade, the cuts were so clean.

This is art? Macy asked jokingly.

But Reagan felt release.

Through the library's French doors Reagan watches a groundskeeper peel tarps off the patio chairs and tables. He has rolled up the sleeves of his blue work shirt. His knuckles are large and knobbed, like irregular stones. Reagan is struck by the urge, almost overwhelming in its intensity, to fling the doors open and take off past him. Bare feet pounding on the springy grass so that her calves end up aching and her lungs burn and her scalp pours with sweat. Maybe he would chase her. She would run at full speed, her feet kicking up leaves. Only to end up where she started. It would not matter, as long as the pull of muscles, the sweat in eyes, the burn in lungs were an obliteration. But Hosts are barred from exerting themselves too much at the Farm, and she would never be allowed to run without shoes. And then there's the issue of the buddy.

She can only take a walk with a buddy. And who would her buddy be?

Reagan ignores the swell of loneliness in her chest and moves toward the window, the UteroSoundz glommed onto her stomach. Two other workmen, farther off, are removing the covering from the pool. Soon, maybe even later today, they'll fill it with water. She can take a dip. That might help: the cold shock and weightlessness.

Weightless is how she imagines Mom: bobbing alone in the inky black. Tethered to reality by the thinnest thread. Reagan's weekly phone call is meant to keep Mom from floating away entirely. She never responds, so Reagan has stopped asking questions. Just talks and talks in the hope that her voice helps. Maybe even kindles something.

Lately, Reagan has been wondering if Mom still exists. The real Mom, not the one who performed for Dad on command. The way the baby inside Reagan's womb exists, even though it is unreachable. Inside whatever place traps her, Mom might still marvel at the symmetry of a full moon—she used to drag Reagan and Gus from their beds to gaze at its perfect roundness. She might still be struck by the hilarity of a subway car full of people, silent but for the screeching of the train's wheels, because everyone—down to the three-year-old sitting next to his nanny—is staring at a phone.

If she's in there, is she happy?

Does she know Reagan's voice, even if she can't say her name?

REAGAN IS AT A WORKSTATION IN THE MEDIA ROOM SEVERAL hours later. In her inbox are two articles from Dad—one about the flat tax, another about a female green-technology investor ("You can do well by doing good, Sweetheart"). It's his way of reaching out; they haven't spoken since their fight about visiting Mom. Reagan knows, from Mom's nurse, that Gus has already dropped by to see her twice since then. But he lives in Chicago. It's not fair to compare them, as Dad always does. And Gus never found Dad's hypocrisy offensive, even when they were kids. Whenever Reagan brought up the latest rumor about Dad's girlfriends, Gus would cover his ears and walk away.

Reagan clicks the Compose button. A window pops onscreen, polyglot legalese reminding her that what she's about to write will be monitored, is subject to the nondisclosure agreements. In other words: keep your trap shut, written in English, Spanish, Tagalog, Polish, French, Chinese, Russian, Portuguese.

Reagan clicks: I agree—but before she can begin typing an email to Dad a new one arrives, this one from Macy. No message, only a video attachment and the subject line in caps: **GALA WAS INSANITY. CALL ME!**

Reagan hasn't spoken with Macy since she became

famous. Or quasi-famous. She was featured in **BusinessWorld,** a magazine Dad has subscribed to for decades and which Reagan has never read. According to it, Macy is one of the top thirty business leaders under thirty. In the **world.**

To Reagan, it seems a little dumb. What does it even mean to be a "top leader"? Who gets to decide? But Dad is bowled over by it. She first heard the news from him, in an email with the **BusinessWorld** article attached, subject line trumpeting: **YOUR BEST FRIEND IS IMPRESSIVE.**

A stream of emails followed this first one. Articles from the **Harvard Business Review;** inspirational quotations; exhortations that Reagan can "make it too," if she only finds where her "passions intersect with the practical." (Did he mean profitable?)

Reagan picks up the phone. The woman who answers Macy's line puts Reagan on hold. To pass the time Reagan clicks open the video clip attached to Macy's email. A man, graying, stands at a microphone. He is talking about Macy, his voice echoing in the cavernous room—how on top of her grueling job selling **blah-di-blah** derivatives, Macy sits on the bank's Diversity Committee and several nonprofit boards; how she graduated summa cum laude from Duke despite being on work-study; her rough start in Baltimore, raised by her grandmother **blah-di-blah,** and how she Pulled Herself Up by Her Bootstraps Through Sweat and Grit and Faith . . . though, ahem—she long ago traded in her work boots for Jimmy Choos. (And on cue Macy sweeps toward him, her strappy, gold stilettos glinting in the spotlight, amid appreciative chortles.)

Reagan feels a twist inside, a spurt of annoyance—or, maybe, envy.

This self-satisfied schmuck is full of shit. Everything he says is true but also wildly false. A fairy tale meant to keep the grandees in the room happy, to maintain their faith in this best of all possible worlds:

Black girl from the 'hood doing right, working hard, playing by the rules. Making good.

Meritocracy, dig?

Except that Macy's grandmother was smart as a whip and educated, too—a middle-school math teacher who owned a home, however modest, back in Trinidad, which Macy visited most summers of her life. Macy's mother's early death was a tragedy, sure, but her life was a cakewalk compared to, say, Jane's. Jane was **truly** poor—developing-country poor, not American poor—and she was abandoned by her dad and mom only to have her grandmother die on her. Jane works her butt off at least as much as Macy ever has—but you won't see **her** winning any awards.

Reagan replays the video. The drape of Macy's red gown, the glint of her steady smile. Framed by the computer screen Macy looks both entirely familiar and completely strange, at once the girl who douses everything on her plate with ketchup but also an alien Macy comfortable in a designer dress cut to show off ridiculously toned arms. She is a lithe beauty walking with ease on four-inch heels and also the Macy whom Reagan caught in flagrante freshman year with a boorish, blue-eyed, floppy-haired pothead—a kid utterly uninteresting in every way except for his pedigree (one of those crusty old families that assure you entry into St. Paul's as well as undeserved pussy and popularity in certain East Coast circles).

"Hey," Macy drawls when she finally gets on the phone, and all is right again. **This** is Macy. Not the mannequin on the screen.

They gossip about a mutual friend's breakup, his subsequent depression and resurrection through hot yoga. Macy gushes about her new boyfriend, the first black man she's dated since before college. He went to Exeter, Harvard.

"He might be the one," she coos, and Reagan's stomach inexplicably drops.

"I'm proud of you!" Reagan says to change the subject. "But not as proud of you as my **dad** is."

It's a joke, and a test. Macy knows Reagan's dad.

"It's not **that** big a deal, Reag," Macy answers, false humility radiating through the phone.

Then: "Shit, I've got to hop."

She promises to email with "full gala details" later.

Reagan stares at the computer screen, the receiver still in her hand. Macy doesn't buy into this bullshit—at least, she never has before. Reagan rewinds the video clip and watches it again, then a third time, studying it as if searching for clues. Macy onscreen. Oxblood dress and tables of white linen and orchids and clanking cutlery; guests in suits and smart dresses, all of them probably top leaders themselves. Or grandmothers of top leaders. Reagan pauses the video and scans the crowd for Macy's grandmother. She restarts the video and watches again.

It's not **that** big a deal, Reag.

Something brushes Reagan's stomach. A flutter, like a bird's wing. The baby? Reagan's heart skips. She leans back in the chair and rests her hands lightly on her belly. She waits. She taps her pointer finger lightly against her skin, breathing deeply to slow her heart, hence the baby's heart. Knock, knock, who's there?

Minutes pass and minutes more. Did she imagine it, that tiniest of movements?

She holds her stomach as she watches the video still playing on her computer. Macy has left the stage. Another Top Leader, an athletic man with pink skin, Irish-looking and smug, is now accepting his plaque. He is nonchalant, even unimpressed, as if all of it—the tables laden with silver and glass, the waiters flitting around the room at obsequious attention, the kudos and applause—were to be expected. Just deserts. Not **that** big a deal.

Will **you** be a Top Leader like this smug asshole? Reagan silently asks the baby boy inside her, suddenly resenting him. Because it **is** a Him. At her last ultrasound, Dr. Wilde announced the news to the camera without even a glance at Reagan. She deflected the Clients' thanks with a wave of her hand, but Reagan could see the self-satisfaction in her eyes. As if she had hand-stitched the fetal penis herself.

But you already **are** the tops, aren't you?

Reagan thinks of the fetus inside her, fattened by organic food, strengthened by custom multivitamins, probably trilingual at this point given the polyglot playlists on her UteroSoundz. And male. And rich.

How could he **not** rule the world someday?

On a whim Reagan begins typing a proposal to **BusinessWorld** for a special issue, TOP 30 FETAL BIGWIGS UNDER 30 WEEKS! There would be ultrasound centerfolds, fetal measurements, and write-ups of fetal diet and hobbies. Descriptions of the wombs the Fetal Leaders inhabit along the lines of luxury real-estate listings. As she types Reagan feels a stirring. Is it him? Is he pumped up, too? Drumming his barely there fingers against her uterine wall in anticipation? Ready to hop—

Reagan is so engrossed in her project that she does not notice the door to the glass cubicle is open. Beatriz, a Colombian Host in her late first trimester, clears her throat. "Are you finished, Reagan?"

Reagan apologizes for taking so long, saves her work, and logs out of the computer. Suddenly, she wants to see Lisa. Lisa, whose head Reagan just ripped off at lunch, but who will understand more than anyone here that all of it—**BusinessWorld** magazine's stupid list, and Dad's unabashed admiration of it, and the self-congratulatory Gala— is bullshit.

"Whoa there!" Ms. Yu says when Reagan almost bumps into her in the hallway. She is with a short Asian woman in black slacks and sneakers.

"Sorry, Ms. Yu. I didn't see you."

"No worries. Reagan, please meet Segundina. She just had her interview, and I'm showing her around the facilities."

Reagan extends her hand and Segundina takes it, looking up from the floor but not at Reagan.

"Reagan's in her second trimester," Ms. Yu says as she readjusts the long strand of pearls double-looped around her neck. "Her Client adores her."

"Well, she hasn't actually **met** me," Reagan answers, directing herself toward Segundina, who is immobile but manages to convey the impression of cowering.

"Not yet, but she tracks everything, and she's very pleased with you," Ms. Yu assures her. To Segundina she adds, "And with Golden Oaks. Reagan's Client is a real world leader, so it's a true compliment to us that she is so taken by our operations."

"Oh, has my Client visited?" Reagan asks with feigned breeziness.

Ms. Yu smiles. "Enjoy the day, Reagan."

Reagan continues to Lisa's room, wondering if she's ever passed by her Client without knowing who she was, and enters without knocking. The room is a disaster—Lisa refuses to let the cleaning ladies in—clothes piled on the rocking chair, a cascade of magazines on the carpet. On the windowsill, a half-dozen half-empty mugs of tea share space with Troy's porcelain sculptures, glossy figures of bulbous women, bright and alluring as candy.

Reagan is flopped on Lisa's unmade bed reading one of her outdated **Artforum**s when the door bangs open. Lisa is unsurprised to see her. Her ponytail is askew and her shirt is on inside-out and she hugs a bunched sweater to her stomach.

"I'm sorry that I—" Reagan begins.

"Stop," Lisa says. "I deserved it. I have a peace offering. Can we walk?"

Lisa stuffs her sweater into a backpack. They walk in silence to the nearest Coordinator Desk and swipe their WellBands in the reader. The Coordinator glances at her laptop screen and scrutinizes Lisa. "Let's stick to the trails today, okay, ladies? And keep it short. It's supposed to rain."

"You don't have to worry about us!" Lisa sing-songs, batting her eyelashes.

Outside, the sky is cobalt and clear. "It doesn't look like rain," Reagan observes, inhaling deeply.

"They're going to track me live, I bet. So we've got to keep walking," Lisa mutters, striding ahead of Reagan into the forest.

"Slow down!" Reagan speeds up to keep pace with Lisa, who is marching down the path, turning this way and that, as if she had mapped out the route beforehand.

"Well, this is fun," Reagan says when Lisa finally stops. She is out of breath. "What's the rush?"

Lisa pants, leaning forward with her hands on her thighs. She smiles suddenly. "There aren't cameras on this stretch yet. Julio said they're installing them later this week."

The path they stand on is short and shaded by trees and, farther ahead, slopes upward to a flat clearing. "We'll see anyone coming way before they can see us."

"Is Troy here?" Reagan asks angrily. "Because if he is, I'm out." She takes a step backward, in the direction of the Farm.

"No. Troy isn't here. Unfortunately," Lisa answers with exaggerated patience. "But I do have a present for you. And Jane, if she ever talks to me again." She unzips her backpack and dumps its contents onto the ground. Along with her crumpled sweater and a couple bottles of water are two cans of Diet Coke and several large Snickers bars. "Surprise!"

Reagan stares at the soda and candy for a split second before bursting into laughter. She laughs so hard she doubles over. She can't stand Lisa, and she adores her at the same time, and she's filled with a stupid joy. She grabs a can, still cold to the touch, and cracks it open, the snap and hiss so loud Reagan cringes. Lisa pops her own can open, too, and they clink, giggling like idiots.

"To your health," Lisa says, holding her can aloft.

"To **your** health."

Reagan tips the soda into her mouth. The chemical sweetness. The fizz in her throat and kick of caffeine. She swishes a mouthful from cheek to cheek, like Dad with his fine wines. She gulps it down and gulps until there is no more, then shakes the inverted can above her mouth to make sure she catches every drop.

Are you amped? she screams silently to Bigwig, feeling supremely alive.

Reagan glances at Lisa, who has also finished her Coke, and starts to laugh again. Midlaugh a burp—wet and fulsome and lasting half a minute—roars out of her mouth.

"Is that your—barbaric yawp?" Lisa can barely get out the words. She is heaving with silent laughter, and tears drip down her face.

Reagan crumples her can and picks up the Snickers bar. She tears the wrapper with her teeth.

Get ready, Bigwig. You're gonna love **this.**

She takes a bite, then crams half the bar in her mouth, and for a moment the world is obliterated by sweetness. Through it, dimly: a chiming. Her WellBand alarm reminding her it's time for the ultrasound. She shouldn't be late, but she can't stop now. She takes another bite. And then another.

JANE

JANE ANGLES HER BODY TOWARD DELIA AS REAGAN AND
Lisa amble past, dipping her head so that her hair
curtains her face. Safely shielded, she focuses on
Delia's lips. What is she saying? Something about
Ms. Yu. That Ms. Yu asked her to have lunch
today with the new Filipina Host, but when Delia
stopped by her room—she is sharing it with the
new Polish girl, the pale one who sometimes sits
with Tasia and your friend Reagan (Delia says
your friend Reagan a little snidely, because it is
clear Jane is no longer friends with Reagan)—she
was nowhere to be found. Delia waited and waited

and finally gave up. She wonders if she will be in trouble.

"Why did you not ask the Coordinators? They can find her with the WellBand." Jane knows this too well.

She forces herself to take a bite of beet salad. She hates the texture of beets, slippery and moist, not quite soft but not hard, either. But Jane is on her best behavior now, and Betsy, the cook who sneaks Lisa desserts sometimes, reminded Jane that beets are a superfood.

"But Ms. Yu cannot be angry with me, because I waited for twenty minutes! And when I get hungry I become dizzy, because of my blood sugar. That is not good for the baby. Do you agree?"

Delia looks worriedly at Jane, who reassures her that Ms. Yu will know that Delia tried her best. Jane scans the room surreptitiously and notices Reagan and Lisa hunched together at a two-person table near the window. So. They are friends again. It makes sense, of course, just as it makes sense that Jane is no longer with them. Reagan and Lisa are from the same world, and Jane is not, and she always knew this.

Still, Jane feels hollow, like something has been taken from her.

Reagan was furious when she first found out that Jane was being punished. Jane was in bed, sapped after her second interrogation with Ms. Yu, when Reagan stormed in demanding answers. At first,

Jane did not notice the depths of her roommate's rage, nor the roots of it. Only that Reagan asked questions, so many, in a voice low and serious.

What really happened? It's not like you to leave the trail. Whose idea was it?

Each question pushed Jane further into herself until she could go no deeper, and then she stopped answering. She did not cry. She only lay inert, allowing the desolation to settle over her, one layer after another: Amalia's visit was canceled. The Clients were angry. Their baby might be sick. It was her fault.

And, looming over everything: she had lied to Ms. Yu, and Ms. Yu knew it, and now Ms. Yu would look at her the way her other employers did.

It was when Jane was working with Mrs. Carter that she learned how people saw her. Before that, she assumed she was invisible to the people she worked for. It was a wet day, the rain drumming against the windows of the study, and she was cleaning spit-up from the sofa when she heard a voice declare: "They seem great—English speaking and diligent and all that. But they lie."

It was the voice of Mrs. Van Wyck, the friend of Mrs. Carter from college. Jane heard Mrs. Carter's gentle protestation (How can you make such a sweeping generalization?), and then the friend began to tell a story about a family in her building. They lived on the tenth floor, where they had combined two apartment units so that they had views from three directions—the husband was a real-estate phenom and the wife was a doctor, and they were rolling in money. Their nanny, a Filipina, had lived with them for six years, helping to raise their two boys. The neighbor often told Mrs. Van Wyck stories about the nanny's deadbeat husband and all the children back in the Philippines whom the nanny supported. Mrs. Van Wyck's neighbor considered the nanny a member of the family, giving her almost four weeks of paid vacation a year and generous birthday and Christmas bonuses. So, when one of the nanny's daughters got sick—a staph infection that started with a sore on her foot but kept spreading—Mrs. Van Wyck's neighbor was the first to tell the nanny to return home, where she was needed. Her neighbor paid for the plane ticket to the Philippines and insisted on helping with the hospital bills, and she was uncomplaining when the nanny called weeks later to ask to extend her stay.

It turned out, Mrs. Van Wyck declared to Mrs. Carter, that the nanny was lying. The cleaning lady outed her, and the nanny tearfully confessed. Her daughter, so the nanny explained, did have a staph infection, but it was never life-threatening. She returned to the Philippines because the daughter was about to marry a bad man—a gambler, a do-nothing—and the nanny had to talk sense into her. Once home, the nanny became mired in the various crises plaguing her other children and their families. The nanny promised to return every cent of the money her boss had given her for the medical costs (she had not spent it; she was not a thief). She promised nothing like it would ever happen again.

Jane, soiled washcloth in hand, stood listening for Mrs. Carter to reply.

"My mother always told me you should swap out your help every few years or they become too familiar," Mrs. Carter finally said, and Jane's heart sank. "I suppose she was right."

"Oh, I could tell you a dozen stories," Mrs. Van Wyck replied. "Missing jewelry, cash, 'deaths' in the family and pleas for help with the fake funeral costs . . ."

"In a way, you can't really blame them. To them our lives seem so easy," Mrs. Carter said.

"But that's exactly why you can't **trust** them."

JANE PRETENDS TO LISTEN TO DELIA'S FRETTING, BUT SHE is watching Reagan and Lisa. Troublemakers, Ms. Yu had called them during the second interrogation. Privileged girls who like to stir the pot but don't have to eat their own cooking. She asked Jane gravely: Do you really want to risk everything for friends who won't remember your name once they return to real life?

She is right. Jane cannot risk any more trouble.

"Lisa is getting fat," Delia notes now, sniggering as she cuts her chicken. "That must make you happy?"

Jane does not answer. After days of pestering Jane

to "spill the beans" about her troubles, Delia now contents herself with the occasional snide remark about Jane's former friends. She assumes that Jane resents them. That whatever break occurred was Reagan's and Lisa's fault.

But this could not be further from the truth. Jane blames no one but herself.

Certainly, Ms. Yu is blameless. She is only doing her job. And Lisa is only guilty of letting a greedy love devour her. How can Jane be angry with her when Jane, too, once felt that same fierceness for Billy? When she, too, made stupid choices because of it? Jane remembers sneaking out of her mother's house in Los Angeles as often as she could to escape the stench of fried fish and Lysol; to avoid the red-faced American boyfriends who padded to the breakfast table in their boxer shorts and ogled Jane's chest while she ate her cereal before school. Even when her mother was crying in the kitchen over another heartbreak, Jane could think only of Billy. When he asked her to go with him to New York, she did not hesitate.

And, of course, Jane does not blame Reagan. Breaking with her is the hardest part. During the weeks of their friendship, they fell into the habit of talking at night, often for hours. Sometimes, Reagan would speak about her family: How smart her brother was, the prestigious job he got right out of college. (Reagan only knew this from her father; she and her brother did not keep in touch.) How her mother filled Reagan's childhood bedroom with watercolors of Reagan's favorite fairy tales—she was so talented; her mother could paint anything.

The mother now remembers only the father's name. Reagan believes he takes a perverse pride in this, because it is proof of her love and his importance.

One night, Reagan told Jane she had decided to get tested for the dementia gene. The mother herself, and the brother, had refused to find out. What would Reagan do if the news was bad? Would it mean she could never—should never—have a child?

Her voice in the darkness was tiny. Jane somehow managed to find the right words. She reassured her friend that every day new medicines were being invented. That neither Reagan nor her baby—if she chose to have one—had a fixed destiny. Things could change.

Jane prayed that this was true, her heart breaking for her friend. Because Jane had Ate, and she would always have Amalia. But Reagan—she was alone.

Jane watches Delia devour her chicken, faintly repulsed. Delia begins complaining about her acid-reflux and saying she hopes the bonus is worth all her aches and pains. Suddenly, she leaps to her feet. "Segundina!"

A small, thickset Filipina trailed by one of the Coordinators approaches the table. Her eyes are glued to a bowl of quinoa, as if she is afraid it will spring off her tray onto the floor.

"Segundina—am I pronouncing that right?—wasn't feeling so hot. But we think she can hold down some lunch now," the Coordinator says and hoots. "Delia, you got this?"

Delia nods vehemently and begins to explain that she waited for Segundina for almost half an hour, but the Coordinator waves her off. "No big deal. Segundina was stuck in Ms. Hanna's bathroom doing her business."

Segundina reddens.

"All righty. Thanks for taking care of her, Delia. Just make sure she's at Dr. Wilde's by two."

Delia makes a show of pulling out a chair for Segundina and dusting crumbs off the spotless seat. "Sit, sit. Eat now."

Jane and the other Filipinas call out various greetings. Segundina responds shyly, her head hanging low as if dangling from her neck by a string. Jane remembers being in her place, those first unreal days at Golden Oaks, everything so new and a stranger's baby in your belly. Several women at the table begin firing questions at her, and Delia repeats them as if she is Segundina's designated interlocutor: What province are you from? How far along are you? Who is your Client?

Segundina's eyes flit from Delia to her tray as she answers. She speaks haltingly. Jane tries to smile at her but cannot catch her eye. Someone arrives in a rush, banging her tray farther down the table and announcing in a hushed voice that she knows what happened to Anya. The attention of the Hosts shifts. Segundina listens silently, looking frightened.

"Do not listen to them. It is very rare, to have this defect," Jane reassures her, although of course Jane worries, too.

Segundina smiles tentatively. She picks up her fork and pushes the quinoa around her plate.

"And if you feel sick, do not force yourself to eat. Your baby will be okay. Many Hosts lose weight in the first trimester."

"Thank you," Segundina says.

The other Filipinas are now trading stories about Down syndrome and miscarriages and other forms of bad luck. Jane finishes her food in silence. She is thinking about the video Ate emailed her yesterday. In it, Amalia lets go of Ate's hand and takes her first, wobbly steps on her own.

Something like pain flowers in Jane's chest when she thinks about her daughter, now over one year old. How did she get so big so quickly? From the videos, Jane has watched Amalia learn to clap, and point to her eyes or tummy on command, and now—walk. And Jane has missed it all. Two weeks ago, Ate organized a birthday party for Amalia at a park near the apartment. Angel was there, and Cherry, and some of Amalia's friends from daycare with their parents. Ate filmed Amalia pulling the toy keyboard Jane sent out of a colorful bag. When Amalia banged on its keys, a song began to play, and she kicked her feet and bopped to the music with a huge grin on her face. Everyone at the party laughed. But watching it from afar, alone and pregnant with a stranger's child, Jane had cried.

"HOW FAR ARE YOU?" SEGUNDINA ASKS SHYLY.

"I am second trimester now."

"You are lucky. You will not have a miscarriage."

Jane, understanding, tells her not to worry so much. Ms. Yu would not have moved her to Golden Oaks if she thought there was any danger that the pregnancy was high-risk. It would not make sense, because Golden Oaks would only lose money. It is a business, you see. Jane notices that she sounds tone. like Lisa, borrowing Lisa's words and her knowing

The baby inside her moves. She felt it move so much earlier than she did with Amalia. Dr. Wilde says this is natural; with second babies you are more attuned to your body. But Jane believes it is because this baby is stronger. With Amalia she was not so careful, eating Big Macs and all those bags of **chicharron.**

Segundina twists a strand of hair and holds the end to her lips, sucking it to a sharp point. Jane tells her this is a bad habit, a good way to give the baby germs. Segundina blushes, and Jane regrets her harsh tone. In a chatty voice, like the one Reagan uses when she is trying to make someone feel comfortable, she asks, "Your name. You are the second child, then? Do you have many brothers and sisters?"

Segundina answers that she has seven siblings.

Jane makes a show of surprise, although she expected this. Farming families are always big. "And all of you are numbered?"

"Prima is my **ate.** I am second. My youngest brothers are Septimo and Octavio." Segundina allows herself a small smile.

"Your parents are smart. Numbers are easier to remember than names!" Jane jokes, and she is glad when Segundina laughs. "And how did you come here?"

Jane means America. She is asking Segundina how she made her way to America, but Segundina thinks Jane is asking about Golden Oaks. They are not supposed to speak about this, Golden Oaks and its ways. It is in the contracts. But Segundina is already explaining, in a nervous tumble: "Before I came here, I was working for a cooking business. My boss told me about Golden Oaks, about how much money I can make. At first, I was not interested, because how do I explain this to my family, that I will carry a baby? Maybe they don't believe me that it is a job. Maybe they think . . . something shameful."

Jane smiles sympathetically, taking note of a Coordinator a dozen yards away.

"I prayed for guidance. And my boss says to me: if you want to help your family, this is the way. My boss, she helped me with the story I told them. It is a lie, but only a **white lie.**"

Jane reassures her that white lies are necessary sometimes. Jane, too, lied to Angel and the others in the dorm in Queens about why she would be away for so long. Why she was leaving Amalia.

"When I was having the shots, I was so sick. I lived in a dormitory—do you know Queens?—and it was hard. Ate Evelyn—that is my boss—she let me stay in her apartment. In Rego Park. She lives with only her baby cousin, who is so easy. Mali only cries when she has the diaper rash . . . And at night, when Ate lets her cry to sleep."

Segundina sees Jane's stricken face and reassures her: "She says this is the way to sleep-train. You see, Ate is an expert with babies."

The noise in the room—clinking of cutlery, jostling of voices—is suddenly muted. Jane stares at the woman, words still streaming out of her mouth but as if from miles away: how she took baby Mali to go shopping while her boss delivered **pancit lug-lug** to a client; how Ate Evelyn told her about Golden Oaks, and her friend Angel loaned her clothes for the interview.

Is this woman talking about Ate? Is she talking about Amalia?

With a shaking voice Jane asks Segundina, "Where is this apartment?"

The address Segundina recites is Jane's, and the baby that Segundina says Ate allows to cry to sleep at night is Mali.

There is a pressure building in Jane's head, a

whiteness like a blizzard. Segundina is still talking, but Jane cannot absorb the words. Something— a scream? a sob?—is filling up her throat.

And then Tasia is standing over her, eyes shining like she has a fever. The other Filipinas have stopped chattering and are staring at Tasia and Jane, several with mouths agape.

"Did you not hear me, Jane?" Tasia asks, as if she has been speaking for some time.

Jane mumbles, "I do not understand."

"I will repeat. The Client of Reagan is not Chinese. I heard Ms. Yu talking on the speakerphone. The mother is American, Jane!"

Jane avoids Segundina's bewildered gaze and looks up at Tasia without seeing her.

"Do you not yet understand?" Tasia asks Jane, her eyes glowing brighter. "This means it is **you** carrying the Chinese baby. You are the only one left. You will be rich!"

Jane stands abruptly, almost tipping over her tray. It is too much, the whiteness in her head. All this commotion. She needs to think. She cannot think here.

Delia is tugging at Jane's sleeve. The smile on her face is gluttonous. Tasia asks if she is excited. The other Filipinas begin talking—to Jane, to Tasia, to each other. So many mouths moving. Jane leaves her tray on the table and rushes for the door.

In the hallway she slumps against the wall. A passing Coordinator asks her if she is feeling all right. Jane nods and stands upright to prove she is fine. She only needs to be alone. She longs for her room, but what if Reagan is there? She cannot face her roommate now.

Jane walks numbly toward the Coordinator Desk. She will ask to go outside. She will tell the Coordinator to assign her a buddy. But at the desk there is a cluster of Hosts. Some are returning UteroSoundz machines; others are queuing to check out for a walk. Several others wear swimsuits, blue-green nylon stretched tightly over their distended bellies. It is a beautiful day, hot for early June, and the trails and the pool will be crowded.

Jane hurries in the direction of the fitness wing, past the exercise room and the stairs to the basement pool and down the hall toward the treatment rooms, where Hosts receive prenatal massages or acupuncture for sciatica and other pains. The lights are dim, and the sound of a river's gentle burbling emanates from hidden speakers. On the verge of breaking into tears, ready to beg one of the Wellness Providers to let her simply lie down in the darkness, Jane flings open a door.

The room is dark. The hallway light illuminates Julio, who leans rigid against the massage table. He is in agony. He grips the table's metal sides as if holding on for life.

A heart attack!

Nanay died of a heart attack. She dropped dead in the rain.

"Julio!" Jane screams, although in her panic his name comes out a whisper.

And then she sees Lisa. She is crouched below Julio, her face buried between his legs and barely visible. She is devouring him, feasting on his flesh in violent, hungry jerks.

Julio's eyes blink open and he squints through the light at Jane, but Lisa does not notice. She continues her attack until Julio places a large hand over her head to still her.

"Jane?" Lisa calls, but Jane has already turned away. She is already walking. She thinks Lisa calls her again, but it is difficult to hear because now Jane is running, and the sound of her shoes on the hardwood floors is deafening.

Jane passes Delia and and another Host, and they are looking at her strangely, like she is a ghost. She runs past a Coordinator who is laughing with Ms. Hanna in the hallway, and they stop laughing and call to her with questions that she cannot answer because she is already gone, past the dining room, past the cluster of Hosts returning from outside with flushed cheeks, trailing clods of earth behind them on the floor.

"Jane?" Reagan asks, standing just in front of her, holding her book and looking at Jane with worry in her eyes, as if there is something wrong. As if Jane is in trouble.

But she is fine.

"No," Jane states and runs faster still, her breath

coming hard now. She does not stop until she sees Eve, Ms. Yu's assistant, sitting at her desk. She is typing on a laptop but lifts her head at the sound of Jane's approach. A smile lights up white against her dark skin, then fades.

"I need to see Ms. Yu," Jane pants. She folds over, hands on her knees, heaving.

"About what?" Eve asks, her voice placid but her brow creased.

"About everything."

ATE

WHEN ATE IS FINISHED STRAPPING THE BABY CARRIER onto her shoulders she glances at Amalia, who sits upright in her stroller teething a toy octopus. "Ready, Mali?"

Amalia is getting too big to carry on Ate's chest, that is the truth. But she is crawling now, and she cannot be set free in the Herreras' home. Ate has spied, during the deliveries of food for Mrs. Herrera's dinner parties, the many tables piled with breakable treasures—Chinese vases patterned in blue, delicate carvings of the saints, thin, capiz-shell bowls filled with pink and white stones from Boracay, where the Herreras bought a house that they rent to rich vacationers.

And pictures. There are pictures covering every inch of every surface of the Herreras' home, all of them framed in silver or gold. Just on the grand piano there are a dozen of them—of Dr. and Mrs. Herrera at various parties, sometimes in traditional Filipino dress; of Dr. Herrera with his famous patients (professional athletes whom Ate does not recognize). Nearby, stretching across most of a wall, hangs an enormous photograph of the family perched on the fancy white-and-gold chairs of the living room. Dr. Herrera and the two boys wear tuxedos; Mrs. Herrera and her daughter don flowing gowns. Ate can imagine Amalia crawling up to it, drawn by the emerald green of Mrs. Herrera's photographed shoe and pawing at the photo with her sticky fingers.

Ate lifts Amalia from the stroller and slides her into the baby carrier, ignoring her yelps of complaint. "Yes, Mali, it is too small. But it is only for a short time."

Ate climbs the three stone steps to the front door and turns back to glance at the stroller. It has rolled off the pathway that cuts through the Herreras' trim front lawn and stands lopsided on the grass. Will someone take it?

She scans the quiet street. No one is outside, perhaps because outsiders are not allowed here. She knows this because Angel's newest boyfriend, an American with thinning hair who flies airplanes for Delta, offered to drive Ate and the **polvoron** and **buko** pie to the Herreras' the morning of the Herrera girl's wedding weeks ago. He parked his car in front of the house and helped Ate and Segundina and Didi and Angel carry the food to the tennis club nearby. When he returned, the back wheel of his SUV was clamped in a boot. The parking ticket jammed under the car's wipers explained that the street was private, only for neighborhood residents. Ate had to pay for the boyfriend's parking fine out of her profits.

How can a street be private? Angel had scoffed.

But Ate liked that a Filipino family lived on the biggest lot on a private street.

Ate turns back to the Herreras' door and lifts the brass knocker, letting it drop with a thud. When there is no answer, she presses the doorbell. From inside the house there is the sound of footsteps. She fixes a smile on her face.

The Herrera boy, the one still in high school, opens the door. He wears bright blue headphones and ripped jeans worn too low, his underwear sticking out, like the blacks. " 'Sup, Evelyn."

Ate was expecting Luisa. She placed her with the Herreras several years ago, and Mrs. Herrera was so pleased with Luisa's diligence that she gave Ate an extra hundred dollars for the referral.

"I am here to see your mother," Ate announces. She speaks loudly because she can hear music spilling from the boy's ears.

"Ma! Evelyn's here to see you!" the boy shouts up the stairs. He gives Ate a cursory wave before slouching off into the house's dim interior.

Ate remains on the stone steps, shifting her weight from foot to foot because Amalia is heavy. Amalia chews on the blue trim of the baby carrier and kicks her legs against Ate's thighs.

"Evelyn! Why is the door open? You will let in the flies!" Mrs. Herrera cries in Tagalog as she bounds down the stairs like a young girl, although she is not young anymore. She wears a tiny white skirt and a collared white shirt and new white sneakers. "Come in, **naman**! Unless you took the subway? Yes? Then go in through the back. Luisa just washed the floors."

Ate has already stepped into the house but now steps back out, down the stone steps, onto the pathway of oval stones that leads to a mudroom at the rear of the house. In the mudroom she wipes her feet thoroughly on a bristly mat. She finds Luisa in the kitchen plucking yellow **kalamansi** fruit from a potted tree next to the window.

"Those are not yet ripe," Ate teases.

"Ate!" Luisa cries, jumping up to embrace her friend. "I told the boy already, but he wants juice anyway. I will add more sugar to cut the sourness."

Mrs. Herrera appears, her tinted hair now yanked

back in a ponytail so tight her eyes bulge slightly. "Where is my tennis racket?"

She instructs Luisa to search the sports closet upstairs and sighs, remarking to Ate in a loud voice that she is surprised Luisa still cannot remember her schedule; Mrs. Herrera has played tennis every Tuesday morning for months. Her eyes fall on Amalia.

"Whose baby is this?" Mrs. Herrera scrutinizes Amalia as Ate tells her about Jane. Amalia stretches for Mrs. Herrera's cheek with her fingertips and coos.

"She is pretty! So white! She reminds me of my Josefina. People always said Josi looked **mestiza,** too."

Ate bites her lip and feigns agreement. Josefina Herrera is the spitting image of her mother. If she squatted down on her haunches, even if she were still stuffed inside her eighteen-thousand-dollar wedding dress, she would look just like the Igorots who come down from the mountains of Luzon, crouching on the roadways in donated American clothes. Brown as mud.

Amalia babbles nonsensically to Mrs. Herrera, who is visibly delighted by the attention. "Pretty baby. Let her out of the carrier, Evelyn. She is too big for it!"

Ate hesitates. She does not want to remain long. She only wants to get her check and go. But Mrs. Herrera is already clicking open one of the carrier straps. She lifts Amalia, kissing her neck, then nuzzling her belly. "So pretty! So pretty! You are so pretty!"

Amalia chortles and Mrs. Herrera kisses her head. "Ah, I hope Josi has a baby soon! She does not need a job—her husband works at Google! You know Google?"

Ate raises her eyebrows to show she is impressed. "Ma'am," she begins, "I am here to collect the balance for the wedding dessert . . . ?"

Mrs. Herrera is dancing back and forth with Amalia and singing. Amalia is thrilled, alternately gurgling and giggling. Mrs. Herrera does not answer for so long that Ate wonders if she spoke too softly. Then Mrs. Herrera turns, still dancing with Amalia, and remarks, "You know many of the **polvoron** cookies crumbled? When the guests took them home, they were like sand."

Ate begins to apologize, even though she had warned Mrs. Herrera this was bound to happen to some of the cookies. Even though she had recommended a different takeaway gift.

Mrs. Herrera shakes her head. "I understand **polvoron** is fragile. But why did you not suggest a different dessert then? You are the professional, Evelyn. You have to use your head."

Ate swallows the retort ready to jump off her tongue. Mrs. Herrera hands Amalia back to her. Amalia clings to the braided gold necklace dangling from Mrs. Herrera's neck and begins to cry when Mrs. Herrera forces her fists open. "I am out of checks. I will pay you when you deliver the **pancit** this Saturday. You can still do this?"

"Yes, of course," Ate says, avoiding Mrs. Herrera's eyes.

"You will need to double the order. We expect more people. I will not pay you more for the extra food—and then we will be even for the problem with the **polvoron.** Do you agree?"

"Yes, ma'am," Ate responds, because what else can she say? She pulls the carrier straps up over Amalia, who still whimpers for Mrs. Herrera.

Luisa returns to the kitchen holding two tennis rackets. Mrs. Herrera chides her that these are the boys'. Mrs. Herrera's new racket has the **blue** over-grip. She sends Luisa back upstairs.

"I will deliver the **pancit** at five o'clock on Saturday," interrupts Ate from the mudroom by way of a goodbye.

"Four-thirty is better," says Mrs. Herrera without looking at her.

As if the half hour makes any difference.

AMALIA, FULL OF MILK, HAS FALLEN ASLEEP IN THE STROLLER, which is both easier and harder for Ate. It is easier because it means that Amalia will not demand attention, and so Ate can focus on her errands. It is harder because it means that when Ate gets to the store she will need to bring the stroller inside. She will need to lift the stroller if there are stairs and maneuver it through narrow aisles and around people who stand in the way and then sigh in annoyance when the bulky bags hanging from the stroller's handles accidentally bump them.

Luckily, the entrance to the MusicShack is easy, with only one step. Ate tilts the stroller to lift its front wheels up over the threshold and enters the store. It is loud, with music blaring and a wall of flat-screen televisions turned to different channels. Ate walks up to a young man wearing a red shirt with a nametag pinned onto his chest. He leans against a tall speaker and types on his cellphone with his thumbs.

"I need to find a music player. And earphones," Ate announces.

The man looks up from his phone and wordlessly saunters away. Ate follows him. They pass the television and computer sections and come to an area full of stereo equipment.

"I need something smaller. Like a Walkman," says Ate, staring dubiously at the large machines surrounding her.

"You know you can download music to your phone, right?" The young man speaks slowly, as if Ate's age has made her stupid.

Ate shakes her head. Roy does not have a phone. He could not talk on a phone even if he did have one. His **yaya** owns one, of course, but Ate thinks what Roy needs is a simple machine for music, and also good headphones, like the ones the Herrera boy had. That way wherever his **yaya** brings him, Roy can listen to music.

Ate says this to the young man without mentioning Roy and describes the Herrera boy's blue headphones with the lowercase **b** etched on the sides. "But the music machine must be very basic," she instructs. "The more basic, the better."

Ate learned about music therapy through Mrs. Carter. They keep in touch, despite how badly things ended with Jane. Most recently, Ate helped Mrs. Carter find a new cleaning woman after hers became ill with throat cancer. Mrs. Carter worried that the cancer was caused by inhaling too many fumes from cleaning products, and she asked Ate to recommend someone who knew how to clean well without using toxins. Ate received not only a referral fee but a new business idea: "organic house cleaning." For this, she could charge a premium, like the grocery stores do for organic bananas.

Mrs. Carter emailed Ate an article about "neurologic music therapy" after seeing it in the newspaper. Several studies showed that such therapy could help people with damaged or diseased brains. There was a company in Massachusetts that used the therapy to help a man with brain damage learn to walk without a cane. Music therapy also helped a young woman who could not speak after a brain injury learn to communicate through song.

Since reading the article, Ate has dreamt often of

Roy. In the dreams he sings to her. In one, he sings that he wants to come to America.

You should write to the doctors about your son, Mrs. Carter suggested in the email. She explained that sometimes doctors will treat patients pro bono. Companies, too, because it is good public relations.

But how would Ate get Roy a visa? How would he travel so far alone? Where would he live?

For now, Ate is taking matters into her own hands. She asked Angel to print as many articles on neurologic music therapy as she could find and, once Ate had worked through them all, she video-called Roy's **yaya** and told her of the plan.

"But how do I do this, **po**?" asked the **yaya.** She was new. Ate chose her from among the dozen or so women Isabel had interviewed for the position, because she was too old and too ugly to find trouble. Not like the other **yaya,** whom Isabel found on Roy's own mattress kissing her boyfriend and wearing only panties.

"You must play music for Roy whenever possible. You must sing to him every day. You must clap your hands to the rhythm of songs and try to get him to sing—even to hum—with you."

On the telephone screen, the **yaya** looked doubtful, and Ate added quickly, "I will pay you a little extra, for the extra work. And if he improves, you will get more."

———

THE BEST HEADPHONES ARE MANY HUNDREDS OF DOLLARS. Ate is surprised by this. Are they so much better than the cheapest pair, which look almost exactly the same, only lacking the logo?

The young man in the red shirt, who is friendlier now that Ate has set aside a music device to buy, explains that the cheap headphones are, indeed, inferior. They are less comfortable. Some of his friends get "crazy headaches" from the cheap ones. The sound quality is shoddy—"like, compare high-def TV to old-school TV." The expensive headphones simply have better **fidelity.**

At the word **"fidelity,"** Ate is sold. It is not like her to buy the most expensive of anything. She is not like Angel, attracted by shiny things; nor like Jane, beguiled by shiny words. But **fidelity** is a different matter. "Fidelity" means faithfulness, and Ate wants this for Roy. She wants the music that filters into his ears, that reverberates in his broken brain, to be faithful to the sounds of the world.

Ate chooses the headphones in green. This was Roy's favorite color when he was a boy.

The young man in the red shirt counts out Ate's money and gives her change. He stuffs the boxes in a plastic bag and reminds Ate to fill out the warranty card. Through it all, Amalia sleeps.

She is still asleep when it begins to drizzle. They

are still only halfway home. Ate stops beneath the overhanging roof of a bank while she stretches a piece of clear plastic over the stroller, sealing Amalia inside. Ate rummages in the compartment underneath the stroller for her umbrella but cannot find it and resumes walking, the light rain slicking down her hair, first polka-dotting and then darkening her shirt. She walks past the street vendors selling cheap black umbrellas from rolling carts. She does not stop for shelter, even as the drizzle thickens into steady rain.

Back in the apartment, Ate puts Amalia in front of the television and dries herself with a towel, wearing a robe from a five-star hotel that a former client once gave her. Her telephone buzzes on the kitchen table. She can see Jane's face in the screen, her eyes rimmed red.

It is not time for their weekly video-call. Ate says a quick prayer that Jane is not in trouble again.

"Jane?" Ate asks, holding the phone up to her mouth. "Are you okay, Jane?"

"Why did you let that woman stay in my apartment?"

"What woman?" Ate asks, buying time.

"Segundina."

"Ah. Yes." Ate pauses, considering her options, and decides to confess. "It was only for a short time."

"But in my apartment! I do not know this woman, and you let her stay in **my** home without asking me!"

Ate is silent, wondering how much Segundina revealed. She did not seem like someone with a big mouth.

"And you leave Mali with her," Jane accuses.

"Only when I delivered food. Never for very long. I did not want to bring Mali to these houses when she could be outside playing. Ay, Jane, you do not believe the houses of these clients! The Ramoses, I told you about them. They are no relation to the old president, but they have his picture in frames all over the house as if—"

"But I pay **you** to take care of Mali, not leave her with strangers!" Jane shouts. On the video she is heaving. She collects herself and in a hard voice asks, "How many times, Ate?"

"I do not understand," Ate answers, though she does.

"How many times? How many times did you leave Mali with that woman?"

"Jane. I did not count. It was never for a long time. I—"

"More than five times? More than twenty? How many times did you abandon Mali for your **business**?"

There is a wildness to Jane's voice that she can barely contain. Ate can hear it, and she decides to apologize before everything is beyond repair.

"You are right. I am sorry."

Jane does not answer. There is only the sound of her breathing, ragged, like something being torn and torn again.

"I took Mali to the music class this weekend as you asked," Ate says finally. She thought it was a waste of Jane's money. Amalia spent the whole hour chewing on a toy tambourine while the teacher, a woman with a ring in her nose and unshaven legs, played baby songs on a guitar. But Ate admits the hairy woman is onto something. She charged twenty-five dollars each baby, and there were at least ten babies in the class.

"Did she like it?" Jane asks after a long pause.

"She bounced to 'Wheels on the Bus.' I will send you the video."

Another silence. Ate tries another approach. "I have a doctor appointment next week. To change my medications. I think it is the cause of my headaches. Do I have your permission to allow Angel to help me with Mali?"

"That is fine, because I **know** Angel," Jane says coldly.

"Yes. I understand."

"Never again, Ate."

"Never again."

Jane exhales shakily. "And I do not want strangers staying in my apartment."

"It is only that I met Segundina in the dormitory and she has hard luck. I was trying to help—"

"It is **my** apartment."

"Yes, yes. You are right, I should have asked you first. This is your home, not mine."

Usually, Jane assures Ate that the apartment is

her home, too. It is both of their homes, because they are family. But now she remains silent.

Ate carefully begins telling Jane about Amalia's latest milestones. How she is walking so much faster now. How she spits out her pureed peas but cannot get enough butternut squash.

"I will bring her to the children's museum tomorrow. She will like the exhibits. She is smart, Jane," Ate says. "I am asking my contacts which are the best preschools in Queens."

"I would like her to go to a good school."

"Yes. She must have a good school," Ate agrees, relieved the conversation has taken a better turn. "I will get Mali now."

She sets down the phone and lifts Amalia off the floor. She hopes this is the day Amalia says "Mama." They practice every time Amalia's diaper is soiled, Ate pointing to the picture of Jane she has taped above the changing table and mouthing: **Mama. Mama.**

"Mali! My big girl!" cries Jane, her eyes immediately bright. She puffs up her cheeks and makes a silly face, but Amalia only stares silently at the screen as if hypnotized.

"Mama. Mama. Mama," Ate whispers in Amalia's ear, bending her head so that Jane cannot see her lips move.

"Do you like animals, Mali?" Jane asks. She begins to make the noises of a cow. Now she is oinking like a pig.

Ate tickles Amalia's thighs until she laughs.

"Is that funny to Mali?" Jane asks, laughing also. She begins to oink again, this time more animatedly.

Ate tickles Amalia again. When she does not laugh, Ate tickles her sides. Amalia squirms. "No!"

"No? You are tired of the piggy? Oh, Mali. You are so smart, talking already, and only one!" exclaims Jane, her face crumpling, her hands stretched toward the screen.

AS SOON AS THE VIDEO-CALL IS FINISHED, ATE DIALS MS. YU. She reports that Segundina has been gossiping and that Jane is unsettled. Ms. Yu promises to keep an eye on things. She informs Ate that the finder's fee for Segundina has been wired to Ate's bank account and confirms that, as with Jane, Ate will receive a small payment at regular intervals throughout the pregnancy, with a bonus upon successful delivery.

"All I ask is that you keep me abreast of things on your end. The information you give me helps me to help **them,**" Ms. Yu explains.

Amalia is tugging at Ate's robe. Ate puts down the phone and lifts her, checking the diaper, which is warm and heavy. Ate kisses the sweet-smelling folds of Amalia's neck as she carries her to the changing table.

Ate does love this baby.

She lays Amalia across the table, gives her a toy to hold, and points to the picture of Jane on the wall.

"Mama," Ate says as she strips off the sodden diaper. The knot in Ate's belly is still there, hard like a nut. It will dissolve by and by, she knows.

She wipes Amalia's bottom, applies cream—she needs to stop by the pharmacy; they are almost out—and fastens the new diaper snugly around Amalia's waist. Before she pulls down Amalia's shirt, she buries her nose in her tummy, wiggling her face so that Amalia screeches with delight.

In truth, Ate never lied to Jane. She was careful about this. Ate **does** believe that Golden Oaks is a good opportunity. She **did** help Segundina because of her hard luck. Of course, this is only a part of the story. Ate never told Jane that Ms. Yu pays for her help in finding Hosts, not only because of the nondisclosure agreements she signed, but because Jane would not understand. She can be simple, seeing only one side when there are always two. Jane would think that Ate's good deeds—because that is what they are; Golden Oaks will change her life, and Segundina's—are contaminated because Ate makes money also. But why should this be so? If the deed is good, does it become less good simply because Ate benefits, too?

"No, no, no," Ate sings to Amalia, who has grown bored and now raises her arms to be picked up. "Because good for you and good for me is good-good-good."

Ate lifts Amalia and carries her to the kitchen. She pours milk into one of the clean bottles in the drying rack and sits at the kitchen table with Amalia upright on her lap. She allows Amalia to hold the bottle. It dips and wobbles as she tries to lift it to her mouth. Ate laughs. "I will help you, Mali." She covers Amalia's pale, smooth hands with her veined brown ones and, together, they lift the bottle to Amalia's lips.

Ate's phone buzzes. On its screen is an image of a young Filipina, the daughter of one of the housekeepers in Forest Hills. Ate believes she might be a good fit for Ms. Yu. It is difficult to tell. Ate sent Ms. Yu several girls before Jane, all rejected. Ms. Yu did not tell her why. Ate didn't even consider Jane for Golden Oaks until she was fired from the Carters', when she became desperate—because how would Jane get another baby-nurse job without a recommendation? How could she support Amalia with the nickels and dimes from her minimum wage?

It turned out for the best that Ate's first successful referral was Jane. Because Ate can keep tabs on her and give Ms. Yu information to help everything go smoothly. Ate believes it is because she is trustworthy in this way that Ms. Yu accepted Segundina. If Ate can prove herself to Ms. Yu, if Jane and Segundina deliver good babies, then this is only the beginning, and the money will be steady, and she can focus on Roy.

Ate answers the phone, feeling a prick of guilt— the girl's mother dreams of her daughter going to college. But the girl is lazy, interested in clothes and boys, not books. For several weeks Ate has been dropping hints to her after church—about a job making big money for someone good with secrets. Little by little, Ate is seeing if the girl might be right.

She can always go to college later—and then she will be able to pay for it herself.

MAE

MAE'S EYES ARE CLOSED. SHE VISUALIZES HERSELF GIVING HER
pitch to Leon. In thirty minutes Mae will unveil
Project MacDonald. The day is new, brimming
with possibility and already fucked—but not, perhaps, irremediably so. She's just got to keep moving, onward and upward.

She had imagined her big day differently, of
course. She was going to wake early, take a quick run
around the reservoir and then, after a light breakfast
(black coffee, poached eggs), a brisk walk through
Central Park to the Holloway Club. Instead, she
spent the night on a too-soft bed in borrowed

pajamas at the overpriced bed-and-breakfast near Golden Oaks where she likes to house out-of-town visitors. The shit storm which broke yesterday after lunch extended far into the night: the black-clad security guards circling Julio as he packed up his locker; the silence of the Hosts lining the hallway; Lisa's rigid face as she was swabbed and sampled.

Lisa's Clients choppering in from Manhattan. Swarms of doctors, huddles of lawyers. Coordinators in pairs, whispering; straightening when Mae strode by.

Strangely the Clients, who upon arrival were rightly distraught, reversed course after a prolonged conversation with Lisa. They spoke with her in her bedroom, door shut, and Mae has no idea (she would kill to have an idea) what sort of black magic Lisa cast to save her soul and salvage her paycheck.

The Clients will not exercise their contractual clawback even though "clearly" the oversight at Golden Oaks has been lax. (In response, Mae hung her head so that Lisa's Clients would not see the relief blazing in her eyes.) They **will** demand restitution if Lisa ends up with an STD that can harm the baby; however, they think the likelihood of this is slight because Lisa swore she and Julio engaged only in oral sex and that she made him get tested first. (It's mind-boggling to Mae that the Clients—Yale and Brown grads, with high-powered careers in tech and fashion, respectively—still trust the viper.) They did **not** want Lisa to be punished.

Before Mae, agog in her chair but hiding it, could formulate a reply the father continued:

Ultimately, the blame for this unfortunate episode rests with Golden Oaks' hyperstringency. Young women, especially pregnant ones, have urges, needs. And wouldn't it be better to accept this fact? Screen male visitors for STDs and regulate sexual interactions rather than criminalizing the behavior, driving it underground, and, ultimately, endangering the baby?

"It's like the War on Drugs, if you follow that debate," the father explained. He wore a cashmere hoodie and unlaced Adidas, and Mae knew he was worth around three hundred million dollars (depending on the current share price of his company). His hand rested on his wife's trim thigh.

"We're libertarians," the wife added, recrossing her legs so that her suede tights made a shushing sound.

Recalling the smug smile that washed over Lisa's tear-reddened face, Mae feels bile rise in her throat. She shakes her head, trying to expel the negative energy, and forces herself to look out the car window. Numerous studies show that gazing at water slows the heartbeat. Greenery, too, has a calming effect. Unable to locate a good patch of trees, Mae locks eyes onto the East River, its frantic gray rush toward the ocean.

Usually, Mae finds this view—of the rivers that wrap Manhattan in a serpentine embrace—elevating. Innumerable times she has zipped up the

FDR Drive or down the West Side Highway and felt a physical upsweep at the sight of the glinting water on her one side and Manhattan's spires on the other. The span of bridges, the toy-sized, green-gray of Lady Liberty, the sailboats and tugboats and taxi boats and occasional fire boats—and, only a strip of highway apart: the blare of city buses, sidewalks seething with pedestrians, deliverymen on bicycles threading through immobilized traffic.

At such moments, Mae is overpowered by a lusty Ayn Randian love of New York, **her** town, its teeming possibilities. Its stink and grime and abundance. She loves that this brash, hulking brute of a city is no physical behemoth but a mere slip of land— separate and apart from the rest of America.

But not today. Today the magic is gone. Mae finds the river oppressive. Ditto for the sky (low and leaden and somehow menacing). Even the city's skyscrapers have lost their glory, diminished by a curtain of low-lying fog.

Mae feels a sudden dread. Goosebumps puckering up and down her arm. Is it foreshadowing? Is she going to fuck it up with Leon?

The car pulls up in front of the Holloway Club. It has begun to rain. Carlos, the Club's ancient doorman, opens Mae's door, his umbrella roofed above her so that not a raindrop falls on her suit. Mae greets him warmly—she hired him when she ran the Club; he was close to retirement age even then but she liked his faded elegance—and feels immediately happier. When she sees that the woman in the coat-check booth is another one of her hires, Mae feels better still. They embrace, Mae asking after her children (twin boys and a daughter from her first marriage); the coat-checker is visibly touched that she remembers. As she hangs Mae's Burberry trench on a padded hanger, the coat checker remarks quietly that the Club isn't the same without her.

The maître d' who greets Mae in the Club's penthouse dining room is new and overly fawning, but everything else is familiar: the framed sketches of the great and the good lining sage-green walls, towers of fresh flowers, antique mirrors angled just-so above the bar, the better to reflect the glory of the glorious who normally fill the room. Mae cannot count how many times, after a long day catering to often persnickety Club Members, she would settle on one of these leather barstools and Tito would swoop over with a single dry martini, extra olives, without her having to ask. Often she would order dinner at the bar, and Tito would introduce her to whoever was slouched on the stools beside her. For whatever reason—the warm glow reflected from the 24-karat gold-leaf-covered ceilings, the cozy curve of the oak bar that seemed to draw together the strangers seated around it—she felt an immediate intimacy with these impromptu dinner companions, whether he (and it was almost always a he) happened to be a nondescript but profligately wealthy financier in town from Singapore, a Hollywood mogul, or a Saudi prince. Some of them even became her friends, at least on Facebook.

She feels a pang and snuffs it. Nostalgia is unproductive. Golden Oaks, not the Holloway Clubs, is the future. And it is her baby. Leon would never admit it, but Mae believes it was one of her offhand comments that got him thinking about a high-end surrogacy venture.

She was only a couple of years out of Harvard Business School, her rotation in the managerial program at Holloway beginning at the New York Club, when she noticed she was spending a huge amount of time defusing the crises of significant others who accompanied Club Members on business trips. Over lunch, she pitched to Leon the idea of a Spousal Division—a new group tasked with programming private shopping and cultural expeditions, arranging childcare, curating a lectures-at-lunch series, and providing any amenities necessary to keep the Members' spouses occupied and happy during their stays.

"Brilliant, Mae!" Leon crowed, adding, "you know what they say: happy wife, happy life."

"Not **all** Member spouses are women," Mae sassed, knowing her boss responded to it.

"All of them but two at my last count. Does that distress you?"

"If women could outsource their pregnancies, **they'd** be the ones running the show."

"They can. Haven't you heard of surrogacy, Harvard?"

"What woman do **you** know who'd trust some random in the middle of nowhere to carry her baby?" Mae parried. "What you'd want, Leon, if you were a juggernaut—like, say, **me**—is a Holloway Baby Farm. You know, to make sure your baby got the Holloway treatment while you were off conquering the world." Mae took a swig of her chardonnay and, sensing Leon's appreciative gaze on her, flashed him a smile.

THE OBSEQUIOUS MAÎTRE D' SEATS MAE AT A CHOICE TABLE near the window. It is the same one she sat at when she invited her mother to the Club, shortly after being promoted to General Manager. Her parents had finally had to withdraw from their country club back home—the annuals were too expensive—and Mae thought her mother would get a kick out of the Club's opulent dining room, the views of Central Park below. Instead, her mother spent the entire lunch complaining about the stalled career of Mae's father, blaming racism one minute and the next, Mae's father himself ("the Chinese are usually great at business, but your dad's clearly missing the gene").

Mae glances at her watch. Time to get her game face on. She opens her briefcase, removes various presentation books and her lucky pen (a limited-edition

Mont Blanc, a gift from Ethan on her promotion to Golden Oaks). She orders a green tea from a passing waiter, silences her phone, and stares unseeing out the window as she runs through the presentation in her head.

There is a hubbub brewing at the elevator, the maître d' making a fuss over someone. Mae looks up to see Leon striding into the room, exchanging pleasantries with various tables of breakfasting Members as he zigzags toward Mae. He wears a custom-made suit, no tie, his hair a little shaggy. The kind of man who plays it a little loose, dreams big, and reeks of success. After Mae's mother met him at lunch years ago, she was aflutter. But Mae knows better. It's why she's never disappointed, and her mother always is.

"Mae! You're looking fantastic as usual." Leon bends to air-kiss her cheek. He asks after Ethan, the wedding preparations. She compliments him on his tan, and he responds that he has just returned from Hawaii, where the surfing was epic.

A waiter slides Mae's tea on the table and places a double espresso and a plate of egg whites next to Leon. Mae hands her boss a presentation book and begins walking him through Golden Oaks' current profit figures.

"It's interesting how much bigger our profit margin is on Premium Hosts, even though we pay them significantly more," Leon interrupts. Mae's presentation lies unopened next to his coffee.

"Yes, I initially underestimated how inelastic demand for them is. But it seems Clients that are willing to pay for them are almost indifferent to price. I'm considering raising our pricing this fall."

Leon stares out the window, forehead creases deepening. "I've been thinking about the rage these days over inequality. The impotence of the middle class, the disappearance of blue-collar jobs . . . Artificial intelligence will only intensify these trends." He pauses to look at Mae.

Mae meets his gaze. She is used to the swerves and doubling-back of conversations with Leon, his penchant for conflating business with Big Issues (global warming, political polarization, wealth inequality). Leon is old-school rich. He believes in the justness of the market and its rewards but also in noblesse oblige. Unlike many of his fellow almost-billionaires, Leon believes in government as a necessary palliative to capitalism's harsh edges. But he is unswerving in his belief that it must never stifle the private sector or the market that animates it, which, despite its imperfections, remains the most efficient and least corruptible way to run an economy. And he believes that people like himself—those winners of capitalism with the generosity of heart and the keenness of vision to discern and help alleviate capitalism's unwitting but real flaws—are the ones who need to lead (but quietly, from the sidelines, no need to alienate Clients or investors or friends . . .).

Mae admires him.

She sips her tea and waits for Leon to expound on his idea. Her stomach growls. Breakfast was an aeon ago. She eyes Leon's untouched eggs, still steaming on his gold-rimmed plate.

"Most of your Hosts come from immigrant backgrounds, yes?"

"Correct. The majority of my Hosts are native to Hispanic countries, various Caribbean islands, and the Philippines, although we do have a smattering from Eastern Europe and other parts of Southeast Asia. And, of course, there are the Premium Hosts."

"I wonder if there isn't an opportunity here to help our **own** struggling middle class in a way that **also** benefits our franchise." Leon pauses again, raising his eyebrows ever so slightly. He likes to do this—propose an idea and let it dangle, like bait on a string.

"Fascinating. How so?"

Leon leans back in his chair, stretching his muscular torso long and folding his large hands behind his head so that his elbows jut out like airplane wings. This is a power pose. Mae read in her business-school alumni magazine that leaders are perceived as more powerful if they take up more space. She uncrosses her arms.

"What if we began sourcing more of our Hosts from lower-middle-class **Caucasians**?" Leon proposes, at first benignly and then with mounting zeal. "They've been hammered for decades—no wage growth, unions emasculated, robots taking their jobs, robot-jobs moving to Mexico or China anyway. I bet we don't have to pay them much more than we pay our immigrant-sourced Hosts, **but**—and here's the nub of it—we could charge a **premium.**"

Mae can feel Leon's gaze on her, gauging her reaction. To buy time as she gathers her thoughts, she parrots a phrase Leon is wont to use during brainstorming sessions: "The idea has merit . . ."

"More than merit, Mae! It's a win-win: bigger profits for us and good jobs—terrific jobs—for the forgotten blue-collar American. Factory work and truck-driving jobs aren't coming back. We're in a postindustrial world, Mae. Service jobs, mostly crappy ones, are the future. Flipping burgers, taking care of old people. **Our** jobs are life-changing. People should be tripping over themselves to land one."

"The issue," Mae says carefully, "is that we may not be able to charge much of a premium. I've found that the Clients who desire Premium Hosts are attracted by the whole package. Not just . . . coloring, but also pedigree: test scores, athletic accomplishments . . ."

"I'm not talking trailer-trash here, Mae," Leon responds with a trace of impatience. "But there must exist lower-middle-class white girls—think wholesome Midwesterners; think state-school grads—who show well but who have no viable career prospects."

Mae considers. Is Leon onto something? Thinking aloud, she ventures, "I suppose we could introduce another price level. Not quite Premium-Premium but . . . **Accessible Premium**?"

"Accessible Premium! Brilliant!" Leon barks, pounding the table with his tanned fist. "The analogy is a diffusion line. Think of high-end clothing designers. Almost all of them have expanded their client base beyond the ultra-rich through more affordable—but still premium-priced, still highly coveted—brands. Think Calvin Klein with CK. Dolce with D&G. Armani with . . ."

"Armani Exchange!" Mae chimes.

Leon grins, clearly pleased that Mae is coming around to his view. He instructs her to dig deeper into the concept and invites her back to the Club in a week's time for a brainstorming session. He belatedly turns to his breakfast, grimaces when he takes a bite of his lukewarm eggs, and signals for a waiter to take them away. The waiter is mortified.

"Anything new at Golden Oaks I should know about?" Leon asks, downing his espresso.

Anya's abortion. Julio and Lisa. Jane and the tick.

"Everything's under control," Mae chirps.

Leon leans forward on his elbows, fusing his eyes with Mae's. "Mae, Holloway's firing on all cylinders. But I'm **most** excited about the growth potential of Golden Oaks."

Mae feels a trill of energy.

"The wealthy—and there are so many more of us these days—are obsessed with their offspring in a way earlier generations just weren't. My mother smoked throughout her pregnancies, for chrissake! It's no longer just three-thousand-dollar strollers and designer baby diapers. The luxury market is moving down the age scale to the newborn and gestational phases, and we've got **first mover advantage.** The Board's considering a second site on the West Coast—I like the sound of 'Redwood Farm'—to pivot toward the Asian and Middle East markets and capture some of the tech wealth. You're the expert; we'd love your input . . ."

Mae could not have scripted a more perfect segue. Her heart lifts, is aloft, would fly out of her mouth on wings if she let it! The room has brightened, the gray outside transmuted into gold. Mae bows her head for the briefest moment, readying herself for the plunge.

She lifts her head and beams a dazzling smile at Leon, sliding the Project MacDonald pitch book across the table. He glances at it quizzically. In answer Mae enlarges herself, squaring her shoulders and planting her hands firmly onto the table in what she has read is another variation of the power pose. She does, in fact, feel more powerful.

"It's funny you bring this up, Leon," she begins. "Because I **do,** in fact, have a few ideas . . ."

———

MAE LEANS HER HAND AGAINST THE STABLE'S WALL FOR balance as she removes her left boot and shakes out a pebble. She rights herself and scrutinizes her surroundings. The previous owner of Golden Oaks built the twenty-horse stable and the riding arena for his daughter, a champion in dressage. She knows she's counting her chickens well before they've hatched, but Leon **did** seem incredibly keen on Project MacDonald yesterday. And these out-buildings could be perfect for a second dormitory.

"Ms. Yu?"

Reagan stands just outside the stable in the sun. She is wearing a white cotton sundress and boots. "I'm sorry to interrupt. Eve said I'd find you out here. Do you have a few minutes?"

"For you I do." Mae leads Reagan to a seating area beneath a pergola a short distance from the stable. "You look good, Reagan. How does it feel to be on the cusp of your third trimester?"

Reagan perches on a wrought-iron chair and small-talks about her recent ultrasound. Mae re-laxes next to her. Closer up she notices Reagan has dark circles under her eyes.

"What is it you want to talk about?" Mae asks companionably.

"I've been thinking about my delivery bonus, now that I'm more than halfway through my time here," Reagan answers. "I'd like your help in giving it to Jane Reyes. Anonymously."

This is a first. Mae proceeds carefully. "That's a

lovely gesture . . . but have you thought it through? You might need the money someday. Maybe for an MFA. You mentioned once that you wanted to get serious about your photography."

Mae's buying time. She needs to draw out Reagan's true motivations, which she may not understand herself. Reagan is someone desperate to do right and who, though she doesn't like to admit it, is also driven by self-interest. Mae needs to strike just the right balance in her approach.

"I did the math. And just with my monthly salary I can pay for a chunk of grad school. The rest I could pay for with loans. I don't really need my bonus. Not the way Jane does."

Mae wishes she'd had time to review the Host Log today. When she skimmed it yesterday morning, there was a note that Jane continued to distance herself from Lisa and Reagan—a wise move, given all she has on the line. Mae assumed Jane was ignoring Reagan only because of her friendship with Lisa. But is there more to it? Did Reagan play any part in the tick episode?

"Is this at all related to your . . . estrangement from Jane?"

Reagan flushes. "It's not about that. I'm not sure why she's . . . Anyway, it doesn't matter. What matters is that I don't really need the money, and she does. Do you know she lives in a dinky one-bedroom with her cousin and her daughter? And before that she lived with six other people **and** her baby in a room half the size of our bedroom here?"

Mae didn't know the part about the six roommates, though she isn't particularly surprised. She's more surprised that Reagan's surprised. It's a reflection of the bubble Reagan lives in that she finds this so shocking. There are several Hosts at Golden Oaks who've come from worse. "You know, Jane's in a good place. Even without your help, assuming the baby's healthy, Jane will do well. Very well."

"But what if she **doesn't** carry to term? What if she gets Lyme disease? Or something happens like with Anya?"

So that's it. Reagan knows about Anya's abortion. Julio must have told Lisa, and Lisa's probably broadcasting it. Mae needs to get Geri on it ASAP, before a panic sets in among the Catholic Hosts.

Mae shifts gears. "But what about **your** goals? Do you really want to go in debt for your MFA? And what about your living expenses? Wouldn't the money come in handy after grad school? Photography doesn't pay—not unless you get some traction."

"I'm not sure I definitely want to get an MFA. I mean, there's something to be said about learning by doing. Or maybe my dad's right, and I should go to business school to learn art marketing as a backup or something. He'd pay for that."

Mae feels a sudden surge of affection for Reagan,

so young and unsure, trying to find her way in the world **and** do the right thing—not just for herself, but for others. Though at her age, Mae was too busy trying to pay off college loans to think this way.

"I went to business school. I don't really see you there," Mae observes, keeping her tone light because her comment might rankle. "You're an artist. I see how you notice things."

Reagan's eyes inexplicably water. "I try. I really try to notice things."

Mae senses this line of inquiry is important, though she isn't quite sure why. "It says a lot about you that you **do** notice. That you care. A lot of people don't see what's around them—the waitress who brings them lunch or the doorman who carries their bags."

Reagan's looking at her lap. Mae can't tell if she's upset. Just in case, she makes her voice as gentle as she possibly can. "Let me ask you. Because it's something I think about a lot. Do you think it helps when we give money away to someone who needs it? Or does it just make **us** feel less guilty that—"

Reagan is agreeing before Mae has finished her sentence. "I wonder the same thing. There are so many people in New York—you pass them every day in the street—who just need help. And you feel complicit because you notice but you don't do anything, not really. Though I have to think even a couple bucks is better than nothing . . ."

"Unless he uses the money for drugs or alcohol," Mae notes. "Not to disparage all homeless people, but . . . many of them are mentally ill. Or addicts. Some of them don't **want** to change their lives."

"You can't generalize, though. Everybody's an individual case," Reagan interrupts, but there is disquiet on her face.

"I have a friend, someone I know from college, who is fabulously wealthy," Mae responds, switching topics. She's learned this from watching Leon— that the insertion of an apparent non sequitur can knock your opponent off track, which lets you control the conversation. She tells Reagan about her friend's newest philanthropic venture, a "cultural exchange" program bringing underprivileged high-schoolers from the Bronx to stay in the Hamptons over the summer. Mae's friend believes the initiative is a win-win: her extremely privileged son and his equally privileged friends will learn gratitude through exposure to poor kids their own age, and the teenagers from the Bronx will be given "something to aspire to," as well as, if they get along with their host families, connections that might serve them well in the future.

"It's awful."

"She means well, though. She's simply trying not to be complicit—as you put it. This is her version of your two bucks."

"She's probably only doing it so her son's got an essay topic for his college applications!"

Mae smiles, having had the same thought. "I told my friend that it might not be the best idea to plop a sixteen-year-old from the inner city in East Hampton. The chasm's too wide. I told her maybe it's better if she used her connections to find these kids jobs for the summer. Real jobs, earning real money, learning real skills."

Reagan agrees. She repeats the cliché about teaching someone to fish versus giving them a fish. It isn't really apropos, but Mae acts as if Reagan has said something wise. She's learned that people—especially young people—just want to feel they are taken seriously.

"Jane will have options after Golden Oaks, beyond even the money. Look at Eve. She'll be the first college graduate in her family, you know. The reality is, charity only helps so much. It's never life-changing the way a job—especially this job—can be. Charity mostly makes the charitable feel good about themselves. Or at least, less guilty."

"But they're not mutually exclusive. I could help Jane and she'd still have options—"

"True. But let's say you use your bonus to really focus on your art. You become a famous photographer. You have money, influence, power. Wouldn't you be able to help Jane and others like Jane much more then? Rather than giving away your money now—and then what?"

Reagan is silent.

"Maybe pursuing your own goals is the best thing you can do. For anyone."

"I know what you're trying to get at. But I just don't buy it. The invisible hand doesn't always work," Reagan says after a long pause. "And anyway, this isn't abstract to me. It's about Jane."

Mae stifles a sigh. She wishes Reagan were more motivated by the money, so that her interests and those of the Clients were completely aligned.

Reagan is staring in the direction of the Dorm. A figure is walking quickly toward them on the path that cuts through the back lawn. It's Dr. Wilde. By the time she arrives at the pergola, she's huffing.

"I should have switched my shoes." She sighs, sliding onto a chair and kicking off her kitten heels.

"You could have called me," chides Mae.

"I needed the fresh air anyway. And it's gorgeous today!"

Reagan stands, avoiding Mae's gaze. She announces that she needs to see Ms. Hanna.

"Reagan, there's no rush on a decision. I'll support you either way!" Mae doesn't want Reagan to leave upset. It **is** lovely of her to want to help Jane. She tries to shoot Reagan a reassuring smile, but Reagan is already walking back to the Dorm.

"I've got good news and bad news." Dr. Wilde places her bare feet on the glass-topped table in front of her chair.

"Good news first, please."

"The STD screen on 33 is clear. Same with Julio. They're clean as whistles."

"Well, that's great!" Mae exclaims, although inside she's conflicted. A part of her hoped Lisa would be diagnosed with gonorrhea or herpes or at least genital warts. Something curable that wouldn't harm the fetus but uncomfortable. Lisa must have been a saint in a previous life to get so many breaks in this one.

Dr. Wilde checks to make sure Reagan is gone. "But there's a development with 82. An irregularity. We found it during her last exam."

The earth tilts. Mae braces herself. "Don't tell me it's another trisomy."

"No. It's a lump. Just above her collarbone."

The earth is tilting again, more precariously this time. Mae closes her eyes, commanding the landscape to still itself. When she reopens them she asks, her voice steady, "What are we really talking about here, Meredith?"

"The lump could be benign, or it could be malignant. The latter is less likely given 82's age. But it's not unheard of for a pregnant woman to develop cancer. My colleague at NewYork-Presbyterian is dealing with a pregnant twenty-eight-year-old with Hodgkin's lymphoma, for instance. Difficult choices."

She's grave, overly so, almost as if she's savoring the drama of the moment and her role in it. Meredith has become a little insufferable since Leon promoted her to Head of Medical Services.

Mae harbors the quiet suspicion that Meredith is angling for her job.

"What comes next?"

"We need to biopsy the growth. And we need to decide what to tell 82 about the biopsy. I'd like to hold off speaking to the Client for now."

Annoyance flares in Mae's chest. There is no "we" in strategic decisions regarding Host policy, and Meredith has no hand in dealing with the Clients. Mae smiles without warmth. "Schedule the biopsy as soon as possible, please."

"We should also probably call Legal and see what the contract stipulates. Do we need to divulge anything to 82 at this point? Does she have any say in treatment? My view is—"

"Leave that to me, Meredith," Mae cuts her off. She is being abrupt, she knows, but the encroachment is too much to bear. "I've got everything under control."

REAGAN

"GOOD MORNING!" A VOICE IN SONG, A BURST OF BRIGHTNESS.
A shock of air as the blanket is stripped away.

Reagan pushes up on her elbows. A Coordinator—
the one with the trim Afro, tinted red—pulls a sundress out of the closet and lays it across her bed,
urging her to hurry, there is a surprise afoot. Reagan,
sleep-stunned, glances over at Jane, but she's already
gone, her bed pristine and pillows fluffed.

"What time is it?" Reagan croaks. Her throat is
dry. "What's happening?"

The Coordinator pulls her upright, gently, and

prods her into the bathroom, handing her the sundress and shutting the door. "There's someone here to see you. Get moving, Honey."

Honey. That isn't Farm protocol. Reagan sits on the toilet. She's tired. She couldn't sleep last night, kept turning over in her mind the conversation with Ms. Yu, round and round. A merry-go-round of half thoughts and reconstructed responses. Reagan hadn't said it right. She came across like a sap, like those do-gooders in college who buzzed outside the student center, clipboard in hand, trying to Save the Bees or Ban Plastic Bags.

She should have told Ms. Yu more. How Jane dilutes their shampoo with water so it will last longer. How her grandmother collapsed in front of her eyes, her entire world pivoting in one instant. She was only fifteen.

"All okay in there?" calls the Coordinator with a rap on the door.

"Do I have time for a shower?"

"No. Sorry, Reagan." The Coordinator chides her to hurry, hurry.

Washed, combed, buttoned, and still half-asleep, Reagan is swept into the Farm's administrative wing, down a hallway she has never set foot in. The Coordinator needs to swipe her badge to access it. She is led into a private dining room, curtains drawn, table already laid.

A tall black woman sits in a Louis Quinze chair,

legs crossed, regal in her pale dress, a scarf wrapped around her head. She stands, extending her hand. "I'm Callie."

"I'm Reagan."

Is she a lawyer? Here to help Reagan transfer her bonus to Jane?

"Please sit," says the woman, gesturing to the chair next to her. "Tea?"

The woman pours tea into a porcelain cup from a teapot etched with flowers, spilling a little. "I don't know why they make these fancy teacups so small!"

She smiles at Reagan, and Reagan finds herself smiling back.

"You don't know who I am, do you?"

Reagan shakes her head.

"I'm the mother of the baby inside you. You're carrying my son."

Everything stops. Reagan's heart. Her breath. Everything in the universe.

"You—" The words are jammed in her throat.

The woman laughs, a warm rumble. "I know. Not what you expected, right?"

Reagan shakes her head. She expected a trophy wife. A failed model married to an oligarch or a titan of industry. She half-expected the Chinese billionaire. But not this. Not her.

"I'm—I'm glad. I mean, I'm glad you're not what I expected," she sputters, not wanting the woman to think she is bothered by her skin color when the exact opposite is true.

The woman laughs again. "I'm sorry it's taken me so long to get here. I've been traveling."

She begins to tell Reagan about herself. How she was born in Ethiopia, the youngest of three siblings. How her father was an engineer for a big oil company in Africa but took a job selling suits in a department store in Maryland to give his children a better life in America. How, since college, she has worked for the same large conglomerate, starting as an assistant, then a sales assistant, salesperson, manager, senior manager, vice president, and upward. Moving from D.C. to Denver to Chicago to Dallas and back again. Baby steps, then bigger steps; breaking glass ceilings left, right, and center. She froze her eggs in her midthirties, but it was not until a decade later, still single, that she realized her time was truly running out. Finding a sperm donor was the easy part. The problem was her womb. She tried to carry a baby herself, multiple times. So many miscarriages she has almost lost count.

"You're my last chance of having a family. Of **being** a family." The mother—Callie—lowers her eyes when she says this. Reagan fights the urge to touch her hand.

Their eyes meet and Reagan shyly smiles.

The door to the room swings open. "Morning, ladies!"

"Hi, Mae." Callie discreetly dabs her eyes with a tissue.

"Did she tell you the surprise yet?" Ms. Yu asks Reagan, grinning and taking a seat next to her.

"I thought **she** was the surprise."

Callie and Ms. Yu laugh.

A stream of waiters arrive bearing bowls of fruit, eggs, yogurt. As Ms. Yu and Callie chat about a Broadway play that Callie recently saw, Reagan's mind races to Macy. She cannot wait to tell her the news: that her Client is black, that she came from nothing and made her life something spectacular, except for one thing: the lack of a child. Without Reagan, she would never have one.

What will Macy say?

It's not that **big a deal, Reag.**

Or will she admit, as she has rarely conceded, that life is sometimes more complicated than easy judgments? That maybe, sometimes, you do the most good when it seems like you're doing nothing much at all.

". . . Diane Arbus?" Callie repeats.

Reagan snaps to attention. "Pardon me, Ms. . . . ?"

"Callie. Please call me Callie."

"Callie was asking if you still like Diane Arbus," interjects Ms. Yu. "I told her about your photography."

Callie pauses for a moment, smiling at Reagan, before revealing the surprise: One of her friends is a trustee at the Met in Manhattan. The friend pulled some strings and arranged a private showing of the upcoming Diane Arbus exhibit just for them. "Only if you're interested, of course," she adds.

"I **love** Diane Arbus."

Callie beams.

Ms. Yu walks Reagan through the schedule: They will fly to Manhattan for the day. See the show. Afterward: lunch. Le Bernardin, if Reagan doesn't mind more fish. A bit stuffy, but the seafood can't be beat. And before heading home, a little procedure, in-and-out.

"What procedure?" Reagan asks, her hand moving to her belly. "Is there something wrong?"

"Most likely everything's fine," Ms. Yu assures her, businesslike and brisk. "Dr. Wilde found an irregularity during your last amnio. We're going to do a few more tests—just as a precaution—and Callie prefers that you do them in the city."

Ms. Yu signals the waiter and instructs him to bring some milk for the tea.

"I'm sure it's unnecessary," Callie apologizes. "It's just I can't stop worrying. Ask poor Mae—I demand every test, second and third opinions galore. I hope you'll forgive me . . ."

"You've become a helicopter parent and the baby isn't even born yet." Ms. Yu laughs, but her delivery is clunky. She doubles down on the joke, pointing out the window at a helicopter glinting dragonfly green on a far field. "You're **literally** a helicopter parent already!"

Reagan cringes. Ms. Yu shouldn't try to be

funny. She sneaks a glance at Callie. Her expression is pained.

"Be careful not to jinx me, Mae. Anything can happen. I'm not a parent **yet.**"

She cuts the cantaloupe on her plate. Reagan can tell she's fighting to hold herself together, even as Ms. Yu, oblivious, babbles gaily about Callie's overprotectiveness.

And in a flash, Reagan **knows.** She knows Callie as if she has slipped inside her skin.

Ms. Yu's clumsy joke, how it pierced; the swoop of sadness, unbidden; furious blinking and forced chatter until the moment has passed.

Reagan understands, with an immediacy that is disorienting, the magnitude of Callie's hope. And for the first time, she is scared for the baby inside her.

"I've been dying to see the Arbus exhibit. I can't think of a better way to spend the day," Reagan says to Callie, meaning it.

Callie, grateful, breaks into a smile.

REAGAN IS COLD. SHE PULLS THE COTTON ROBE—OPEN TO THE front, as instructed—tighter around herself. There is no sash. The robes at the Farm have sashes.

The clinic is a private one, with a waiting room out of an interior-design magazine and fresh flowers in the bathroom. On the walls of the examination room hang photographs of still waters—a lake mirroring a row of trees in autumn, a green bend in a wide river. Reagan jumps off her chair to study them. She's never been drawn to taking pictures of landscapes, only people. She wonders if this means anything.

Reagan's still not sure why she's here. She gave up questioning Callie after she echoed, several times, Ms. Yu's hollow explanations ("irregularity," an "abundance of caution"). The only reason that Reagan isn't anxious is that Callie herself seemed calm, even cheery, when she dropped Reagan in the hospital lobby after lunch.

Reagan hops onto the exam table, her legs dangling. She runs her hand along the curve of her stomach. She can imagine him now, the baby she carries: a cap of black hair, cocoa skin. Dark eyes, like his mother's.

You're one lucky kid, she says to him affectionately.

Callie, it turns out, has a wicked sense of humor. She had Reagan choking on her fish at lunch with her snarky comments about the other diners in the restaurant (the ladies with their designer handbags who were dressed to the nines for no other reason than to impress each other; the geriatric with his buxom companion—affectionate niece? friendly caregiver? gold-digging mail-order bride?—holding hands at the table behind them).

At the exhibit, Callie surprised Reagan with her

deep knowledge of Arbus. They liked the same pictures. Callie wants to take Reagan to a Walker Evans exhibit next month.

The Coordinator—the one who was waiting in the hospital lobby when Callie and Reagan arrived—enters the room trailed by an Asian nurse in pale-green scrubs. Reagan can't believe the Farm sent her. As if she'd make a run for it with Callie's son in her belly. Was the Coordinator at the museum, too, skulking behind a sculpture? At the restaurant behind a potted plant?

"This is Nancy," introduces the Coordinator. "She'll be helping us out today."

Reagan greets the nurse and ignores the Coordinator, whom she can sense is watching her.

The nurse announces that she will take Reagan's vitals. She sticks a thermometer under Reagan's tongue, wraps a blood-pressure gauge around her upper arm. The Coordinator leans against the closed door, arms folded. Reagan fights the urge to rip off her robe, give her a show.

A buzzing sound. The Coordinator pulls a phone from her pocket. "Gotta take this. I'll be outside if you need me."

Reagan acts like she didn't hear her and fixes her eyes on the nurse's friendly face, the tiny blackheads on her nose. The nurse is humming a pop tune.

"You look so cute pregnant!" She removes the thermometer from Reagan's mouth and clucks with approval. "Is this your first?"

A hesitation. "Yes."

"Boy or girl?"

"I'm carrying a boy."

"Blood pressure is good," the nurse remarks, adding, "he will be handsome if his daddy is handsome. You are pretty."

Reagan thanks her, wondering for the first time what Callie's sperm donor looks like. What she looked for. Did she want someone black? Smart? Tall?

"I have a boy and girl, but the girls give trouble later! The boys love their mothers," the nurse says.

Reagan smiles as if in agreement, but of course she knows nothing. She may never have a baby of her own. And Callie, someday not so far in the future, will take away her son. Reagan used to wonder about this: how she'll feel after the delivery; if, having carried the baby for so long—felt him kick and turn and heard his heartbeat innumerable times—it will be hard to separate. But now Reagan knows it won't be. She can tell that Callie is a good person, truly good, which is so rare. Callie will raise him right. And their story, the one Callie will tell her son, will begin with Reagan.

REAGAN FINGERS THE BANDAGE TAPED OVER HER COLLARBONE and follows the Coordinator across the grass. Behind her, the helicopter rises. A hot wind beats against her back, whips her hair.

She is wearing new clothes. She ended up spending

the night in New York because the procedure took longer than expected, and Callie didn't want Reagan to fly home in the helicopter at night.

"I guess Mae's right. I guess I **am** a helicopter parent," Callie said ruefully in the hospital lobby after the procedure.

The Coordinator joked, because she was still there: more like an **anti**-helicopter parent.

Callie dropped Reagan at a fancy hotel in midtown, apologizing repeatedly that she couldn't stay with her. The bellboy, who walked Reagan to her room even though she had no bags for him to carry, told her the hotel was bomb proof. Reagan stayed up most of the night watching horror movie after horror movie to distract herself from the procedure, the gash below her neck.

"You feeling okay?" asks the Coordinator, stopping several yards from the back entrance to the Dorm. She had appeared in the hotel restaurant at breakfast and canceled Reagan's coffee order. They didn't speak the entire helicopter ride.

Reagan nods, picking at her collar.

"Stop fussing with that bandage," the Coordinator says, staring at Reagan's hand until she lets it drop to her side.

They enter the Farm through the library, which is empty except for a figure in light blue—the color of the housekeeping staff's uniforms—crouched in a corner dusting a shelf of books. At the desk Donna, one of Reagan's favorite Coordinators, greets her.

"Welcome back!" She takes Reagan gently by the wrist and scans her WellBand into the reader. She says to her colleague: "Thanks. I'll take it from here."

Reagan smiles at Donna with gratitude before realizing that she is the "it" in the sentence.

"Come on, let's get you settled." Donna leads Reagan to her room as if she has forgotten, in her one day away, how to get around the Farm. "How're you feeling?"

"I'm okay, thanks."

"Do you need anything? Snack? Juice?"

Reagan shakes her head, wishing Donna would leave.

The door to her bedroom is ajar. Reagan gasps when she steps inside. Jane's bed is stripped clean, the striped mattress somehow indecent in its bareness. The shelf above it is cleared of her belongings except for a few books, and her closet is empty.

My God, what happened to Jane?

"Jane's got a private room now," explains Donna. "And that means you do, too!"

A flood of relief—Jane is okay, her baby is okay—and then bafflement. "Why?"

Donna slides the closet door shut, folds back Reagan's comforter, and urges her to lie down. "We-ell, she's been having trouble sleeping. If it's not her bladder waking her up at night, it's **you** dealing with yours," Donna says jauntily. Reagan recoils. She didn't mean to bother Jane when she used the toilet at night. She always left the lights off, fumbling in the darkness for toilet paper.

Reagan shuts her eyes against a sudden press of tears. Donna pulls the sheets over her legs and draws the curtains closed. She tells Reagan to sleep; she's under no obligations today.

Reagan remains silent, still afraid to open her eyes lest she cry in front of Donna, who might report her outburst to Ms. Yu, who would send Psych to visit her again.

So Jane asked to be moved. Good for her. She must be overjoyed; she never had a room of her own. Even in high school when she lived with her mom, she slept in the TV den.

"Get some sleep," Donna urges her before shutting the door.

Alone in the dimness, Reagan cries. She does not move to wipe her face. She's alone, and there is a hole in her body where there used to be a lump. **When did you first feel it?** the doctor asked her in the clinic, and Reagan had looked up at him, confused. **What lump?** She'd never noticed it before, she confessed, knowing how strange that sounded. But the lump wasn't so big—she explored its contours while the doctor was readying for the biopsy, sneakily, as if breaking some taboo by touching her own flesh.

How could she possibly keep track of all the different ways her body has been morphing, anyway? Her stomach ballooning, nipples darkening, veins a starker blue against her skin, discharge from her breasts, white streaks in her panties. The one time she noticed something off—a pink lump on her left nipple, tender to the touch—she was told by the nurse it was a clogged duct, no big deal, and instructed to take warm showers.

"The chances are high there's nothing to worry about," the doctor boomed.

Reagan asked him, a growing panic, What **is** there to worry about?

Both the nurse and the Coordinator stepped toward Reagan then, but it was the nurse who spoke. "You are young and healthy, miss. We are just being extra careful because of the baby."

The doctor grinned. "Relax, Dear. There's really nothing to fret about yet."

He smiled down at her, teeth straight as a picket fence, and whiter. She closed her eyes, the "yet" echoing in her head. She began to pray to keep herself from falling. She didn't stop praying until it was over.

OUTSIDE THE CLOSED DOOR OF REAGAN'S NEWLY PRIVATE room, she hears movement. Breakfast must be over. There is a shriek of laughter, loud shushing. Reagan sits up. She studies Jane's bed, deserted; the books on the near-empty shelf. She takes a closer look. They are the books Reagan gave her. An offhand gift. Reagan thought she might like them.

She shoves her feet into moccasins, ignoring the tightness in her chest. She doesn't want to stay here, alone, with these rejected books in this rejected room. She walks down the hall without a fixed plan and finds herself standing in front of the media room.

Because she needs to know.

She finds a workstation, logs in, and types:

lump near collarbone

In an instant, the screen is filled with information.

Health Conditions Related to This Search Include:

Lymphoma
Hodgkin's lymphoma
non-Hodgkin's lymphoma

Her stomach somersaults.

She forces herself to keep reading. Lymphoma and non-Hodgkin's lymphoma mostly occur in older patients. But Hodgkin's lymphoma **attacks adolescents and adults.**

It attacks.

Before she can chicken out, Reagan clicks on the link and braces herself for the onslaught.

But the screen is unchanged.

Reagan jiggles the mouse and clicks the Hodgkin's

lymphoma link again, then a second time. A third. Click, click, click. She opens the **BusinessWorld** website as a test with no problem, but when she retypes **Hodgkin's lymphoma** in the search engine the screen freezes.

Reagan walks to the neighboring cubicle. One of the South American Hosts, Ana Maria, is bent over her keyboard typing an email in Spanish.

"Sorry to bother you, but is your computer working?"

"I have no problems," Ana Maria says.

"Can I search something really quickly? Mine's glitching."

Yes, Ana Maria answers. She rolls her chair back several feet to give Reagan room. But here, too, the links for Hodgkin's lymphoma are static.

Severed.

Reagan thanks her, a banging inside.

Why are they blocking her? What are they hiding?

"Hi, Ana Maria!" It's Donna. "Reagan, I've been looking for you."

Reagan swallows, stares.

"I thought you might want to catch up on your UteroSoundz sessions since you were away yesterday," Donna says, cocking her head. She holds up a device, already uploaded with Reagan's playlist, and flashes a crinkly smile.

Reagan accepts it silently.

"Anyway, it's much too nice a day to be stuck in here!" Donna chitters, her hand on Reagan's shoulder, leading her out of Ana Maria's cube. "I saw Tasia out by the pool. Why don't you keep her company?"

"I have to call my mom!" Reagan blurts. "I call her every week . . ."

Donna frowns slightly, then grins. "Of course you do! Let's get you back to your workstation then. Are you still logged in?"

Reagan says she is. She picks up the phone, presses 9 for the dial tone, and calls Mom's nurse. Behind her, Donna is silent, but Reagan can sense she is there.

"Hi, Kathy. Can I talk to my mom?"

When Mom is on the phone—Reagan only knows because the nurse tells her so, because Mom almost never speaks anymore—Reagan begins to talk. She talks about her trip to New York and Diane Arbus and the photograph of the boy in the park holding the toy grenade, the way his free hand is tensed like a claw. She talks about **Infinite Jest** and the recent full moon, how Reagan stood at the window in the middle of the night to contemplate it.

"You would have liked it, Mom. It was so bright."

Behind her, Donna coughs.

"I miss you," Reagan whispers, not wanting Donna to hear. She hasn't said the words to Mom in years, but she realizes they are true.

"Mom . . . can you please say something?"

If you say something, it means I'll be okay.

She presses the receiver tighter to her ear, straining to detect a sound.

"Do you remember Kayla, Mom? Is it like that?"

Kayla Sorenson was a friend of Reagan's from elementary school. She had bright orange hair the color of a carrot and a round face covered in freckles, and she whinnied like a horse when she laughed. The summer before fourth grade she was diagnosed with brain cancer. An aggressive glioblastoma, Reagan heard Mom murmur to Dad. He was crying in the kitchen; Mr. Sorenson was one of his closest friends. Reagan had nightmares after every visit to the hospital. She imagined the glioblastoma as a black nothingness eating away at Kayla's brain and the roundness of her friend's face and her smile.

One night, Reagan woke to find Mom at her bedside, shaking her awake. "You were having a nightmare, Sweetie. You were yelling in your sleep."

"What's going to happen to Kayla? When she dies? Where does she go?" Reagan was sobbing, her face buried in Mom's chest.

Mom kissed her forehead and walked to Reagan's window, parted the curtains, and stood behind their heavy folds. Reagan tried to make out her shape but couldn't.

"Can you see me, Sweetie?"

"No-o!" Reagan cried.

"Am I here?"

"Yes, but I can't see you!"

Her mother began to sing. "Puff the Magic Dragon." She'd sung it at bedtime for as long as Reagan could remember. She sang it again and again until Reagan's crying subsided. When she stopped, the silence in the room was different. Reagan still doesn't know how long she lay in the dark, alone but not alone. When Mom emerged from the curtains sometime later, she slipped into Reagan's bed, her body so warm. "You won't be able to see Kayla, and you won't be able to hear her. But she'll be there."

WHEN REAGAN HANGS UP THE PHONE, DONNA IS GONE. REAGAN returns to her room on wobbly legs, conscious of the cameras aimed at her from their mountings on the walls. She slips inside and slumps against the closed door.

"I am sorry!"

Jane is standing at the bureau holding one of the books she left behind. She wears a guilty expression.

But they are her books; Reagan wanted her to have them.

"I forgot my address book. And then I saw these. But I was only looking—"

"They're yours, Jane. I gave them to you," Reagan says.

"I am sorry . . . This is your room now—"

Reagan takes three long strides toward the bureau, scoops up the books, and thrusts them toward

Jane with an aggression she doesn't intend. "Take them. Please, take them."

Jane is shaking her head, moving swiftly to the door.

"Take them." Reagan's voice cracks.

"I have an appointment—"

"They think I have cancer."

The words freed from her head, loose in the world, are monstrous.

"There's a lump. They did a biopsy. That's why I was in New York. The Client took me, and a Coordinator followed me. The whole day, she followed me, and now Donna's following me, and—"

Reagan is crumpling. She might be falling, but Jane is there. Jane puts her arms around Reagan as if Reagan is something small. She is propping her up and shielding her, too, her words falling around Reagan like snow.

MAE

MAE CHECKS HER WRISTWATCH. IT'S ALMOST NINE. SHE CLEARS her throat and announces to the gathered women— they are all women in the room—that Leon will arrive in an hour and they have a lot of ground to cover. Becca, an associate on the Host Management Team, hurriedly fills her cup with coffee, plucks a mini-quiche and a forkful of fruit from the refreshments table, and takes her seat.

Mae takes a moment to glance out the window at Central Park. God, she's glad she didn't have to schlep upstate today! She was so pleased to have the extra hour and a half at home this morning that she let Ethan have a quickie even **after** she'd showered.

She crosses her legs primly and gazes at the half-dozen women seated around the conference-room table. Her team. Her inner circle.

"For those of you who haven't been to the Holloway Club until now, I hope it meets your standards," Mae says jokingly. There's a murmur of appreciation, comments about the décor, the famous decorator who masterminded it.

Mae cuts them off. "The reason we're here is so I can give Leon the most robust update possible regarding one of our most important Clients. She's on the brink of making a substantial investment in our operations."

Mae glances around the table to make sure everyone is listening. "This investment will allow us to finance a truly transformative expansion of Golden Oaks. But it's up to us to make that happen."

Mae pauses to allow the import of her words to sink in—for herself as much as for her staff. She can barely believe it, still. She was in the middle of a wedding-dress fitting, standing on a low platform in front of a three-way mirror at the Carolina Herrera shop on Madison Avenue, her strapless, silk gazar gown billowing around her in ivory folds, when her phone buzzed. One of the attendants retrieved it from Mae's bag and read aloud Leon's number flashing on its screen. I'll take it! Mae shouted, dashing through the scrum of seamstresses so abruptly she almost ripped her antique-lace train.

"Project MacDonald gives me a hard-on!" Leon barked, and Mae, holding the phone against her cheek like a caress, resplendent in her ivory dress, glowed.

"Unsurprisingly," Mae continues, "whether or not our Client makes this investment is tied to the success of her pregnancies. So let's start with a review of 84. As we all know: a stable and happy Host produces a healthy baby, which produces a—"

"Satisfied Client," Becca chimes.

Becca's an eager one. Her ambition rubs some of the others the wrong way, but healthy competition pushes everyone to be better. And Mae respects Becca's hunger. That's what success boils down to, really, what separates the middling from the great. Many of Mae's friends wrote off Mae's first job after college—as a personal shopper at Bergdorf's—as a ploy; a way for her to get steep discounts on designer duds until she landed a husband. But none of her girlfriends ever had to work. What they missed was that personal shoppers—if they're good— could make great money. And Mae was good; she had a knack for connecting, for being whatever and whoever was demanded—the blessing of being a halvsie, of being on financial aid at a rich kids' prep school, of constantly straddling worlds.

Mae's friends also missed that the best personal shoppers had repeat clients, and these clients were rich, and some of them were powerful. Mae's two biggest ones—the CFO of a bulge-bracket investment bank (size 6, wide in the hips, with a penchant for pencil skirts and jewel tones) and the wife of a mind-bogglingly rich real-estate tycoon (size 4, wild about prints and peplum, loved to show a hint of cleavage)—became her friends. Both wrote glowing recommendations for her to HBS.

Becca's got the same kind of commercial instincts. The Arbus show, for instance, was her brainchild. She used to work in the photography department of one of the big auction houses. She had a hunch that Arbus's photos of freaks and outsiders would appeal to Reagan—and she was right.

"Becca, why don't you start us off?" Mae suggests.

"My pleasure! So, we just upsold the Client to a private room for 84. Of course, we prefer Hosts to room together, but given 84's recent troubles with the tick, we thought it best to isolate her. This means 82 now has a private room, too, so we can monitor both of their visitors and the frequency of them more easily."

"We should also frame 84's room upgrade as a reward for her cooperation with the incident between Julio and 33," says Mae.

"Good idea!" exclaims Becca, typing a note on her device.

"And how is 84's disposition? Geri, want to step in here?" Mae turns to the large-boned woman to her right.

Geri, the Director of Coordinators, has a background in psychiatry. She leans back in her chair. "I talked to my girls, reviewed the video feeds. 84 seems fine, much less fragile than post-tick episode. She's spending a lot of time with other Hosts from the Philippines."

"Actually," interjects Becca, "Host 84 recently started spending time with 82 again. There's been an increase in bedroom visits, and they're eating lunch together more."

"82's not the issue," Geri snipes. "33's the troublemaker. It's interactions with her that we should be tracking."

"And 96," adds Mae, shaking her head at the memory of Segundina's face, blotchy and swollen from a violent bout of sobbing after Mae docked her pay. She doesn't enjoy punishing Hosts, particularly those like Segundina, who already have such challenging lives in the outside world. But she had no choice in the matter. Actions must have consequences, and Segundina knew she was contractually barred from speaking to anyone about how she was recruited. "Incidentally, how are we doing on keeping 96 and 84 from interacting?"

Geri reports that Jane's and Segundina's newly reengineered schedules mean they do not cross paths except occasionally at mealtimes. "And 96 is running scared after she spoke with you, Mae. She won't come within ten feet of 84 if she can help it."

Mae checks the agenda on her device. "The next question is how we keep 84 out of trouble for the duration of her pregnancy. We can't afford another snafu."

"I've got someone monitoring her video feed at regular intervals," says Geri. "But without sound, this isn't a hundred percent."

Becca pipes up. "We could assign her a dedicated Coordinator?"

"We could," Mae responds. "But that's expensive. It seems to me there might be a more efficient way to keep 84 in line."

Mae looks around the table to see if anyone is on her wavelength. Becca wears a quizzical look; the others avert their eyes as if fearing Mae will cold-call them.

"Ladies," Mae begins, adopting the vaguely professorial tone she uses when presenting her team with a learning opportunity, "the key to a well-managed organization—whether it's a Fortune 500 company or a start-up, a refugee camp or a hospital system—is having the right incentives. People respond to them. Full stop."

Around the table, heads nod. Several women, Mae observes, are tapping notes onto their devices.

"The question is less 'how do we more effectively monitor 84' and more: how can we incentivize 84 **herself** to behave optimally?" Mae tries to make eye contact with her team, most of whom are still staring at their devices. Mae flashes her most disarming smile. "Don't hold back, ladies. There aren't wrong answers. We're simply brainstorming."

After more urging, several women lift their hands into the air.

"Increase 84's cash bonus?"

"Let her skip her least-favorite fitness classes?"

"Give her unlimited massages?"

"All fine ideas," Mae says. "But I'd postulate that each of you are considering incentives from **your** perspective. The first step is to ask what incentivizes **her.**"

Becca's arm rockets high. "Amalia!"

"Exactly," Mae answers. "84's primary motivator is her daughter. This is what we target."

"You mean rescheduling the visit," Geri states.

"The carrot can be as effective as the stick." Mae asks Geri to come up with a proposal for what such a visit would entail and advises her to schedule it at least several weeks out. This way they can maximize the period in which 84 is incentivized to be on her best behavior.

Mae proceeds to the medical update. Usually, this is where Meredith steps in, but Mae excluded her from today's meeting. She's busy adjusting to her newly expanded role and, to be honest, Mae's still annoyed about her pushiness since her promotion—not least because it was Mae who recruited her to join Holloway five years ago!

Mae exhales hard to expunge the negative energy and rattles off 84's medical report.

"Can we get to 82? Is the lump . . ." Becca's voice trails off.

All eyes shift to Mae.

"I know you're all worried, so I'll cut to the chase," Mae says. "The lump is **benign.** The doctors tell us the growth doesn't need to be removed until after delivery."

Chatter explodes, the tension broken.

"We haven't yet told 82 the good news because the doctor only texted us this morning." Mae's voice breaks through the din.

"Is there any reason **not** to tell her?" interjects Becca. "Like, maybe so 82 stays out of trouble? Because she's friends with 33? Because her baby's so important?"

Mae looks at Becca in surprise.

Geri snorts. One of the Coordinators points out that increased levels of cortisol in the Host have been found to have long-term effects. Fiona from Legal posits that Golden Oaks might be legally obliged to inform 82 of her condition.

"In any case, it seems **very** cruel to let her continue to believe she has cancer," Geri snipes.

Becca reddens. Mae intercedes. "All ideas are welcome in this space. No judgments, please."

They are interrupted by a rap on the door. The receptionist announces the arrival of their guest. Mae tables the discussion and, minutes later, Tracey lopes into the room. She wears black jeans and a striped shirt, her hair no longer straightened but

voluminous and wild. Large, crescent-shaped ear-
rings tug at her earlobes. She looks much younger
than she did when in character.

"Your timing is impeccable, as usual," Mae says,
standing to greet her. They exchange air kisses.

"What's the news on Reagan?" Tracey asks.

"All fine. The lump's benign."

"Thank God!" Tracey sinks into the chair Becca
has pulled out for her.

"For those of you who haven't had the pleasure
yet, this is Tracey Washington. She's a local legend in
the theater community in Seattle," Mae introduces.

Tracey guffaws. "Are you a legend if you're only
known locally?"

"Tracey also teaches drama at a public high school
in the Seattle-Tacoma area and runs an after-
school program for inner-city youth."

"And in case Mae hasn't told you," Tracey says,
"Holloway made a big donation to our programs. So
thank you."

Appreciative murmurs ripple around the table.
Mae notices that Becca claps her hand to her
chest as if her heart needs buttressing. Only Geri
looks unmoved.

"And, of course, Tracey's our Stand-In for 82's
Client," says Mae. "I know this program is new
to all of you except Geri. It's new to us as well.
Though we've been developing the idea for some
time, we've never actually utilized a Stand-In until
now. I thought it was worthwhile to fly in Tracey

to meet the team. I want everyone to understand our rationale in going this route so we can analyze what worked and what didn't, and we can do even better next time."

"Kaizen," pipes Becca, referring to Mae's mantra, one she has drilled into her underlings' heads in meeting after meeting. "Continuous learning!"

Geri rolls her eyes again.

"We opted for a Stand-In from the West Coast to minimize the risk that any of our Hosts have run into her in the past," Mae says. "But I'm getting ahead of myself. The idea of a Stand-In was Geri's. Geri, do you want to talk about the thought process behind it?"

"Yes. Well. 82 is what I call a seeker. She's looking for purpose. She does harbor vague ambitions of 'getting serious' about photography, but she hasn't fully committed to the idea. My sense is that she fears failure; the ease of her life means she's never truly worked hard to achieve anything."

"I saw this a lot with the trust-fund kids at Christie's," Becca interrupts. "They're **really** insecure."

Geri pointedly ignores Becca. "I felt from observing 82 that carrying a baby for the current Client wouldn't fulfill her need for meaning. Therefore, I proposed to Mae that we use a Stand-In. Someone to be 82's 'dream client.' Someone who would make carrying the baby a meaningful experience for her."

Mae interjects. "Clearly, a Stand-In isn't necessary for most Hosts. But given the importance of the baby 82 carries, and 82's 'seeking' nature, it seemed worthwhile. It also gives us a new revenue stream because we can charge extra for Stand-Ins."

"We were not convinced we absolutely needed Tracey. She was simply an insurance policy," Geri says.

Tracey chortles. "I've been called worse!"

"Over the past few weeks, it became clear a Stand-In **was** necessary," Mae continues. She describes the satirical "Top 30 Fetal Bigwigs Under 30 Weeks" essay found on 82's online files and her request to donate her bonus to 84.

"To me, the offer to forgo her bonus was the deciding factor," explains Geri. "It implied that 82 felt carrying an anonymous baby wasn't meaningful enough in itself."

"So, we gave her meaning. Well, Tracey did— and quite masterfully. Tracey, do you want to talk about this briefly before we open up to questions?" Mae asks with a glance at her watch.

"With pleasure." Tracey makes eye contact with each person around the table as she speaks. "Okay, well, Geri gave me the download on Reagan. Sorry— I mean: 82. That she's looking for **something.** So that's how I played it. The underdog thing, the self-made thing. All the good stuff Geri and I came up with in prep."

"And how did she respond?" prods Mae.

"She ate it up. She really did. And the exhibit? That was a **fantastic** idea."

Becca straightens in her chair, beaming.

"Those pictures really got 82 talking about all kinds of things." Tracey shakes her head. "She's a nice girl. She really is."

"All this is important, even with a clean biopsy. It can only help us if 82 feels a connection, even affection, for the mother and therefore the child."

Around the table, heads bob.

"Couldn't 82 have just met her real Client? I mean, she has such a moving life story herself." It is Becca again, playing the contrarian. Mae approves. Women don't rock the boat enough.

"The Client does not want to be known," Geri snaps, not even looking up from her device.

Becca, chastened, drops her head. Mae adds gently, "But even had the Client been open to meeting 82, we might still have opted for a Stand-In. Our Client isn't gifted interpersonally. She can come across as . . . cold. A rapport might not have developed between her and 82. The Stand-In strategy allowed us to use Geri's research to create a faux-Client with the best chance of forging a real connection with 82 . . . the best chance of helping 82 want—of her **own** volition—to make the right choices for the child."

Around the table, heads nod again, Becca's most vehemently.

Mae opens the floor to questions for Tracey. Several hands wave in the air. Tracey fields each query with aplomb. She really is a pro. Mae would love to use her again. She considers the Stand-In strategy a success. One more positive development to include in the update for Leon.

"Excuse me!" says Becca, who has been waiting to ask a question for some time. "Ms. Washington, when you were at the gallery—that was **my** idea, I used to work in the art world before Holloway—how did the Arbus photos specifically help you make a connection?"

A self-serving question, but a good one to end the meeting on.

Tracey takes a moment to gather her thoughts. "Well . . . at the exhibit, like I said, 82 really opened up to me. But there was one photo that was key. I knew it would be there, because Geri and I went over the pictures in prep. It was of this dwarf man in a bed wearing a little brimmed hat. 82's standing next to me, and I say: Look at this guy. He's a freak by any standard, and yet he looks so sure of things.

"I let that sink in a while, and I can tell she's thinking hard. So, then I say: It took me a long time not to feel like a freak in this country, and I'm still working to achieve that kind of certainty."

Tracey pauses, allowing the silence in the room to ripen.

"And what did she say?" Becca interrupts, rapt.

"Well, she turns to me and says, like she's trying to reassure me: I think it's okay to be uncertain, as long as you're trying to do the right thing . . . And then I ask **her:** Do **you** think you're doing the right thing, Reagan?"

Tracey looks up and down the table, making sure her audience is with her. Becca has her hand clasped to her chest again. Even Geri looks captivated. Or at least, interested.

"And she answers me, all serious: Yes, I do."

Tracey's face breaks into a smile. "And that's when I knew we had her."

ATE

"ELLEN, THANK YOU."

Ellen is looking into the mirror of her compact and dusting powder on her forehead.

"I know you are busy."

Ellen looks at the camera, her big eyes filling the screen of the phone Ate holds. "When does his **yaya** come back?"

"Soon. She is already on the way back from the hospital. Her father is stable. It was a small heart attack."

Ellen's voice becomes a whine. She was always the whiniest of the four—wanting another cookie or the shoes in the shop window. "Ma, I'm supposed to meet Hans for lunch. He's Danish! You know Denmark? His flight is in a few hours already!"

"Roy is your brother." Ate fights to hide her annoyance. Ellen never visits Roy, only Isabel does, but Isabel is working, and Ellen is free during the days. Ellen was not so selfish before. Ate worries that she has become spoiled without a mother to guide her and because of the money Ate keeps sending.

"Even if I leave before his **yaya** returns, Roy is okay. How can he get in trouble just sitting there?" Ellen grumbles, testing Ate, but she has the decency to avert her eyes.

"Is Roy wearing the headphones?" Ate asks, choosing not to fight with her daughter, even though anger now burns inside her heart like a hot coal. "They are expensive. Yaya says he will not wear them."

Ellen glances to the side, presumably at Roy, and shakes her head.

"The music can help him," Ate explains. "I have read articles. I am working very hard, saving money to bring him here. For the therapy."

"I want to come also! Save money for me! I will bring him to New York!" Ellen smiles at the camera, the kind of smile that is hard not to return. It is the way she must smile at her boyfriends.

The problem is that she is too pretty. When you are too pretty, the other parts of you do not become strong.

There is the sound of a door shutting, and Ellen announces gleefully that Roy's **yaya** has arrived. She blows Ate a kiss and disappears. The **yaya** appears onscreen, apologizing for having to leave so suddenly. Ate asks her to move Roy's wheelchair to the laptop, to adjust the camera so Ate can see him, and then to make him lunch. He might be hungry. Ellen does not know how to cook and probably did not feed him.

"Roy, look at the camera so Mama can see your eyes."

Her son does not respond, only continues staring straight ahead.

"**Guapo na guapo!** You are so handsome! But you need a haircut. I will tell **Yaya.**

"Roy, did you see Ellen came?" Ate asks. "She was so happy to see you. She does not come more often because she is busy. She will try to come more.

"And, **Hijo:** you must wear the earphones. Only until I bring you here for the doctors. I am working very hard to do this. But the cooking business, it is harder than I thought."

An insect buzzes around Roy. Ate's fingers itch to swat it away, but what can she do?

"Angel, she has an idea. Remember I tell you about Angel? The one with the American boyfriends, the orange hair? Angel has a client. The client is going to Disney for vacation during Christmas. You remember Disney? Mickey Mouse? Snow White? All that?

"Christmas time is very busy at Disney. The lines will be long, and the client's children are still small. Disney sells special bracelets that allow people to skip the long lines, but they are very expensive. Angel's client is clever. She located a guide, someone special like you: maybe in a wheelchair, maybe a little slow. Disney lets special people skip the long lines. Hiring someone like this—it is cheaper than the Disney bracelets, you see."

Ate looks at her son hopefully. He stares now to the side, in the direction of the door. Maybe he is wondering where Ellen went. Maybe he is missing her. They were so close when they were children.

"Angel will ask her client if there is an agency for these special guides. Perhaps this agency can help with your visa. Perhaps they will hire you when I bring you to America. Disney is too far away; the music doctors are in Massachusetts. But perhaps you can get a job at Six Flags. Six Flags is like Disney, but closer. A job is good, because it gives you purpose."

Roy burps.

"Roy! When you burp like that, you must say, **'Excuse me.'** That is the polite way."

Ate falls silent. If the agency cannot help Roy with the visa, how will she get one? She thinks of Cyntia, who lived in the dorm in Queens years ago. Ate ran into her last week on Atlantic Avenue. She told Ate how the Mulroneys—Cyntia is still working for them after all these years—are sponsoring her eldest son. Their lawyer is rushing to arrange the green-card application before he turns eighteen. It is easier that way with Immigration.

Ate has many clients who respect her. They send her Christmas cards and ask her help finding a new nanny and email her newspaper articles. But she has no one like the Mulroneys. She does not work for her clients long enough for them to love her in this way. A love big enough to include her children.

In fact, Ate had counseled Cyntia **not** to stay with the Mulroneys. It was eleven years ago, and Cyntia needed to support her sons back in Davao. The Mulroneys were friends of a client of Ate's, and they needed a baby nurse. Ate recommended Cyntia. When the Mulroneys asked her to stay on after the four-month job to become their nanny—both parents worked, the mother made more money than the father—Ate told her to refuse.

"There is more money in baby nursing than nannying!"

But Cyntia preferred one family, one job. She did not listen to Ate—and now she will be reunited with her son. And she will own an apartment, a one-bedroom in Flushing that the Mulroneys helped her buy. Ate did not believe Cyntia at first—what kind of clients would do all this? But the mother got a big job, she is now big-time at her bank on Wall Street, and she said to Cyntia: My success was only possible because every morning when I left for work and every time I stayed late in the office, I didn't worry about my children—because of you.

Dios ko. I do not know.

"I do not know if I made the right choice." Without thinking, Ate has said this aloud. She looks at Roy, who stares into space as if he did not hear her. She explains, "But most families are not like the Mulroneys. You remember I tell you about my friend Mahalia? She was a nanny for seven years for a family, and when they moved, they did not even give her a severance!"

The insect that has been buzzing around Roy lands on his cheek. Ate thinks it must be a fly, because a mosquito would have bitten him long ago. But she does not like to see it there, resting on her son's face as if he were a plate of food.

"**Hijo,** there is a fly . . ." Ate says, her voice trembling.

Roy. Do **something.**

JANE

JANE WALKS TOWARD THE CONFERENCE ROOM WHERE MASS IS held on Sundays. She peers through the pane of etched glass on the door. Behind the oval-shaped table usually used for business meetings stands Father Cruz. Arrayed around him in several rows of conference-room chairs are a dozen or so Hosts, heads bowed. Carmen sits self-importantly at the electronic keyboard near the window, waiting for him to signal her to begin a hymn.

In the past, the Catholic Hosts would gather in the screening room on Sundays to watch Mass celebrated on television. It never occurred to any of them to ask Ms. Yu if they could hold a real Mass at Golden Oaks until Reagan suggested it. Jane was nervous to approach Ms. Yu, so Reagan did, and Ms. Yu agreed.

Jane hurries to the dining room. She is skipping Mass. She could not possibly sit through it today.

In the corridor one of the cleaning ladies is vacuuming the carpet. She turns off the machine when Jane approaches. Jane was trained to do this, too, in the retirement home. You were not supposed to have the machine on when one of the visitors walked by.

The dining room is almost empty, only a few early risers sipping noncaffeinated drinks, half-asleep. Sundays are sleep-in days, with no scheduled activities until midmorning. Bed is where Reagan is, Jane knows, because she is not a morning person. Or so she is always telling Jane, as if this is something fixed in her nature, like the type of her blood or the color of her skin. At the retirement home Jane often started work before seven. When she baby nursed Henry Carter, she woke whenever he did, at any hour of the night. If Reagan is a morning person, then that makes Jane a whole-day person, which is more of a person than Reagan. If you believe Reagan.

Jane laughs, because she is happy.

"Hi, Jane," says a Coordinator, slowing her steps to chat. She asks Jane how she is feeling and tells Jane about her daughter's birthday party the previous week. They lit fireworks, because it was only days after the Fourth of July, and her daughter was terrified by the noise. The Coordinator squeezes Jane's arm and leans close. "I heard about your daughter's visit!"

Jane hesitates. The familiar tone, the friendliness, are still new to her. It is how the Coordinators are with her now that it is widely known which baby she carries. And since she told Ms. Yu about Lisa and Julio.

Or, maybe, it is Jane herself who is different.

"Yes, I find it hard to wait," Jane admits, and a boundless joy fills her.

"I hope you and your daughter have a wonderful time!"

Jane approaches the serving counter. It is so early that the only foods laid out are fruits and yogurts. She waits for the muffins, daydreaming.

When Ms. Yu called her into her office the other day, Jane's immediate thought was that the baby contracted Lyme disease, despite the medications. Instead, Ms. Yu announced that she "managed to convince" the Client to allow Amalia a belated first-birthday visit in a month's time—and not only that, she would be allowed to stay with Jane **overnight.**

"I kept telling her that the tick incident was an aberration. You're a model Host. You want what's best not just for yourself, but the whole Golden Oaks family," explained Ms. Yu, beaming.

Jane knew Ms. Yu was referring to Lisa and Julio. How she "ratted them out," as she overheard Tasia whisper to another Host at lunch not so long ago. The visit with Amalia was a reward, or a bribe, or both.

And, still, Jane will get to see her daughter.

They spoke about logistics, even though the visit was still weeks away. Ms. Yu recommended a bed-and-breakfast in a nearby town and a toy shop where Jane could buy Amalia a gift. "And I assume your cousin—Evelyn, is that her name?—will be bringing your daughter?"

At the mention of Ate, Jane felt heat rising in her chest. She knows she should forgive her—Ate is old and has many burdens—but she cannot. Not yet. Every time Jane thinks of her daughter alone with Segundina—the confusion Amalia must have felt, the sense that she was being abandoned yet again— fury explodes in her body. For all Amalia knew, sitting in her stroller in a random park with a strange woman, neither Jane nor Ate was ever coming back.

Since their fight over two weeks ago, Jane has not spoken with her cousin. At first Jane was the one avoiding the video-calls, but now she thinks Ate is avoiding her, too. Jane called several times in the past week but only got voicemail. Ate is stubborn. She is not used to being wrong.

"Jane!" Betsy, the cook, appears in the kitchen doorway, wiping her meaty hands on her apron. Through the open door comes the clanging of pots and the sound of running water. "Need something, Hon?"

"Hon" for "Honey." This, too, is new.

"I am only waiting for the muffins . . ."

"They're just out of the oven. Lemme run back and get you one. What kind?"

Jane protests. She is not in a rush; she is happy to wait. But Betsy insists and returns moments later with a small plate of muffins: blueberry-bran, banana-chia, and, "between us," one chocolate-chip banana muffin, the kind Betsy sometimes makes for Lisa. Jane's eyes linger on the crown of melted chocolate on the banana muffin before handing it back to Betsy with a shake of her head.

"Ms. Yu won't mind this once." Betsy winks.

But Jane will not risk Amalia's visit for a little sweetness.

Jane takes the plate of still-warm muffins and brings them to a table in the rear of the dining hall. From here, through the floor-to-ceiling windows, she can watch the alpaca as they graze in the nearby fields. She spies them now, furry heads bent to the ground. Near the edge of the herd, she notices a miniature one: white, with a scrawny neck and spindly legs. It lifts its head and seems to stare across the field at her. A baby. They lock eyes, or so it seems.

Beautiful. The world can be beautiful sometimes.

Jane crumples her napkin. She cannot let Reagan sleep through such a beautiful day.

"Hi, Jane." A Coordinator passing in the hallway greets her.

"Good morning!" Jane looks the Coordinator in the eyes.

Reagan's room is dark, the curtains still drawn. She is flung across her bed as if dropped from somewhere high above—on her back, with one arm dangling off the bed's side. She is not supposed to sleep this way. They learned of it in class. Sleeping on your back can prevent enough blood from reaching the baby. It is also not comfortable. When Jane rolls unthinkingly onto her back at night, she immediately finds it hard to breathe.

"Wake up!" Jane sings again, but more softly. She places the plate of muffins on top of the big blue book Reagan is always carrying with her and nudges her friend's shoulder.

"No-o," mumbles Reagan, turning onto her side.

Jane gazes at her friend's sleeping form. It was not so long ago that Reagan believed she was sick. She was scared, and so was Jane, but Jane could not show it. Jane sat by her friend's side in Ms. Yu's office when the results of the biopsy came in. She held her friend's hand, which was hot and moist, like a child's.

It was also this scare that brought Jane back to Lisa, but only because Reagan begged her. Reagan had a migraine, and the Coordinators would not let her out of bed. She worried that Ms. Yu might not be telling her the whole truth and wanted Lisa to find out anything she could.

Confronting Lisa—Lisa with the sharp tongue and mean mouth; Lisa whom she had ratted out—was the last thing Jane wanted to do. But how could she refuse?

"I didn't expect to see you" is what Lisa said when she found Jane at her door. Her hair was twisted up in a towel. Jane's stomach flopped like a caught fish.

"I have news about Reagan," Jane whispered, eyes checking the hallway for Coordinators.

Lisa pulled Jane into the room and listened closely as Jane explained about the growth, the biopsy results.

"We have to make sure that's the full story," Lisa said. "And that they treat her if she needs to be treated."

"But of course they will treat her," Jane ventured, thinking of Princesa, the Filipina with cancer at the dorm in Queens. She had no money, she was not from America, and even she was getting treated.

"Not necessarily. Not if it puts the fetus at risk. What we need is to know what her contract says. Which life takes precedence."

"But Ms. Yu told us there is no cancer," offered Jane timidly.

"Ms. Yu is a liar, Jane. Don't you get that? We have to be prepared for anything."

Jane stood then, because she had nothing more to report. She was worried if she stayed too long in Lisa's room the Coordinators would get suspicious. And she was afraid of Lisa. As she moved to the door, Lisa grabbed her arm. Her grip was strong, like Billy's.

"Quit avoiding me," Lisa said, her voice calm. "You did what you had to. I get it. Okay?"

Jane nodded, her heart beating so fast. Once she was in the hall, she had to fight herself not to run.

REAGAN IS FINALLY AWAKE. SHE AND JANE SIT IN THE DINING hall eating their muffins and watching the alpaca. There is a loud tittering. A group of Filipinas has entered the room. Delia is there. Carmen. The very-pregnant Host carrying twins. Trailing the group is Segundina.

"She is here," Jane says in a low voice to Reagan, her heart quickening.

As if Delia could hear them from across the room, she begins to wave her arms. "Jane! Jane!"

"Segundina," mumbles Jane. "She has seen Amalia more than I have seen her this year."

A bitterness fills Jane's mouth. She imagines Segundina texting her friends in the Philippines as Amalia, diaper soaked, whimpers next to her. That is why Amalia developed the diaper rash. Segundina admitted as much the first time they spoke. Jane remembers this now.

"But that's not her fault. She didn't know."

Reagan is trying to calm her. And, of course, she is right. Segundina is not the one at fault. It is Ate. Ate with the two faces. Jane says this to Reagan, who hesitates.

"And yet, even your cousin was only trying to help someone in need," she suggests, adding quickly, "not to excuse her behavior."

"Each time I call her, I go to voicemail. She is avoiding me."

"She's probably just busy." Reagan mentions the video from yesterday again, the one where Amalia is dancing to a song on the radio. Jane knows her friend is trying to distract her.

She stares at the serving line, where Segundina waits with an empty tray. How did Ate come to know her, anyway? And why did Ate choose to help **her,** out of all the women with hard-luck stories drifting in and out of the dorm in Queens?

Jane realizes she knows nothing. She did not ask enough questions when she confronted Ate about her deception. Jane was so angry, her mind so clouded, that she was driven to shout at Ate and shout at her more until the rage inside settled and she could sense—in Ate's voice, usually sure, always right—shame.

Jane stands and brushes crumbs from her skirt. "I will talk to her."

"Jane, don't—"

Jane walks away before Reagan can get to her feet, leaving her tray on the table for Reagan to clear. She can hear her own heart pounding. She can see ahead of her the table where Segundina sits, Segundina and Delia and the others, the chandelier that Jane loves exploding above their heads. Segundina is hunched over her plate like she is eating from a trough.

"Segundina," Jane says, standing over her, knowing she should turn around and walk away but unable to move. The noise at the table drops. Several Hosts stare openly at Jane, not even pretending to mind their own business.

Segundina looks up, and Jane is surprised to see that she is afraid.

"Sit, Jane!" Delia urges, sliding over so that Jane can take the seat between her and Segundina. "Sit before the Coordinators see."

"How is your **baby,** Jane?" asks Carmen. Jane has never liked her. She has heard Carmen whisper, loud enough so that Jane can hear, that she thinks Jane is stuck-up, following the Americans like their pet, thinking she is better than the others because of the baby she carries.

"He is fine," Jane answers, her voice tight. No one speaks, as if waiting for her to say more.

"Did you receive your third-trimester bonus? Mine was not big—but yours must be very big?" asks Delia eagerly. She has told Jane, with longing in her voice, how lucky Jane is to carry the Billionaire Baby.

Jane shakes her head, flustered by the bombardment. The other Hosts are eyeing her and exchanging glances, talking in quiet voices she cannot quite hear.

"What province are you from?" asks Jane, turning to Segundina.

Segundina twists the napkin in her hands. "I am from Visayas. Bohol . . ."

"Visayas? Ah. Then how is it you know Ate Evelyn?"

Segundina hesitates, her eyes shifting around the table.

"I know her also. She is my cousin," Jane explains, trying to keep the impatience out of her voice. "But how do **you** know her?"

Segundina's voice lowers to a whisper. "I know Ate Evelyn from the dormitory in Queens."

"How often did Ate leave the baby with you—"

"No more questions!" Carmen hisses. "This is not allowed. You know that, Jane."

"I am only talking," Jane retorts, looking around the table for support, but no one meets her eyes. Not even Delia.

"Only talking so that you can report her again!" Carmen is leaning so far across the table that Jane can see the flare of her nostrils, the pockmarks on her face.

Jane, startled, looks at Segundina, who has covered her face with her hands.

"Did you get in trouble?" Jane asks her. "Because of me?"

"Do not answer her, Segundina! You will only lose more money. She does not care about the rules because soon she will be rich, too!" Carmen is speaking in Tagalog now, her words flying.

"I did not report her!" Jane replies, but without anger, only surprise.

"Then who?" Carmen snaps.

Jane's mind races. Did Reagan tell Lisa? Did Lisa tell Ms. Yu?

"When did you get in trouble?" Jane asks Segundina, switching to Tagalog.

Segundina lifts her head from her hands. "It was the day after we spoke. Ms. Yu called me into the office—"

"Excuse me, ladies!" the Coordinator standing behind them is the one Jane spoke with earlier. The one whose daughter celebrated her birthday with fireworks. Everyone around the table falls silent. "Have you forgotten that it's English-only at Golden Oaks?"

Segundina and Jane look at each other guiltily. Carmen sputters, "Ma'am, it is only that . . ."

"Oh hi, Jane. Didn't see you there," the Coordinator says, and her friendliness makes Jane ashamed.

In a milder voice, the Coordinator announces that she understands that their home language is a source of comfort, especially for Segundina, who is still new. "But you need to stick to English, ladies. Otherwise, the rest of us feel left out!"

The Coordinator moves away, stopping well within earshot.

"Let us go now," Carmen announces, attempting an exaggerated American accent. She gives Segundina a glare and stands. Segundina stumbles to her feet, piling her silverware and napkin on her tray. She avoids looking at Jane. The other Hosts sit quietly, watching their departure. Eventually, conversation resumes; food is eaten. Jane notices but ignores the surreptitious glances in her direction.

Segundina's fearfulness. Her punishment.

Who told Ms. Yu?

Reagan would never confide in her. Lisa hates her.

Could it be that she and Segundina were over-heard that day by one of the Coordinators? But no Coordinator was near them, Jane is almost sure of it, she is always so careful.

Unless—

Jane looks around the table. The Hosts picking at their eggs, sipping their green juices. Gossiping and laughing and sneaking looks at her. Many of them were sitting beside her and Segundina that day. They all have ears, and mouths, too.

They all need money.

Jane takes a breath. She closes her eyes, gather-ing herself.

"Jane!" whispers Delia so urgently that Jane's eyes flutter open.

"Yes?"

Delia leans close, her lips inches from Jane's ears. "Jane! Tell me: what will you do with your money when you are rich?"

REAGAN

REAGAN WAKES INTO A HOT HAZE. SHE IS BURNING. THE SUN shifted while she slept, and she no longer lies in the pool umbrella's shadow. Her skin sticks to her bathing suit. She fumbles for the glass on a nearby table and gulps the sun-warmed water. She stretches. The pull in her muscles, this gorgeous lassitude.

She catches herself humming. Loses herself in the sky above, endless and blue. Inside, Callie's son stirs. He likes to move when Reagan is still and lie still when she is moving. She says a wordless hello. Savoring the sun on her skin, the bloom of her stomach. No cancer, no more fear or paranoia (that Golden Oaks is out to get her, that Ms. Yu is lying to her).

She's done with that.

There is nowhere else she'd rather be than here, stretched on this chair, the heat making her heavy and Callie's baby inside her. And her body healthy and strong.

When Callie came to visit the other day—a bottle of nonalcoholic bubbly to belatedly celebrate the good news that the biopsy was clear—she brought a picture of herself and her brothers as children. In the photo Callie was barefoot, hair in beaded braids, sandwiched between her lean-faced siblings who stuck pink tongues at the camera. Reagan tried to imagine a baby version of the older boy, the handsomer one. Callie told her he was stubborn and smart and a little wild.

Reagan thinks of Callie's baby tumbling in her womb. A stubborn, smart, slightly wild boy who will see the light only because she is carrying him. A boy who might end up a titan of industry or inventor of a fuel-free flying electric car. Or senator. Governor. President! A boy who will grow into a strong, right-thinking black man, like his strong, right-thinking mother.

She gets goosebumps. She cannot help it, even though Lisa scoffs when she tells her so. ("A trust-fund kid is a trust-fund kid is a trust-fund kid.")

But Reagan sees things differently now. She does not fault Lisa. It's only that Lisa does not—

cannot—understand. She has never inched to the edge of the abyss and stared death in the face. She doesn't recognize that life, the very act of it, is blindingly, stupendously courageous and also—breakable. A single twig cracking in a forest is enough. One mutant cell.

The other day during lunch Reagan had an out-of-body experience. A zooming out, as if in a film, to a bird's-eye view of everything below: the dining-room clamor, the tables of women bathed in midday light. And in each of them—chattering, chewing, sniggering, sulking, teasing, laughing; black, brown, bronze, pink, peach, cream—a living thing.

In an instant, the room was transformed into a hallowed space, more so than a church. No cardboard wafer not-melting on the tongue, no drone of prayers or incensed air too thick to easily breathe. And yet, there was a sacredness in the room's abundance.

"Did you miss the news alert that there's no such thing as **sacred** anymore? Everything's for sale. Including everyone in **this** baby factory," Lisa responded, wiping kale-pesto sauce off her mouth. "I think you're just on a survivor's high. It's understandable given what you went through."

She added, less kindly, "Or you're brainwashed. The Farm's good at that."

Reagan let the dig pass. It wasn't that Lisa was wrong. Golden Oaks **did** make money, probably lots of it, by making a business out of pregnancy.

Some of the Clients **could** carry their babies themselves but chose not to for reasons—vanity or purportedly jam-packed schedules—that Reagan didn't really respect. And Lisa's Clients shouldn't have lied to her that the mother's endometriosis rendered her unable to carry a baby on her own. Lisa learned the truth—that the mother had started modeling again and didn't want to risk ruining her figure—only when she was already pregnant with Baby Three. Lisa is, understandably, resentful.

But many more of the Clients at Golden Oaks were desperate, but unable, to have children on their own. Like Callie. Reagan knows that what she feels cannot be faked—a sense of rightness about carrying Callie's child. Maybe for the first time in her life: the knowledge that she is doing something inarguably worthwhile.

That's what Lisa cannot see. It's what Dad could never understand. He keeps sending her articles about people not much older than Reagan accomplishing fabulous feats (the Persian American woman at Stanford working on a cure for Ebola; the Ohioan with an MFA-MBA who started a string of artisanal home-goods-and-jewelry shops in a resurgent Detroit). He claims that the "key" to success in life is plugging away at something for ten thousand hours (Bill Gates! Yo-Yo Ma!).

But you don't have to be a top leader, or a best-selling writer, or an art-world darling to make your mark. Running simply to run faster is pointless. The constant striving—for what, really? The adulation of strangers? More Instagram followers? A fawning article in some dumb magazine—ultimately empty.

Reagan is jolted by a kick, stronger than usual. She places her hands on her tummy and smiles. She catches the next kick right in her palm.

I've got you, she tells Callie's son.

A SHADOW FALLS ACROSS HER FACE. JANE LOOMS. SHE HANDS Reagan a bottle of water, vitamin-infused.

"Thanks." Reagan presses it to her throat. A bead of water drips a cold trail down her neck, her chest.

Next to her, Jane pushes a chaise into the shade and settles herself. She attaches a UteroSoundz to her stomach and takes off her hat. Her hair is matted and oily. "I still cannot reach my cousin."

"I'm sure she just forgets to charge her phone. My grandfather's like that," Reagan says, sitting up. Jane hasn't spoken in person to her cousin, or Amalia, in over three weeks, though she receives daily videos. "Can I see the clip from yesterday again? Where Amalia's doing the animal sounds?"

"Ate is never in the videos she sends me. I have reviewed them," Jane says. Her voice sounds strained. "I believe this is because she is not there. She is leaving Mali with strangers, and they are the ones filming my daughter. That is why Ate will not call—because then I will know the truth!"

"Your cousin's not in the videos because **she's** the

one filming them, silly!" Reagan is making an attempt at lightheartedness, but Jane only shakes her head. There are bluish circles under her eyes. She told Reagan she's been having trouble sleeping.

"I do not trust her anymore. My cousin is ambitious. My Nanay used to say this about her. Ate already owns many properties in the Philippines, but still she thinks only of money."

"Jane," Reagan says firmly. "Old people are bad with cellphones. They forget to charge them. Your cousin loves Amalia, and she's great with babies. You've told me that!"

"Only with Clients' babies," Jane says bitterly. "She would never leave a Client's baby with a stranger."

Jane is fumbling with her drink, trying to twist open its cap. She mutters under her breath, like the homeless man who loiters outside Reagan's building in New York, the one Reagan had to report to the police one night after he wouldn't budge from her doorway.

"Why don't you try **not** to worry until you see Amalia? She'll be here next week—"

"I do not know if my cousin will bring Mali! She does not return my calls. She sends only the videos. She writes nothing to me about the visit, because she does not want to come!"

"And why—"

"Because she is too busy! With her cooking and her money-making . . ."

"You don't know that, Jane. You're basing this on—"

"Or she is hiding Amalia from me!"

"Why would she **possibly** do that?" Reagan tries to keep the exasperation out of her voice.

"She dropped Amalia one time. I did not tell you? I only discovered it from the bruise on Amalia's face during a video-call. Maybe even then, it was not Ate who dropped Amalia but someone else. Maybe it was Segundina!"

Jane's voice is shrill. Squeezing the drink bottle between her thighs, she twists its metal cap, face reddening with the effort. Without warning, she slams it against her chair. A spray of glass and the ground, glittering.

"Jane!"

The lifeguard is shouting questions as she clambers down from her elevated chair. A Coordinator emerges from the pool house with a rolled-up magazine in her hand.

"Do we have a problem?" the Coordinator asks, standing over them.

The lifeguard gives her side of the story, pointing occasionally at Jane. Jane stares into the distance with a blank expression on her face, still gripping the cracked bottle, a drop of blood on her arm.

"It's just these dumb drinks. They're hard to open," Reagan interrupts, trying to draw the Coordinator's attention away from Jane. She holds up her unopened bottle and begins babbling about the beverages she wishes Golden Oaks would order, asking the Coordinator if Golden Oaks would ever loosen its rules on caffeinated drinks, even just occasionally.

"It's not up to us to decide policy," the Coordinator says. She holds out a hand to Jane, who does not seem to notice. "Let me see that bottle."

Reagan thrusts her drink at the Coordinator, chattering about the heat wave, willing Jane to say something—anything—before the Coordinator gets suspicious, calls Psych, cancels Amalia's visit again.

"These aren't even twist-offs!" the Coordinator exclaims. She confiscates both bottles and tells the lifeguard to call Janitorial about the broken glass. "I wonder what idiot ordered these."

Out of nowhere, another Coordinator arrives bearing a tray of fresh drinks in plastic bottles. Jane snaps out of her torpor. She notices the gash on her arm and, with a sheepish glance at Reagan, wraps a towel around her shoulders to hide it. The cleaning woman arrives and begins to sweep the broken glass from the tiles. Jane watches her guiltily, but when she stands to help, the Coordinator shakes her head.

"Sit back down, Jane. Glass can cut."

As soon as they are alone Reagan grabs Jane's drink, yanks open the cap, and bangs the bottle down on the table. "There."

"I am sorry, Reagan."

"Just stop acting like an insane person!" Reagan snaps. "Unless you actually don't ever want to see your daughter."

It's a mean thing to say, but Reagan feels mean. She ignores Jane and her sad, teary eyes and tries not to wonder why Jane insists on doing exactly the wrong thing at exactly the wrong time.

She shuts her eyes and tries to sleep, but the image of the red bead on Jane's arm is stuck behind her eyelids, the red bead bleeding into a red streak. It's incredible that a tiny piece of glass can do that. At Golden Oaks, all the meat is precut, because Hosts are not allowed to wield knives. But Reagan could have slashed open the Coordinator's face with a sliver of glass.

She turns away from the pool and the lifeguard and Jane.

The day has turned ugly. This beautiful day.

"I do not know what to do," Jane says, and she sounds so forlorn Reagan is forced to sit up again. She checks for the Coordinator, who is entering the pool house.

"Look, I'll make you a deal. If you stop acting **erratic,** I'll get Lisa to help."

Jane nods, almost imperceptibly.

"Good. Now I'm going to take a nap. And you should, too. You clearly need sleep."

Reagan folds her arms across her stomach and closes her eyes again even though she knows sleep is impossible. She is too agitated. Everything is too

close, like sitting in the front row of a movie theater: the roar of a jet; the rapid shifting of Jane's
eyeballs under her closed eyelids; the Coordinator,
reemerged into the sun, standing near the towel bin,
thwacking the rolled magazine against her thigh.

Everything inches away. Too clear and too vast.

"It's all good," Reagan says to her friend, but she
is uneasy. The sky overhead is a clear, limpid blue
and yet the day feels suddenly dark. Reagan looks
around the pool—at Jane, at the other Hosts sweating under the sun's hot glare. All these humble,
bloated bodies, and the crushing sky above, and the
shards of glass that may still lie, unnoticed, on
the ground.

LISA'S NOT IN HER ROOM. REAGAN PUSHES ASIDE A PILE OF
clothes on the bed and lies down to wait. It's been
a week since Reagan asked Lisa for help in getting
information about Jane's daughter. Since then,
Jane's become even more frantic. Just this morning
she tried to follow Segundina into a fitness class to
interrogate her about Amalia. Reagan just barely
managed to stop her.

Reagan notices that Lisa's windowsill is clear. She
must have already packed Troy's sculptures. Lisa
was told yesterday that her Clients want her in New
York right away. They managed to book a photo
session with a famous fashion photographer, who

will take pictures of the Boys interacting with (kissing, hugging, palming) Lisa's bare belly.

"Are naked pictures in your contract?" Reagan had joked when Lisa told her she was leaving within twenty-four hours. Inside, Reagan was devastated.

"Honestly, my Clients have seen more of me than Troy has. They're **very** involved in the delivery," Lisa said. "Daddy and Mom stationed at my knees. It's weird, I will not lie to you. Luckily I'm in so much pain I almost don't notice Daddy's got a zoom lens stuffed up my snatch."

She cackled. "You'll see."

Reagan's chest tightened. She wasn't ready to think about it: delivery, delivering. She'd seen countless videos of live births in class, and yet she couldn't imagine the scene with herself in the starring role. Would she cry out or grit her teeth and bear it silently? Would she need stitches? Tasia once told her about a Host who was almost ripped in two, the baby's head was so big.

Would Callie be in the room?

Reagan asked Lisa if she'd return to the Farm after the photo shoot. She was barely thirty-five weeks along, after all. But Lisa responded that the mother was type A "to the extreme" and was worried that Lisa might deliver early, as she did with Baby Two. They were keeping her in New York until she was induced.

"At least they set me up in a swank hotel. The

one all the presidents stay in that's bomb proof. We wouldn't want Baby Three to get bombed." Yawning, she plunked down next to Reagan and, unexpectedly, dropped her head against Reagan's shoulder. They sat in silence, Lisa resting on her friend, her breath growing even. Reagan tried to keep as still as possible, but she couldn't control Callie's son, who kicked inside her. The tightness in Reagan's chest became an ache. She missed Lisa, and Lisa hadn't even left yet.

REAGAN WAKES TO FIND HER FRIEND SITTING AT THE FOOT OF the bed, nudging her and telling her to wake up.

"I'm worried about Jane," Reagan mumbles sleepily.

Lisa doesn't respond. She wears a troubled expression.

"What's wrong?" Reagan sits up. "Did you find out something about Amalia?"

Lisa begins pacing. "Evelyn Arroyo. She's on the Farm's payroll."

Reagan thinks back to what Jane has said in the past about her cousin. "That can't be right. There's **no** way she's a Host. She's old. Like, grandma-old."

"She's a Scout, not a Host."

Reagan looks at Lisa blankly.

"Scouts find Hosts. They're like headhunters. The Farm has a bunch of them on retainer. They've got Scouts for the Philippines, Eastern Europe, South Asia, the islands . . ."

Reagan's mind is racing. Segundina is from the Philippines; Segundina lived in the dorm in Queens; Segundina worked for Jane's cousin.

"We can't tell Jane until she's more stable. She'll do something nuts and get the visit with Amalia canceled . . . unless you think Jane's right? That Evelyn's keeping Amalia from her?"

Dread washes over Reagan. And guilt. She's dismissed Jane's worries about her cousin for weeks.

"I wouldn't put anything past them. I knew this place was rotten, but I honestly had no idea how bad—" Lisa's voice catches. She sits next to Reagan and takes a deep breath.

"What is it?" Reagan asks. "Lisa, you're starting to freak me out."

"Callie—"

Reagan's hand moves to her stomach. The baby. Callie's son.

"She's not your Client. No one I talked to knows who your Client is."

"I don't understand . . ." Reagan's mind is swirling, because she **knows** Callie. They understood each other from the first moment they met.

"I don't, either."

MAE

"CAN YOU GET MY SUNGLASSES?" MAE CROAKS. HER HEAD IS pounding.

Katie pads onto the balcony in an oversized T-shirt and flip-flops. She hands Mae her sunglasses and slumps into the chair opposite her. "Christ, how much did we drink last night?"

Mae shakes her head, taking a gulp from the exorbitantly priced, jumbo-sized bottle of Evian she scavenged from the hotel fridge in the wee hours of the morning. She picks up a cock straw and holds it up against the horizon.

"That about sums it up," Mae states, eyeing

the oversized, pink-tinged plastic boner silhou-
etted against a distant sliver of white sand and blue
ocean. She shakes her head. "I can't believe I used
to be friends with these people."

"They're nice . . ." Katie says amiably. She shakes
two tablets out of an aspirin bottle on the table and
swallows without water.

"They peaked in college."

"But we cared about that stuff in college, too.
You more than I, you"—Katie sniggers, choking on
her water—"Kappa Kappa Gamma poster girl!"

"All right, all right . . ." One of Mae's sorority
sisters unearthed and brought to Miami a sixteen-
year-old pamphlet published by their sorority featuring, as its cover girl, Mae Yu at age twenty. Mae
knows it well. Her mother sent laminated copies
to all her friends and hung a framed copy in their
entryway at home, Mae being her mom's last hope
of achieving the life she felt she was meant to live.

"Those highlights!" Katie begins laughing again.
"You were blonder than I was!"

"How else to fit in with all of your Barbie dolls?"
Mae retorts, but she begins to laugh, too. Her
laughter turns into a fit of coughing and, as Mae
wheezes, she is filled with regret over the pack (or
two? or three?) of cigarettes she chain-smoked the
night before. She hasn't smoked since her early
twenties, and her lungs today feel like they're made
of lead. She also hasn't done tequila shots in a decade; nor has she ever made it a habit—even in her

twenties—of grinding against buzz-cut, shirtless, gold-chain-wearing dudes at cheesy dance clubs 'til two in the morning.

"Honestly, though. No one works anymore. They all leave their kids with their nannies all day and—I don't know—exercise," Mae grouses.

"I leave my kid all day . . ." Katie smiles.

"Yes, but you **work.** I could never stay at home, even with kids. Could you? Could you give up your independence like that? Rely on your husband for literally everything—I mean, not just money, but your entire identity?"

Katie is pensive. Her mother was a stay-at-home mom, like Mae's was, but she actually seemed happy with her choices. Mae spent every Thanksgiving during college but one with the Shaws at their second home in Vermont. It was where she first learned to ski, during an early snowstorm sophomore year. Mae used to marvel at how Mr. and Mrs. Shaw held hands while the family watched movies after dinner, but she also knew marriage was a crapshoot. That Katie's parents had lucked out. Not every couple completes each other.

"I think, if I hadn't started Exceed, if I didn't have something I really believed in—I could be happy staying at home with Rosa," Katie says eventually. "And, obviously, if I didn't need to work for the money."

"Well, **I** couldn't," Mae says emphatically. "I love Ethan, but I'd never put myself in that position. My mom would've left my dad years ago if she could make it on her own."

There is a knock. A muffled voice announcing room service.

"I ordered bacon-and-egg sandies while you were sleeping. And coffee," Katie says. "All on your tab, of course."

"You are **genius**." Mae trails Katie into the bedroom suite.

A young dark-haired man wearing a black jacket and tie rolls a table into the room.

"On the balcony's fine." Mae picks up her bag and fishes inside for tip money.

The waiter pushes the rolling table as close to the balcony as possible and transfers the covered silver trays and the crystal glasses and a bottle of champagne to the wrought-iron table outside. Mae hands him a fifty.

"Do you need change, ma'am?"

"No, I'm set." Mae picks up the champagne bottle by its neck and studies the label. It is a gorgeous Armand de Brignac, the color of liquid gold. She only recognizes it because she shared one once with a Client when she was still running the New York Holloway Club.

"Katie, this is fantastic. Did you order this?"

"No, ma'am," interjects the server. "It was sent to the hotel last evening when you were out. With this card."

He hands Mae a small milk-colored envelope.

She rips it open, anticipation making her hands so clumsy that she tears the note, too. She holds the two pieces of the card together and reads the message, scrawled in Leon's hand:

Congrats, Mae. Assuming all goes well w/the bambinos, she's in for the $. Next up: Project MacDonald. Enjoy the weekend. You deserve it.

A wave of exhilaration spills over Mae. She's landed Madame Deng!

"Let's open it!" Mae cries, handing the bottle to the server.

"Seriously?" asks Katie, glancing at her watch. "It's not even noon . . ."

"It's past noon in China!" Mae, pressing Leon's card to her chest, pirouettes across the carpet. She pulls Katie to the balcony, her heart so full it could burst. Katie is laughing. Mae faces the ocean, the soldierly palm trees, the untrammeled sky. She slings an arm around Katie, stretches wide the other as if trying to embrace the whole gorgeous world.

There is a pop, and the cork whizzes past their shoulders. Champagne fizzes onto the balcony floor. Mae gives a whoop and lifts a glass to be filled. The first one is for Katie, her dearest, most loyal, most beautiful friend. She takes the second glass, stuffs another fifty into the server's palm, and shouts, facing open sea: "A toast!"

"To you and Ethan." Katie squeezes Mae's arm.

"To never peaking!"

"To good friends."

"To the future!"

They clink glasses, splashing champagne—probably a couple hundred dollars' worth, by Mae's reckoning—across the balcony floor.

And they drink.

AN OVERWEIGHT MAN THUMPS PAST MAE, KNOCKING HER outstretched feet with his roller bag. She stares coldly at him, retracting her legs. The hangover from the champagne she and Katie polished off this morning is finally hitting her, and she is grouchy.

"I still don't see why you exchanged the tickets I bought you," she complains. Without them, Katie doesn't have access to BestJet's Premium Lounge, and Mae feels like a jerk leaving Katie alone to wait for her plane in the main terminal.

"I'm smaller than you are. Business class is a waste of money on me." Katie sets her phone down on her lap and digs into the side pocket of her overnight case for earphones.

"Maybe I **wanted** to waste my money on you."

Katie shrugs. A toddler standing on the seat next to Mae begins shouting, and Mae scowls. Katie grins at her. "You don't need to wait with me."

"Of **course** I'm going to wait with you," Mae says. Her flight to New York is two hours after Katie's to L.A. She'll hit the Premium Lounge once Katie has boarded.

Katie's phone buzzes. "Sorry. It's one of our

principals. I've got to take this." She slides ear buds into her ears and stands, mouth moving as she walks away.

Mae watches her for a moment, noting Katie's scuffed flats as she paces around a bank of chairs, the generic leather backpack slung over one shoulder. In college, Mae used to raid Katie's closet for her cashmere sweaters, her superior denim. She wonders if Katie's parents still subsidize her rent.

Her heart twists. There's no fortune to be made in running charter schools, and now Katie and Ric have Rosa to raise. Katie doesn't even have a regular babysitter! Every morning before seven she drops Rosa at daycare on her way to work. She's on duty all weekend while Ric goes to school for his master's. Katie rarely complains, but it must be exhausting.

The shame of it is that Katie could have done anything. She graduated summa cum laude from Trinity, nabbed internships on Capitol Hill and at J.P. Morgan during college. But she was always a save-the-world type. And stubborn. When Mae advised her their senior year to make money first and **then** rescue the downtrodden masses—Katie had offers from two of the premier consulting firms— she only said, **Oh, Mae.** As if Mae were the one being impractical.

Mae should set up a college account for Rosa. She should send Katie and Ric on a getaway weekend, a respite from the grind that is their life. It isn't fair that the fruits of their labor are so skimpy.

They work hard, the two of them, and yet combined they'll make—at best—half of what Mae will make this year. A tenth if Mae's hunch is right and her bonus, what with the Madame Deng deal, is as big as she thinks it will be.

Mae's phone bleeps. It's an update from Geri reporting that all is now copacetic with Jane. The incident over the weekend was slight—a mishap with a water bottle. Geri recommends that Golden Oaks moves to all-plastic drinks bottles out of an abundance of caution. She adds: Jane hasn't tried to approach Segundina in days.

In truth, Mae isn't all that worried, because Jane doesn't have the incentive to court trouble. She needs her bonus, and she loves her daughter. Those two things will keep her in line. And the fact that she took a stand and outed Lisa, who was more or less Jane's friend, shows that Jane is eminently sensible. She won't bite the hand that feeds her.

"Sorry about that." Katie sighs, sliding back into her seat.

"All okay?"

"Yeah. Well, no." Katie runs a hand through her hair. "So, our newest school is 'co-located.' That means we share space with an existing public school. It was a total dropout factory. Its student body's down to, like, half of what it was five years ago."

"Well, that's smart. They probably had excess capacity."

"But it's political, too. The parents of the

existing school are pissed that we're there. They think we're diverting funding away from them—which we aren't, but they don't believe us. Suddenly, we're **the Man,** coming to screw them." Katie laughs ruefully.

"Aren't their kids better off, too, though? I thought that's what the money was for." Mae had made a big donation to Exceed two years ago. She thought it was for school extras that the government couldn't fund—basically everything.

"They are. I mean, **we** think they are. We built this incredible art studio—both schools use it. We're upgrading the school gym . . ."

"They should be grateful you're there!" Mae explodes. She has zero tolerance for ingratitude.

"I guess it's hard, though," Katie muses. "Our kids have laptops and field trips and teachers who actually give a shit, while theirs . . ."

"That's envy, not rational thinking."

"I don't know. Life isn't fair. But it's not always shoved in your face like that. And as a parent . . ."

"I'd like to give my goddaughter a gift," Mae announces abruptly, not interested in yet another debate over inequality with Katie. It's a buzzword so overused it has almost lost its meaning. "I was thinking of a general-education account. Ethan says it's better than a 529 plan because you can use it before college. Like, even for preschool."

"Oh, Mae!" Katie smiles the prettiest smile. "That's so nice of you! But my parents started a

college account for Rosa already. And we'll probably send her to Exceed when she's old enough."

Mae is stunned.

"Katie! You cannot—you **cannot**—send Rosa to
one of your schools!" She glances at Katie to see if
she's crossed a line, but Katie looks unperturbed.
"You know what I mean. The kids at your schools
aren't **like** her. It's an insane idea."

"Ric and I are still discussing it."

"It's preposterous!" Mae cries. A parent's job is to
give her child the best she possibly can.

"We think our schools are pretty good."

"You know I think what you and Ric are doing
is important," Mae says. "But you can't jeopardize
Rosa's future for abstract ideals that—"

"They aren't abstract to us."

"You can believe in something and not **act** on it!"
Katie raises an eyebrow.

"All of us do it every day," Mae snaps. "How
many people believe in . . . I don't know . . . fighting terrorism but don't enlist in the army? Or feel
bad when they see a homeless guy in the subway
but then get out at Fifty-ninth and buy an overpriced handbag instead of donating to charity . . ."

"We haven't decided anything yet. But we're leaning toward sending her to Exceed," Katie says with
a firmness that signals the end of the conversation.
Mae bristles.

A woman's voice cuts through the airport hubbub
and announces that Katie's flight to Los Angeles will

begin boarding momentarily. Katie announces that she needs a coffee. Mae watches her friend weave through the airport throng in the opposite direction of her departure gate. The nearest coffee stand is halfway down the terminal. If she misses her plane, Mae will force her to accept a business-class ticket back to California, and they will wait together in the Premium Lounge where the air doesn't smell like McDonald's and the coffee is organic, and free.

A disembodied voice announces preboarding. Mae watches the young couples tugging small children through the mob of waiting passengers. Her phone pings—Ethan asking if she'll be back in time for dinner with his boss. The bank where he works has been laying off traders left and right— like everyone else, they're pouring money into artificial intelligence—and Ethan wants Mae to help him ingratiate himself with his boss. She texts him a thumbs-up emoji and thanks her lucky stars that rich people like to be catered to by actual humans. Robots will never run Golden Oaks.

There is another announcement that boarding for BestJet's Platinum members is about to begin. Mae texts Katie to hurry. She then swipes her phone and opens the Bergdorf website. She is looking for nude heels. Her rehearsal-dinner dress is a vivid scarlet, and any other color will clash—except, now that she thinks of it, gold. A matte gold. Nothing sparkly.

The crowd clustered around the ticket agent parts to allow BestJet's First Class passengers to board, followed by its Gold-Level members, Business-Class travelers, Silver Medallion, and finally its Elite ones. With each subsequent boarding announcement, Mae pauses from her shoe quest to scan the terminal for Katie.

When she finally returns to the gate, Mae scolds her for cutting it so close.

"You've forgotten how long it takes to board Economy," Katie teases, handing her a Styrofoam cup.

Mae throws her arms around her friend and squeezes. "Thanks for my tea. And thank you for coming."

"I wouldn't have missed it for anything," Katie answers, pulling back from Mae's embrace so she can look Mae in the eye. "I know it took you a while to come around to the whole marriage thing. And it's not always easy—but worthwhile things never are. And Ethan's wonderful."

"He is," Mae agrees, knowing it's true. Ethan is kind and good and steady. Since she met him at HBS, he's never once disappointed her.

"And depending on someone can be pretty nice," Katie adds.

Mae watches her friend walk to the back of a long line, where she begins to chat with the harried-looking woman in front of her. The woman pushes a cheap stroller in which a baby wails; two toddlers in matching basketball jerseys flank her and, jointly, try to yank up her shirt.

Dear God. Why do parents let their children run

amok like that? When Ethan and Mae have kids, they're going to raise them old-school.

Katie leans down to speak to the toddlers. They grudgingly release their mother's shirt. Katie then takes one in each hand and leads them, with the other trailing behind, to the front of the line. She speaks with the airline attendant, who takes their tickets.

Katie turns to wave at Mae.

"Brilliant!" Mae shouts to her above the airport's din, flashing a thumbs-up sign.

Katie shakes her head. Mae can almost see her mouthing, **Oh, Mae.** As if Katie didn't just find a way to cut to the front of the line.

"Love you!" Mae shouts. Her friend lifts one of the now-crying toddlers into her arms and waves, the sobbing child waving tentatively along with her, and they disappear down the jetway.

JANE

"HELLO?"

Jane did not expect anyone to pick up the phone. She called her apartment again because she cannot simply sit still, knowing what she now knows.

"Hello?" asks the voice again.

"Who is this?" Jane asks. The voice is not Ate's. It could be one of the Filipinas she allows to live in Jane's apartment before she sends them to Ms. Yu. Maybe Ate charges them for the bed, which is actually Jane's bed. Ate will make money any way that she can.

"This is Angel."

"Angel!" Jane is momentarily relieved.

"Jane? Are you still in California?"

"Yes. I—"

"Is the baby easy?" Angel asks, though she sounds preoccupied.

"Yes, very easy," Jane lies. "Angel, I need to speak to Ate."

"Ate is not here," Angel answers after a pause. "I am only watching Amalia for a little while, because Ate has things to do."

"What things?" Jane demands, trying to contain her anger. It is not Angel's fault that Ate has left Amalia again.

"Ah, you know Ate. Always busy! She has many cooking jobs." Angel laughs a forced-sounding laugh.

"So, she is always leaving Mali with you?" There is an explosion inside Jane, white and searing, because if Ms. Yu is paying Ate, why does she still abandon Amalia for other jobs? Does her cousin think of nothing in the world but money?

"No, not **always,** Jane! She is only busy today!"

Jane hears a childish yelp, and her heart lurches. "Is that Mali?"

"Yes, Amalia just had a nap. Ate put her on a sleep routine. Now I am letting her watch a little **Sesame Street.** Elmo is her favorite."

"How is she, Angel? I see her only in videos, because Ate does not call."

"She is healthy. And headstrong!" Angel chuckles, and Jane feels a trickle of relief.

Jane asks Angel if they can video-call. She wants to see Amalia in real life with her own eyes. Angel apologizes: her cellphone is not working; she is behind in her payments again.

"But I will see if Amalia will talk to you now."

Jane hears fumbling, the sound of tinny voices from the television, Angel's lowered voice trying to coax Amalia into speaking. Jane presses the phone to her ear. She can hear—she thinks she can hear—Amalia breathing, and her eyes grow wet. "Mali. It is Mama."

Angel's voice is cajoling. "Ma-Ma. Ma-Ma. Like we practiced!"

"Mama loves you, Mali," Jane whispers, her chest too small for all it holds.

There is more fumbling, muffled voices. Almost as if Angel is talking to someone in the room.

"No more TV. Talk to Mama," she hears Angel announce suddenly. The background jangle of the television stops.

"No-o!" Amalia protests. Angel is urging Amalia to hold the phone.

"No!" Amalia shouts again, followed by: "Eh-mo! Eh-mo!"

"No Elmo until you speak to Mama," Angel admonishes. Amalia begins to cry, and there is a thud and a clattering, and Angel is reprimanding Amalia for throwing the phone across the room.

"You almost hit Ate!" is what Jane hears.

Ate?

"I am sorry, Jane," Angel says into the receiver, slightly out of breath. "Amalia is cranky."

In the background, Amalia bawls.

"Angel. Is Ate there?"

"Ate?" Angel echoes, as if she does not recognize the name. She hesitates, and the words rush from her: "No, Jane! I already told you: Ate is busy with a cooking job! She is not here!"

"Did you not just say that Amalia almost hit Ate?"

"No!" Angel answers too quickly. "I was telling her not to throw the phone like that. She throws things. She has a hot head, Jane! Always losing her head, especially when she is sleepy!"

"Why is she sleepy if she just napped?" Jane asks, because did Angel not just say this? That Amalia had only woken from a nap? That she is on the sleep routine?

"Ye-es . . . she did nap," Angel answers, flustered. "But it was . . . ah . . . not a good nap. It is that Amalia has a cold. She is congested . . . It is difficult to sleep when a baby is congested."

"But did you not just say Amalia is healthy?" Jane cries, engulfed.

"She has an ear infection," Angel admits.

"Another one! Her fourth?" Amalia has had at least three ear infections since Jane left for Golden Oaks.

"I do not know about the other ones," says Angel matter-of-factly.

"But you told me she is not sick!" Jane is furious. Because why is Angel saying one thing and then its exact opposite?

"She is a healthy girl!"

"But you **just said** she has an ear infection!"

Jane is met with silence. She fears, for a moment, that Angel has hung up the phone.

"Angel. Do you hear me? Angel! Did you take her temperature?"

"Babies get ear infections!" Angel cries, exasperated. There is a scrabbling sound, like Angel is digging a hole. Amalia still wails in the background.

"Angel?"

But Angel does not answer. She is not listening to Jane. There is only an indiscernible murmur, rising and falling.

"Mali?"

"I put Amalia in her playpen," Angel answers, her voice crisp.

"Who were you talking to? Just now?"

"No one!" Angel retorts.

"Just now. You were talking to someone—"

"That was only the TV!"

But did she not just turn the TV off?

"I have to change Amalia. Her diaper is full. You call us later. Okay? We will call you later!"

Jane does not even have time to say goodbye.

And how can Angel call Jane when she does not have a phone number?

Jane dials her apartment again and listens to the phone ring. She lets it ring ten times. Twenty. Thirty.

But Angel is stubborn.

JANE BURIES HERSELF UNDER HER BLANKETS, HUGGING HER knees to her chest tighter and tighter still, as if compressing herself will shrink the fear inside her. She has tried to call her apartment two more times since she spoke with Angel this morning, but no one answers.

When Lisa and Reagan told Jane the truth about Ate a week ago, they first asked her to sit down. Reagan took her hand, and Lisa stood by the door, as if Jane might try to flee. But what could she have done, even if she ran?

"Scouts excel at finding prospects who are rule-followers, secret-keepers, nontroublemakers," Lisa said.

A strange sensation rattled Jane as Lisa spoke—as she learned of her cousin's betrayal. It was as if she were being picked clean and left bare. A brutal bareness, but one that left her clear-minded. Because it made sense. Ate would do anything for money.

"You are right," she said to Reagan. "Everything has strings."

Now Jane knows it is worse than she'd thought. Amalia is sick. After the phone call with Angel this morning, Jane rushed to the media room and researched **chronic ear infections** on the Internet.

She learned that left untreated, they can cause paralysis in the face and then spread to the brain! Jane immediately pulled up the pictures and videos Ate sent over the weeks. Dozens upon dozens, and Jane studied them all. In the more recent pictures, she noticed Amalia looked pale. In the videos, her face seemed rigid, and she was too subdued.

It is Ate's fault. She has been too busy with her business schemes to pay attention to Amalia. She has been leaving her niece with strangers, Filipinas fresh off the boat who do not know what they are doing, who might be sick themselves.

But it is Jane's fault, too. She learned from the Internet that the best way to prevent chronic ear infections is to breast-feed your baby for its entire first year of life. Jane did not do this. She left Amalia for Mrs. Carter, and then she left her again for GoldenOaks.

Jane envisions Amalia. In her mind's eye her daughter is tiny—like the wrinkled things from the videos they are forced to watch in class, the ones filmed in intensive care: babies in see-through pods that keep them warm, pump air into their half-formed lungs. A warning to the Hosts about what could happen if they did not take care of the babies inside them.

Jane has to find Amalia. She has to take care of her daughter, too—not only this baby inside her. Because if she does not, who will?

———

EVE IS SORTING CREAM-COLORED CARDS INTO STACKS, humming.

"Ms. Yu needs to see me?" Jane asks, tilting her wrist so that Eve can see the message from Ms. Yu on the face of her WellBand.

"Go on in. She's finishing up with another Host. She'll be in soon."

Jane enters Ms. Yu's office but does not sit. She does not know why she has been summoned. She fears Ms. Yu somehow learned of her conversation with Reagan and Lisa last week. Or perhaps Ate, who has no loyalty, reported that Jane is unstable, that she shouted at Angel this morning and must be watched.

"Do you want a drink?" Eve pipes from the doorway.

Jane declines. She notices a small dome of glass on the coffee table in front of her and picks it up, pretends to study it so that Eve will leave her alone. Trapped inside the glass is a fragment of New York City. The buildings are rendered in such detail that Jane, despite the drumming of her heart, cannot help but admire the workmanship: the tiny windows punctured in the miniature skyscrapers, the fish scales of the Chrysler building gleaming silver.

"Those are for Ms. Yu's wedding. She's picking party favors. She's deciding between that and something from Tiffany's," Eve says airily.

Ms. Yu sweeps into the room. Her hair, as always, is gathered in a loose bun at the nape of her neck, and today she also wears glasses.

"Hi, Jane." Ms. Yu waves at Eve to dismiss her. "I'm sorry I'm late. There's an issue with another Host . . . another **two** Hosts, actually. Not everyone's as easygoing as you are!"

Jane returns the paperweight to the table.

"What do you think?" Ms. Yu asks. When Jane does not answer, she continues gaily, "If you look closely, you can see the building where my fiancé and I are getting married."

Jane does not look closely. She does not look at the paperweight at all.

"Please sit, Jane. By me." Ms. Yu pats the chair next to her. "How are you?"

Jane fights to keep her voice steady. "I'm fine. The baby is healthy."

"Yes, you've been doing a wonderful job," Ms. Yu remarks. Her warm smile leaves Jane cold. "I hope you know, Jane, how much I appreciate your attitude and your help. I don't think I ever explicitly thanked you for letting me know about Lisa and Julio."

Jane lowers her eyes. She looks at Mae's hand. The ring on her finger is a new one, with a blue stone the size of a dime.

"And that only makes what I'm about to tell you more painful," Ms. Yu says. "We have to cancel Amalia's visit. The Client has gotten cold feet. I'm . . . I'm so sorry, Jane."

Jane studies her hands, the hangnails and chapped skin, hiding her eyes from Ms. Yu because she is afraid Ms. Yu will see the terror in them. Because this can only mean that Amalia is much sicker than Jane had feared. She is too sick to travel, and they will never let Jane go to her. Because the Billionaire Baby comes first, and hospitals teem with sick people and viruses with no cure.

"I—I understand," Jane whispers. Because she does.

"Of course you do. You're a real professional. I wish every Host were like you! My job would be so much simpler!"

"Thank you." Jane stands. She can no longer remain in this office with this woman. "Is that all?"

"Yes, it is." Ms. Yu takes Jane's hand as she turns to leave. Her eyes shimmer. "I'll continue to try my best to get you a visit with Amalia. I give you my word. Don't give up hope."

Jane's voice is stony. "I have not given up hope."

MAE

TEAM UPDATE

cc: Becca, Geri, Fiona, Maddie, Ana

Had an update call with Madame Deng this morning (four-thirty a.m. EST—get me another coffee!). She is pleased with the results from 82 and 84.

Topic broached by Deng's team: implantation of more of Deng's less-viable embryos. 96 as test case—but do we wait and see or move forward? Let's convene Monday to discuss. Be prepared to share your recommendation, pros/cons.

Off the top of my head, pros: revenue upside; Client satisfaction. Cons: will likely damage our track record for "successful implantations," which impacts marketing and future Clients. Unless we segment track-record into Viable Implants versus Second-Tier ones? Also, potential ethical considerations (be prepared to discuss).

Quickly: 84 handled news of visit cancellation well. The cancellation was unavoidable due to illness.

Need to find a "carrot" to compensate 84 (for visit cancellation; for good behavior since Tick Episode). Considering an outing. Some ideas: a concert (does she like music?), expensive restaurant (does she like Thai? Chinese?), play? Should we include 82? A "girls night out"? May make 84 more comfortable to include a peer; authority figures make her visibly nervous.

Keep up the good work.

My best,

Mae

PS Another agenda item for Monday. Please review attached studies. We discussed this trend at last month's "big-picture" powwow: wealth and empathy inversely correlated, ie: the richer you are, the less empathetic. New studies out from Stanford and Chicago. Prepare for brainstorming session on how these learnings should inform our modus operandi, esp. our dealings with Clients vis-à-vis Hosts. Does this argue for increased usage of Stand-In Clients to build rapport? etc.

REAGAN

"YOU WARMING UP FOR YOUR WALK?" THE COORDINATOR behind the desk asks.

Reagan looks up at her, confused.

"You're going to wear a path in that rug!"

Reagan had not noticed she was pacing. She forces a smile, but her mind is on Callie. On who she is and what she's hiding. **Whom** she's hiding.

Why would her Client work so hard to hide her identity? What does it mean?

A Host approaches the desk. Black hair, tan skin, a face of flat planes and angles. Reagan recognizes but doesn't know her.

"Oh, Amita. There you are. You okay being Reagan's buddy?" chirps the Coordinator. She chatters about how fresh air is the best cure for morning sickness as she takes Amita by the wrist and swipes her WellBand into the reader.

"You'll want to tie your hair back," the Coordinator remarks, handing Amita a hairband. "And tuck the ponytail into your jacket . . . It'll be harder to find ticks on you, because of your coloring."

Once the Coordinator is satisfied, Reagan and Amita walk outside. It is unseasonably cold. All morning it rained, short bursts followed by long lulls. Amita pulls the hood of her waterproof jacket tighter around her head, but Reagan flings it off, glad for the wetness on her face.

"Is this your first time carrying?" Reagan asks, to distract herself from thinking about Callie. Whoever Callie is.

"Yes," Amita answers. She tells Reagan that she is seven weeks along and the morning sickness has been bad. She adds, quickly, that the discomfort is a small price to pay for such a good job with such good pay.

"And you?" Amita asks. They are now walking on the path, and their shoes crunch on loose gravel. Around them water drips from the trees.

Reagan answers that it's also her first time carrying and that she's already in her third trimester. As she speaks, her stomach lurches.

"And you carry what kind of baby?" Amita picks her way around a puddle.

Reagan sloshes through it. "I—"

She stops.

She carries what kind of baby?

Only a week ago, Reagan knew the answer; she would have announced it with pride: I carry Callie's son. He's smart, stubborn, and a little wild. Every day I wish him well a thousand times in a thousand different ways, towers of wishes, like cairns on a mountainside—that he will be healthy and upright and strong; that he will steer clear of trouble and ugliness and bad neighborhoods and racist cops; that he will use his plenty to repair the world.

But what does Reagan really know about anything? She doesn't even know what kind of baby lies within her—boy or girl. Black or white or blue. Stubborn or docile, smart or stupid. Whether it's the offspring of a self-made millionaire or a murderous dictator. Or a billionaire enriched by manufacturing bombs or one of those oily pharmaceutical-company bosses, jacking up the prices on lifesaving drugs so she can buy a private jet while millions sicken. Or a Middle Eastern autocrat who won't let his girls go to school, who rejoiced when Malala was shot in the head. Or a fat-cat financier who peddled bad mortgages to uneducated Floridians and bought an island in the Caribbean while their homes were foreclosed on.

She only knows the baby's mother isn't "Callie,"

and she has no way of finding out more: Lisa is gone, and Reagan trusts no one else at the Farm besides Jane.

"Callie" with the rumbly laugh and off-color jokes that made Reagan laugh so hard she cried. "Callie" who managed to get Mom an appointment with the best Alzheimer's specialist in the country and who brought Reagan a book of Arbus's pictures and inscribed it: **With love and gratitude.**

Was that even her handwriting?

What kind of person fakes this?

Amita is still waiting for Reagan to answer her question. A squirrel darts across their path and up a tree. "Does your Client keep the baby's sex a surprise?"

"Yes," Reagan says, feeling sick. "My Client likes surprises."

IT BEGINS TO RAIN WHEN AMITA AND REAGAN ARE ABOUT TWO hundred yards from the Farm. A drizzle and then a downpour, the indifferent sky a dirty white.

"Do you mind?" Amita asks, bracing herself against the wind, which has begun to gust.

"Of course not."

Amita streaks across the gravel and grass to the back entrance, the one closest to the examination rooms. At the doorway she calls to Reagan to hurry.

The rain is coming down heavier, but Reagan doesn't pick up her pace. She leaves her hood down and her jacket unzipped so that it flaps in the wind.

The world is blurry through the thick rain, rivulets coursing down her neck. She removes the elastic band from her hair so that it hangs tangled long and wet, like seaweed.

A Coordinator is waiting for Reagan under the eaves, exuding impatience. She holds the door open and pushes Reagan inside, squawking at her (hurry! the baby! soaked!), as if a little water could do the baby any harm. As if the baby weren't bobbing in liquid already. The Coordinator hands Reagan a towel and robe, sighing dramatically. She swipes Reagan's WellBand and sends her to a room to dry off.

The examination room is even colder than it is outside. Reagan leaves her sodden clothes in a lump on the floor. She doesn't put on her robe. Her body is slick, water dripping from her like rain off wet leaves. She spreads herself on the exam table, allows herself to pool on the stiff leather that covers it.

She stares at the mobile suspended above her head. Red ovals and black swirls. Inside her, the baby moves, and for the first time since she met Callie, Reagan does not feel tenderness for him.

For it.

Is the baby even a boy, or was the ultrasound staged, too?

Whose baby is this?

And what is the meaning—of the nausea and migraines and back pain and swollen feet, of the tears she shed when she first heard its heartbeat or the pride that filled her when its kicks grew strong—if it is, all of it, a sham?

Reagan's heartbeat picks up speed as she comes to a decision. A thrum of anticipation, because she knows now what is right.

She's going to help Jane. She's going to help Jane find her daughter.

She doesn't care if she breaks her contract, gets sued, loses every cent of her bonus. She won't let the Farm, nor Ms. Yu, nor Jane's billionaire Client use Amalia, a mere child, as a pawn. Or leverage. As punishment or reward.

"How're you doing, Reagan?" asks the nurse. She is trailed by an assistant, who shuts the door.

Reagan spreads her legs without being asked. "Cold and wet, but very well, thanks."

Reagan smiles calmly. She can do this, too.

"That's the spirit!" says the nurse, smiling back. She places her hands on Reagan's ankles, and Reagan doesn't recoil. Only spreads her legs wider as the nurse leans toward her, pale eyes skittering over Reagan's cold skin.

THE LIBRARY IS WARM, THE CRACKLING OF SINGED WOOD AND a smoky smell that reminds Reagan of Thanksgiving. She checks her watch. After the walk with Amita and the horrible tick check, Reagan went to find Jane. She wanted to start strategizing right away, but Jane was late for her weekly prenatal massage.

Jane only managed to tell her that Amalia was very sick, and they didn't have much time.

"I must find my daughter soon," Jane whispered, just before a Coordinator appeared to berate her for keeping the masseuse waiting.

Reagan stares into the fire. Its red-rimmed leap and curl.

How will she get Jane out of the Farm so quickly? Without money, without transportation? And the WellBands tracking every move?

She doesn't see a way to pull it off without help from someone on the outside. Macy, ideally; she would jump at the chance. But how can Reagan reach her without tipping off Ms. Yu? Every call, every email coming out of the media room is recorded. There is no other way (is there any other way?) to send a message to the outside world.

The only answer is to find someone at the Farm to help them. Reagan reels through the possibilities: the Coordinators, the nurses, the kitchen staff, the cleaners. The groundskeepers, the security guards, the nurse's aides, the receptionists. So many people, and she doesn't know any of them. Certainly not well enough to ask for help.

How can it be, when she has been at the Farm for so long, that the only non-Host who knows her at all, who feels any sort of warmth toward her, is Ms. Yu?

And Ms. Yu is a liar.

Out of nowhere, Reagan yearns for Lisa. Her foul mouth and irreverence. Lisa who is obnoxious, unsympathetic, and rude, who rubs so many at the Farm the wrong way. Yet who has friends here—real friends who would risk themselves for her. And not just other Hosts. And not just through plying sex, although there is that.

Lisa would know whom to trust. But she's gone, swept away to New York by her lying Client three days ago when Reagan was at a fitness class. Reagan didn't even get to say goodbye. Lisa had warned her this might happen. The Farm hates goodbyes—too fraught, too often complicated by overemotional Hosts.

Reagan covers her face with her hands, willing an epiphany. Thinking so hard her head hurts and wondering if Dad is right, if she's the kind of person who likes humanity in the abstract but has little interest in actual people. He always tells her that feeling sorry for people isn't the same as loving them, much less helping them.

But at least she tries. At least she notices.

Reagan retreats to her room. She needs to write out the possibilities. She thinks better on the page—a visual learner, as Mom used to say when she taught Reagan how to make study cards to prepare for tests in school.

There's a sheet of paper on Reagan's bed attached to a leaflet from a local theater. The note from

Ms. Yu says that Callie "raved" about their outing and is inviting Reagan on another one. A play in a few days in Great Barrington. **My Fair Lady.**

Are you up for it? Ms. Yu writes, although it isn't an invitation but a command.

Reagan tosses the note aside and sits on her bed.

The beginnings of panic, a dark bird fluttering.

She yanks open the drawer of her nightstand, rummaging among the loose paper and cast-off pens for her notebook. She flips through the pages covered in lists to her latest entry: notes on MFA programs strong in photography next to a list of business schools Dad says are strong in "art markets and cultural management."

She turns to the notebook's first blank page, or what should be the first blank page. But it isn't blank.

In blue ink, scrawled in script that is not hers:

Infinite Slog 40

Lisa's handwriting, Lisa's joke. Reagan's been trying to finish the book the entire time she's been at the Farm.

"Only a true narcissist thinks he has that much that's interesting to say," Lisa liked to needle her.

Reagan walks to the window and draws the curtains closed, her heart banging. She takes **Infinite Jest** from her bookshelf. For a moment, she simply presses her palm against its creased blue cover.

With a deep breath, she flips to page 40. In the margin, in pencil, Lisa has jotted a website address. Next to it: **Comments?** On page 41, another website address. A website about photography. A website about early-onset dementia. Websites that Reagan might peruse anyway, where Reagan could type comments without attracting anyone's attention.

Reagan closes the book and hugs it to her chest, thinking of the play, wondering if it could work. And for the first time all day, she smiles.

JANE

MS. YU IS TELLING JANE ABOUT **MY FAIR LADY**. IT IS A PLAY, says Ms. Yu, though it was made famous by a musical. A movie-musical really, from Hollywood's heyday, starring Ms. Yu's favorite actress. Audrey Someone. She was the epitome of elegance; but Ms. Yu digresses! She wants to talk to Jane about a local production at a little playhouse in the Berkshires, not far from Golden Oaks . . .

Jane is trying halfheartedly to follow what Ms. Yu is saying, but her mind today is like a fly. Flitting in circles, landing only to buzz upward again. She does not know why Ms. Yu called her into the office. She is careful to expect nothing and everything at the same time. She fears that, somehow, Ms. Yu can sense that Jane is changed. That she is, on the inside, a different kind of person.

With a start, Jane remembers that Reagan told her to pay attention. What Ms. Yu says might be important. Jane is not sure how, but she trusts her friend, and she forces herself to listen. Ms. Yu is now talking about different theater companies in the area, including an incredible one that focuses on Shakespeare, but Ms. Yu thought that Shakespeare might be too hard for Jane to follow, what with the old English.

Jane tries not to think about Ate and Angel—Reagan warns that if Jane seems distressed she might raise suspicions—but it is not easy. Jane cannot help but wonder how much Angel knows about Golden Oaks and Ate's relationship with it; whether Angel, too, thinks Jane is a sheep to be led.

Above all, she wonders when Ate decided that Jane was a product to sell. Was it in the months after Ate had to stop baby nursing, or earlier? When Ate counseled Jane to leave Billy, helping her move to the dorm in Queens, even paying for Jane's bunk—was that an act of kindness or part of a bigger plan?

Jane is afraid that she is losing her grip on herself. In her room in the dead of night, when all is quiet except the hum of the air purifier, she cries—violent, ugly cries with her face mashed against her pillow. Sometimes the terror is so big that she cries without tears, a silent anguish, doubled over like something vital has been torn from her body.

Jane can see Amalia in these moments. Nurses hover over her but they each carry Ate's face, and they are not caretakers but Ate-faced guards.

Ate—who greeted Jane at LaGuardia Airport when she arrived with Billy from California, young and unsure and stupid with love. Ate who scolded her for not finishing high school, who believed she could do better.

"I think you'd really like it," Ms. Yu is saying.

Jane's eyes dart to Ms. Yu. What is it she would really like? And how could Ms. Yu know?

"The story may have resonance for you," Ms. Yu continues, "because the main character, Eliza Doolittle—isn't that a terrific name?—raises herself up. She goes from a life with few prospects to one with many. The way you're doing." Ms. Yu brings her teacup to her lips and looks at Jane with raised eyebrows, as if waiting for an answer.

Uncertain of the proper response—why did Jane not pay attention?—Jane says: "It sounds interesting."

"So you'll come along tomorrow?"

Jane hesitates.

"Reagan will be at the show with her Client, too. It'll be frivolous, but fun. A girls' outing."

Jane's interest is piqued. Is this what Reagan meant when she said Ms. Yu might tell her something helpful? Is this part of Reagan's plan?

She lowers her eyes to hide the turmoil in them,

hope mingled with fear and the smallest flicker of defiance. "Thank you, Ms. Yu. It will be my first play."

"It's my pleasure," says Ms. Yu. Her voice softens. "Jane, I still feel terrible that we had to postpone your visit with Amalia. I know nothing can compensate for how much you miss her, but I hope this outing can take your mind off things for a night."

Jane still averts her eyes. As if a play will make her forget her daughter.

She responds in a quiet voice. "I do not worry about Amalia, because my cousin Evelyn is taking care of her. She is a top baby nurse. Evelyn Arroyo."

When Jane utters Ate's name she looks into Ms. Yu's eyes.

Ms. Yu gazes placidly at Jane, not even blinking. A smile washes over her face, and she exclaims, "I look forward to finally meeting her when we reschedule Amalia's visit!"

Jane stares at Ms. Yu disbelievingly. The radiance of her smile, the naturalness of the lies that fall one after the other from her wicked mouth. There is no way a person like this will allow Jane to see her daughter. Not until Jane has safely delivered the Billionaire Baby. And by then, it could be too late.

LATER, REAGAN CONGRATULATES JANE FOR KEEPING HER COOL. She is almost giddy, bouncing around her bedroom in her bathrobe and explaining to Jane that the play **was** her idea. It is part of her plan. Reagan knew she had to get Jane out of the Farm somehow. She suggested inviting Jane to Ms. Yu yesterday without knowing whether Ms. Yu would bite.

"And she bit!" Reagan crows, doing an exuberant jig before finally sitting down on the rocking chair near the window.

"You will be there also," Jane states, shivering. She has felt cold ever since she left Ms. Yu's office, even though it is a hot day.

"With my fake Client."

"And then . . . ?"

"Well, I haven't fully hashed that out yet. But getting you out of the Farm is the first step. The hardest step," Reagan assures her.

Jane's heart plummets. This is the plan? To go to a play?

Reagan, noticing Jane's expression, rushes to her side. "Don't **worry,** Jane. I'm going to the media room now to get in touch with Lisa. We don't have much time, but she's way ahead of us. She's been laying the groundwork for some kind of escape ever since she found out about Callie and your cousin. You know how paranoid Lisa is. And she hates this place."

Jane smiles along with Reagan, feigning an optimism she does not feel. She watches her friend dress herself with a growing sense of despair. Jane is grateful to her, of course, for wanting to help. But she worries, watching Reagan hum as she pulls on socks, that Reagan is too optimistic, too trusting that things always work out for the best. She also worries that Lisa, free now of her Clients and rich with the bonus from her delivery, might already have forgotten how smart Ms. Yu is, how she notices everything.

If Jane runs, will they not catch her?

And if they catch her, what then?

"I'm off," Reagan announces, jaunty.

"Remember: they can read what you email," Jane warns.

"I'm just going to surf the Web. Post a few **comments** on some websites . . ." Reagan rests her hand on the knob and turns to Jane. "This is going to work. I can feel it. You'll be with Amalia in no time."

JANE TUGS AT THE SWEATER THAT BARELY BUTTONS OVER HER stomach. She is wearing a dress. Reagan made her put it on.

"You have to seem **excited,** Jane. Ms. Yu has to believe you're looking forward to this . . . this 'treat,'" admonishes Reagan, leaning over Jane with a lip pencil.

Jane cannot answer, because Reagan begins coloring her mouth.

"You have to get Ms. Yu to let her guard down. This is your first play, right? Act like you're thrilled about it. Otherwise, none of this will work—oh, crap," Reagan drops the pencil. Her hands are jittery. She is nervous, too.

"I will. I will act eager," Jane assures Reagan,

watching her retrieve the pencil, feeling a surge of affection for her.

"And grateful. Ms. Yu eats up gratitude." Reagan scrutinizes Jane's face. Jane squirms.

"You look pretty," Reagan concludes. She plucks a jar of pale cream and another one of pale powder from her makeup bag. "But you look tired. Stay still, and I'll make your eyes look brighter."

Jane makes her face immovable as Reagan uses her pinky to pat cream beneath Jane's eyes, trying to erase the dark circles there. Jane was up all night turning the plan around in her head: Does she really have the courage to risk it? Will it really work? But then she would think of Amalia, and her worries for herself would balloon into terror for her daughter. Because Jane is running out of time.

She knows this because, last night, she tried to reach Ate one final time. It was early evening, after the long huddled talk with Reagan; after sitting with the Filipina Hosts for a dinner that Jane could barely force down her throat. She slipped away before dessert to go to the media room. It was almost empty because most Hosts were still eating or making their way to the screening room, where a romance-comedy featuring two famous Hollywood actors was playing.

In one of the cubicles Jane dialed Ate's number, but her call went to voicemail. Her call to Angel ended the same way. Then Jane had the idea of trying the phone line at the dorm in Queens. Why had she not thought of this before? She had to run back to her bedroom to look up the phone number in the date book she kept in her nightstand.

A man's voice Jane did not recognize answered after only two rings.

"I am waiting for a call from Manila," he said impatiently.

"I only need a minute to speak to Angel. Angel Calapatia. Do you know her? She—"

Before Jane could finish, the man interrupted: "She went to Queens hospital."

"She is sick?" Jane felt as if her heart had stopped.

"No, no," the man answered, exasperated. "She went with the baby. The little girl—ay, that is my phone call. My cousin—"

Jane does not remember hanging up the phone. She does not remember how she made it to Reagan's room. She was suddenly there and asked Reagan, simply: "Do you believe this can work?"

Reagan said yes. And that was enough.

THE THEATER IS SMALL BUT BEAUTIFUL. THEY SIT IN THE second row, middle section: Ms. Yu nearest to the aisle, then Jane, then Reagan's Client and Reagan. In front of them, on a small sunken platform, perches a group of musicians. They are bunched in a semicircle, like a huddle of birds around a heel of bread. Immense scarlet curtains stretch heavily across the stage. Jane imagines commotion behind them, actors tiptoeing to their places, helpers rushing around with props.

Jane fans herself with her program even though she is not hot. It gives her hands something to do. She glances up at the ceiling, white and gold and carved into intricate patterns, three large chandeliers floating above their heads like stars.

"Excited?" asks Ms. Yu, giving Jane's arm a squeeze.

"Yes. Thank you, Ms. Yu." Jane tries to make her voice lively.

"I'm so glad I could bring you to your first play. And you look so nice!"

One of the Coordinators—there are two of them, they rode in a separate car to the theater—appears and whispers something in Ms. Yu's ear. Jane turns away to make it clear she has no intention of eavesdropping. Next to her, Reagan's Client is speaking to Reagan in hushed tones. The Client—Callie, she told Jane to call her—laughs suddenly, low and throaty, and Jane once again feels a pinprick of doubt about Lisa's information. How can this woman—who is so nice, with the type of laugh that makes you feel like laughing also—be a fake?

The lights begin to dim. Someone coughs. A strand of music wafts upward from the pit in front of them, a lone violin, and then a gathering. The curtains part. Jane senses Ms. Yu's eyes on her, and she puts a half smile on her face.

Her stomach drops, because it is beginning.

The stage is filled with flowers. Flowers in carts,

flowers in tubs. A spill of them. Behind the flower stalls there are buildings of stone, painted of course, but they look real, and behind them the sky. Marbled and gray. A woman is selling flowers, shouting. A man in a suit, a tall hat, crosses her path and they begin to speak. Jane is struck by the strangeness of it all, of sitting in the darkness watching an illuminated world onstage. And all those flowers.

She feels suddenly a great disquiet, as if she herself is what is unreal, and not the actors going about their business onstage. As if this plot of Reagan's is part of an act, too: impossible and unbelievable.

Can it be that in an hour's time Jane will attempt to walk out of the theater doors and disappear?

"Are you following the storyline?" Ms. Yu whispers, leaning close.

Jane realizes she has been frowning. She smooths her brow, turns to Ms. Yu, and feigns confusion. "I am not sure who the men are."

Ms. Yu explains in a whisper what is happening onstage. The men are wealthy and educated, and the flower girl is poor and ignorant; the men will try to better her.

Jane thanks Ms. Yu and fixes her eyes straight ahead of her. She tries to pay attention, but she cannot absorb a word. There is only a quickening inside, a growing dread.

The audience titters, and Jane titters.

The audience is rapt, and Jane is rapt.

Minutes pass, and more minutes. Jane's heart

beats faster. Intermission must be around the corner. She feels as if she is trapped in a dream. She digs her nails into her palms, harder still so that what she feels is pain, sharp and solid.

There is an abrupt blackness and, around Jane, applause. When the lights come on only a moment later, everything has changed. The platform holding the musicians is abandoned, a sheet of music splayed on the ground; the aisle is already filling with people, the mild buzz of everyday conversation, as if it is not remarkable that an entire world has been swallowed by the long red curtains.

Jane tries to catch Reagan's eye, but her friend is speaking to Callie. She is talking too quickly, Jane notices. She is twisting a strand of her hair the way she does when she is anxious.

"Well? What did you think?" Ms. Yu asks.

"I loved it. Thank you for bringing me," Jane says, but her voice quavers. She drops her eyes, horrified that she is already ruining the plan.

Ms. Yu, thankfully, misinterprets. She places her arm over Jane's shoulders, pulls her just the slightest bit closer, and says gently, "You don't have to thank me, Jane. You deserve this. A night free of worries."

Jane stares down at her lap.

"Reagan has to use the bathroom!" Callie tells Ms. Yu, making a joke about third-trimester bladder issues.

"Me also," Jane says. Her voice holds firm.

Ms. Yu asks them to wait for the Coordinators.

Callie comments that the actress who plays Eliza is a rising star on Broadway; she cut her teeth in local theater and spends every August back in the Berkshires. The two Coordinators appear out of the throng holding bottled waters, which they hand to Ms. Yu. Ms. Yu asks them to take Jane and Reagan to the bathroom and, if it's not too much trouble, to get Ms. Yu a bottle of Pellegrino instead; she prefers bubbly water to still.

Jane and Reagan follow the Coordinators up the crowded aisle and into the lobby. They thread their way to the staircase and follow the flow of foot traffic downstairs, where the line to the women's bathroom is fifteen-people deep.

While the red-haired Coordinator waits with Jane and Reagan at the back of the line, the dark-skinned one marches to the front to speak to the bathroom attendant. The red-haired Coordinator asks them about the play; she and her colleague did not get to watch it. Reagan chats with her about the performance, trying to draw Jane into the conversation.

The Coordinator at the front of the line signals.

"Go on," says the red-haired Coordinator. She trails behind them as they make their way to the bathroom entrance. Jane avoids eye contact with the women they are skipping in line.

It is cramped in the bathroom. There are five stalls and across from them, only three sinks. Several women wait their turn, arms crossed or glancing at their phones; others wash their hands and a couple of younger women peer into the mirrors hanging above the sinks, touching up their faces. There is the sound of a toilet flushing, and a middle-aged woman in a fringed shawl emerges, smiling at Reagan's belly. The bathroom attendant motions to Reagan, who steps into the vacated stall; the sound of the lock; from somewhere, a child asks its mother for more toilet paper.

Jane steps forward a few steps, the two Coordinators right behind her.

There is no way this will work.

"Are you enjoying the play?" asks the dark-skinned Coordinator. Jane notices she has a slight accent. She forces herself to speak, to buy Reagan time: it is her first time in a theater, she found the play hard to follow at first, the stage was so beautiful, so many flowers, she wonders if they could be real?

And then, the sound of retching. Rasping and violent.

"Reagan, are you okay?" asks the Coordinator who was speaking with Jane.

Reagan moans, the sound of heaving and more retching, the Coordinators moving toward the stall.

"Unlock it, Reagan," commands the red-haired Coordinator. Her face is grave.

"There's blood." Reagan's voice is wan and small and even though Jane knows she is faking, that her words are as false as the magic world behind the red curtains, she grows afraid.

"Oh God . . ."

But who is saying this?

The Coordinators burst into action, one pulling at the handle of Reagan's stall, the other on her knees, trying to see under the stall's door. From inside, the sounds of upheaval, of a body in rebellion.

Jane digs her nails into her palms, because this is it. Just like she and Reagan talked about.

She takes one step backward, then another, each step taking her farther from the commotion until several women stand in front of her, like a buffer; backward still until Jane is absorbed by the women surging forward, a faceless group of the curious and the concerned.

A child—it must be the child in the stall next to Reagan's—begins to shriek. The sound of a child shrieking, and around Jane the crush of bodies begins to reverberate with panic and fear. A woman's voice shouts: "She's collapsed! Call 911!"

Around Jane, a murmuring: a pregnant woman . . . collapsed . . . was there blood? . . . Ohmygod . . .

Several women are on their cellphones, calling for help. A man rushes forward yelling that he is a doctor.

Jane takes the stairs as fast as she can, using the railing to pull herself faster. She does not have a great deal of time. This Reagan told her repeatedly. Once she is on the move, she has to **move.** If they stop you inside, say you are getting help. If they stop you outside, say you felt faint and needed fresh air. But move, move, move.

Jane's throat is dry. As she pushes her way through the crowded lobby she pulls the scarf from her pocket, pale yellow with a darker print. She drapes it around her head, across her shoulders.

Move, move, move.

The glass doors are lighter than they look. She fights the urge to glance backward, to check if she is being followed. She waits for the hand to grab her shoulder, to yank her back, but she is outside—the air is heavy, the sky is darkening—and the doors close behind her. People walk along the sidewalk; several smoke cigarettes near the theater doors. Somewhere in the distance, an ambulance wails.

Jane fumbles with her WellBand until it is unfastened. She frantically scans the pedestrians on the sidewalk, as Reagan had counseled her, until she spies a woman approaching. She walks a dog, a small gray one, and there is a canvas bag slung over one shoulder, the ones that people use for groceries. Jane sees a loaf of bread jutting from it, a green frill of lettuce.

Before Jane can doubt herself, she asks the woman for the time, just as Reagan instructed. When the woman pulls out her cellphone to check the clock display on her phone's screen, Jane drops her WellBand into her canvas bag. She does not hear it fall.

Jane thanks the woman, who wishes her luck.

She walks quickly in the other direction, hunching, as if walking against the wind. But it is a windless night, and cloudless. The stars above are sharp as broken glass.

Take a left out of the theater, Reagan had said, then left again. Left and left again, Jane mutters in her head, feeling a thousand eyes on her.

She turns the corner, and it is there: the black hatchback with the rainbow sticker on the passenger window. Just as Reagan had described.

She gulps, fighting the urge to sprint to the car. She refuses to succumb to the relief that surges inside her until she has opened the door, slid inside, felt the whoosh of cool air from the car's vents. Her scarf has fallen over her eyes, but she does not adjust it. For a moment she allows herself to sit, slumped, in her seat; to feel her heart slow and her muscles unclench. Behind her closed eyelids, her eyes are wet.

"Magandang gabi," says a voice, a man's. Familiar.

The car begins to pull away from the curb.

Jane sits up, pushes the scrim of her scarf off her face with her hand and turns, because she had expected Lisa.

Troy grins at her. "Hey, sweet Jane. Where we headed?"

MAE

FOR A MOMENT, MAE ALLOWS HERSELF SIMPLY TO BREATHE. She shuts out the clamor around her. She ignores the cacophony within. She breathes with her entire being, exhales, expelling the muddle and the panic and the stress and the fury.

"Do you want to go with Reagan in the ambulance?" the Coordinator asks, her voice tentative. Mae's eyes snap open. The Coordinator's red hair is askew. She is flustered, as well she should be.

Mae stands in the center of the lobby as various personnel from Golden Oaks—they arrived quickly, cars of them—eddy around her. The doors to the theater are closed. The second act, delayed by the hubbub, has started—the show, after all, must go on—which makes everything more difficult. Jane could be hiding inside the theater, under cover of darkness, or in the wings, digging through the costume racks for a disguise.

Mae shakes her head, dispelling the images. Useless, all of them.

"I believe that 82 is most likely fine. I believe the real problem here is that you've lost 84," Mae says coolly. She pulls her device from her purse and swipes it open. She senses the Coordinator shifting from one foot to the other, unsure whether to stay or go. She is one of the highest-rated Coordinators at Golden Oaks, which is why Mae had entrusted her with Madame Deng's Hosts. Clearly, Tech needs to rethink its algorithms.

The Coordinator clears her throat. "Should I . . . should I go with her?"

Mae allows her gaze to rest on the Coordinator for several uncomfortable seconds. It is in times of crisis that one's true nature comes to the fore. This one turns out to be a total incompetent. "I would think, yes, that one of you should be with 82 at all times, lest you lose a second Host tonight."

The Coordinator reddens and darts away. Mae, swallowing her ire, pages through the messages on her device. The Panopticon team is claiming it sent an alert to the Coordinators when Jane's WellBand locator moved fifty yards beyond the perimeter of

the theater. There is another message from Security
with a map showing the path that Jane's WellBand
took, ending in the farmhouse kitchen of a white
colonial ten minutes from town, where it was found
in the bottom of a housekeeper's bag of groceries.

Hal, Golden Oaks' Head of Security, approaches.
He is an imposing slab of a man. Leon wooed him
away from the Special Services by quadrupling
his salary.

He reports that his team has finished interrogating the housekeeper. He confirms that she spoke to
a pregnant Asian woman fitting 84's profile outside
the theater earlier in the evening while running errands for her boss, a weekender from Manhattan
with a craving for freshly baked bread with his
dinner. The housekeeper said that 84 was walking toward the town center, due east, when she last
glimpsed her. Security is now fanned out along the
streets looking for other witnesses. Another team is
discreetly making the rounds inside the theater, in
case 84 doubled back through the side entrance and
is hiding inside the building somewhere, biding her
time to make a run for it later. They are still waiting
for the theater to pull its security-camera footage.

Hal's update is interrupted by a bleep. Mae
holds up her forefinger, mouthing **one minute,**
and swipes open her phone. Eve reports that she
has tried Evelyn Arroyo several times on her cellphone without luck. No one is picking up on Jane's
home line, either. She asks if Mae wants to get

patched through to Leon, who has just landed in the Philippines on a surfing trip.

A frisson of nervousness shoots through Mae's body. Leon will be beyond irate. The ink on the deal with Deng is barely dry. What if she reneges?

Mae types: **Not quite yet**

Within seconds Eve texts again: **What about Madame Deng?**

Mae swipes off her phone. She cannot risk answering Eve until she has spoken with Fiona, the only person she fully trusts in Legal. Mae needs to understand how much she is contractually obligated to inform Madame Deng, and when, and whether there is any wiggle room.

The second Coordinator approaches and hands Mae a glass of Pellegrino. "Megan accompanied 82 to the hospital. I have a helicopter on standby in case we need to get 82 to New York."

Mae takes a sip of the water, savoring the clarifying fizz in her throat. She takes another sip, slowly, forcing the Coordinator to wait as she finishes her drink, letting her stew in her failure. Mae hands her the empty glass.

"I asked Security to go, too," says the Coordinator. "Given our screwup tonight, I thought we should take extra precautions."

Mae glances at the Coordinator with grudging approval. At least this one owns her mistakes. Mae decides to give her a chance to redeem herself somewhat. "The Panopticon is scouring all outgoing communications from 84 and 82 over the past month. Stay on top of this. And remind all the Team Heads to dispense information to their people **only** as needed. There's too much at stake."

The Coordinator bites her lip and hurries off. Mae signals to Hal.

"Ma'am," begins Hal after surveying the room to make sure they cannot be overheard, "I've got to raise the possibility that we have a kidnapping situation here."

Mae allows him to outline his theory even though she knows he has it wrong. He simply doesn't know Jane. It's a matter of what is in and out of character. Jane would never hurt the baby or even threaten to do so. She's Catholic, for one thing, riddled by guilt, fearful of damnation. More than that, she's a rule-abider. She has neither the constitution, nor the imagination, for rocking the boat. Which is why Mae knows that someone put her up to all of this. Reagan, most likely—the logs show that they've spent significant time together of late, though this raised no red flags at the time. And it was, now that Mae thinks of it, Reagan who broached the idea of inviting Jane to the theater.

But why? To what end? Reagan is a lost soul looking for meaning. She would never wittingly lead Jane astray.

"So we've got to find her daughter. It only helps to

have leverage in these types of situations," concludes Hal. "I can send a team by chopper to Manhattan and have the child isolated within the hour."

Mae gazes at Hal but is thinking about Amalia. Jane's child. Is she what this is about? Could Jane—her hopes of seeing her daughter dashed time and time again as visit after visit was canceled, her hormones wildly unbalanced due to the exigencies of pregnancy—have risked it all simply to lay eyes on her daughter?

It is ludicrous. Entirely irrational. Possibly criminal.

But it has the feel of the truth.

Mae laughs joylessly, pity for Jane sluicing through her with such suddenness that her eyes moisten.

Oh, Jane. You silly, stupid, sentimental girl. What have you done?

"Ms. Yu?" asks Hal.

"I have a hunch about something . . ." Mae doesn't finish her sentence. "It can only help our cause to find Amalia, I agree with you. But it requires a light touch. We'll go together."

"IS THERE NO WAY AROUND THE TRAFFIC?" MAE ASKS HAL. HE is squeezed in the seat next to the driver. His buzz-cut head almost touches the car's ceiling.

"Traffic everywhere, ma'am. BQE always bad on Fridays." The driver shakes his head.

Mae leans back, aggravated. Outside, there is an eruption of honking. A large van blocks the intersection. A wave of pedestrians spills across the street, surrounding their car so that Mae feels like they are marooned in an ocean of bodies. Disquiet seizes her, an uneasy premonition that at any moment the throng will turn into a mob and begin smashing their fists against the windows, pelting them with stones.

The van makes its turn. Mae's driver begins to inch the car forward but is forced to brake abruptly as pedestrians continue to pour past their hood.

"It's **our** light!" Mae cries angrily.

The driver flashes an apologetic smile through the rearview mirror. Mae returns it.

How does he do it, this man? Day in and day out? Endless traffic, pushy drivers, suicidal pedestrians, impatient passengers, bad pay, bad air, parking tickets, bills, children, maybe even grandchildren from the looks of him.

How does he not explode?

"The Panopticon just briefed me," the Coordinator sitting next to Mae announces. She reports that Reagan hasn't communicated with anyone outside Golden Oaks in months except her mother and father and her roommate in New York. "She only emails with the father. And the mother never speaks. The convos with the roommate are clean."

Mae frowns. Then who could possibly have put Jane up to this? Or could it be that Mae completely misread her favorite Host—that Jane, behind her mousy, frightened mien, is actually a conniver?

Before she can pursue her thoughts, the Coordinator continues, "84's also clean. She's made hundreds of attempts to contact Evelyn Arroyo in the past month, but they never connected."

"Hundreds?" Mae asks, incredulous.

The Coordinator swipes through her device and corrects herself. "Over a hundred, 108 attempts, between emails and calls."

"Daily?"

"The frequency increased over time. This past Tuesday, for instance, 84 sent Ms. Arroyo six emails and made five calls," the Coordinator hands Mae her device.

Mae studies the distribution of Jane's attempts to reach her cousin. Her mounting frenzy is clear from the data.

"How was this not detected by Data Analysis?" Mae struggles to keep the anger out of her voice.

"The emails are clean, so no flags were set off. 84 only requested that Ms. Arroyo return her calls."

Mae closes her eyes, head swimming. She is certain now that Jane fled in search of her daughter. That the weeks in which she was cut off from her cousin—and Amalia—caused some sort of psychological rupture. It can happen, Mae knows from the stories in the news. The last straw. The pressures of the world growing increasingly unbearable. You can only bend so much before you break.

She sends a text marked **Highly Confidential** to Geri explaining her theory.

Need response ASAP, how to handle, and if she's a danger to herself or fetus.

She settles back into her seat, feeling jittery. Her phone bleeps. Geri agrees with Mae that some sort of "break" occurred, but she's confident Jane poses no threat to the baby. She also agrees that Jane is not the type of person to believe in her own agency; someone else planned the escape.

But who?

And how did Mae miss it? Jane's oceanic despair.

Mae swallows hard and looks out the window, at her reflection in the glass. It is her fault. She took her eye off the ball—too consumed by her wedding and Project MacDonald.

Mae is whipped forward as the driver slams on his brakes again to avoid hitting a taxi that has swerved into their lane to pick up a passenger.

"What an asshole!" Mae exclaims.

Her driver flashes the same gentle smile into the mirror.

The car begins to move. The Coordinator leans forward to murmur something to Hal. The question of who planned the escape nags at Mae, and she is suddenly irate with Reagan, who knows more than she is letting on. Mae calls Geri and tells her they need to ramp up the pressure. "Get the Coordinators involved—and Tracey, too."

Mae's phone bleeps again. Fiona from Legal. She

is researching whether in New York State the fetus is considered a "person" in the legal sense; if not, then Jane (and Golden Oaks) can't be found guilty of "kidnapping."

The distinction could be mitigating.

Mae sighs in annoyance. Lawyers. Mitigating circumstances or not, they will lose Madame Deng's investment if they do not find Jane ASAP.

"Almost here!" the driver announces, with a note of triumph.

It is a nondescript block. The buildings are low-lying and utilitarian, with a variety of stores occupying the ground floors—bodegas, a laundromat, a check-cashing storefront. Metal grates are pulled closed over darkened windows except the chicken-wing shop, which is open for business, blinking neon green and bustling.

The car pulls to the curb. Mae asks Hal to wait outside and make sure the backup team stays out of sight so that Jane isn't scared off. She tells the Coordinator to follow her and record everything, just in case. It's always better to have too much data than too little.

A family passes—a woman pushing a stroller, a man piggybacking a small child wearing a swimsuit. Two women in halter tops and bright lipstick hover over a cellphone.

Mae strides up to Jane's building, climbs the stairs, and presses the button to her apartment. She announced herself as Jane's boss. A woman's voice, accented, murmurs, "Okay," and there is a click as the building's front door unlocks.

The lobby is dusty and hot and smells of stale food. There is a child's sun hat on the floor, pink with tassels, and Mae pockets it because it might be Amalia's. At the least, it's a good icebreaker.

The Coordinator is right behind her. She grins at Mae. "That was easy!"

Mae fingers the pink hat in her pocket.

Poor Jane.

She turns to the stairs and begins to climb.

REAGAN

THERE IS AN IV JABBED IN REAGAN'S ARM. HER EYES ARE closed, and she listens to two women talk about Jane. The security team found the WellBand, but Host 84 is still missing. Where can she possibly be?

Reagan contains the smile that threatens to spill onto her face. She's meant to be unconscious. Beneath the hospital sheet she crosses her fingers.

Go, Jane. Go!

A door opens. Hallway noises amplify, then quiet. Footsteps approach. Someone is hovering near her, over her. Reagan remains immobile. The footsteps recede, and the women start talking again. One of them says, in a clear, sure voice, that the police are being called in because it's a kidnapping. Jane Reyes kidnapped the billionaire's baby.

Reagan's eyes flutter open, and for a moment she's blinded. The lights. She turns her head, shielding herself, but her movements are too abrupt. Reagan slams her eyes closed, but it's too late.

"Reagan?" says a flinty voice, something grazing her arm.

Lisa said they would never call the police.

"Reagan, we're glad you're awake."

Lisa said the Farm does not want to be known. The videos are enough to keep Jane safe.

"We saw you open your eyes. Sit up. Sit up now," says the voice, insistent hands on Reagan, pulling her forward, upward. Rougher than they need to be.

Will they arrest Jane?

"Have some water. There's a good girl. You don't need this IV anymore, do you? You're fine, aren't you?"

Reagan's eyes are open now. She's never laid eyes on this woman, although she wears the uniform of a Coordinator. Curly hair, an unremarkable face, but her eyes are unforgettable—hard and small and gray, like the pebbles Reagan used to throw at the birds at their lake house; Mom served lunch outside whenever it was nice, the teak table right by the water. The birds liked to steal Gus's food. He never fought them off. Reagan had to do it for him.

"How are you feeling?"

"Better," Reagan replies softly, because she's meant to be weakened after her ordeal. Her eyes skip across the room looking for the other speaker.

"That's quite a scare you had."

Reagan doesn't answer. There's something about this woman she doesn't like.

"The doctors found nothing wrong with you. You must've eaten something bad for dinner," the woman says in a shiny, cheerless voice. She has removed Reagan's IV. She is now tugging at Reagan's sheets but so roughly that Reagan is jostled.

"They're checking the food logs to see what you ate tonight. We'd hate to have other Hosts get sick, too," she continues, now tucking the edges of the sheet under the hospital mattress so tightly that Reagan feels trapped. "You'd hate that, wouldn't you, Reagan? To have another Host get into trouble?"

Reagan stares at her. "Of course."

A device bleeps. The woman swipes it open, and she makes a face. Reagan realizes it's meant to be a smile.

"Good news. Your Client's here. Callie's been very concerned about you."

Reagan doesn't trust herself to speak.

The door swings open. "Oh my God, Reagan. I've been so worried!"

Callie envelops her, sagging against Reagan in fake-relief, with fake-affection, and the smell of her perfume makes Reagan want to vomit.

"How are you?" Callie asks, taking a step back to study Reagan's face.

Her forehead furrows, implying worry. She twists her fake-trembling hands so fiercely her knuckles whiten.

Fear hits Reagan, a cold splash. The whitened knuckles, the tremulous hands. Reagan would swear it was real if she didn't know better.

Who is this woman? What are they up against?

What have she and Lisa done to Jane?

As if on impulse, Callie springs toward Reagan. Another envelopment, tighter than the first one. "Wipe that worry from your face. You're okay now. You're okay."

Reagan closes her eyes, feeling but trying not to feel Callie's palm rubbing her back, the heat from the cheek that lies against her hair. She's too rigid, she knows; she exudes wariness. Reagan forces herself to soften. A glacier melting. The coming of spring.

"Oh, Honey," Callie murmurs.

The intimacy of her voice is a violation.

"I'm glad you're feeling better," Callie says after a time. She pulls a chair nearer to the bed. She lays her hand on Reagan's, a gesture of affection. Or ownership. "They say it's probably some kind of food poisoning."

Reagan takes a sip of water. Then another.

"That must have been scary."

Reagan doesn't answer.

"But you're here and on the mend. And my baby's

fine. That's what matters, that you and my baby are fine." Callie squeezes Reagan's hand.

My baby.

Whose baby?

And where is Jane?

"Your friend Jane," Callie begins, as if in answer to Reagan's thoughts, "is still missing. Poor thing, she must be scared, too."

Reagan tightens her grip on her glass. She tries to sound offhand. "Does anyone know where she is?"

"Oh, don't worry. They'll find her," Callie replies. "They've got the whole security team on her. And now likely the police, too. Or was it the FBI? I think kidnapping is considered a federal crime. Although Jane didn't seem like the kind of person to harm a baby."

"She's not!" Reagan blurts. "Jane wouldn't hurt a fly—"

"But why run off then? She must know that her Client would be worried sick."

Reagan scrabbles for words. She needs the exact right ones, in the right combination. She needs "Callie" to understand. To speak to Ms. Yu for them.

"—that's exactly how Jane feels," Reagan says urgently, trapping Callie's hand in hers. "She's worried sick about her own baby. Do you know Jane's a mother, too?"

Her voice breaks. Callie blurs, and Reagan swipes at her eyes.

"Do you think she went to find her daughter?"

"I—I don't know," Reagan responds slowly.

How did Callie know that Jane's child is a girl?

"I know you two are close. If you had to guess—where would she go?"

Callie is picking at the nubs of her jacket. She acts like she doesn't care whether Reagan answers or not. But she does care. She's quivering with attentiveness, like an insect's antenna.

"I think she's probably not thinking totally straight. Because she hasn't seen her daughter for so long, and she's worried about her. Amalia's been really sick," Reagan says carefully. It's a good seed to plant, that Jane's not in her right mind. The unstable broth of her hormones, the stress of late pregnancy, the terror for her child.

Will that be enough to save her?

"What kind of sickness?" Callie asks.

"Ear infections. A lot of them. You know, sometimes they can spread to the brain." Reagan fakes a certainty she doesn't feel. "You must understand how that could make you crazy, that kind of worry over your child. How it would eat at you. Because **you're** a mother, too."

Her eyes flit to Callie's, and Callie looks away. Just for a second, and then she's back in character, meeting Reagan's gaze with equanimity and warmth.

"Of course. Of course I understand."

"So she's not thinking straight," Reagan continues with more assurance. "Maybe she had food

poisoning, too. Like me. Maybe she got sick somewhere near the theater. Have they checked the area?"

Callie purses her lips, looking at Reagan like
she sees something new there. "They have."

"Well, maybe she went for a walk to get air, because
she was feeling nauseous. And then she started
vomiting, like I did. And someone took her in and
helped her, because she's pregnant. I'm sure she'll
turn up before too long." Reagan now speaks
briskly. "And what a shame, to get the police involved. All the attention and all that publicity."

Callie's smile flickers. "I'm on your side, Reagan.
Can't you see that?"

Fuck you, Callie.

"I'm on your side," she repeats. "And on Jane's,
because she's your friend, and therefore she's mine.
I only want to help."

That makes two of us, Reagan thinks but does
not say, and suddenly she is exhausted. And sad. A
sadness so vast she feels likes she is drowning in it.
She is sad for Jane and for Amalia, and for Anya
and Tasia and Segundina, and Jane's cousin and
her children, and Mom, poor Mom erased like that
and alone.

Because nothing is going to change.

Reagan feels her eyes grow wet and grabs the pitcher
on the table next to her, muttering that she is thirsty.
But it's heavy, and she splashes water across her torso
as she tries to fill her half-empty glass.

Callie jumps up, swabbing at Reagan's stomach with a wad of tissue paper. The woman with the flinty eyes arrives out of nowhere bearing a towel and a fresh hospital gown.

"I'm fine," Reagan protests, but the woman ignores her, yanking loose the cord that holds Reagan's dressing gown closed.

Reagan crosses her arms quickly to cover herself, but the woman forces Reagan's arms open and into the holes of a new gown, knotting it closed as if Reagan were a child.

Callie sighs. "I wish you'd let me help you. And Jane. Especially Jane. Because you'll land on your feet. But someone like her . . . She doesn't get second chances. This isn't a game for her."

"I never thought it was a game," Reagan answers.

JANE

OUTSIDE THE HOSPITAL'S REVOLVING DOORS, SEVERAL PEOPLE
wait. A bearded man with pale arms smokes a cigarette and stares up at the sky. An older one leans
against a column laughing into a cellphone. Behind
them, a woman sits in a wheelchair. She looks pregnant, even though she isn't anymore. Every few seconds she glances worriedly at the car seat at her feet,
as if the newborn strapped inside will somehow in-
jure itself. Jane remembers being this woman, waiting for Billy in the same spot, her stomach emptied
and soft.

"I'm going to wait for you here," Troy says to

Jane. He has turned the engine off, and the new-found silence in the car allows street noises to invade: music thumping out of the open windows of a passing van; an angry exchange of horns somewhere up the block.

"What if she is not here?" Jane says to her hands. She looks up at Troy. It is the first time she has met his gaze since he picked her up outside the theater, hours ago. She barely spoke during the car ride, answering his many questions with as few words as possible. Trying to forget that she has seen him, every part of him, in the gray-green dusk beneath the trees.

Not that her shyness stopped Troy from telling her story after story, making the car ride pass more quickly than it might have—how he met Lisa at a festival in the desert, topless in the bonfire's light; about the videos that Lisa filmed in secret of the goings-on at the Farm using a tiny camera Troy had smuggled to her during one of his visits.

"I've made montages from the videos. And sculptures. They were gonna be for this big thing I'm working on—a show but more than that. An indictment. But then Lisa said you needed them, which is cool," Troy said before rambling about consumerism and commodification and Venus figurines, one unearthed recently that was at least thirty-five thousand years old and still so powerful, so many thousands of years later. "Man, the pregnant female form is just **awe**-inspiring."

Now Troy's stories have dried up, and he stares at Jane with an intensity that makes her squirm. Outside a siren wails, drawing nearer. Jane asks again, panic flicking at her insides: "What if she is not **here**?"

Jane's car door clicks open, Troy unlocking it with the press of a button. "Go and see. If she isn't here we'll find her at your apartment."

Jane forces herself out of the car. She turns back to thank Troy, embarrassed that she was not friendlier during the car ride, and notices that he has been holding his phone, tilted up at her. Filming.

He smiles, the slow-spreading smile Jane remembers from the time she met him in the forest. "For posterity's sake," he explains without a trace of embarrassment, now aiming his phone camera openly at her face.

Jane walks toward the hospital's glass doors, shivering a little despite the night's heat. She is conscious that behind her Troy is likely still filming, capturing her stilted waddle. Reconsidering his opinion of the pregnant female form.

Jane pushes through the revolving door into the hospital lobby, not allowing herself to think or feel. A security guard glances at her, and she seizes up inside, but he soon turns with a yawn to the phone in his hand.

"Obstetrics is on seven," the man behind the information desk says to Jane when it is her turn in line.

"No, I—I am looking for my daughter . . ." Jane apologizes.

"Name?"

"I am Jane Reyes."

The man gives Jane a look, the kind she has received so often (from Billy's parents; from the haughty daughter of her favorite patient in the retirement home). "Your **daughter's** name?"

"Oh," Jane flushes. "She is Amalia. Amalia Reyes."

The man types on a keyboard, the light from his computer screen reflected blue green in his glasses. He begins shaking his head. "She's not registered here."

"But I know she is here. Since last night!" Jane flattens her hands on the counter.

A look of annoyance drifts across the man's face. "What can I say? She's not in the system." He shrugs and, angling his head away from Jane to show he is finished with her, asks the woman in line behind Jane if he can assist her with anything.

Jane, angry, demands: "Angel Calapatia! Check her name. Please. Also: Evelyn Arroyo. She is my cousin—"

The man shakes his head, but he obeys. He asks Jane to spell out the names and, grudgingly, clacks at his keyboard. Behind Jane there is a small thud, and the woman in line begins to scold her son for dropping his juice cup. His shirt is brand new, and now it is stained.

"Tenth floor," the man says to Jane curtly, staring past her to the upset mother, the crying boy in the sticky shirt.

In the elevator, as the doors close and the metal cube begins to rise, Jane's breath comes with difficulty, as if the air has become thin. She leans against the elevator wall—cold, metallic—to steady herself.

I am having a panic attack.

Jane recalls how the psychologist at the retirement home handled the patients who had such attacks. She made them trace the outline of one hand with the forefinger of the other, breathing slowly as they did so. Jane watched as she emptied the wastebaskets: the old people outlining their own bodies; tracing where they ended and where they began.

Jane tries this now, calling to mind the psychiatrist's voice. She told Jane once, as Jane cleaned her office, that the method calmed the old people because it gave them a sense of control. As the psychiatrist lifted her coffee mug to allow Jane to better wipe down her desk, she added: because what do we really control but how we react to life's curveballs?

She winked at Jane, though Jane did not understand why, and still doesn't.

The elevator doors open. Jane, still tracing her hand, sees a woman behind a desk. Everything is a blur but the woman's round face. The woman does not grow angry when she cannot find Amalia in the computer. She only squints at Jane behind her old-fashioned glasses shaped like cat's eyes and asks if she should check under another name.

"Evelyn Arroyo," Jane says. "I am her cousin."

"Ah, yes. Room 10-11." The woman points down the hall.

Jane begins walking. She passes a man outside room 10-02 with a gloomy face and big sweat stains under his arms. From room 10-05 Jane hears muffled voices and a peal of laughter. Several doors down Jane glimpses a woman in pink scrubs pulling the sheets off a bed.

Oh God, please. No.

Outside of room 10-11, Jane stops. The door is closed, a nondescript door painted white with a strip of frosted glass at eye level. She places her hand on the door's handle but, overwhelmed, turns away. She finds herself at the end of the hallway in front of a window without curtains. The sky outside is gray and half-lit by the city lights. On the bottom pane of glass is the smudged handprint of a child. She must have stretched tall to make the mark. How could she have known that there is nothing worth seeing outside, only a dirty city under a dirty sky?

Jane drops her head and prays. For once, the prayer is not meant for Amalia but for herself. For strength, so that she can endure whatever is to come, no matter how bad Amalia's condition. And for self-control. So that when Jane finally lays eyes on Ate—Ate whose job is to snare fertile Hosts for the Farm even as she pretends to mother them, these ignorant, trusting Filipinas—Jane will be able to bite her tongue long enough to ensure that Amalia is safe.

She pushes open the door.

The room is white and small, divided into halves by a blue curtain hanging from a metal rod. The front half is vacant. Through the part in the curtain, Jane sees a bed, and a lump covered by a dull green blanket that is too big to be Amalia.

Jane freezes. "Ate?"

"Another visitor, Evelyn," announces the nurse who hovers over her cousin, adjusting this and that. Ate does not respond. Her eyes are closed, and there is something unnatural in her stillness.

Jane stares, speechless, her head spinning. Or perhaps it is the room that spins.

The nurse, noticing Jane's confusion, explains, "She's been slipping in and out since surgery."

"Surgery?" Jane crosses the room in one swift motion. She stands close to her cousin, unable to speak.

"You're related to Evelyn?"

"I'm her cousin," Jane answers. "What is wrong with her?"

"She had a mitral valve replacement. She's just out of ICU. She got a few extra days in there because of an infection."

Jane leans closer to her cousin, who takes up far less space than she should on the hospital bed. She touches her hand. A foreign object.

So this is why Ate has not returned Jane's calls.

The nurse is dragging over a chair so that Jane can sit. Jane thanks her without taking her eyes off her cousin's face.

Jane has been imagining this moment all day and much of the previous night, the moment when she would confront her cousin about the betrayal: Why? Why do you put your pocketbook before your family?

She would say it in a voice so sharp it could draw blood.

But, here.

Now.

Jane stares at Ate, willing her to speak. Just one word, one sentence. Some sign that Ate is okay. After she collapsed at the Carters', she was weak but still herself—snapping at Angel, cajoling Jane to replace her.

But here is Ate's face: sunk into itself.

Here are her cheeks: so hollow.

Her mouth—the mouth that is always moving—is inert. One more furrow in a face creased with furrows.

Jane dares to touch Ate's hand again, and when there is no movement, she stifles a sob.

"I thought Angel would've told you," the nurse explains, a note of apology in her voice.

"You know Angel?" Jane asks, wiping her eyes with the back of her hand.

"She's visited every day. Yesterday she brought Evelyn's niece. What a cutie."

Jane's heart skips a beat. "Amalia was here?"

"It's not technically allowed, but we thought the baby might give Evelyn a reason to fight . . ."

"How is she?" Jane blurts. She places her hand on the bed to steady herself.

"The baby? Oh, she's a spirited one. She wouldn't let Angel hold her! She kept squirming away and marching around the room like she owns the place. Angel says she . . ."

There is a roaring in Jane's ears. So loud she cannot distinguish the nurse's words. They run together, a cascade, swirling around Jane and lifting her.

Amalia is well.

Jane shuts her eyes to hold back a flood. She is shaking. The nurse begins telling another story—how when Amalia was placed on the bed to kiss Ate goodbye she took the old woman's face in both hands and kissed her—and Jane is lifted even higher, dizzyingly high, suspended somewhere beyond Earth's pull by the blunt force of the nurse's words.

Amalia is well.

Jane is crying openly, not bothering to wipe her face. She is crying, and she is melting, and she is awash in an ocean of gratitude.

The nurse is pressing a box of tissues into Jane's hands, mouthing words of comfort that she has probably repeated too many times to count. "She isn't in pain. She knows you are here."

Jane jolts upright. There is still Ate. Ate stretched on the bed, who has not stirred.

"How serious is this with my cousin?"

The nurse equivocates, then apologizes. "It's better if you talk to the doctor himself. But, I think, the sooner Evelyn's children come to see her, the better."

Jane has only been punched once—that boyfriend of her mother's with the snake tattoo around his ankle—and it felt just like this: a blow, the sudden loss of air.

". . . Angel said she told Evelyn's children the gravity of the situation. So they can make arrangements to come."

"But how?" Jane demands. The nurse does not understand. It is not so easy. They will need visas. Money. And what of Roy?

"You mean the disabled one? Angel told me about him, poor thing. Well, he probably can't. But Angel said the daughters could, the other son . . ."

A burst of rage disorients Jane. Why would Angel say all this when she knows the difficulties? If it were so simple, why has Angel not seen her own children in so many years?

Or was she trying to protect Ate? To shield Ate, even in her unconsciousness, from the nurse's pity?

Jane takes Ate's hand. Her bones fragile as a bird's.

Ate did hate to be pitied. Angel is correct in that.

"In any case, from what Angel told me, the disabled

one wouldn't know what's going on with his mom anyway," says the nurse.

"His name is Roy," Jane says but so quietly the nurse does not seem to hear. Roy; not the Disabled One.

"I have a boy," says the nurse, almost absently.

Jane strokes Ate's hand.

"You're young still, but you'll understand when you have your baby," the nurse says, glancing at Jane's stomach. "There's no bigger nightmare for a mother than not being able to protect her child. Before she lost consciousness, Evelyn kept repeating his name. Roy this, Roy that."

The nurse snorts. "At first I thought it was her husband she kept calling for. But Angel told me about **that** good-for-nothing."

Jane tightens her hold on Ate's hand, as if Ate is falling and only Jane can catch her. The bony fingers so thin Jane might break them if she squeezed any harder.

Of course, it is about Roy. Everything Ate did was for him.

Shame fills her. Jane is so ashamed of herself she feels ill.

"Honey, are you okay?" asks the nurse, concerned.

Jane barely hears her. She is thinking how many plane tickets she can buy with her savings; she wonders if Ms. Yu would ever give her an advance.

Something enormous presses against Jane's chest. The weight of her grief and her sticky shame. Jane folds her arms on Ate's bed and lays down her head so that it rests against Ate's body. She half-expects to feel Ate's hand on her forehead, pushing away the strands of her hair and berating her for not wearing it back in a ponytail, as Ate used to do when Jane was pregnant with Amalia, hanging over the dorm's toilet, the morning sickness that always struck at night.

A hand touches her shoulder and for a moment Jane allows herself to pretend. Then she looks up at the nurse.

"I'm gonna give you a second with your cousin, okay? Press the button if you need me."

Jane presses Ate's hand to her face. She never thanked Ate for helping her with Amalia. She didn't thank her enough for too many things to count.

"I am sorry," Jane whispers. She speaks louder, in case somehow Ate can hear her. "And I understand. Because I would do anything for Mali, too."

ATE

ATE IS REMEMBERING: HER MOTHER'S FACE IN THE WINDOW OF their crooked house. The sound of her father coughing. And this:

"Follow Tito Jimmy."

Ate is with her boys. The room is teeming and hot. Several hundred people—all of them men, at least as far as Ate can see—sit in row upon row around a raised platform. It is a Tuesday afternoon, and should they not be working?

Ate keeps her thoughts to herself. She has come to ask Jimmy for help. It is not easy to raise four children alone. And he is doing well, that is what everyone says, making big piles of money from men such as these.

And he always was kind to her, even when her other in-laws were not.

Roy halts abruptly so that Ate bumps into him.

"Why do you stop, Roy? Go, go!" Ate does not want to lose Jimmy. The throng is so thick, and the hall is no place for little boys. Or women.

Roy still does not move. He shrinks backward as though trying to melt into his mother. Ate swats his backside and gives him a small shove. "Romuelo, help me. Hold Roy's hand and follow your Tito!"

With Romuelo tugging on Roy's arm and Ate pushing at his back, they inch forward. Ate glimpses Jimmy's head bobbing several yards ahead of them. Everywhere, she smells men—the staleness of sweat long dried, the sting of cigarette smoke; alcohol, even though it is still early in the day. And, everywhere, there are eyes on her. Ate does not flatter herself; she knows she is nothing to look at—her husband, before he abandoned her, liked to remind her of her plainness—but here, in this room, it only matters that she has breasts to fill up her shirt and an emptiness between her legs. She presses forward, a thousand eyes scraping over her body in assessment. She grabs hold of the back of Roy's shirt.

Jimmy stands near the platform, in the second row. He waits until Ate and the boys approach before ordering the men already seated in the row to move. "You, you, you, you," he barks, pointing to each man in turn, making sure that Ate and her sons can see him. "Do you not see a lady? Do you not see the children? Move now!"

The men shoot dark looks at Ate as they shuffle past her, but they obey. Jimmy manages the hall. His thugs are scattered around the room ready to escort anyone making trouble outside, where they will be taught a lesson, and they know it. Ate thanks Jimmy profusely for the seats and tells her boys to thank their **tito,** too.

"It is nothing! It is not every day my nephews visit me." Jimmy chortles. He pulls a thick wad of money out of his pocket and hands Romuelo and Roy five hundred pesos each.

"For your wagers." He winks at Ate, and she flushes. She does not want her boys gambling. Already it is in their blood, this vice. But she bites her tongue.

Romuelo, who has been staring at his uncle with admiring eyes, is so overwhelmed by his sudden riches that he throws himself at Jimmy, burying his head in the bulge of Jimmy's stomach. Jimmy laughs, his head tilting back and eyes falling closed in the exact manner of Ate's husband, back when Ate's husband used to laugh so freely that he forgot himself. Ate wonders, fleetingly, whether he laughs this way now, with that woman, rid of the burden that Ate and the children represent.

Jimmy ruffles Romuelo's hair and tells him to sit. The fight will start soon.

They take their seats, Jimmy nearest to the aisle so he can talk more easily to the many men who approach him. Next to Ate, Romuelo is fidgety with excitement. Roy sits quietly, his eyes wide and watchful. Romuelo peppers Ate with too many questions—Are these the cocks that were tied outside Tito Jimmy's house? Can he keep the money if he wins his bets?—but Ate ignores him. She is waiting for the right moment to speak to Jimmy. Surely, he will help. He was always kind to her, after all.

"So," Jimmy says at last, taking a tug from the cigarette he holds in his fingers. Ate notices that he needs to cut his nails. They are long and yellow. "So my brother has left you."

Ate's face burns. Of course, Miguel must have confided in Jimmy. They were close once, and crisis can draw people close once again. Maybe Miguel asked Jimmy for help already; it would have been a humiliation for him, bowing low before the little brother he had spurned for so long. Maybe Miguel is here, sitting somewhere in this big hall, already drunk and ready to squander whatever money Jimmy lent him.

"I already know, Ate Evelyn. He called to ask me for money months ago. He had already run out of what he took from you." Jimmy exhales a stream of smoke out of the side of his mouth to spare Ate.

"Is he here?" Ate spits the words, despising herself for even asking. But she has not seen her husband in almost half a year.

"He does not talk to me since I refused to help him. Giving him money is like throwing it away." Jimmy shrugs, dropping the cigarette onto the floor. "But you know this."

Ate drops her head. There is an unexpected gentleness to Jimmy's voice that cuts her.

"Plus," Jimmy continues, lighting another cigarette using an ornately carved lighter he keeps in his pocket, "he thinks I am a big man now. But he does not know how much money it takes to make money. He does not know how tight my boss is."

Ate's heart sinks. She does not like the way Jimmy is talking, already preparing excuses.

"It is very hard without him. I am working, but it is hard with four children," begins Ate.

Jimmy squints, as if trying to make out someone in the distance. Ate continues, not knowing what else to do. "I . . . I ask if you can help a little. I do not like to have to ask. I ask only for the sake of the children. Your nieces. Your nephews—"

"Ah, but, Ate Evelyn, did you not know that I am engaged to be married? My wife, she wants many children!" Jimmy grins, and the sharpness of his teeth makes him look like a wolf.

"I did not know. Congratulations to you both," Ate murmurs, crestfallen.

"I will give you a little money now, of course, of course. We are family! But I cannot commit to more when I must save for my own family, too." He removes the thick stack of cash from his pocket and begins counting out bills, leaning toward Ate conspiratorially as he does so. "And this business looks better than it is. My profits are not always tied to the size of the crowds."

Shame fills Ate. But she smiles, a brittle smile, refusing to reward Jimmy with her disappointment. She takes the handful of bills Jimmy pushes into her palm and considers flinging them into his wolf-face, but instead she clicks open her handbag and sets the money in a side pocket. "Thank you, Jimmy."

There is a sudden roar from the crowd. Jimmy jumps to his feet, and Romuelo with him. Roy slips his hand into Ate's. The first cocks are being brought out, one on each side of the platform.

"So which will be the winner, eh?" Jimmy asks the boys.

Ate thinks of the cock in her childhood home. How he strutted in the dirt, chest puffed. He had mean yellow eyes and dirty brown feathers, and he was the undisputed king of his nothing-special plot of land.

"We attach razors to their claws," Jimmy says in answer to a question of Romuelo, who is excitedly interrogating his uncle about the unfolding spectacle.

Roy visibly cowers in his chair, watching the goings-on through splayed fingers.

"It is only a little blood spilled," Jimmy remarks, eyeing Roy dismissively. "It is only a part of the fight."

One of the cocks squawks, spreading its wings—gray and black plumes that, in the harsh overhead lights, are inexplicably magnificent—and flaps into the air. For a moment Ate thinks it will continue rising, beyond the reach and noise of the manic crowd. And then it is yanked back earthward by its handler, a man in a sleeveless shirt and baseball hat, because the fight has not yet begun.

"AMALIA!" SAYS A WOMAN FROM FAR AWAY, ACROSS A VALLEY.

Ate tries to open her eyes, to see who this Amalia is, but they are so heavy. Her body is heavy, too, as if filled with sand.

Will Jimmy help them?

"Ate," says the voice, and Ate feels something soft and wet on her hand, nuzzling. The wet nose of a dog.

But who allowed Blanca to climb onto the bed? Mama will not like it! She does not like Blanca to be even in the house. She is a guard dog, not a person. Mama will be angry.

"She kept calling for him," says another voice, but it is difficult to hear because of the baby crying. Ellen does not usually cry so quietly. She must be hungry, then.

But Ate is tired. Her legs will not move. She will cook by and by.

Someone is shushing Ellen. Someone is soothing

her. "It is okay. It will be okay," says the voice. Isabel? Isabel knows how to comfort. That is why she is a good nurse.

The white cock was covered in blood, but it did not stop fighting. Both cocks hovering, as if dangling from strings, their wings spread wide and the feathers at the ridge of their heads jagged. Their hateful yellow eyes. The white cock pounced, quick as lightning. A spurt of scarlet against the black one's feathers, and Roy started screaming. He would not stop, only covered his ears with his hands and screamed and screamed.

Get him out, he is a disturbance! Jimmy yelled to her, even though the entire room was roaring.

She hurried Roy up the aisle, jostling and jostled. He dropped the money from Jimmy, and she scrambled on her knees to retrieve it, something hitting her in the head as she did so. Romuelo remained in the hall with Jimmy, mouth agape and mesmerized by the fight. Roy, too, was rendered speechless. Even outside, in the sun and the relative quiet, Roy only curled into himself, weeping, but silently.

Did they always hate each other, or were they taught? Roy asked later at home, his brother asleep next to them clutching a wad of his winnings.

Ate cannot quite remember the sound of his voice.

Is Yaya doing the music therapy? Why am I paying her if she will not do as she is told?

Ate will ask Mrs. Carter for help. She has not spoken to her in some time, but Mrs. Carter is kind. Ate will approach her on bent knees with her pride cupped in her palms like an offering and beg her, please. Please find a doctor for my son.

"I am sorry. I am sorry, Ate."

There is a warmth on Ate's cheek. Blanca on the bed again, probably bringing in the fleas. Ate tries to shove her off before Mama notices the transgression. But she is too weak to lift her hand.

MAE

MAE SETS HER DEVICE ON THE SOFA AMID A SCATTER OF Amalia's things—junky, plastic, made-in-China toys and puzzles and dolls that will break within weeks and end up not-rotting in a landfill for the next several millennia—and tries to ignore the knot in her stomach. She considers calling Ethan, just for the reassurance of his voice, but decides instead to do a guided breathing exercise. She needs to clear her head. She retrieves her device, logs into Zen in Ten, her preferred meditation app, and chooses "Focus and Clarity (Ten Minutes)."

She closes her eyes, trying to ignore the sweat

pooling in her armpits. Jane's apartment is uncomfortably hot. There is only an air conditioner in the bedroom. Mae takes a breath, then a second one. She is midway through her third cleansing breath when her device bleeps.

An email has arrived from a sender Mae does not recognize. The subject line reads:

You'll find this interesting, Ms. Mae!

Usually, Mae would delete it. Her last laptop was hijacked by a computer virus when she clicked on an email masquerading as a birth announcement from a friend. But what if this message is from Jane, or whoever put her up to running away?

Mae's finger hovers over her device. She clicks. There is no writing in the body of the email, but there is a video attachment. She opens it.

There is, at first, only light, a corona of it, its edges wavering like water. Then sky, a merciless blue, and a line of trees almost showy in their greenness.

A mowed field, the split-rail fence past the pool.

Why the scene, idyllic by any definition, elicits foreboding rather than peacefulness, Mae doesn't know. A trick of the camera, perhaps. Or maybe Mae is simply framing it, since she knows the video's intent. Its implicit warning.

The grassy field morphs into a close-up of water. The sun glinting off its surface every which way, like light off broken glass. Standing in the dazzle: silhouettes, backlit by the sun. Their arms are raised, some sort of sun salutation. As the camera moves, their sturdy outlines give way to fleshiness, and flesh—the protuberance of stomachs, globular breasts smashed behind blue lycra. The jiggle of fat on a dark, upraised, water-slicked arm. There are choppy close-ups then. The Hosts' faces scrubbed of expression. Bodies moving in unison, like marionettes—which Mae knows is the whole point. Then, as Mae expected, a cut to the teacher. Of course it would be Jenny, because of all the Pre-Natal Fitness Instructors, she is the most Aryan, almost laughably so: preternaturally tall, lithe, pale even when toasted pinkish by the sun, her hair ridiculously light, unbelievably fine. Sunlight made gossamer. The kind of sorority sister in college who made Mae feel ethnic.

Mae admits the next shot is beautiful, even though it is about as subtle as a hammer on the head. Jenny stands on the raised platform used by instructors so that Hosts in the pool can easily see them and follow their movements. Her arms are outstretched, the setting sun bathing her in a golden glow. She is luminescent, her skin so smooth you want to rub it with a soft cloth to enhance the sheen. Below her the Hosts—of course it would be a class where they are all black or brown—look inconsequential, dark flotsam bobbing in still water.

The footage cuts to an interior shot, now in black-and-white, of the changing room in the pool house. The lighting is bad, or more likely whoever made the video manipulated it so that the room is shadowy, the Hosts' faces almost indistinguishable. They are in various stages of undress. Udder-like breasts, chunky backsides, stretch-marked bellies. The feel of the footage is claustrophobic—cattle in a holding pen, pregnant internees during wartime—which is such a crock, such a malicious warping of reality. The real changing room is lovely. All white-washed walls and gleaming stainless-steel fixtures, big skylights cut into the ceiling. Not that you would guess it from the faux-chiaroscuro hack job that Mae is watching unfold on her device.

Suddenly, "Golden Oaks" materializes onscreen in swirly pale-green font, superimposed over a montage of black-and-white stills (tables of pregnant women in matching Golden Oaks cashmere; a row of Hosts with shirts shoved up over their bellies on which UteroSoundz machines are attached like large, flesh-eating slugs—obvious pictures that are no less emotionally potent for their obviousness). "Golden Oaks" fades to black and the names of various websites and blogs and social-media sites and eminent news organizations scroll down the screen, one after the other.

This thing is a loaded gun. It would go viral in a heartbeat.

And she would lose control of the narrative just as Project MacDonald is taking wing.

Is it Reagan's doing? She understands the power of

an image. Who could have helped her? Because someone did. All devices—phones, cameras, iPads—are confiscated as soon as Hosts arrive at Golden Oaks.

What is it they want?

Mae forwards the clip to Geri and Fiona. She then asks Eve to set up an Internet filter. Mae wants to be alerted ASAP of any mention, anywhere, of Golden Oaks on the Internet, blogosphere, social media, YouTube. Anywhere at all.

Because if something leaks before she's briefed Leon, before she's managed Deng's expectations, Mae is screwed.

Mae's device bleeps again. Her heart thuds, but it's only the security team stationed at the dormitory in Queens. Jane isn't there. They are questioning the residents, but everyone is skittish. They seem to think the security team has been sent by INS to root out immigration violations. Should they play on these fears—without actually lying, of course—to try and elicit more cooperation?

Negative, Mae texts back, instructing them to stand down, only text her if Jane appears.

Mae restarts Zen in Ten. She listens to the sonorous voice wafting into her ear canal, dutifully relaxing her throat muscles, then her tongue. But her thoughts keep intruding.

It's now been more than three hours since Jane disappeared, and the drive from Golden Oaks to the city takes two and a half hours on a bad day.

Eve reports that the Taconic is clear, the FDR flowing; it isn't traffic that is holding up Jane.

So where is she?

An image flashes in Mae's head: Jane wheeling too quickly around one of the Taconic's tight curves, losing control; the car—a flimsy rental—skidding into a stone wall, chunks of glass spilled across the asphalt. Jane's body smashed against the steering wheel.

Mae exhales. She forces herself to smile. The very act of smiling, Mae has read, releases endorphins.

Another bleep. It's Leon demanding an update. He canceled his day's surf trip and is stewing in a hotel in Manila awaiting news.

"I expect you to put out this fire, Mae," he said when they spoke earlier by phone. His voice was so calm it scared her.

Mae is sure, now, that Jane fled Golden Oaks to find her daughter. Angel, Evelyn's friend, explained everything to Mae in a torrent when Mae first arrived in the apartment: that Evelyn had been unwell, that Angel had been helping take care of Amalia while her friend was confined to bed, that Evelyn collapsed five days ago and was rushed into emergency surgery. They've been dodging Jane's calls and emails because they didn't want her to worry and do something rash, jeopardize her job.

Which Jane ended up doing, anyway.

Which means Jane just risked everything over a horrible misunderstanding.

Mae begins typing, ignoring the churning in her stomach. The best thing she can do for everyone involved is to keep Leon from doing something stupid—calling Deng, bringing in the police—until she speaks to Jane.

Mae informs Leon that 84 left Golden Oaks in a misjudged attempt to help with a family emergency and that she presents no threat to Deng's baby. Mae explains that, with Geri's help, she knows which pressure points to use to compel 84 to return to Golden Oaks without force. Mae then outlines the Worst-Case Scenario before Leon can ask for it. She reminds him that Deng's eight viable fetuses were implanted in eight separate Hosts: 70, 72, 74, 76, 78, 80, 82, 84, with a less-viable/high-beta fetus implanted in 96. Three (70, 72, 76) spontaneously aborted within the first three weeks of implantation. Hosts 74 and 78 miscarried in weeks four and five, respectively. 80's was terminated due to trisomy. Although the success rate thus far has been disappointing, Mae believes it's served the purpose of demonstrating to Deng the exceedingly steep challenges Golden Oaks faces in attempting to bring her fetuses to term, given the advanced age of Deng's eggs and her husband's sperm at the time of fertilization.

Should things with 84 go south and the Worst-Case Scenario come to pass—which, Mae takes care

to emphasize in her update, she does not expect—
Deng would still retain the primary fetus carried
by 82, as well as a potentially viable fetus in 96.
Additionally, because 82 is a Premium Host, and
because the fetus she carries is the male one, the
revenue outcome would still be very attractive for
Golden Oaks.

The key in this unlikely scenario, Mae types, her
stomach lurching, is to avoid the "gross negligence"
revenue-clawback mechanism in the contract.
This entails spinning the narrative properly—
emphasizing the fragility of Deng's fetuses and
downplaying, as much as legally permissible, any
issues with 84 that might have led to the fetus's lack
of viability. Legal is reviewing the contract to see
how much the narrative can be finessed.

Mae attaches to her update the latest medical results on 82's fetus from the hospital where Reagan's
confined, as well as a back-of-the-envelope calcula-
tion on how much revenue they'd lose if something
happens to 84.

Leon replies within seconds: **82 is not enough.
We need and Deng expects 84.**

Mae's stomach flips again. Her hands, she notices, are shaking. She tries to restart Zen in Ten,
but for some reason the app won't open. She forces
herself to take a deep breath.

Her device bleeps with an urgent text from Hal.
84 is outside the building.

Mae's heart is in her throat. She forwards the

message to Leon and Geri and gets up to find the bathroom. It's so full of junk—stacks of diapers, unwrapped rolls of toilet paper, a deep fryer, still in its packaging—that it is difficult to open the door.

Mae sighs as she shoves boxes out of her way to make room for herself in front of the sink. She can't believe people live like this. Certainly, Evelyn didn't seem so slovenly when Mae interviewed her for the Scout position.

Mae washes her hands. She sprinkles water on her face, taking care not to smudge her eye makeup, which has held up well. Leaning toward the mirror she applies powder to dull the shine on her forehead and begins to outline her lips.

It's a new color. **Sunrise.** The woman at the Chanel counter said it would suit her.

She's thinking of using it on her wedding day.

JANE

JANE, STEPPING UP TO HER BUILDING'S FRONT DOOR, CAN FEEL
Troy watching her. He is parked in front of a fire
hydrant, engine off, windows rolled down. He
told her he would wait for her and, afterward, they
would need to return her to the Farm.

"But take your time. You deserve to enjoy your
daughter," he had said almost gently. Jane's eyes had
watered, of course. Troy was holding up his camera
phone as he spoke, not even hiding it, but Jane did
not care.

Jane has no keys. The Farm took them on the
first day, along with her cellphone, her wallet. "For

safekeeping," they told her then. Jane presses the button to her apartment and listens to the familiar ring. A long silence follows and, heart sinking, Jane turns to the car and shakes her head. But Troy is looking down at his lap, likely editing video on his phone.

Jane presses the button again. She leans into the speaker: "Angel, are you there? It is Jane!"

There is a crackling, followed by a long guttural buzz. The front door clicks open. She steps into the building, relief flooding her, and she inhales the familiar stew of mildew and take-out food.

Home.

Amalia is only three flights above where Jane stands. She should be in bed by now—if Ate were in charge, she would be—but Jane does not know Angel's rules. Maybe she lets Amalia stay up watching television. If Amalia is awake, even so late, Jane will not be angry. Amalia will look up from whatever it is she is doing, and she will see her mama at the door and totter wildly into Jane's arms.

Or she might be shy. Amalia might hide behind Angel's legs when she sees her mother. In this case, Jane cannot allow herself to feel hurt. It is understandable that Amalia might be wary with her; she was just a baby when Jane left her for the Farm.

There is a lump in Jane's throat. A nervousness she did not expect.

She should have brought Amalia a gift. The thought is a remonstrance. Troy would have lent her a little money. The gift did not have to be big. Only to have something to give.

Jane blinks back her disappointment. She squares her shoulders. There will be time later for presents.

She begins the long climb up the stairs, clutching her stomach with one hand, the other tugging on the railing. She notices how grimy the walls are, the sickly yellow tinge of them. She did not notice before how dirty the building is.

Outside of her apartment door, Jane pauses. She wipes her feet on the mat that Ate bought as a housewarming gift. Thinking of her cousin, Jane's stomach flips. How much does Amalia understand about Ate's sickness? Has she felt alone without her, and without Jane?

She arranges a smile on her face and knocks on her front door.

"Hi, Jane."

It is Ms. Yu. Ms. Yu has just opened the door to Jane's apartment.

Jane closes her eyes and opens them again, but Ms. Yu is still there: her hand resting on the doorknob, her pink lips smiling.

"Come in, Jane," Ms. Yu says, opening the door wider, stepping aside to allow her in.

Jane hesitates. Is this a mistake? A trap?

But here is the green carpet and the listing coat rack that tips if you do not balance the jackets properly. There is the refrigerator that seems to hum louder at night.

"I asked Angel to take Amalia out for a bit," says Ms. Yu. "We thought it would be better this way. So that you and I can talk more freely."

We.

Is Angel working for Ms. Yu, too?

Ms. Yu swoops past her—a fleeting whiff of her perfume—and shuts the front door. She gets a glass from the cupboard, fills it with water from the faucet, and sets it down on the counter before taking a seat on a stool. There are three of them—one for Jane, one for Ate, and one, eventually, for Amalia. That was the plan. The stools were one of Jane's first purchases for the apartment when they moved in.

"Come have some water. I'm sure you're thirsty after such a long night."

Jane's heart pounds as she approaches Ms. Yu. She peeks at her from under lowered lids.

"When will Amalia come back?" Jane keeps her voice strong.

Ms. Yu gestures to the empty stool next to her. "Sit, Jane. Please."

Jane remains standing. "Did they go to the dormitory?"

Ms. Yu smiles the calming smile she has used on Jane so many times before. "Angel and Amalia will be back soon enough. I asked one of our Coordinators to accompany them to a restaurant for a snack. Amalia was **extremely** excited for a treat. I promised her vanilla ice cream."

Amalia's name rolls off Ms. Yu's tongue effort-
lessly, as if she has uttered it a thousand and one
times. Something dark and barbed shoots through
Jane. She senses, in Ms. Yu naming her daughter, a
flag planted.

What if they do not let her see Amalia, even
now? What can Jane do? Can she call Troy somehow and—

"So, how'd you get here, Jane? I remember you
told me once you hate driving," says Ms. Yu, her
manner conversational. When Jane does not answer, Ms. Yu continues. "He must be bored waiting
in the car out there."

Jane looks up quickly. How does she know
about Troy?

Jane forces herself to accept the silence that she
normally tries to fill as she thinks of a plan.

"I don't think he's your boyfriend. You haven't
been in touch with anyone except your cousin
since you arrived at Golden Oaks," Ms. Yu muses.
"So I have to guess it's one of Reagan's friends.
Incidentally—she's miraculously healed. We're of
course keeping her in the hospital as a precaution."

Jane pinches the fabric of her skirt, trying to ignore the anger building inside her. She must keep
control of herself until she knows Amalia is safe.

"No matter," says Ms. Yu. "Security is talking
to your friend now. He's parked in front of a fire
hydrant, which of course isn't legal. They'll have to
run his driver's license, I expect."

Ms. Yu is shaking her head. "Jane, Jane. What were you thinking?" Her voice throbs with sympathy, but Jane refuses to be drawn in. Not again.

What now? What do they do now?

"It's taken all of my efforts to keep the authorities out of this situation," Ms. Yu begins.

Jane's throat burns with thirst. She eyes the cup of water that Ms. Yu set on the counter but refuses to take it. She swallows with difficulty and reminds herself that this is her apartment. Paid for with her own money. She turns her back on Ms. Yu and retrieves another glass from the cupboard. She drinks one glass of water, then refills it and drinks another.

"The problem," says Ms. Yu placidly from behind her, "is that kidnapping is a federal crime."

Jane spins to face Ms. Yu. "But I—I am not—"

"The baby you carry isn't yours. You signed a contract attesting to this and you're bound, by this contract, to take care of the baby to the best of your ability. Running away in the dead of night, not letting anyone know where you were going, entrusting the baby to an unknown driver, subjecting yourself to the risks of a car accident without the means to seek help should you have needed it—"

"But I was always going to—"

"It was reckless. It was dangerous," says Ms. Yu sharply. She gives Jane a penetrating stare and holds it, then sighs. "Some of my colleagues think it shows your lack of fitness to take care of your own child, much less someone else's."

Jane falls back against the sink, her legs suddenly too weak to hold her. Ms. Yu is still talking—pink mouth moving, white hands waving in the air.

". . . so I insisted to them you must have your reasons. This simply isn't like you. But your flight makes my judgment look bad, too. I'm not in the strongest position to help you even if I was convinced that you had no other choice . . ."

Ms. Yu is only trying to scare her.

Reagan and Lisa say this is how they control you. By making you afraid.

". . . and if the Client chooses to pursue this path, by deeming your flight a kidnapping, well then . . ."

But Reagan and Lisa do not know everything. They did not even think of this possibility—that the plan could endanger Amalia. They came up with it so quickly, in the hours after Ms. Yu invited Jane to the play. Reagan insisted that it was Jane's chance, possibly her only chance, to find Amalia. They were too rushed to think of everything; they were convinced that the videos—

"But there are the videos," she hears herself interject in a voice eerily calm.

Ms. Yu's eyes widen for a half second. "The videos. Oh, yes. I received them. They're quite beautiful, actually. It's a shame I don't know who sent them to congratulate him on his artistry."

Jane does not dare look Ms. Yu in the face.

"What do you think those videos accomplish, Jane?" Ms. Yu is smiling, and her voice retains its outward friendliness, but inside there is something different, something steely and cold.

Jane wipes her hands on her skirt.

"One of the videos mentioned websites, social media, YouTube. Is that the plan? To release footage of Golden Oaks far and wide? To 'out' us, as it were?"

Ms. Yu is no longer smiling. Her face frightens Jane. Jane should never have mentioned the videos. She should never have listened to Reagan and Lisa.

"Or is the plan to release the names of Clients? To blackmail them?"

"No!" Jane cries, shocked that Ms. Yu would even think of this. "No, they never said anything about—"

"And who is **they**?" Ms. Yu pounces.

Jane shakes her head vigorously. She closes her eyes, feeling their wetness.

"Who put you up to this, Jane? This isn't like you. It doesn't seem like Reagan's handiwork either, but she's the obvious one to blame. Or was it the man outside? Did he come up with all of this?"

Jane is still shaking her head. Refusing to open her eyes.

What has she done?

"Are you going to take the blame again, Jane? Like you did with the tick, when the fault so clearly lay with Lisa? Like you did with your husband, carrying the brunt of the separation—the expenses, your daughter?"

Jane does not bother to wipe her eyes.

"You don't deserve it, Jane. To always be the one to give and give and give. To never get your due. It simply isn't fair."

Ms. Yu hands Jane a tissue.

"Think of the mother of the baby you carry," Ms. Yu says quietly. "Because it matters less who came up with this plan than for you to understand why what has happened is so harmful."

Jane can feel Ms. Yu studying her. She blows her nose.

"Can you imagine what it's like to not know where your baby is?" Ms. Yu asks. "Because that's what you put the mother through tonight. For several hours, the mother had no idea whether her child was in the hands of someone caring and careful, or someone selfish and possibly dangerous."

Ms. Yu pauses. Jane balls her hands, which have begun to shake.

Can they take Amalia from her?

"Imagine," continues Ms. Yu, "having no inkling whether your child is injured or sick or in the gravest of danger. Do you have any idea how painful that is to the mother who trusted you? How painful it is **not knowing**?"

A sob rises in Jane's throat. She stifles it, or tries. She hears herself saying, "Of course I know."

"Oh?" Ms. Yu is watching her, unmoved. Ms. Yu does not believe her.

"Why else am I here?" Jane cries, something inside her bursting.

Ms. Yu shrugs, a tiny lift of her narrow shoulders under the crisp ivory jacket she wears. "It doesn't make sense, Jane. I already promised you I'd figure out another visit for your daughter. You knew she was in fine hands with your cousin."

"My cousin is dying," Jane spits, surrendering, not even caring that Ms. Yu sees her swollen, wet, ugly face. She stares at the refrigerator. There are pictures of Amalia held up with magnets, a calendar from the laundromat down the street with Ate's handwriting on it marking down doctor and other appointments, a yellow flyer titled **Warning Signs of a Heart Attack.**

"Angel said she was recuperating?"

Jane, her voice so thick she is surprised Ms. Yu can understand her, tells her everything: learning about Segundina; finding out that Ate worked for Ms. Yu; Amalia's ear infections and the long weeks that Jane could reach no one to check on her daughter—not Ate, not Angel, no one at the dormitory in Queens.

And then the hospital, and Ate, and Roy.

Jane does not mention the escape. She does not mention Reagan or Lisa or the theater or the drive, and Ms. Yu does not ask.

What Ms. Yu does say is, "Jane. I'm sorry. I didn't know things were so serious. When Evelyn canceled Amalia's overnight visit, she only told me she was feeling a little 'off' and didn't want to worry you."

She pauses for a moment, as if thinking hard about something. "And I hope you know that—that she brought you to me because she truly believed Golden Oaks would help you to improve your life. And Amalia's."

"She did not need to lie to me," Jane says, pressing a ball of tissues to her face.

Ms. Yu sighs. "In retrospect, it probably wasn't the best way to do things. But she thought it best at the time. You just have to trust, Jane, that she had your best interests at heart."

Jane looks up at her, incredulous. "How can I trust anyone?"

Ms. Yu sighs again. She shakes her head in what seems like sorrow. "I can see you were in a difficult position. And that you were overcome with worry about Amalia. And that you felt you had no one to turn to . . . Oh but, Jane. You were just so close. And now—"

Jane swallows. "Now, what?"

Ms. Yu shakes her head again. "I simply don't know."

MAE

MAE NOTICES THAT THE WAITER IS BALDING. A PATCH OF SCALP the shape of Australia gleams at the crown of his head as he stoops down to set the tray on the ottoman. He's older than he looks at first glance.

"Have you been working here long?" Mae asks him. She doesn't recognize him from her days managing the Club.

The man straightens the teaspoons so that they are perpendicular to the tray. "No, ma'am. It is my first month."

"Congratulations."

His accent—some kind of Eastern European

one—is heavy. Mae used to advise such heavily accented employees to take accent-reduction classes online. Clients hate it when they have trouble understanding the staff. Why allow something remediable to impede your career?

"Thank you, ma'am."

Mae considers recommending such a class to the waiter, but he has already turned away, and Mae knows she's only trying to distract herself from the call she just had with Leon.

She pours herself a cup of tea and gulps it down, then pours herself another. She didn't sleep much last night even when she knew Jane and Amalia were safely ensconced with a Coordinator at a hotel, and this morning she was up with the sun and out the door before Ethan had even stirred.

Mae has seen Leon get angry often during her years working with him—he has a temper, and shouting, for him, is a form of exorcism. But she's never heard him as furious as he was last night. Not that she can blame him. Leon has every right to be angry. Mae's fuckup—her lack of rigorous oversight, her complacency—put not only Madame Deng's baby in jeopardy but also their big plans for Golden Oaks' expansion.

Luckily, Leon didn't see it quite this way—or, at least, he professed not to. For some reason (his affection for her? her humility in the face of his ire?) he pinned most of the blame on the Coordinators and on Jane herself. Mae knows she narrowly dodged a bullet—her reputation dinged but not eviscerated. Her favorite HBS professor always said that no failure is a true failure if you learn something from it, and Mae is committed to learning from this monumental snafu so that it never happens again. She's rethinking Golden Oaks' visitation policies—perhaps they should be loosened, particularly for Hosts who have young children at home. Or the opposite: maybe they shouldn't hire Hosts who are already mothers because their loyalties, inevitably, lie elsewhere.

Mae's phone bleeps. Leon is speaking to Madame Deng this morning (evening in Asia) to discuss the previous night's happenings. He will tell her their edited story, cleared by Legal: 84 left Golden Oaks due to a family emergency and the Coordinators failed, in the rush, to ask Deng's permission first—a breach of protocol but a minor one compared to the full story. Who knows, though, how Deng will react? Wealthy people are used to mastering their universes. Even a whiff that Golden Oaks isn't wholly in control could be dire.

Heart pounding, Mae answers her phone. But it is only Eve. She reports that Jane, escorted by Security, is five minutes from the Club. Attached to her text is the new contract, which Mae skims.

The phone pings again. This time it's the wedding planner. The florist says she's found a vendor for the dark-pink peonies Mae wants for the table arrangements, but they're hothouse flowers—peonies don't grow in the fall—so buying them in October will be expensive: does Mae care?

No! Mae wants to scream, though she very much does. She's micromanaged every detail of her wedding down to the exact shade of ivory of the raw-silk, 134-inch round table linens—but this was when she'd imagined her wedding as a glorious celebration on multiple levels: of her nuptials to Ethan, obviously; of Madame Deng's babies, who are due days before the ceremony; of Deng's investment; and of Golden Oaks' ambitious expansion and her own role at its helm.

Mae texts the wedding planner to hold off. She needs to rein in her spending until she's certain the Deng investment is moving forward.

There is a loud knocking at the door and Jeff, one of Hal's men, pokes his head into the room. "You ready, Ms. Yu?"

"Hi, Jeff. Yes, I am. Please send her in."

Jane enters. Her face is drawn, her eyes dark holes. She clearly didn't sleep much, if at all. Thank God Leon, who'd expressed interest in joining the conversation via video feed, is tied up with Madame Deng.

"Hi, Jane. Please sit. Can I get you some tea? We have herbal—"

Jane shakes her head and sits, rigid, on one of the tufted slipper chairs across from Mae. "The men would not allow me to see my cousin."

Mae didn't expect Jane to be so direct; she'd

hoped to break the news to her gently. "I'm sorry, Jane. Your Client doesn't want you spending any more time at the hospital."

Jane opens her mouth to speak, then drops her head and stares at her clasped hands. Mae imagines how terrible Jane must feel to know she's not allowed to see her cousin when her condition is so dire. But the Client has a point, too. The Client will do anything to make sure her child is safe, the same way Jane will.

"The issue is that we don't know how long your cousin will linger," Mae says. "The doctors say it could be days. Or weeks. There's too big a risk you could catch something at the hospital. Just the other day there was a case of staph on Evelyn's floor . . ."

"I can stay in a hotel," Jane interrupts. "I can pay using my bonus."

Mae steels herself. "You're not getting a bonus for delivering the baby, Jane."

Jane meets Mae's gaze. It is so quiet that Mae can hear Jane swallow.

"I understand the pressures you were under," Mae fights the urge to reach for Jane's hand, knowing that without the bonus Jane is back to where she started: a dead end. "I explained the situation to my boss. But he simply won't budge. He feels that paying you a bonus when your contract clearly states that an infraction of this magnitude would result in—"

Jane speaks in a rush: "I will ask Angel to keep Amalia in the dormitory in Queens. I will use my rent money to pay for a hotel. I have a little savings."

"Your Client doesn't want you at the hospital, and she doesn't want you here in the city," Mae interjects, before Jane can get her hopes up any further. "It's not just the air quality here in Manhattan, or the lack of safeguards. She worries about the stress on you—the toll—of watching your cousin . . . Of seeing your cousin ill."

Jane falls silent. She is staring at her hands again.

"Jane, I know you don't want Evelyn to be alone—"

"I will not leave my cousin alone."

"I don't want that, either," Mae agrees, a little surprised at the hardness in Jane's voice. "So this is what I propose: we fly Evelyn's daughters to New York. Angel's already been in touch with them. Our legal department is seeing about getting their visas expedited."

"My Client will do this?" Jane asks, surprised.

"Well, no . . . It's not the right time to . . ." Mae is momentarily flustered. "I would like to help. It would be my pleasure to pay for the tickets."

"But why?"

This is not the response Mae expected. She was ready for a profusion of thanks, maybe even tears.

"I want to do this for you. And for Evelyn," Mae explains, feeling awkward. "You both work hard—harder than most people I know."

"And if my cousin dies?"

Mae ignores the pit that has opened in her stomach and forces herself to press onward. Regardless of her personal feelings, there's work to be done, however difficult. "If your cousin . . . passes . . . while you're still carrying, the Client will allow you to return to New York for the service. As long as you're not dilated more than three centimeters . . ." Mae shows Jane the relevant section in the contract displayed on her device. "If you're dilated three centimeters and the baby is at least thirty-eight weeks, she will also accommodate you . . ."

Jane stares at the contract but does not seem to see.

"You'll still get your monthly stipend," Mae says, knowing this is small compensation. "There will be no other ramifications for your actions. Besides losing the delivery bonus."

Jane presses her hands together, falling silent again. Mae assumes she is praying—for Ate, or maybe for guidance—and waits. She is filled with sadness, big as the ocean. For Jane, for Evelyn. For Evelyn's daughters, who will see their mother for the first time in decades only to say goodbye, if they even make it to New York. For her sons. Bad luck on top of bad luck. The stories are always the same.

"I want Amalia with me," Jane announces with an abruptness that makes Mae jump. "If Amalia is near me, even though my cousin is sick, I will be calmer. This is what you can tell my Client. She will agree because she worries about my stress and the baby."

Mae gazes at Jane. She looks different suddenly. It could be the light—the sun is streaming through the window now, full force—but Mae doesn't think so.

"I can certainly broach that idea with the Client," she says carefully.

"And Reagan," Jane says. "She should not be in trouble. She did nothing wrong. I believe it was the food she ate at Golden Oaks that made her sick."

Mae pretends to take notes on her device to buy herself time. Convincing Leon to let Amalia stay with Jane will take some doing. But this second request is a no-brainer. They were never going to tell Madame Deng that **both** of her remaining Hosts went rogue. Not that Jane needs to know this. "Is that all?"

Jane nods slightly and reaches for the pot of tea on the table, which wobbles in her hand. She pours herself a cup and refills Mae's. Mae watches her sign the contract. She's so young, a whole lifetime ahead. But what kind of life?

Mae comes to a decision: she will give Jane some money to tide her over until she finds a new job. This won't be easy—Jane lacks skills and a high school diploma, and she's persona non grata at Golden Oaks. But Mae must know someone in her circle who needs help around the house—with childcare or, maybe, cleaning. Obviously, the pay won't be great. Jane and Amalia will probably have to move back to the dormitory in Queens. It's no way to raise a child, but what other option does Jane have?

Mae's mind continues flipping through the possibilities. And then an idea strikes her, a way to stop Jane from freefall. It's a big step, maybe too extreme, and she's not sure how Jane will react. "Have you thought about what you're going to do next?"

Jane does not hesitate. "I will do whatever it is I need to do."

EPILOGUE

TWO AND A HALF YEARS LATER

"STOP KICKING, MY HAPPY ONE," JANE SAYS TO VICTOR. HE IS kicking his legs against the changing pad. Above him, the mobile with the airplanes spins.

He chortles suddenly, as if one of the airplanes is doing tricks specially for him. He is jolly, always so jolly, and he smiles now at Jane with his mouth spread so wide she laughs. "Silly happy baby boy."

Amalia stomps into the room. She insisted on dressing herself this morning and wears a neon-pink tutu and the pajama top with frogs on it. "I want to go outside!"

"I am not ready yet, Mali," answers Jane, taking

a scented wipe from the dispenser and swiping Victor's bottom.

Amalia stares at the mess with distaste. "Yuck," she says, and marches off.

Jane watches Amalia's bright silhouette disappear around the corner. She is jealous of the baby, Jane knows. She loves him and hates him at the same time. Jane understands this; how you can hold both feelings in your heart, equally fierce.

Jane transfers Victor to the yellow chair, her favorite, in the corner of the room. It was not so many hours ago that she sat here holding him, knowing that she should let him cry but allowing herself to rock him to sleep. She enjoys these moments—the house still, even the crickets silenced, and the world only Jane and Victor and the yellow chair in the pool of lamplight.

Jane did not take the time to enjoy Amalia in this way when she was small. They were living in the dorm in Queens then, Jane still shell-shocked that she had left Billy. When Amalia woke at night Jane worried about disturbing her bunkmates. This worry led to others—how she would find a job, who would help with Amalia, whether Billy was right, that Jane would go to Hell for seeking a divorce—until the blackness had lightened to gray and it was almost morning.

"Now? Can I go outside now?" Amalia has returned. She added to her outfit the sparkly cowboy hat that she wore for Halloween trick-or-treating last year.

"Only a few more minutes, Mali."

Amalia glares at her mother, hands on her hips and head cocked to one side. In this stance she reminds Jane so much of Ate that her heart hurts.

"Be patient."

Amalia turns on her heels. Jane can hear her thudding down the stairs. The screen door bangs. Through the window, she sees Amalia tearing across the grass without shoes on. Jane is half-angry. It was only last month that Amalia, barefoot, stepped on a bee and was stung. She hobbled around for half the day insisting that Jane carry her.

But Jane is also half-glad. During the last parent-teacher conference, Amalia's preschool teacher recited to Jane the different ways that her daughter bucked the rules (she would not wear her smock when painting; she found it "challenging" to take turns on the swings). "She's a good girl, but very strong willed."

The teacher said this with a shake of her head, as if it were something shameful. As if being a **good girl** and being **strong willed** were in conflict.

No one has ever described Jane as strong willed.

Jane pulls on Victor's pants and lifts him to her chest. He really is so easy, rarely fussing. Amalia at this age was a handful, Ate used to say. Is it because Victor knows, somehow, that he was born into an easier life? Is it because boys are more comfortable in the world than girls?

Jane glances out the window again. Amalia is now crouched in the grass hugging the neighbor's dog. It is a black dog, big, and believes their yard to be his also. Jane does not like it when Amalia plays with the dog in this way—hugging it, rolling on the grass entangled with it—as if it is not, at heart, an animal.

Amalia defends it: But he is trained, Mama! He does tricks!

And he does; the neighbor showed them: Sit. Shake. Play dead.

But Jane knows that the tricks are on the surface only. That if threatened, the dog will revert to what it truly is, the way Nanay's dog nipped Jane once when it thought she was trying to steal its bone. Of course, Amalia does not listen to her warnings. And what is Jane to do—lock Amalia inside the house all weekend long?

"You will be a good listener," Jane tells Victor, kissing his fat neck. She is carrying him down the stairs when she hears Amalia shriek.

"MAMA!"

The dog. Amalia is too rough with the dog.

Jane bolts outside, Victor bouncing on her shoulder and laughing as if it were a game. But Jane is not playing games, and she is ready to do what she must—kick the dog, grab her daughter with her free arm and run with both children into the house.

"Push me, Mama!" Amalia yells. She has climbed

onto the wooden swing that hangs from a branch of the large tree in the middle of the backyard, and the dog is nowhere to be seen.

"Mali!" Jane scolds. "You scared me!"

Amalia dips back her head and sings, "I'm rea-dy!"

Ate would have spanked Amalia for behaving in this way. Like a queen, demanding this and that. She always said the worst thing you can do to a child is raise it with too much softness, because the world is hard. But Jane is not sure. There are people who move through the world like they own it, and the world seems to bend to their demands.

"Say 'please,' Mali."

Amalia kicks her legs as Jane tries to push her, but it is difficult with only one free arm. Jane's other arm holds Victor, who squirms but does not cry, gurgling and wetting her shirt with his drool. She should go inside and start his lunch soon. She is going to make pureed squash. It was Amalia's favorite when she was starting on solids, or so Ate had told Jane. And Mr. Ethan's shirts need to be ironed. He and Ms. Yu are not back from the wedding in St. Barts until tomorrow, but Jane wants to finish the ironing before the handyman comes to fix the faucet in Victor's bathroom.

Jane can imagine Reagan rolling her eyes at her, the way Jane worries over her chores.

"And do they **make** you call them Mr. Ethan and Ms. Yu?" Reagan had scoffed when she last visited, a month ago. "You **live** with them, for fuck's sake!"

It is true that Jane and Amalia stay in the apartment above the garage, but it is not their home. This is what Reagan does not understand. Ate taught Jane the importance of a "respectful distance" when living with clients, because if they feel you are in the way too often or observing them too closely, they might look for someone new.

Only last weekend, Jane was preparing breakfast when Amalia's bouncy ball escaped down the hall. Amalia chased after it, too loud as usual, and Jane should have gone after her. But the scrambled eggs were almost done, and Ms. Yu does not like them overcooked. By the time they were plated, Mr. Ethan had escorted Amalia back to the kitchen. He was smiling—Mr. Ethan is always nice—but he asked Jane if he could "have a little space," just while he finished up a conference call.

Jane, mortified, had berated Amalia before sending her up to their apartment, which she was not allowed to leave the rest of the day.

"More pushing!" Amalia shouts.

Jane knows she is a little tough on her daughter sometimes, but they cannot take their situation for granted. Jane can still remember the dread she felt when Ms. Yu told her she would not get the big bonus from Golden Oaks. Her mind immediately raced toward backup plans and possibilities, none of them good: reconciling with Billy; begging her old supervisor at the retirement home for her job back or asking Angel to find her a position—nannying, cleaning, it did not matter—with a rich family.

"Mama, why can't I **convince** you to push more?"

Jane stares at her daughter in surprise. "**Convince?** How do you know this word, Mali?"

"From Mae!"

"Ms. Mae," Jane corrects her, so that Amalia cannot sense the awe in her voice. Amalia only needs to hear a big word once to know how to use it. Ms. Yu says it is because Amalia is gifted. When she found out that Amalia—only three and a half—was already reading a little, Ms. Yu bought her a set of Dr. Seuss books, and they are Amalia's favorites.

It is acts of generosity like this that prove to Jane that Ms. Yu is not a bad person, as Reagan insists. Reagan despises Ms. Yu for lying to them at Golden Oaks, for taking away Jane's bonus, and for her manipulativeness—but could Ms. Yu have done anything differently without losing her job?

Jane does not believe people are as free as Reagan thinks they are. Sometimes a person has no choice but hard choices, like the one Jane made to be here, living without true privacy among strangers. There are days when Jane misses her apartment in Queens and its comforting nearness to the dorm. In this town, almost everybody is white and blond, even at church. But she made the right choice for Amalia.

And Ms. Yu is kind when she does not need to be. After Jane delivered Madame Deng's baby—the infant girl was taken away before Jane had even seen her face—Ms. Yu came to see her in the hospital. She asked Jane what her plans were, and when Jane responded that she didn't know, Mae told her she had an idea.

"Ethan and I are ready to start a family—we just don't have the time!" Ms. Yu had laughed. Then she asked Jane to be her surrogate. She told her that there was an apartment on their property where Jane and Amalia could live rent free during the pregnancy and, if things worked out, maybe even afterward.

Jane was floored by Ms. Yu's generosity, and still is, most days. It is true, as Reagan likes to remind her, that Jane routinely works much more than the forty hours a week she is paid. But it is also true that without Ms. Yu, Amalia would not be in a good preschool. Ms. Yu spoke to the church and arranged the financial aid. And without the free apartment, Jane would have spent all her savings. Now, the money left over from working for Mrs. Carter so long ago, and Jane's salary from Golden Oaks, sits in the bank. The money is not yet enough to make life easier, but it gives Jane comfort to know it is there, growing steadily with the **compounding.**

"Mae lets you live here because it's a **great** deal for her. Not an act of generosity," Reagan said during her last visit, her voice ugly.

"It is both," Jane had answered. "I am grateful."

MAE LIFTS HER SUITCASE OUT OF THE TOWN CAR AND WHEELS it toward the house, her heart lifting at the thought of seeing Victor a day earlier than planned. Her flight to Los Angeles isn't until later this evening, so she'll get most of the day with him. If the weather holds she can take him to their country club, and they can sit by the pool and enjoy the Indian summer.

Leon was profusely apologetic when he called to tell her he needed to cut her long weekend short, but honestly, Mae was glad for the excuse to leave. Ethan's friend, the groom, is nice enough, but his bride is beyond vapid, and her bridesmaids even worse. Mae couldn't have handled another discussion about the latest-greatest boutique cardio class or the newest cellulite-blasting injection.

And it didn't hurt that Leon sent his plane to St. Barts for her.

In any case, Mae wouldn't have missed this opportunity for the world. She feels terribly for Gabby, the Head of Investor Relations, of course. An emergency appendectomy is no picnic. But it does mean that Mae will run the meeting on Monday with Deng and the other investors who bankrolled Red Cedars. It's always good to make connections. You never know where they might lead.

It's hard to believe it was not even three years ago that she first pitched Project MacDonald to Leon. Since then, Golden Oaks has almost doubled in size, and Red Cedars launches in months! The client list for their new outpost includes some of the biggest names in Silicon Valley, a mining magnate from Indonesia, several Chinese billionaires half-based in Vancouver, and a third-generation banking scion from Japan.

Whatever the mind can conceive and believe, it can achieve.

Mae enters the house—the door is unlocked, she'll speak to Jane about that—and slips off her shoes. She hears Jane talking to someone in the kitchen and feels a twinge of annoyance. It's fine if Jane has friends over, but she should know enough not to entertain them in the main house, even when Mae and Ethan are away.

"Surprise!"

"Ms. Yu!" Jane jumps up from her chair, cellphone in hand and a guilty expression on her face. Mae has asked Jane not to use her phone when she's with Victor. "I am sorry. I lost track of time . . ."

Mae reaches for her son. "Hello, handsome!" As soon as he sees his mother, Victor beams, and Mae's heart floods with happiness.

"I am sorry I was using the phone," Jane says, arranging a burp cloth over Mae's shoulder.

"I'm not back from Cali 'til Wednesday, so I'll need you to work late the next few days." Mae pointedly ignores Jane's apology. She notices a picture on the counter. "What's this?"

"Reagan gave it to me."

Mae studies the image with interest. It is a photograph of Reagan's mother—the family resemblance is clear. In it, the mother is half-turned from the camera, the sun flooding her face so that she glows, and she is smiling with what looks like joy.

Mae is impressed. She knew Reagan was into photography, but she had no idea she was actually talented. Mae helped her get into a group show recently out of kindness and, quite honestly, residual guilt. Years ago, when Reagan confronted Mae about the Callie/Tracey switch after delivering Deng's baby, she was angry, which Mae had expected, but also deeply hurt. Mae realized only then that "Callie" must have been a sort of mother figure to Reagan.

In any case, getting Reagan into the show was a cinch. One of Mae's Clients bought a building in Gowanus years ago for his artist-son as a studio-cum-performance-cum-gallery space, and he seems to host a new exhibit every other month for his various bohemian-trustafarian friends.

"Shouldn't she put this in the show?" Mae asks. "It's beautiful."

Over the whir of the food processor, Jane explains that Reagan thinks the pictures of her mother are too pretty. "She wants to take pictures that 'make people see.' That make them angry. Like the one she showed me . . . it is famous. A refugee boy dead on a beach from trying to escape Africa?" Jane unplugs the machine. "I do not really understand why being angry is better."

Mae kisses Victor's neck. Clearly, nothing has changed for Reagan, even with all her good fortune. When she delivered, Leon insisted on increasing her already huge bonus by fifty percent to reward her for being "the good Host." The money freed Reagan from her father's dictates and then some—the last Mae heard, Reagan bought an apartment in Williamsburg and footed the entire bill for her MFA. And yet Reagan's still fundamentally dissatisfied. It just proves that in life, attitude's everything. Reagan's trapped in a cage of her own making.

"Some people can't be grateful for what they have," Mae says, setting the picture back on the counter. "What a shame, though. Her photos would sell."

The screen door bangs. Amalia hurls herself around Mae's legs. "Mae!"

"**Ms.** Mae," Jane reprimands from behind the sink.

"It's okay, Jane." Mae ruffles Amalia's hair as the little girl begins recounting a book she read that morning.

"Mali. Ms. Mae is tired from the airplane. Let her rest."

Mae waves Jane off and urges Amalia to continue. It's important to encourage her interest in books and learning, which Jane doesn't do enough.

She's so hard on her daughter, constantly nagging Amalia about her manners, her loquaciousness, almost as if Jane's trying to force her into the rigid mold of Good, Obedient Asian Female. But how many Good, Obedient Anyones truly make it in the world? Honestly, and Mae would never say this aloud because she doesn't like to boast—living with Mae and Ethan is the best thing that could have happened to Amalia. She'll be exposed to a different way of being. She'll get to see, every day, what a strong woman and a strong marriage look like.

It's the least Mae can do for Jane. And Mae's grown fond of Amalia. She's extremely bright. She could go places with the right guidance.

"Mali, enough. Go wash your hands and I will make you lunch," says Jane. When Amalia starts walking to the mudroom's bathroom, Jane reprimands her, "Not here. In the apartment."

"Jane," Mae chides. "Feed her here." Mae's told Jane that on the weekends, she and Ethan prefer that they have the house to themselves. But Ethan's still in St. Barts, and Mae's in a good mood.

"Thank you, Ms. Yu."

Mae kisses Victor's stomach, and he chortles. "Oh, Jane. I meant to tell you. My mother's coming on Thursday. Can you make sure the guest room's set?"

"Of course," Jane says. "It is good your mother will visit. It has been a long time."

Mae watches Jane scoop pureed squash into one of the BPA-free plastic bowls sold on the new

Golden Oaks website. Mae's mother was atrocious to Jane during her last visit—criticizing how Jane burped, bathed, dressed Victor; sniping at Amalia so that the little girl steered clear of the main house for the duration of Mae's mother's visit. Mae explained to Jane later, by way of apology, that her mother wants to move to Westchester to help care for Victor. She resents Jane, but it isn't personal.

And yet—here's Jane, telling Mae that her mother's visit is a **good thing.** Reagan could learn a thing or two from her friend, who's mastered the art of turning life's lemons into lemonade.

Mae feels a pang of guilt. Her mother's been unmoored since Mae's father passed away. And Ethan and Mae **did** build the apartment above the garage with aging parents in mind. But Mae's mother isn't all that old yet, and honestly—she'd drive Mae crazy with her unsolicited advice and incessant complaints. At least until Red Cedars is up and running, Mae needs Jane close by.

"Hi bye!" Amalia yells. The mudroom door slams, and Jane sees her daughter running across the grass, screaming for the neighbor's dog.

"She is too wild." Jane shakes her head.

"She's spirited," Ms. Yu answers. "I'm happy to feed Victor. Go get her."

Jane walks outside. She sees that the black dog has heeded Amalia's calls and is scampering in circles around her. Amalia is trying to grab his tail.

"If you roughhouse with the dog, it will rough-house back," Jane warns.

The air smells of cut grass and grilled meat from a barbecue somewhere down the street. It is hot for October. Jane watches her daughter, wondering how she is not afraid of this big dog, or her teachers, or Ms. Yu. Wondering how she became so brave and so smart.

Ms. Yu says the school down the street is ranked in the top ten in the state. Next fall, even though Amalia will only be four, Ms. Yu thinks she should start kindergarten.

"We'll need to get her tested, " Ms. Yu said. "But she's clearly smart enough."

To go to this school Amalia needs to live in the school zone, and so Jane has been devising a backup plan. Ate always had one, and Jane now understands why: nothing is guaranteed, and no one is irreplace-able. On the bulletin board in church, Jane has seen advertisements for nannies, both live-out and live-in. If Ms. Yu tires of Jane, or if Ms. Yu's mother moves in, Jane will try to find work with someone in the neighborhood. The difficulty will be find-ing an employer who will allow Amalia to live with them, too. Jane will need to entice them with extra services—free weekend babysitting or cooking, or both. And Jane must learn how to drive, so she can take the children to their lessons and sports. Reagan owns a car now and said she would teach her.

———

"MAMA!" AMALIA IS SCREAMING. THE DOG HAS STOLEN HER HAT.

Mae watches from the window as she feeds Victor his milk. Jane has her hands on her hips and is saying something to Amalia. Probably scolding her. But no, now she's holding Amalia close and wiping her face with the corner of her apron. Jane's harsh with her daughter, but she's a good mother. And she's been unremittingly wonderful with Victor.

Mae wonders if Ethan is right. If they should consider having another child soon. She just turned forty, and Ethan's even older, and they don't want to be geriatric parents. They still have viable eggs stored with Golden Oaks. And it might be nice to have kids close in age. Ethan and his brother are Irish twins, and they're best friends.

"I hope we have a little girl, a little Mae," said Ethan when they were lying on the beach in St. Barts over the weekend, smiling the smile that still makes Mae's stomach flip.

He asked her if she'd consider carrying the baby herself this time. Mae was startled, and then furious. What was he implying about their first pregnancy? And how selfish for him to propose a "real" one, when it wouldn't alter his life at all!

Ethan apologized and then explained in his gentle way, "I know you'd bear the brunt of it, but I'd be with you every step of the way."

Mae is far from convinced. But on the plane ride

home she did recall the look of wonder on Ethan's face the first time he felt Victor move. They were in the kitchen, and it was just after dinner, and Ethan and Mae stood close to Jane with their hands on her stomach, feeling their son kick. Mae did feel a stab of—something. Jealousy, maybe, or longing.

Maybe it **would** be a worthwhile experience to go through a pregnancy together. All the marriage books say that new, shared experiences are what keep couples bonded. They would take pregnancy classes, and at night Ethan could sleep with his hand glued to her belly, and when she delivered he'd be at her side, feeding her ice cubes and coaching her on her breathing exercises.

Then again, Mae makes more money than Ethan, and pregnancy might slow her down. And she feels like she's pulled in seven different directions as it is. Plus, her womb is way older than Jane's, so there's more risk involved.

She hears, suddenly, her mother's voice in her head, the judgment when Mae told her they were using a surrogate, and again when Mae told her Jane would live with them to help care for Victor. "You're missing out. You're sidelining yourself from your own life."

This from a woman who had the housekeeper care for Mae every afternoon while she was at the club playing golf!

And yet, two weekends ago, when Jane and Amalia spent a night with Reagan in Williamsburg, it had been nice—exhausting, but nice. Just Mae and Ethan and Victor. She and Ethan puttered around the house—it was hard to make plans when Victor still napped three times a day—and cooked together. At night the three of them lay in bed watching a movie. Ethan made it only a third of the way through before he fell asleep, Victor splayed on his chest. Mae was content just watching them.

AMALIA HAS STOPPED SCREAMING, BUT SHE STILL CRIES.

"I will get the hat for you," Jane assures her.

The black dog is galloping back and forth across the yard, the cowboy hat clamped in its jaws. Jane calls to it, but when it approaches she grows afraid. It is a big dog. Powerful. Reagan has told her that dogs can sense fear, and it makes them bold.

"Come," Jane orders, making her voice hard.

The dog nears. Jane manages to grab the hat, but the dog will not release it, and it is stronger than she is. It breaks free, delighted, and begins to zigzag across the grass.

"Bad dog!" yells Amalia.

Jane has seen the neighbor play fetch with the dog. She finds a stick on the ground and, with thumping heart, begins to wave it in the air until the dog notices and approaches. Jane, terrified, throws the stick as hard as she can across the yard. The dog drops Amalia's hat onto the grass and streaks away.

Amalia runs for her hat and beams at Jane. "Thank you, Mama!"

She begins to dance a triumphant jig, hands on hips and bare feet stomping. The sun overhead glints off the sequins of her hat so that Jane is, momentarily, bedazzled.

Amalia runs toward the swing but is distracted by a fallen tree branch, and she takes it in her hands and begins riding it like a horse.

"I'm coming to save you, Mama!"

Jane laughs at her daughter, watching her shoot imaginary bad guys with her fingers before dropping the branch, bored. She skips across the grass, holding on to her hat with one hand and gesticulating to the black dog with the other, trying to get it to come nearer.

"Be careful, Mali," Jane warns. Her breasts have begun tingling, which means she will have to pump milk soon for Victor. Ms. Yu bought the best kind of pump, so it does not take long, and Jane can fold laundry while she makes milk so as not to waste time.

"Mama, look!" Amalia cries. A gust of wind has filled her skirt, and she is spinning, bright pink blooming around her like a flower.

"That is pretty, Mali," Jane says, something pulling at her heart. She thinks of Ate and her rough-gentle hands on Jane's head when she was sick, and the reading glasses that balanced on the very end of her nose when she explained things, and the brusque way she told Jane to stop crying, she would find a way without Billy, Ate would help her.

Jane wishes she were here. In the sun, on the grass behind this big white house, watching Amalia. Because she would know then that things were going to be different.

"MAMA!"

"Yes, Mali?" Jane asks, feeling pain and joy, both, as she watches her daughter begin to run.

"Mama, push me!" Amalia shouts, climbing onto the swing and flinging off her hat.

Jane shakes her head, walking to retrieve it from the grass before the dog steals it again. Amalia should take better care of her things. She is about to say so when her daughter begins to shout anew, "Hurry, Mama. Hurry!"

Jane takes her place behind her daughter. She can push harder now, without Victor to hold, and both arms free. "Hard or soft, Mali?"

"The hardest!" cries Amalia. "The highest!"

AUTHOR'S NOTE

THE FARM IS A WORK OF FICTION. BUT IT IS ALSO, IN MANY ways, true: inspired by people I have known and the stories they have shared with me.

I was born in the Philippines. When I was six, my parents, siblings, and I moved to southeastern Wisconsin. In many ways, America's heartland was wholly different from the world we'd left. And yet, because my father's family had preceded us in emigrating to Wisconsin, and because of the tight-knit Filipino community that had already taken root in the area, I grew up straddling two worlds: our old one, preserved in clamorous weekend

gatherings filled with Filipino friends and family
and too much food, and our new one, where my
little sister and I were two of the four Asian kids in
our elementary school.

After high school, I headed east to attend
Princeton University. My world was blown open,
and not just intellectually. Princeton was the first
place I encountered truly great disparity—in wealth,
in class, in experience and opportunity.

Years later—after stints in finance and then
a career switch to journalism—I decided to take a
break from the working world to spend more time
with my young children. I realized one day that
the only Filipinos I knew in Manhattan, where I
lived with my family, were the ones who worked for
my friends—baby nurses, nannies, housekeepers,
cleaning ladies. My husband and I ended up hiring
a wonderful Filipina nanny for a time, too.

Perhaps because I am from the Philippines and
am chatty and curious about people by nature, I became friendly with many of the Filipina caregivers
in my orbit, as well as others from South America
and the Caribbean and elsewhere in Asia. I listened
to their stories—about errant husbands and difficult bosses; about the dormitory in Queens where
beds are rented by the half-day to save money and
how the money saved was sent halfway around the
world to support children or parents or nephews
back home. I saw the daily sacrifices these women
made in the hope of something better—for their

children, if not for themselves—and the enormous obstacles standing in their way.

The gulf between their lives and possibilities, and mine, is vast. I often wonder if it is even bridgeable in our society today. And despite what I've been told countless times in my life—that I am the embodiment of the "American Dream"—I know this chasm has as much to do with luck and happenstance as it does with any kind of merit.

In many ways, **The Farm** is a culmination of a running dialogue I've had with myself for the past twenty-five years—about just deserts and luck, assimilation and otherness, class and family and sacrifice. I didn't write it to come up with answers, because I don't have them. Instead, the book is meant to explore—for myself, and hopefully for its readers, too—questions of who we are, what we cherish, and how we see those who are different from ourselves. I hope **The Farm** might serve as a window to the "other" side of these divides, from wherever readers approach it.

ACKNOWLEDGMENTS

WHEN I STARTED **THE FARM** SEVERAL MONTHS SHY OF MY forty-first birthday, I hadn't written fiction in two decades. This isn't to say that I took a twenty-year hiatus from writing—to the contrary, I wrote and write nonstop; it's how I digest the world. But I shied away from the act of writing stories, which I'd loved to do ever since I was a child.

So it was with no small measure of trepidation that I began to write **The Farm.** Luckily, I have people in my life who nudged, cheered, cajoled, and carried me along the way. I am grateful to my earliest readers, Annie Sundberg, Sara Lippmann, and

Rachel Sherman of the Ditmas Writing Workshop, who believed in the promise of **The Farm** well before I did. To the friends who read draft after draft and offered insight and encouragement over the years, I owe a huge debt: my younger sister, Joyce Barnes, Courtney Potts, Krista Parris, Marisa Angell, and, especially, the wonderful writer and friend Hilary Reyl. Nick Snyder and Kyle Clark: without your late reads, I might still be tinkering with the book; thank you for telling me it was ready to send into the world.

My agent, Jenn Joel, understood **The Farm** and what it means to me on her very first read. She was then and remains its stalwart champion, and mine. I am lucky to have her on my side. At Random House, Susan Kamil and Clio Seraphim, wise and incisive editors, took the manuscript and helped make it truer to itself.

I was born in the Philippines but grew up in Wisconsin from the age of six. My understanding of my birthplace in all its complexities and, more important, of family, was shaped by the tight-knit Filipino community in Milwaukee and, especially, my **titos** and **titas** and cousins, with whom I spent countless weekends of my childhood.

My big sister and brother, Guia Wallace and Jon Ramos, have looked out for me ever since I was a kid, and my little sister, Joyce Barnes, is still my favorite playmate. I love you all.

Dad, you always believed I would write a book

someday. I wish you were here to see that you were right. Mom, it's from you that I learned to love words and stories. This book begins with you.

Owen, Annabel, and Henry: It is my life's greatest privilege to be your mother. Thank you for all your pep talks when I was in a rough writing stretch and for the celebrations when things began to fall into place. And, of course, to David. You are my ballast and my inspiration and, hands down, the most generous human I know. I love you.

ABOUT THE AUTHOR

JOANNE RAMOS was born in the Philippines and moved to Wisconsin when she was six. She graduated with a B.A. from Princeton University. After working in investment banking and private-equity investing for several years, she became a staff writer for **The Economist.** She currently serves on the board of **The Moth.** She lives in New York City with her husband and three children.

Instagram: @joanneramosthefarm